A WOMAN WHOM SOCIETY COULD NOT CONTROL

She was Claire Cottington, exiled from the court of Queen Victoria for her shocking indiscretions. As her last chance for respectability, she accepted the proposal of an English Lord old enough to be her father.

A MAN WHOM DANGER COULD NOT DAUNT

He was Major Colin Whitecavage, the legendary "Sword of Pandeish," the forbidden lover of an incredibly lovely Indian princess. He was the man chosen to escort Claire Cottington on the long and treacherous voyage to the East.

When these two came together, only one thing could happen. And when they arrived in the whirlwind of passion and violence that was India, anything could. . . .

The
Jasmine Veil

The Jasmine Veil

Gimone Hall

A SIGNET BOOK

NEW AMERICAN LIBRARY

TIMES MIRROR

NAL BOOKS ARE AVAILABLE AT QUANTITY DISCOUNTS
WHEN USED TO PROMOTE PRODUCTS OR SERVICES. FOR
INFORMATION PLEASE WRITE TO PREMIUM MARKETING
DIVISION, THE NEW AMERICAN LIBRARY, INC., 1633
BROADWAY, NEW YORK, NEW YORK 10019.

SIGNET TRADEMARK REG. U.S. PAT. OFF. AND FOREIGN COUNTRIES
REGISTERED TRADEMARK—MARCA REGISTRADA
HECHO EN CHICAGO, U.S.A.

SIGNET, SIGNET CLASSICS, MENTOR, PLUME, MERIDIAN AND NAL
BOOKS are published by The New American Library, Inc.,
1633 Broadway, New York, New York 10019

First Printing, April, 1982

1 2 3 4 5 6 7 8 9

PRINTED IN THE UNITED STATES OF AMERICA

PUBLISHER'S NOTE

1

Claire Cottington had done many a daring thing, but nothing so daring as what she planned tonight. If her plot succeeded, she'd have the last laugh on everyone! On her peers in the London social set, who had been snickering at her. Even on Queen Victoria, who had banished her from court and had sent her home to Cottington Crest. Claire's turquoise eyes, the color of the sky at sunset, glinted with purpose. But sunset was hours past, and only in Claire's eyes did such hues dance and shine, when the rest of Cottington Crest was sleeping.

Beyond, the moonlit moor beckoned. Claire knew she had been mad to arrange a tryst with William Rutherford. Some said the moor was an enchantress of destruction; some said the same of Claire Cottington. Surely neither was the truth.

Claire had grown up in the big moorstone mansion at the edge of Dartmoor, and to her the dangers of its rocky coombs and blanket bogs were only an exciting facet of the country she loved. Grown men had lost themselves for days in the moor, going about in circles, pixy-led. Horses stumbled into mires; light played tricks, making objects seem nearer or farther, larger or smaller; herdsmen were sometimes seized by inexplicable terror even in familiar surroundings.

None of this had ever deterred Claire from riding far and wide over the moors. She loved the wild streams, the exhilaration of steep tors. She had never ridden on the moor at night, but she wasn't frightened. She knew the way to Raven Tor as well as she knew the way to the granite gateposts of Cottington Crest. It was a silly superstition that the raven was a bird of ill omen. Who would believe such a thing in this enlightened year of 1854?

Every pore of her body throbbed with eagerness for her adventure to begin. Claire crept from her bedroom and tiptoed down the hall, pausing to listen with satisfaction to the soft snores emanating from behind the oak-paneled door of her mother's bedchamber. Dear Mama! Claire longed to wake her and confide. But Mama had a weak constitution and would never be able to stand it. Better tomorrow when they would savor the triumph together. The thing must be done, and done now. Soon Papa would be home from London, and he was not so sound a sleeper as Mama. In London, Claire had brought disgrace upon him, but tonight she would remedy that. He would return to Cottington Crest to find his only daughter betrothed to the new Lord Rutherford, the inheritor of the immense wealth and lands of Thistlewood. Even now Lord Rutherford waited for her, restless as a prowling fox.

Tonight the trap would be sprung. Tonight the bridegroom must be caught!

Lighting a lantern, Claire slipped a cloak over her silk-lined riding jacket and habit skirt of riflecloth and went quietly out into the night. In London, Claire had had exquisite gowns, but she did not need fine clothes to make her beautiful. The shimmer of her eyes; the delicate tones of her skin, creamy and fragrant as a white gardenia; the softness of her thick midnight-dark hair, done in twin clusters would cause any gentleman to lose his heart.

She looked so innocent in her daintily-plumed felt riding hat that a man would have staked his life she was a victim of malicious gossip, no matter how many stories about her he had heard.

Surely it wasn't Claire's fault that the Earl of Sudbury had been thrown from his horse while taking the jumps at London Downs! Claire had only been a little bored that day, and to enliven the event, had offered her first dance of the evening to the winner. It was the Earl's own doing that he had attempted a jump that was too high, but people had said the unkindest things!

The near riot at the yachting party hadn't been Claire's fault either, but wagging tongues had attributed the fray to Claire's scandalous appearance in bloomers. There had been a stampede to be near her, but she had not been responsible for someone's having been knocked into the water by the boom. From there, things had gone from bad to worse.

Bloomers had seemed so practical, and Claire had loved the silver-buttoned vest, flowing jacket, and crimson necktie she had worn with the outfit. It was unfair that the next day Mama had sent everything to the Missionary Society.

Worst of all had been the duel. It had begun over the auctioning of a harmless wicker picnic basket tied with green ribbons and containing roast pheasant, peaches, and wine. Claire had prepared the basket to benefit an orphanage, and she did vaguely remember that she had spoken to both gallants about the plight of the dear children. But had she really urged both to bid for the basket, hinting that she yearned to share it with each, intimating delights beyond those of digestion? She had only wanted her basket to bring a high price for the little orphans.

Claire had been shaken when the pair had come to blows, and the challenge been given and taken. When neither had been seriously injured, she had tried to carry the matter off with aplomb, and had called it amusing.

Her majesty had not been amused, and she had suggested to Claire's father, Sir Henry Cottington, that Claire might find it pleasant at Cottington Crest for a time.

Claire loved Dartmoor, but for once she was not happy to be there. The wide expanses of heather, the song of thrush and meadow pipits did not ameliorate her despondency.

She was humiliated.

But then a kind fate had sent her Lord William Rutherford. Had she been in London, she could not have met him when he returned to inherit his title and Thistlewood after many years on the Continent. She had seen him first at his uncle's funeral, winsomely handsome in his black dress coat with its high, silk-lined collar; and when the service had been over, she had expressed her condolences and invited him to visit Cottington Crest, should he be melancholy.

In less than a week, William Rutherford, bored by Dartmoor, had felt overwhelmed with grief for the uncle he had scarcely known and had sought the drawing room at Cottington Crest. He had danced admirably, and he sat a horse well. She told him she remained at Dartmoor because she found the hubbub of London unendurable. It was a blatant lie, but William proclaimed it refreshing.

William was smitten; and Claire, for her part, liked him as well as any of her London beaux. She even persuaded herself that she was in love with him; and when on a warm July evening he stole a kiss on the veranda, Claire, nearly swooning, told herself it was from passion, not from the heat or from the tightness of her stays. She had had a half a dozen earnest proposals in London and had accepted none. She would have become engaged to Lord Rutherford in an instant, but Lord Rutherford did not ask.

William was canny. He was well aware of how eligible he was. He was not certain that he was ready to settle down with a wife at Thistlewood. Claire, of course, was not really ready to settle down either, but that was not what mattered. She would be twenty-one soon, and the time had come for her. The time had come, too, she decided, for William Rutherford.

Lord Rutherford valued his freedom, but tonight she would make sure there was something he wanted more.

A collie, sleeping near the door, waked and growled; and Claire reassured the animal with a soft word. The dog rose loyally to follow her, and for an instant she considered taking it along for comfort in the darkness. Then, with decision, she whispered, "Lie down!" She didn't need protection. She could handle herself perfectly well alone.

Despite so many of her recent escapades having gone dangerously awry, Claire was undaunted. As she rode along a path through moonlit fields, a fresh cool breeze stirred her hair and made her draw the cloak more closely about her. Rain was coming; soon the moon and stars would be enveloped in clouds. Beyond the granite gateposts of Cottington Crest, Claire left the road that ran toward the village and struck out on a track toward a remote turf tie, traveled in summer by pannier donkeys carrying peat. She crossed a stream, the water glistening pearlescently in the moonlight. A black Galloway cow stared at her as she galloped past. Farther on she came to a hutment, built there in ancient times, and began to climb up to Raven Tor, careful of clitters of loose rock that might send her and her mare plummeting downward.

Claire's excitement grew as she reached the peat cuttings. Here and there, vags of peat, cut in flat blocks, leaned together forlornly, where they had been set to dry. The peatcutter had left his cottage for the winter, but a lamp gleamed forth at the window. Claire caught her breath. Lord Rutherford was here, as he had promised.

Claire felt giddy. She was almost grateful to the Queen for having sent her here where misbehavior was so simple. Had she been in London, it would have been too dangerous to arrange such a meeting. But who was to know what went on in the wild reaches of Dartmoor?

Not that Claire had made the assignation lightly. She had given William ample opportunity to propose marriage in some more conventional way. But she had grown impatient, and she had come to dread the day when the post came up from the village with the *London News*, announcing the engagements of her peers in Mayfair.

Today's social page had told of the approaching nuptials of Eliza Woodridge and the oldest son of Count Penninton. "That plain little thing!" Mama had cried. "He was mad about you, Claire, not two months ago, and now *she* has got him! And to think, we won't even be able to attend the wedding!"

Mama had been so upset that she had had to repair her agitated appearance with a dusting of pearl powder. Worst of all, the mail had also brought a seemingly belated invitation to a ball given by Jenny Bainbridge and her mother. "It's tomorrow," cried Mrs. Cottington, in horror. "We won't even have time to plan new gowns!"

Claire knew it had all been done on purpose, for ever since Jenny had returned from a London season without a fiancé, she and her mother had been hotly on William's track. So Claire had devised a plan of her own, and when William had come to tea, she had whispered it into his ear.

"The moon will be full tonight and the turfcutter's cottage at Raven Tor has a wonderful view. I have always wanted to see the moor by moonlight from there. Don't you think it would be lovely, William?"

Surprise had flickered on his sophisticated features, but only for an instant. His wordliness was one of the things she liked about him. He was not easily thrown out of stride, and quickly he was assuring her that he would relish the sight. Ardently he kissed her hand as he took his leave, as unruffled as though there had been nothing unusual about meeting a girl of fine family alone in a peatcutter's cottage.

Mist suddenly covered the moon as Claire approached the rough plank door. Now there could be no romantic view of the moon, but Claire was unperturbed. Neither he nor she cared a fig for the view.

"Claire, my love!"

"Oh, William!"

Her words were swept away by his kiss as she stepped over the threshold. Her cloak fell from her shoulders as he pulled her into an embrace. "Do make a fire, William," she said, breathless, pulling free.

"Really, dearest, we'll be too warm." He hid his flash of ill humor beneath a smile and reached to encircle her tiny waist with his arms.

Claire moved cagily out of reach. "It's going to be chilly with the storm coming on, William. We'll need the fire."

"Oh, very well." William became more cheerful. "It may be a black mist coming in. We may have to stay all night."

"All night!" Claire had carelessly not considered the possiblity of the most dreaded of Dartmoor terrors. Enwrapped in its coils a traveler might experience utter panic. It was like suddenly being struck blind. She ran to the window and peered out, her throat tightening as she saw that the house was enveloped in fog as though it had been encased in cotton batting. In an instant the landscape had been blotted out. No one, no matter how familiar with the moor, could traverse it in such a mist.

Fearfully, she returned to watch as William took out flint and steel and struck a spark. His blond hair, fashionably waved, with full side whiskers, shone in the firelight. He looked so pleasing, with each little twist of his hair just so, like a cluster of buttercups, and his features all so regularly made, that Claire's resolve returned. How furious Jenny would be when Claire announced her engagement to William at Jenny's own party!

Lord Rutherford turned and smiled at her. "You're quite right," he said. "It's better with a fire." He slipped off his frockcoat. Claire was not alarmed until he unbuttoned his waistcoat and pulled off his Wellington boots.

"William, whatever are you doing?" she cried.

"Why, I'm getting comfortable. Let's not play games. Come, I'll help you."

He reached for her, catching her easily and opening the mother-of-pearl buttons that secured the front of her cambric blouse. Claire gasped, but the touch of his hands on her breasts was oddly pleasant. She sighed and fastened her arms about his neck. His fingers leaped to other tasks, struggling to loosen her whalebone corseting. He knew his business, because before she realized what was happening, Claire felt his mouth against her nipples, which leaped erect under his caress.

Claire tried to recover her composure. "William, stop! That's enough, William!" she ordered in her best tone of command. He had been more familiar than she had expected, she thought, trembling, but now she had him where she wanted him.

The passion in his face was obvious; in fact it almost frightened her. She had never seen a man so flushed with desire, but she knew what it meant. It meant that he must have her. He could no longer deny the urges of love. He would have to relinquish his freedom and propose marriage, for he could not dream that Claire would allow him to ravish her, except in the marriage bed.

She waited for him to grovel at her feet, to plead with her to marry him and admit him forever to the paradise she had allowed him to glimpse.

But Lord Rutherford did not grovel. With a muttered curse he lunged for her, and she felt the sleeve of her gown rip as she instinctively tried to evade him. The minutes passed in a blur of confusion and arousal; for William was, by his own lights, a gentleman. He had never taken a woman against her will. The challenge lay in making his will her will, too. Therein was a large part of the satisfaction Lord Rutherford derived from illicit sexual encounters.

He had expected little resistance from Claire, for not only had she been flirtatious, but he had guessed accurately at the sensual nature that lay just below her ladylike exterior. William had known such women before, frustrated by the bounds of upper-class morality, who, after suitable pretense, had been only too pleased to allow him to satisfy their lust. On the Continent, he had been a boon to married ladies in particular, allowing them to soothe their needs with no risk of complication. With his looks and breeding, he had been the perfect lover. He had never made a spectacle of himself by urging any of his conquests to forsake all for him. Indeed, he never wished it. And in the occasional instance that some lady fell hysterically in love with him, he had known how to make a quiet, graceful exit.

William had been uncertain about Claire. She wasn't married, and so she was a special danger to him. Aware that a trap was being laid for him, he counted on his own cleverness to evade it and make away with the bait. He had never really believed that Claire preferred Cottington Crest to London. Rather, he smelled scandal, scandal which might easily involve someone's bedroom. William had no intention of being carried off as a trophy, but, on the other hand, he considered Claire ripe for plucking. She excited him as no woman ever had; and if he had been in the market for a wife, he would have delighted in allowing her transparent little scheme to succeed.

He had not intended to rip her clothing, but she had jerked away so sharply that it had been unavoidable. It had added a primitive quality to the encounter, which, combined with the mist and earthy setting, gave an uncontrollable edge to his desire.

But unfortunately for William, the incident also alerted Claire to the seriousness of her predicament. William had to dispense with the gentle caresses that so many times had placed a woman at his mercy before she was aware that she had surrendered.

Claire was as determined to have her way as William was to have his, but she had led a protected life, and she had not dreamed of such sensations as now possessed her, overwhelming her plans. When he had ripped her gown, a torrent of feelings had burst forth, just as a torn sack of grain would have spilled its contents. Claire allowed him to kiss her again, parting her lips to admit his insistent tongue. She pressed herself against him, moaning as his hands explored her body. Then came a gasp of wild amazement, drawn up like a whirlwind from the pit of her being, as he worked his way beneath her crinoline.

With a cry of victory he threw her onto the rough-hewn bed that filled one corner of the cottage. Quickly he was atop her, lifting her skirts, spreading her legs, whispering endearments, working at the fastenings of his trousers. If he made her pregnant he would have to marry her, and he would do so, even without her father's pistol pointed at his head. He was a man of some honor, and he knew that as master of an estate like Thistlewood, he would have to marry someday. But an impending heir was the price of his proposal at this point in his life.

Claire thought otherwise. Part of her ached to surrender. There was a peculiar sensation between her thighs, but she reasoned that if William were as upset as she, she would soon have his declaration. He *was* dreadfully disturbed, she could see. He was breathing hard and sweat was running in a stream along his forehead, dripping into the cleft between her breasts as he kissed her neck. Claire felt as though she were suffocating herself. Heat seemed to rise from inside her as though William had built a fire there instead of in the hearth. It had been a mistake to have the fire. She might ruin everything by fainting, she thought in panic.

Claire jammed her legs together. "William, you must behave yourself," she said weakly. "Oh, do open a window!"

He gave a grunt, vastly more annoyed than when she had urged him to start the fire, but he rolled off her and hurried to do her bidding. He, too, was afraid she might faint and ruin things.

When he returned, she had pulled herself together, straightening her skirts and trying to rearrange her hopelessly disheveled curls. He kissed her again, and she responded, gulping in the cool, wet air that made the ruffled curtains stand out stiffly. William felt his attainment at hand. She had had her chance when he had released her to open the window. Now she was lost!

But Claire had a core of steel he had not intuited, and she resisted as he shoved her down again. "William, stop!"

Unthinkably, he did not stop. She pushed his handsome face away, using both slender hands, and unwittingly she gave him an advantage. He was able to grasp both her wrists with only one of his hands, while the other worked at removing her skirt. Her bodice, which she had tried to rebutton, flew open again as he flung her down.

His hand slid over the smooth skin of her stomach, trying to lower her skirt and petticoats, and at last Claire gave way to pure terror.

"William, I never meant. . . ." she sobbed. "I am not the kind of woman to do such things unless—unless. . . ."

He gave an ugly laugh, passion having swept away his reason. He had forgotten that he was too honorable to take a woman against her will. He had never been tempted so strongly before, never wanted a woman as much as this one, never known any to display such desire and yet fight him with such will. He knew now that she was a virgin; he knew it without the proof that he was sure would soon be his. Her sudden, genuine fear could mean nothing else.

"You *are* that kind of woman, Claire! I'll show you!" he cried. He was exultant. He would be the first to teach her the transport of the flesh. It would be a night that neither he nor she would ever forget. After tonight he would possess her body and soul; she would beg to have him meet her and love her time and again, until he was sated with her. He had lost count of the number of mistresses he had left broken-hearted.

But never had he had one like Claire—so sensual, so calculating, so innocent, all in the same explosive mix.

Married! That was the word with which she had intended to end her sentence, but it was a word that he never would allow her to mention between them. He let his face furrow with anger as she attempted to speak again.

"Please, William." Her voice was a desperate wail. Wild with anticipation, William reached into his already gaping breeches for the means with which to master her.

Claire's desire had fled. This was no longer simply a titillating game which she would win. She was bewildered, for she had never seen this dark side of the male nature. Always she had been catered to, deferred to, obeyed. She intuited that she was about to be humiliated and disgraced more profoundly than by the punishment of the Queen.

But Lord Rutherford had made a mistake. When he had reached into his pants, that necessary maneuver had caused him to release Claire's wrists. In a flash she seized a pillow and hit him over the head with it so hard that the covering split. He was unhurt, of course, but the suddenness of the blow disoriented him. Bringing her knees up under him, she unseated him, knocking him breathless in a rain of goose down. Not pausing to think how ruined her life would be if she killed him, she grabbed up the poker he had used to stir the fire. Surely her life would be ruined if she did *not* kill him!

She tried to hit him over the head, but he deflected her hand and she rammed his stomach instead. Lord Rutherford's face drained of color. Claire stepped back, aghast, thinking she had stabbed him. But that was impossible. The poker was blunt-ended after all, and the white of William's face was the white of ultimate arousal. He must have her and have her now, or die; not of any wound, but of desire!

The knowledge that she was willing to have him dead inflamed him. He reached for her with a strangled cry, and unable to escape him anywhere in the cramped cottage, Claire flung open the door and ran outside. Immediately she was lost from view in the cold cloud of fog.

"Claire!" he called.

She could not seen him; neither could she tell where he was from the sound of his voice. The queer acoustics of the fog made the sound echo from every side. It seemed to come from only a few steps away and at the same time to come from the top of the tor. She had no idea which direction she was going; she only prayed that she would not make a circle and wind up at the cottage again. She thought of her horse, but she could not retrieve the mare. Even had she known its whereabouts, she could not have ridden it or even led it safely down the tor.

She felt her way along, sometimes crawling on hands and knees, feeling the ground before her so that she would not plummet into some ravine. She wept softly, convinced that William was searching for her.

The fog had saved her from him, might not it as easily deliver her to him again?

She knew at least that she wanted to go down, but when the slope began to level, she could not find the hutments that should have been beside the track. She began to wander aimlessly, hoping that by some stroke of luck she would come to a landmark she recognized. Another fear began to take hold of her: suppose that she could not find her way back to Cottington Crest, and her absence were discovered in the morning?

She would be in disgrace again. Claire did not think she could stand the smirks and stares another time. Jenny Bainbridge would be in gossipy raptures; Mama would faint; Papa would stroke his Dundreary whiskers and ask in long-suffering tones why she would not behave like other young ladies.

It was a question that he had asked before. And Claire had no better answer than before. "I don't know, Papa," she would have to say.

She had been walking more than an hour when she came to a stone avenue, a line of menhirs, erected in ancient times. It gave her her bearings. If she followed the track carefully from here, she would arrive at a stream; and since streams all flowed out of the moor, she had only to follow it. But Claire's relief was short-lived. She remembered a reason why she was afraid to follow the stream.

She sank down against one of the stones and gave way to tears. She must conquer the fear or be disgraced. It was a fear that most would have thought foolish, but Claire had spent her life near the moor and knew truths that were beyond reason. Claire might have sat there all night, had the shadow of a man not come out of the fog. The man might not have seen her, though they were no more than ten paces apart, if she had not imagined him to be William and screamed.

The man, who was leading his horse, whirled and instinctively whipped out his revolver. He put it away as he gazed at her in astonishment. A woman! Alone on the moor! He stepped closer. She looked as wild as the moor itself. Her hair was disheveled and her clothing torn. Her turquoise eyes had an intensity that was unusual, not the humble gaze of a peasant girl or the demureness of the lady her finely-cut riding habit purported her to be.

The man, who wore the uniform of a regiment of the Army of Bengal, had never been on the moor before tonight, but he had heard tales. Perhaps she was a mirage, or perhaps some supernatural apparition waiting to lure him to doom.

The idea of an apparition occurred to Claire as well. Hadn't she heard talk among the herdsmen about sheep that were not sheep, but changed themselves into various forms? He seemed almost as if he had been born of the mist. His black hair had the same soft fury, and his dark eyes burned with impatience. His body seemed spare and muscled; his lean cheeks had been tanned by some more powerful sun than the one that shone on the moors. The flapping of his military cape in the breeze added to the illusion that he had come here in some unnatural way.

She was almost more frightened of him than of Lord Rutherford. How different he was from William, who had a meaty look to his well proportioned figure and whose face was often pink from ale.

How could she had imagined for a second that he was William?

She felt an odd thrill, as though he stirred something lost to her conscious memory. She experienced a sense of *déjà vu*, and her soul filled with inexplicable longing. She had no chance to think where she might have seen him before he spoke to her.

"I beg your pardon, miss, do you know the way off the moor?" He thought it a foolish question. She was lost, else why would she be sitting there?

But she answered simply, "Follow the track from here to the river. The stream will lead you out. It's no more than a mile away."

"Shall we ride together, then? Where is your horse?"

"I've lost it."

"Then it's lucky I came along. We'll ride double."

"No, thank you," said Claire.

"Why not?" he asked bluntly. "Are you going to sit there all night? If you're waiting for someone, chances are he's not coming." That was it, he thought. She was waiting for her lover. That explained why she remained although she knew the way out. That explained the look in her eyes that was neither that of a peasant nor a lady. He understood her now. He relaxed, laughing to himself at the strange way she had made him feel. He had become addled from his years in India. His superior had been right to send him on leave.

"I'm not waiting for anyone," she protested. "It's not that. . . ." She hesitated, knowing what thoughts he was having.

He regarded her through the shimering fog. Her sleeve was ripped from the shoulder, and he found himself staring at the soft flesh beneath. It annoyed him to think of a man's touch profaning it.

She followed his glance and blushed. "I tore it on a hawthorne."

Remembering his manners, he averted his eyes. "Are you sure you don't want to come?"

For a moment she didn't answer, and he felt a lift of his heart, thinking she'd changed her mind. Then she said, "I'm sure." He wondered why the idea of leaving her bothered him. It wasn't his business to save her, either from the mist or from whatever immoral course she had embarked upon.

Turning away, he vanished into the fog. She should have gone with him, she thought. It had been her only chance. But she had been too frightened—of the thing that lay beyond. Now that he had gone, the desolation of the moor was unbearable. She leaped to her feet, crying out, "Wait! Wait!"

She was terrified that he was already too far away to find her again or that he would not try; but in a moment he appeared, and she shivered with relief.

She was glad that he made nothing of it, but wordlessly held out his hand, to help her mount behind him. She had never ridden double except with other children, when she had been a child herself, and it unnerved her to have to embrace him, pressing her breasts against his straight, stern back, her hands locked about his hard rib cage. She seemed to go limp as she cling to him, her face lying against his shoulder so as not to see the terrors that lay ahead.

As they neared the ancient cyclopean bridge, an icy chill began inside her, as though she were starting a high fever. She quivered helplessly against him and heard the horse whinny in alarm.

"What is it? What's happening?" cried the soldier, as his

mount reared and fought for its head. He was the last to be affected by the terror, but as he twisted to look at her, she saw the bewilderment in his eyes and knew he felt it, too.

"The bridge," she called as the horse bolted onto it. "It's haunted!"

He gave an exlcamation of dismay or disbelief, but he had no leisure to debate the veracity of her words. The horse had gone mad, and he needed all his wits to control it.

In the center of the bridge, the animal braked suddenly and reared again. Claire felt her grip shaken loose and clutched wildly for the man in front of her. But he was out of reach, and she was flying free, floating over the parapet as gracefully as a hawk, diving down toward the cold, rocky, moorstream. She screamed once, and the fog made the sound echo from some distant tor. The splash echoed also, and then the fog was silent.

2

Sunlight poured into Claire's bedroom window at Cottington Crest. The damask draperies should have kept out the light, but Claire had opened them to gaze out across the path and assure herself that no one had been watching her return to the house.

The fall from the horse had stunned her, but she had missed the rocks and landed in a shallow eddy, her head pillowed on soft heather. When, her body aching, she had recovered her senses, there had been no sign of the soldier who had shared her adventure. Claire was convinced he had been a specter whose evil purpose had been to lure her to the bridge. But if she had not gone with him, she would not be safely home this morning, and oddly she thought of him with warmth.

Bruised but unharmed, Claire had followed the intricate course of the river until she had emerged from the black mist at last. A graying of the sky had foretold dawn, and Claire had only just had time to reach the safety of her bed before any of the servants were up and about.

Sighing in the comfort of her feather mattress, Claire remembered the thrill she had felt at the sight of the soldier. It occurred to her that he might have been the apparition of a real person. Colonel Maxwell Todd was not dead, but that was the person she had been reminded of.

She had been only fifteen when Colonel Todd had come to Cottington Crest, wearing that uniform. He had been thirty-six and a friend of her father's, but Claire had lost her heart. It had been a callow love, her very first; but it had been so

15

profound that it had immunized Claire to the myriad infatuations of other girls. Perhaps the reason that Claire had never accepted any of her beaux was that beside Colonel Todd, all seemed hopelessly inadequate.

When Colonel Todd had left Cottington Crest, bound for Calcutta, Claire had languished for months. Mama, little guessing that Claire was old enough to suffer the pangs of unrequited love, had dosed her with tonics, made her wear woolen stockings when it was damp, and even taken her on a holiday to recover her health. Claire had been humiliated; but she had had one perfect memory for comfort.

In honor of Colonel Todd's visit, there had been a ball at Cottington Crest. Claire had been allowed to wear her first grown-up evening gown, low off the shoulders with a falling border of lace. Colonel Todd had waltzed her onto the veranda, kissed her forehead and, plucking a blossom from the wreath of pink roses in her hair, begged her permission to take it to India.

"Have they no such roses in India?" she had asked.

"No," he had replied, "nor women as lovely as you."

Had he even thought of her once? For at least a year she had hoped so. *She* thought of *him* every day. But it was too much to imagine that he thought of her. He had had grand things to do. He was to spearhead Governor Dalhousie's reforms in Bengal, and Claire had loved to take her embroidery and slip into the corner of the drawing room to listen to him converse with Papa on all that he hoped to accomplish. Papa, who had served in India himself before inheriting Cottington Crest, would draw on his pipe and murmur, "It will be difficult, Max."

But Colonel Todd, his eyes alight with vision, would talk on and on about education and improvement of living conditions and equality, about hospitals and railroads to be built and barbarous religious practices to be stamped out.

Claire had never known a man with a dream before. She had never known a man with interests beyond investments and horse racing. Perhaps that was why she had fallen in love.

After returning from the moor, Claire had dreamed of Colonel Todd. In her dream she had danced with him, so brave, so distinguished, with a thread of gray in his side whiskers. But in her dream Claire was not fifteen, and it was not her forehead that the Colonel kissed.

She had awakened in confusion. Something else was wrong with her vision. The Colonel had not had gray in his whiskers after all. In her dream his hair had been black, and the insignia on his uniform was that of a major. Dark eyes, instead of the Colonel's gray-blue ones, laughed at her.

Wheatears twittered in the garden outside, reminding Claire of the day ahead. She sneezed and decided she had caught a cold in the mist. She would have a red nose for Jenny Bainbridge's party, but she would have to go, of course, or abandon William to Jenny.

William! What a mistake she had made there. She'd been a skillful flirt, and thought she'd known all there was to know about men. But she'd known nothing. She could never have guessed at the terrible force that had seemed to drive Lord Rutherford. Claire had pretended helplessness on many occasions, when it had suited her purpose, but until last night she had never guessed at her female vulnerability. But she was warned now!

Claire suspected that William would be more difficult to manage after their rendezvous, but she was no less determined than before to cement their relationship. She was only more cautious. It even seemed to her that certain aspects of marriage might be enjoyable, contrary to whispers she had heard.

The day that had begun so blissfully with the dream of Maxwell Todd had gone sour. Claire might have stayed abed all morning with the excuse that she was resting for the evening, but she was ravenous and she could smell sausages and shirred eggs.

Claire selected a morning dress of Pekin silk with an open robe and bishop sleeves. Her hair was a disaster, still laden with bits of white fuzz. Claire unwound her tangled curls and fastened them in rags before going down stairs. Had her father been home, Claire would have never dared to appear *en deshabille*, but it seemed silly to put on a show for Mama.

Brooding over the dismal prospect of the Bainbridge's party, Claire was halfway across the dining room before the sound of a male voice penetrated her thoughts. The gentleman was half hidden by a Greek jardiniere planted with palms, and by the time she caught sight him, it was too late to retreat. She could only stand there gasping, her hands flying involuntarily to the bundle of rag curls on her head. Mama managed to make the best of it. Mama usually did. She'd had practice enough with a daughter like Claire.

"Claire, dear," said her mother, "may I present Major Colin Whitecavage of the Bengal Army? He's come all the way from Delhi with a letter for Papa."

It was he, of course. His face registered surprise as he stumbled up from his chair and bowed, almost upsetting a Queensware sugar bowl.

"I'm pleased to make your acquaintance, sir," Claire stammered, equally stunned, and taking a step backward, turned and ran for the stairs.

Before long her mother followed, chiding gently. "I declare, dear, you must be more careful about your appearance. I'm afraid you gave the Major quite a start. He's a bachelor, and unused to seeing ladies undressed. They are very proper at the Bengal Club, so your father always said. Of course, in those days most of the officers married natives—quite a disgusting thing—but Major Whitecavage says that has changed." Mama sighed, reminded by the waving flags in Claire's hair of all that had happened in the dining room. "The Major's a hero of some sort, I believe. The Sword of Pandeish, they call him, according to his letter of introduction. Wasn't there something about that in the papers some months ago? The Major was very uncommunicative on the subject. But you always read those stories about India."

Claire did read everything she could find about her father's old regiment—Colonel Todd's regiment. She remembered the story about the Sword of Pandeish. He and his sepoys had been sent to the little hill-country kingdom of Pandeish to supervise the building of a road. The treacherous Rana had turned on him and attacked unexpectedly. Against overwhelming odds the Major had turned a near defeat into victory and Pandeish had been subdued.

Yes, she knew who *he* was, the question was, did he recognize her? Had it been only her rag curls that had caused his surprise. Had she run away before he could be sure she was his companion of the moor?

"I am not interested in the Major," said Claire petulantly, not sharing her information.

Mrs. Cottington was startled by Claire's reaction. She herself had thought the Major attractive, even exciting. For these very reasons she had been displeased by his arrival. She had ascertained that he was the third son of the family and had only a modest fortune. Also she was afraid he might return to India when his leave was over.

Mrs. Cottington had a horror of India. She herself had

been betrothed to Claire's father just before he had left for his tour of duty in Bengal. She had waited three years for his return and had never regretted it. India was hot and smelly. In India, peaches tasted like turnips, camels reeked like drains, and the cockroaches were as big as mice. So Mrs. Cottington had been told by women who had gone there and lived to be sorry they had. Mrs. Cottington had known women who had gone out and not lived at all. One had one's choice of disgusting ways to die.

Mrs. Cottington would not have been interested in Major Whitecavage as a husband for Claire, even if he had been eligible, which he wasn't, despite his aristocratic family. The instant she had seen the Major, Claire's mother had been terrified that Claire would fall in love with him. Claire had failed to fall in love with so many suitable men that it seemed almost as though she were looking for someone unsuitable. The idea had become an obsession with Mrs. Cottington, and it gave her nightmares.

But here was a bit of luck. Claire wasn't taken with the Major. Most likely it was because she'd made such a fool of herself in front of him. To judge by the look on the Major's face, Claire hadn't impressed him favorably either. For once Claire's carelessness had worked to advantage. Mrs. Cottington felt easier.

"Papa will enjoy him so when he gets home tomorrow," she chattered. "It will be nice for him to have someone from his old regiment to talk to, and we will create a sensation when we bring him to the Bainbridge's soiree."

Claire gave an audible groan. If she spent an evening in his company he'd be certain to recognize her. Perhaps she should feign illness. Her cold. Female trouble. But that would mean abandoning William to her rival.

"What are you planning to wear tonight?" her mother wanted to know.

"The yellow. William is fond of yellow."

"Splendid," said Mrs. Cottington, glowing with maternal satisfaction. Her daughter was becoming sensible at last. Perhaps the displeasure of the Queen had sobered her. If so, it was worth the mortification Mrs. Cottington had suffered. If Claire had set her cap for Lord Rutherford, nothing would stop her. "Do wear your peacock pendant; it goes well with the yellow gown," she advised happily.

That evening Mrs. Cottington was resplendent in a gown of mauve silk. A deep bertha of lace frills spilled over the bodice, obscuring the short little sleeves and the line of her ample bosom. Silver thread in the material accented the silver strands in her hair, fastened in an elegant chignon which suited her maturity. Mrs. Cottington was not quite the faded beauty she was in terror of becoming; but this fear had influenced her to lace her stays too tightly, and her face already looked flushed and a little startled. As they rode through the summer evening en route to the Bainbridge's soiree, the older woman fanned herself and gasped gently, like a fish gulping air at the edge of a pond.

Claire frowned at her mother, slightly embarrassed. If only she dared to tell Mama the dangers that lay before them tonight! Claire had great respect for her mother's abilities in the realms of social warfare, but this was beyond her powers. Would the Major give her away? Would there be another scandal? Suppose that William had been seen leaving the moor this morning as well?

She studied the Major across the jolting carriage. As she looked at him, he sighed and tapped his boot against the floor. He did not seem happy to be going to a party, nor did he seem the sort to enjoy it. But why shouldn't he seem the sort? He was bound to make a sensation. Claire supposed it was because she still pictured him in her mind's eye as he had appeared in the mist. His lean, tanned cheeks, his dark, whipping hair and uncompromising mouth had given him a savage look. He seemed too raw and primitive for Jenny's party, and merely to look at him made little currents of alarm begin in her stomach.

Nonsense, thought Claire. He was like any other man, to be managed with a smile and a well-batted fan. She must not fail to manage him, or her reputation could be shattered. She had been determined to prove to herself and everyone tonight that the Queen's displeasure could not spoil her popularity. Now the evening was ruined. Along with party souvenirs, the guests might take away with them the tale that would be her final undoing. If he were a gentleman he would not give her away. But was he? Something told her he was different from the men she had known. Perhaps he played by different rules. She shivered and pulled her shawl closer about her.

Colin Whitecavage looked bemusedly at the girl on the other side of the carriage. This morning in the dining room of Cottington Crest, he had had only a glimpse of Miss Cottington, and he had been certain that his eyes had deceived him. The image of the girl on the moor had remained in his mind, superimposing itself on the ridiculous visage of Miss Cottington. Mrs. Cottington had been right about his not being used to seeing ladies under such conditions. Claire had looked to him like a package wrapped in white ribbons by a madman.

But now he saw that Miss Cottington did resemble the girl on the moor. Major Whitecavage was astonished. Surely she could *not* be that girl! Despite the resemblance there were important differences. In her yellow silk gown, its skirt looped up in ribbons, her silk evening slippers decorated with rosettes, and her dainty gloves of straw-colored kid, Miss Cottington could not be mistaken for the wild temptress of the mist. It wasn't just the clothes. This girl's demeanor was different. She was polished and cool, whereas the girl of the moor had seemed to burn.

The eyes—he thought. He had never seen eyes like the eyes of the girl on the moor. Her eyes had been aloof and distant, yet warm and compelling. They had been strangely innocent, yet flickering with the secret fires of womanhood. And the color—the shade of the Bay of Bengal at sunrise! Those magnificent orbs might have been a trick of the fog, not to be seen by mortal man except on such a preternatural night. The girl had been an apparition, he thought, though he was not usually a superstitious man.

When he had been able to check his terrified mount, he had tried to return to the bridge to look for her, but he had not been able to find it again, and it had not been until dawn, when the mist had lifted that he had encountered a herdsman who had directed him there again. The girl had been gone. He had wondered if the stream had carried away her dead or injured body, and having searched its course for a mile, felt foolish and frustrated.

It had been in his mind, a variation of his constant nightmare—in which he dreamed of the woman he had loved and the various horrible deaths she might have died. Waking or sleeping the outcome was always the same. She was gone— *Tamila*, the woman who had eclipsed all others. His heart constricted as he thought of her. He should not have loved her, but how could he have helped himself? He thought of Pandeish and the blood and fury amid which she had been lost to him forever. The Major was not looking forward to waltzing the night away in the company of adoring maidens, pale, brittle imitations of womanhood like the girl sitting across from him.

His thoughts became too painful, and forcing his mind away, he caught her glance. He gave a start. By God, her eyes *were* the same! *She* was the same! She dissolved any doubt he might have had by blushing as she realized he knew her identity.

Colin was not glad to make the discovery. He would sooner have had her an angel of the mist. Instead, she was only a spoiled little wanton whose devastating beauty might make her a danger to the sanest of men.

Colin wished with all his heart that Colonel Maxwell Todd had not made him privy to the contents of the letter he had been entrusted to deliver to Sir Cottington. Since Pandeish, he had been acutely aware of the hazards even honorable women posed to the men who loved them. In the right circumstances what destruction might a woman like Claire Cottington not wreak? Would he be the instrument to place her in those circumstances?

He told himself it could not be helped; he had a duty to perform and must perform it with the same strength of will that he led men into battle. He had no choice to make. He had come to deliver Max's letter, and deliver it he must. If he told Max what sort of woman Miss Cottington was, Max would not believe him, though they were dear friends. And after all, he had no evidence. But he knew. He knew a man had been involved in her adventure on the moor. Would it be different if he had evidence?

Then, before he or Claire could quite gather their senses, the carriage came to a halt, the wheels crunching on the crushed stone of the curving oak-lined drive. The tall windows of the Bainbridges' ballroom were thrown open, and the sounds of violins and laughter drifted out.

Mrs. Cottington became animated, patting at her hair, checking her flounces and the little jeweled bottle of smelling salts she always wore dangling from a chain at her waist. Many women carried such bottles for ornament and to suggest their delicacy, but Mrs. Cottington had formed the habit from necessity after Claire's debut. One never knew what jolts an evening might bring, and the smelling salts had more than once saved her from embarrassing collapse.

This evening, however, Mrs. Cottington had worn the bottle simply because it went well with her gown. She was all smiles as she allowed herself to be handed from the carriage by her unexpected bonus of the night, the handsome young major, who was bound to entrance the company, producing floods of envy and gratitude for her who had brought him.

Etiquette decreed that the Major dance first with her, and she was anticipating that privilege. As was usually the case, the mere proximity of a party made Mrs. Cottington feel almost intoxicated.

Having handed Mrs. Cottington down from the carriage, Major Whitecavage gave his hand to Claire, and gingerly she took it with her own small gloved one. That tiny hand became insignificant in his large one, toughened from years of handling guns and horses. But he did not seem to marvel at this difference of anatomy as many another man had with less cause. His hand closed over hers in a businesslike way, gripping it so roughly that Claire almost squealed with pain. Her ego was bruised as well. Claire was proud of her pretty little hands.

Major Whitecavage offered her his arm. She accepted, her fingers still smarting, her chin tilted up, her smile frozen, and her eyes bright with tears that remained unspilled by great effort of will.

Heads turned as they entered the ballroom—Claire Cottington, reprimanded by the Queen, but here nonetheless, as beautiful as ever and with a very attractive man in tow. Major Whitecavage frowned, aware of the titter that went around the room. Miss Cottington had a reputation, it seemed. Well deserved, no doubt. He sensed her trembling beside him, and he wondered if it were because she was afraid that he would give her away.

"Claire, dear, introduce me!" A giggly voice roused Colin from his reverie. Beside Miss Cottington was a girl in pink. Matching ribbons fluttered in her hair, which bounced in long, golden curls toward the mounds of her partly-exposed breasts, soft and round with apple-blossom tints.

"Miss Bainbridge, may I present Major Colin Whitecavage of the Bengal Army?" Claire was saying.

Jenny Bainbridge flicked pale lashes. "Major Whitecavage! Oh, but I've heard of you in London, sir. You fought some dreadful battle with the heathen."

"A dreadful battle, yes, but not with heathens, Miss Bainbridge. Hindus and Moslems—but devout."

"Hindu, heathen, what on earth is the difference, Major? You are merely being modest."

"Oh, I assure you that it would be easier to fight almost

anyone than Hindus, Jenny," Claire put in mildly. "They are formidable enemies because they aren't afraid of death."

"Not afraid of death! What an idea, Claire! Everyone is afraid to die." The subject made Jenny uncomfortable, but she smiled brightly. *Laugh and the world laughs with you* was Jenny's favorite dictum. Jenny wanted to laugh, and she wanted the handsome Major to laugh with her. The orchestra was playing her favorite waltz.

"It's because they believe in reincarnation," said Claire. "An honorable death means a higher position in the next life. They strive for perfection."

"Perfection? What could be as perfect as this waltz, Major?" Jenny turned blue eyes on Colin. "I adore dancing."

"Then will you do me the honor?" The Major offered his hand. She took it, flushing prettily as though surprised and flattered, as though she had not practically forced him to ask her. She had bested Claire with empty-headed feminity, to which men so readily acquiesced. But Jenny was not so empty-headed that she did not know exactly what she was doing, and she gazed up adoringly at the Major as they waltzed across the floor.

Colin, stealing a glance over her shoulder, saw a mischievous smile at Claire's mouth and rather wished he might have continued their conversation. Certainly her understanding of the Hindu religion spoke in her favor. There were officers' wives in the cantonments of British India who did not understand as much, or care to. He returned the smile and felt his mood lighten. He almost felt that he liked her. Why should he like her? After last night he didn't want to like her.

Claire's smile faded when Colin returned it. She had not really been smiling at him at all. The conversation had reminded her of Colonel Todd, to whom she owed her knowledge of India. She had listened with close attention to everything he had said to Papa, and she had even dared to ask him questions herself, such had been her interest. The challenge, the possibility, the wildness and diversity of the country had intrigued her as much as the Colonel himself.

Now Claire thought of the hazards of Colin's dancing with Jenny and positively frowned. Jenny was a notorious gossip, skilled at extracting information. Jenny had her antennae out, and who knew what a man might say to please an appealing creature like Jenny.

"Claire!" William was at her elbow, and he, too, was gazing at the Major and Jenny.

"Good evening, Lord Rutherford," she said distantly, but her heart began to pound. Memories of the previous evening returned, and she felt lightheaded. With Jenny preoccupied with the Major instead of William, Claire had an opportunity to salvage the situation. She still might triumph, she thought, if she could get Lord Rutherford to proclaim himself.

"Dance with me, William," she commanded, and before he quite knew how it had happened, he had taken her in his arms.

No sooner had he done so than both were suffused with the emotions of their encounter in the turfcutter's cottage. Claire's breath quickened at the touch of his hand, gloved in primrose kid, and her breasts grew tight with unseemly remembrance. Lord Rutherford became agitated, holding her so close that she was shocked and excited to feel his body though his black evening trousers.

She gave him a moony, lovesick glance and allowed her thighs to brush against his. *Now, William, now,* she thought, registering the effect she had had on him. Let him murmur his proposal of marriage! How grand it would be to announce her betrothal right here under Jenny Bainbridge's nose! What a coup! Papa was not present to do the honors, but Mama could do as well, giving consent, and under the circumstances Papa would be happy enough. Jenny would be furious at having Claire announce her claim to William at the very party Jenny had given in hopes of snaring him herself. She could thank the charming Major for distracting Jenny from William tonight.

William Rutherford knew what Claire intended, and the room seemed to close in upon him. The scent of roses in pearlware bowls was suddenly overpowering. He required fresh air, and waltzed Claire dizzily onto the veranda.

He wasn't thinking clearly or he would have realized that taking Claire onto the veranda was playing right into her hands. Once there, in the cool darkness, he could not possibly prevent himself from embracing her and kissing her passionately.

Claire responded, slipping her slender arms about his neck and pressing her soft lips against his. The gilt buttons on William's claret-colored coat trembled, betraying volcanic upheaval within. He struggled to fix his mind on his freedom instead of on the longings of his body. An announcement of his engagement would not make *him* happy, any more than it would make Jenny or Claire's London admirers cheer. But William could not seem to remember why not.

Why, after all, shouldn't he propose to Claire? She was beautiful; he desired her. He had been to the very brink with her, and the experience had nearly been his undoing. He could find no thought to counter the thought of how much he wanted her.

The tryst should have been *her* undoing, and would have been, he was sure, if it had not been for the mist. William allowed his finger to stray to her bodice, hoping against hope for another assignation.

But Claire was a quick learner. "William!" she reprimanded, removing his fingers as though they had been spiders crawling toward her cleavage.

Lord Rutherford could have wept. Last night she might have surrendered and become his mistress, but the opportunity had fled. She had become the proper Victorian maiden, and there was only one way he could possess her. Lord Rutherford had survived as a bachelor thus far simply because a key seemed to turn inside him at the crucial moment, locking his wayward emotions safely inside him. Now, mentally, he tried to turn that key. He listened helplessly for the comforting click in his brain that would seal away his impulses.

But tonight Lord Rutherford did not hear a click. Instead, he heard his own voice, desperate with passion, pleading, "Claire, my darling, please marry me! Say that you'll marry me!"

He backed up a step in surprise and stared at Claire, while she, still gasping from their tussle, stared back in equal astonishment.

"Oh, dear me, William, this is most improper," said Claire, regaining herself. "You haven't even asked Papa's permission to address me so. I should go back to the company this minute!"

William very nearly exploded. Damn women! She had what she wanted. Why couldn't she just admit it? Why did women have to play these games? To think this was the same girl who had offered to meet him alone on the moor. If he had managed better there, he would not be in this fix now.

"I shall speak to your father the instant he returns! I will be at Cottington Crest at dawn to wait for him! If he is there already, I shall require him to receive me in his nightshirt," William promised wildly.

"I suppose that would be all right," Claire murmured. She,

no more than he, understood the game she was playing. Why had she brought up Papa at all, when Mama would do? Why had the fact of his proposal frightened her? Now she had done herself out of her wish to announce their betrothal tonight.

"Then we'll be engaged, love!" he cried happily. He took a ruby ring from his finger and folded it in her palm. "This will seal the bargain."

"It is not an engagement ring, William," she said dazedly.

"You shall have my grandmother's ring, sweet. But until then, this one will be on a ribbon around your neck."

He kissed her ardently, leaving her too breathless to speak assent; but William took that for granted, and departed well satisfied. He had given up his freedom, but she would make an excellent mother for the heirs of Thistlewood, and soon the longings of his body would find release. He was relieved, too. A certain story was beginning to circulate on the dance floor.

Jenny Bainbridge, in a sour mood, had twitted to him about it. He had repaid her by treading on her toe in consternation. Soon everyone would know that he had had a tryst with Claire on the moor. He might well have paid a greater price than loss of freedom for his ill-advised escapade. Sir Cottington was a renowned marksman.

William knew that his groom must be responsible for the gossip. When he'd returned to Thistlewood at dawn, he'd had Claire's mare in tow. He'd told the boy to deliver the animal discretely to Cottington Crest. The same boy had driven his carriage this evening; and no doubt he was sharing the tale with other drivers, his tongue loosened by the brandy that the servants were wont to pass among themselves while waiting for their masters. Thank heaven Claire had not been a married woman! Then the damage could not have been so quickly remedied.

Claire hurried to find her mother and give her the wonderful news. But Mama was embroiled in a game of whist and resisted her daughter's attempts to speak to her privately. "Later, dear," she begged, "after I've played this hand."

So Claire danced with this admirer and that, all of whom noticed her radiance. Colin Whitecavage was the hit of the evening, of course. Jenny Bainbridge kept him rapturously in tow as much as possible, and all the ladies asked Claire about him, while casting yearning looks after the Sword of Pandeish. Claire answered all questions off-handedly, no longer concerned with the soldier who had thrilled her so strangely in the fog.

"Do you mean you have not danced with him, Claire?" someone asked, incredulously.

"Oh, I must, of course. I simply haven't had a chance," she said indifferently.

Then he was beside her, requesting a waltz. She danced away with him, remembering her injured hand and thoroughly expecting to be trampled. Instead his firm hand at her waist guided her with amazing lack of effort. Surprised, she gazed into his unsmiling eyes and felt dazzled, as if the golden flecks in the night of brown had been a hundred fires. She lost her bearing in a sense of wonder.

Soon, too soon, the dance was over, and Jenny rang a little bell and announced in a tone of naughty delight that they would all play hide and seek.

Before long, the garden, laid out formally in a maze of hedges and paths, rang with shrieks and laughter. Claire took refuge behind a thorny bush. In a moment the branches moved, and someone slid down beside her in her hiding spot.

"There's not room for both of us here, Major," she observed.

"You would not say so if I were William Rutherford," he answered.

"That is none of your business, my dear Major," Claire bristled. "You have made conquests yourself tonight."

So he had seen her on the veranda, she thought, the darkness covering her blushes. How ungallant of him to mention it. No doubt he had thought the worst, just as he had on the moor. That was his way. No doubt it was because he was worse than William with women.

He smiled ruefully, his mood obviously foul. "My conquests were quite unintentional, I assure you. Women who pant after a man to hear of the bloody deeds life has required of him sicken me. I expect better of women."

"Perhaps you expect too much."

"Undoubtedly," he agreed. An anguished expression came over his face; and Claire, not knowing that he thought of her, Tamila, the Rani of Pandeish, who had given more than he could ever have asked, wondered if he were in physical pain.

"I tried escaping to the veranda," he went on, "but I was forced to abandon the idea because of the way in which it was occupied. And now I am to be chased about the garden like a rabbit in a cabbage patch. I haven't been so disadvantaged since I fought the Russians in Crimea. Can you imagine how foolish I feel to be playing this childish game? I have been away from England too long for it."

"I suppose you've forgotten the rules," she said recklessly. The rules allowed a young man to steal a kiss, should he encounter a member of the opposite sex in her hiding spot. As soon as the words were out of her mouth she wanted to call them back. She knew suddenly that he had *not* forgotten, and that a kiss of his would not be of the decorous variety she was used to receiving on such occasions.

She had only wanted to devil him, sensing his disapproval of her, and now as he bent toward her, she backed away, tangling her lace bertha on the thorns of the bush. Then his mouth was on hers, and she forgot that she had been kissed before in any way by any man. She struggled, unaware of whether she was pushing him away or embracing him. Her Victorian soul was shocked at the ecstasy that tingled down to her silk slippers, while her sensual nature rejoiced, wanting the moment never to end.

The sound of ripping material brought them both to their senses. Both stared down at her ruined sleeve, both remembering the tale she had told about tearing her jacket on a hawthorne on the moor.

Major Whitecavage laughed insultingly. "I do believe you are destined to collide with every thorn in Dartmoor, Miss Cottington. Stay here, and I'll go fetch your shawl."

He left her trembling, unnoticing of the angry red scratch on her arm. The bush stirred again, and Jenny Bainbridge came in next to her, giving a little grunt of disappointment as she realized the gender of her partner in hiding. Claire was certain that Jenny had thought the Major was the occupant of the bush. Then Jenny's eyes fastened on the wreckage of Claire's gown and she forgot her pique.

"Claire, what's happened? Are you all right? Has someone. . . ." Jenny's concerned voice held undertones of hope.

"I've torn my gown, that's all. It was so stupid, and this is a Worth dress, too." Claire pointed to the bits of yellow material clinging to the thorn.

"Oh, what a pity!" Jenny was genuinely distressed. "The lace is ruined. But I'm sure it can be fixed, Claire. We could take off this row, and the sleeve can be patched. I'll go and get you a cloak, and you can go upstairs. I'll send my seamstress up to you. There'll be no need for you to go home and miss the rest of the party."

Finally Claire understood Jenny's concern. *There'll be no need for you to go home and take the fascinating Sword of Pandeish with you,* she meant.

"Thank you, Jenny, but I've already sent someone to fetch my shawl. Could you be a dear and check on Major White-cavage for me? I'm afraid he may not be enjoying himself. I think he went into the tool shed."

"Oh certainly, Claire!" Jenny looked as though she'd been asked to eat a bowl of ripe strawberries. Clutching her pink skirts, she tripped off through the moonshadows with her ribbons fluttering.

It seemed to be taking the Major a long time to retrieve her shawl, Claire thought. Maybe she'd been ill-advised not to take Jenny up on her offer. Had the Major been intercepted by someone appealing and left her in the lurch? How little she knew what to expect of him! In all her experience as a London belle, she had never been kissed as he had kissed her. Even William's lusty kisses could never compare. When William had aroused her, it had only been with animal feeling. It had been no more than an imitation of what she had experienced with Colin Whitecavage.

She was shamed as she had never been by any of her escapades. To think that he had kissed her in such an indelicate way! He had done so because he thought her the sort of woman who gave her favors lightly—to an unknown lover on the moor, to Lord Rutherford on the veranda. Oh, why hadn't she told him that William was her fiancé? But then he would not have kissed her as he had! And Claire herself had, at the moment, forgotten she was betrothed.

She heard his footsteps returning, and he ducked beneath the bush, her shawl in his hand. Her shoulders burned in the cool autumn air as he slipped it around her. She sat unmoving, stunned at his very touch.

"Claire, hurry, we must leave right away," he said, and she noticed more than anything else that he used her given name for the first time and without having obtained permission to use it. On his tongue it sounded like a temple chime, reverberating softly in the midnight air.

"Leave? But why? The party will go on for hours yet." She wanted the party to go on—and on. She would arrange for him to find her in the shelter of the privet hedge, behind an ancient wisteria, amid the wispy, concealing arms of a willow. Would he follow her and kiss her again and again as custom said he might? He would; he must. It could not be necessary to leave.

"It's your mother, Claire," he explained. "She's ill. I've put her into the carriage, and we have only to offer our thanks to our hostess before we go."

Claire jumped up in alarm, almost leaving her shawl on the same branch that had snagged her dress. Mama was rarely indisposed, but Claire remembered the dreadful weeks after their return from London, when Mama had lain abed with the draperies shut. She had refused to eat anything but her favorite onion broth, fed to her by Claire; and Claire, afraid her mother would die, had been in an agony of remorse. She had made promises to herself of good behavior should her mother regain her health, and perhaps her immense gratitude to William for having sparked her mother's recovery had contributed to their romance.

Having murmured her appreciation to Mrs. Bainbridge, Claire rushed out to the carriage. She was aghast at the sight of her mother, cringing in a corner of the vehicle, her face pale and haggard. The contrast to her earlier demeanor— when she had come to enjoy a ball in the company of a handsome officer—was incredible.

"What's wrong?" Claire cried. But Mrs. Cottington could not speak. She could only cling to Claire's hand with her own cold, trembling one, and clutch her little bottle of smelling salts as though her life depended on it. Her eyes were wild in her white face as she emitted little sobbing syllables of which Claire could make no sense.

"You had better loosen her stays," said the Major.

"No, don't you dare," Mrs. Cottington recovered enough to say.

The Major looked irritated at her display of vanity. "I'll look out the window, of course," he sighed, but still Mrs. Cottington fought Claire's hands away. Die, she might, but it would be with her twenty-three inch waistline intact!

As soon as the carriage came to a halt in front of the house at Cottington Crest, Claire alerted the household. Mama was whisked upstairs and put to bed by able servants, dosed with brandy and camomile tea. "I'll send someone for the doctor," Claire said anxiously. "Perhaps the Major will go."

"Claire, no." Her mother's voice was a whisper. "Send everyone out of the room. I must talk to you."

As soon as it was done, Mrs. Cottington grew calmer. "Oh,

Claire, you cannot imagine! It's too awful." She wept exhaust-
edly into her lace handkerchief.

"Come now, it can't be that bad," Claire encouraged.

Mama sat up. "It's worse! You wouldn't say that if you
heard the story they are telling about you!"

"You mean they are still talking about the Queen's sending
me home?" Claire felt a chill of premonition. Had the Major
given her away? He was the only one who knew.

"Oh, it can't be true, naturally. But truth matters little
when a story is as scandalous as this one."

Claire gritted her teeth. It could be nothing else. "Do you
mean the tale that I was on the moors last night?"

Mrs. Cottington was amazed. "Why, Claire, you've heard
it! How can you be so composed? How could you just go on
as if nothing had happened? It's your generation, I expect.
Nothing fazes any of you!"

"Mama, it's true," Claire said. "I was with William. . . ."

Mrs. Cottington's large bosom heaved. Her lacy nightcap
quivered. "True! I shall die!"

"Mama, it will be all right. William has——"

At that moment they heard a commotion in the drive.
"That's Papa carriage!" Mrs. Cottington cried, and before
Claire could give her her news, she fainted.

3

Colin did not wait for morning to deliver his letter. He asked for an audience with Sir Cottington at once and was ushered into his presence. Sir Cottington, looking worn, greeted him wearing an alpaca lounging jacket, and offered him a cigar. Colin declined the cigar, then accepted a glass of brandy. Sir Cottington was grateful to have a respite, even at this hour, before he dealt with new difficulties concerning his daughter.

Her troubles in London had been bewildering enough, but now he had come home to find his wife ill because of her again and some upsetting story sweeping the neighborhood. Would it never end?

But Sir Cottington loved his daughter. He was a man with understanding beyond his time, and he recognized that Claire was an exceptional woman. She was out of kilter with her confining society, but was it society that was really out of kilter with nature? Claire was like the single stalk of corn that had shot up in a barren field where a hundred less vital seeds had failed to germinate.

He did not like to think of her spirit being crushed in marriage. But what choice did he have? Claire must be married, and soon. Perhaps it was already too late. He had spoiled her, his wife said. He supposed it was true.

He sighed and looked at the young officer before him. Colin Whitecavage. The name meant something. He was the one who had so distinguished himself in Pandeish. His presence caused the older man to be suffused with thoughts of his youth, when he and Maxwell Todd had ridden side by side. As mere newcomers, "griffins," they had traveled up the

33

Brahmaputra River to Assam during the first Burmese War. The country had been dense jungle, filled with unfordable rivers, infested with malaria. The enemy had resisted from clever stockades of bamboo hidden in the trees; but the British had held on until cold weather and triumphed at last. Those had been the finest days, Sir Cottington thought. India was different, now that the memsahibs had come. Native society and British were more set apart now, and men and women of different colors did not mix so easily. But India was still India, he thought with a touch of yearning.

The presence of Major Whitecavage made Sir Cottington's homecoming less a trial. Tonight he would sip brandy and chat about India. Tonight he would hear news of his old regiment; he would relive his golden days. He did not regret having given up his commission to come home to marry, he told himself; but oh, what days they had been, the days of his lost youth!

Here, too, was an unexpected bonus: a letter addressed to him in the handwriting of his dearest friend, to be read after their pleasant conversation.

But his conversation with Colin Whitecavage was not exactly pleasant. Sir Cottington could only conclude that the Major had been touched by the sun, for he made very little sense at all. Sir Cottington wanted to reminisce of conquests and battles, but the arrogant pup did not want to listen. The Major was ranked too high for his age. It had gone to his head.

The Major wanted to talk only of unimportant civil matters, intimating that some day there would be mutiny. The Sword of Pandeish, indeed! Major Whitecavage was an old woman!

"The Hindus are shocked by the abolition of the Kingdom of Satara, and our refusal to pay the pension due the Nana Sahib, the Peshwa, titular head of the Maratha Confederacy," Major Whitecavage ran on. "And the Moslems are equally distressed at the annexation of Oude. There will be trouble——"

"Nonsense, my boy. Our annexation of the Punjab has not caused trouble. It's as peaceful as Devonshire there, and the Sikhs are fierce fighters."

"Yes," agreed Colin, "I fought in the Sikh War. But John Company has sent good men to the Punjab."

"Maxwell Todd in Delhi is a good man," mused Sir Cottington.

"Yes, but there are not enough like him. And even he does-n't fully comprehend. Max strives for justice according to the British way of thinking. He does not unbend to the Eastern ideas of our subjects."

"Humph! Should think not! Our duty's to raise 'em up."

Major Whitecavage seemed flustered at having said any-thing in the least uncomplimentary about his friend and men-tor. "What I mean, sir, is that India is more dangerous than ever before—especially for a woman."

Sir Cottington frowned and wondered if Major Whitecav-age had come home to marry as he himself had done. India was dangerous for a woman, but how he had missed his Mar-garet when he'd been a young blade! The Major's seemingly pointless remark reminded Sir Cottington of things about himself that he had hoped to forget—of the succession of na-tive women he had had installed in a small cottage behind his bungalow, ostensibly to cook for him and clean his rooms.

Eager to read Max's letter, Sir Cottington yawned; and the Major, taking the hint, excused himself. Sir Cottington put on his spectacles and spread the pages before him. Maxwell Todd wasn't a man to write letters. Sir Cottington hadn't heard from him for years.

The letter was long, filled with descriptions of Max's en-deavors. He wrote of having been present at the opening of the first railway, twenty miles long, from Bombay to Thana; and spoke with enthusiasm of another to be constructed from Calcutta to the Raniganj coalfields. He had hopes for the new forms of the civil service and Lord Dalhousie's new depart-mental plan of government. But the Army of Bengal was in a sorry state, he wrote, and the job was more difficult than he had expected.

"You were right, Henry," Max wrote. "I have not had a vacation since I have been here, except one visit to the hill country to a conference at the Governor-General's summer home at Simla. But I will not give up; this is an historical op-portunity, the likes of which will not soon be seen again. I must go on, but I cannot go on alone."

Then came the astonishing part of the letter, and Sir Cot-tington readjusted his spectacles in surprise. "I have learned the hard way that a man is not sufficient unto himself. I need a wife, Henry, but where am I to find one who is not a mere toy? One to believe in me and stand with me, shoulder to shoulder? The women here cannot think past the next tea party! In all my life I have met only one woman who inspires me to marriage. She was scarcely more than a child at the time. I am speaking, of course, of your daughter, Claire. She is in my thoughts constantly. I have never forgotten her; she is the one who could relieve me of my nightmare of loneliness. The difference in our ages is great, but some things go beyond age! I dare to hope that she remembers me and feels kindly disposed toward me. I beg you to ask her, and if she is willing, send her to me! I will be a considerate husband and will build her a house in the hills at Simla to make her life as comfortable as possible. My dear friend, if you had a son, I know you would not hesitate to send him to India, caring for it as you do. Send India—and me—Claire instead!"

When Sir Cottington had finished reading Colonel Todd's impassioned letter, he sat for a long while in a state of bewilderment. Send Claire to India, what an idea! It was true that he would have been delighted for his son to serve in his regiment, but Claire! He shuddered at the thought of the tears Mrs. Cottington would shed. He didn't think he could stand it himself; Claire was his only child.

On the other hand, there were certain advantages. The sort of partnership Maxwell had in mind might suit Claire, utilizing energies which she had hereto squandered in scandalous frivolity. Like Lord Rutherford, Sir Cottington had stock in John Company, and his voice was sure to grow stronger should Claire wed a prestigious man like Maxwell Todd. Sir Cottington might even be elected to the board, where, having first-hand knowledge of the country, he could make himself listened to. The idea pleased Henry Cottington, and he even chuckled as he lighted another cigar.

He knew now why Major Whitecavage had seemed such an alarmist. Claire appeared such a delicate girl to go to India. But the Major knew nothing about Claire. He did not know the problems. She had become involved in a scandal that would not be easily forgotten. What could be more perfect than the timing of Colonel Todd's letter? Claire could be spirited out of the country, but spirited out with pride, since marriage to Colonel Todd would be anything but shameful. Max would not stay in India much longer. No one could stand the climate forever. Max would come home, at least for a time; and if fate were kind, Claire would have no children until they were home again.

Sir Cottington thought a while longer and, having downed another brandy to fortify himself, went upstairs to wake his wife.

Claire, in her room, heard her father's footsteps. She tensed, wondering if he were coming to speak to her. But Claire had nothing to fear, for once, not with William's ring in her possession.

However, Papa's footsteps went past her room and into her mother's. Claire sighed, but did not go back to bed. She rather wished that Papa *had* come in to talk to her. She couldn't sleep.

Tonight she had become engaged, and Colin Whitecavage had kissed her. It was a disturbing combination. Claire was badly frightened. She was frightened because she had liked his kiss. Most certainly she would never allow him to kiss her again. He had shown himself a cad, for no gentleman would ever have repeated the tale of her journey on the moor. She hated Colin Whitecavage, and she flung a pillow at her wall to prove it. He thought her immoral, and she thought him no better. But why, why, had his kiss unnerved her so?

She ought to forget about Major Whitecavage. Tomorrow her engagement would be announced. She ought to be thinking of that. She had worked hard for her moment of triumph. She ought to be ecstatic. But Claire imagined herself the mistress of Thistlewood, she imagined herself on her wedding night, and she felt frightened and alone. She and Mama had shared everything until now. But tonight Claire had not even been able to tell her mother about her success. Mama had fainted, and that had seemed to presage the future. When Claire thought of her marriage bed, she did not think of being together with the man she loved. She thought of herself as she had been in the peatcutter's cottage. Alone with William. *Alone.*

Claire's attention was arrested by voices in her mother's bedroom. Mama was weeping.

"Oh, Henry, please! You cannot even consider it!" she sobbed.

Claire began to listen intently, wondering what punishment he was planning for her latest escapade. Would marriage to Lord Rutherford turn out to be a punishment itself?

"We must at least think about it," said Papa, giving no clue. "It may be the best thing for Claire, considering."

"Oh, but I'm sure that Lord Rutherford will ask for Claire's hand. He was seen coming home at dawn and so is involved in the story. Claire admits——"

"That would be an advantageous match, of course. But so would the other. Perhaps we should let Claire decide."

"Let Claire decide! How can you say that when you know how Claire is? Promise me you'll burn that letter, Henry!"

"But I can't do that. Suppose Lord Rutherford doesn't propose? Suppose I must duel him? He will not make a good husband should I aim wrong and kill him. Anyway, I do not like the idea at all. We need an alternative. Claire cannot go on as she has!"

"No. . . ." Mama's voice was tremulous as she agreed. "Oh, Henry, India is so dirty—so vulgar—so—unfashionable!"

"Colonel Todd is none of those things, my dear. He will marry her and take good care of her. It's obvious that he loves her. I'll let you read the letter."

"But he is more than twice her age and——"

"And so able to offer her more than a young man just starting out."

"Not more than Lord Rutherford!" said Mama sharply. "He has inherited his."

"True. I agree that we will say nothing to Claire until Lord Rutherford has been given the opportunity to declare himself. But then we must urge Claire to accept Maxwell Todd's offer of marriage. Egad! How will we persuade her? Maybe she doesn't even remember him."

A shiver of rapture ran down Claire's spine. She was afraid that she had fallen asleep after all and was dreaming, for certainly this was all her dreams coming true! Maxwell Todd loved her! She could go to India as his bride! Of course she would! Hugging herself, she spun in a little circle, her silk nightgown billowing in moonbeams. She knew she had been waiting for him all along. All these years he had been waiting, too, dreaming of her just as she had been dreaming of him. How wonderfully poetic it was!

As she spun, something clinked painfully against her chest. She glanced down and saw William's ring. She could not marry Maxwell Todd! She was already engaged to William. Well, not officially engaged, but he would speak to Papa tomorrow! And if Papa learned William was willing to marry her, he would not consider Colonel Todd's offer. What was Claire to do?

In the morning all the servants tiptoed cautiously about. In their quarters it was whispered that Miss Claire had "done it" again.

Whenever Miss Claire had "done it," everyone shuddered, from the butler to the newest upstairs maid. For then, Mrs. Cottington, who was usually sweet and lenient, was likely to fly into tantrums and make dismissals over dust on a bannister or an overdone roast. This time things appeared worse, because Miss Claire was in a state herself, and at breakfast reprimanded the maid on three different occasions because her tea was cool. Actually the tea had been steaming each time, but Miss Claire had sat morsely in a brown study until it had become tepid. The last time had been most confounding, for Claire had absentmindedly sweetened her tea with four lumps instead of two and, gagging on the result, flew into an unprecedented rage.

At least no one was there to see it. Mrs. Cottington had taken breakfast in her room, and the Major had been up early and gone out for a ride. One would have thought that Major Whitecavage would have lolled abed, for he had danced the night away and was on leave besides.

But no sooner had dawn pinked the sky than here he came, traipsing down most shockingly to the kitchen itself to request a slab of bread and a hunk of sausage. He had consumed the meal at the kitchen table, scandalizing everyone. It was only sensible, he said, since the dining room wasn't prepared. He did not want to sit about and wait until breakfast time or even to cause anyone the added trouble of serving him early.

The cook feared that Mrs. Cottington would find out. In her present mood, heads would roll. But by mid-morning the inhabitants of the kitchen received another shock, which melted the Major's indiscretion to insignificance. Miss Bainbridge's driver arrived to inquire after Mrs. Cottington's health and took a cup of tea. He wheedled a piece of jam cake out of cook to tell the tale he was splitting to tell anyway; and when he had told it, he was irately banished from the kitchen at the end of a broom. Miss Claire did get into fixes, but no one of the establishment of Cottington Crest was about to believe the filth that poured out of that fellow's mouth! Claire was their pet.

Colin had enjoyed his morning's ride. The autumn meadows had been lush with harebells and dogdaisies which soon would be gone. He had watched swallows diving over a newly-harvested field, feasting on insects uncovered by the scythe. Suddenly a white butterfly had soared up, higher and higher, its course steady as though reaching for the mare's-tail clouds in the cerulean sky. He let his heart lift with it and shared the ecstasy of its small, determined wings.

And then the swallows had seen it and come for it, dark, graceful, and swooping, sunlight brilliant on the rosy hues of their breasts. The butterfly was caught, and fluttered in a beak, as, pursued by jealous companions, the bird skimmed away. But the butterfly struggled free. At first it catapulted downward; then, regaining itself, it went up, up. Again it was caught—by another swallow. Again it regained freedom. Colin began to be interested and to hope that the butterfly would live. Time and again it was caught. And time and again it escaped.

Then it was caught for the last time. He waited to see it flutter free and intsead saw nothing. The Sword of Pandeish frowned. It had been inevitable, and Colin did not like the concept of inevitability.

Colin felt that his life was full of white butterflies. He was a white butterfly himself. So was Maxwell Todd. And all the men who had followed him and died on the battlefield of Pandeish. Tamila. Most of all, Tamila.

It had been inevitable that he love her. Colin tethered his mount and lay in the grass, thinking of the day he had come upon Tamila unaware in a little courtyard of the Rana's marble palace. He had been dumbfounded at the sight of her unveiled beside a trickling fountain. She had looked at him with dark eyes and made no move to cover her face. After that, whenever he had come to the palace on state occasions he had felt those eyes watching him from behind the tatties. Much later, there had been stolen nights on which he had scaled the wall to the zenana to love her among silken cushions. Those nights he had known he might die for. Those nights had been worth dying for. He himself had been willing to die, but he had not been willing for others to die.

The cool September field became the battleground of Pandeish, where blood had flowed onto sand and, drying, had been stirred aloft into clouds of vermilion dust. Water had been scarce that day, and men had broken caste by drinking from the brass lotas of those of inferior station. It had taken every ounce of his leadership to retain leadership, for they had seemed hemmed in on every side. But he had found a way through the rocks, and his men had followed, under incredible fire. Many had followed him only to die. They had gone to their graves admiring him, never knowing that he had provoked the attack. He had emerged a hero, but he had his terrible secret to bear—a secret a thousand times worse than Claire Cottington's secret of her tryst on the moor.

Pandeish had been peaceful, its fiery Rana like a somnolent old tiger on his throne until Colin had come.

Tamila had suffered, too, he was sure. Perhaps the worst of his burden was that he did not know how she had suffered or what sort of circumstances she lived under now. He believed in his heart that she did not live at all.

Tamila had been fearless, afraid only for him. Had she died, too, departing the earth like the butterfly, leaving only empty sky? Empty. His life was empty sky without her.

Had she died a suttee? Had she chosen that way to atone for the sin of loving him? Had she been dragged drugged to the fires by her enemies? He would never know, he thought, for it was not often that a Westerner penetrated the confines of the zenana. He would never be allowed to return to Pandeish.

In the sweet grass the Major relaxed finally, as he had not been able to do on the featherbed behind the walls of Cottington Crest. He needed rest; indeed, he had been ordered to rest.

He might have been court-martialed; but Colonel Todd would not permit things to turn out so. Colonel Todd knew how Colin loved India. He had had much to offer there; perhaps he still did. Colin had come home to England a hero and been given the choice and the responsibility of deciding himself whether to return. But, of course, even if he returned, it could not be to Pandeish or Tamila.

Colin felt weighted with his responsibility. He wished again that Colonel Todd had not made his privy to the contents of the letter he had been charged with delivering. Colin had boundless respect and affection for his superior, who had been such a friend during the years of his Indian service. But Colonel Todd's dreams for India were not always practical, given the native temperament and the condescending attitude of the majority of British in India. Maxwell Todd would never give up, Colin thought. He would destroy himself with trying. India would destroy him, as it had many a lesser man.

Colonel Todd was a white butterfly. And what of Claire Cottington? Would she become a white butterfly, too

Colin thought of the sweetness of her kiss. He had not expected such haunting freshness. The emotions her kiss had aroused had made him restless all night. Was she, after all, the right woman for Max?

Her strange appearance on the moor and the passionate encounter he had witnessed with Lord Rutherford had confused him. He had meant to speak more plainly to her father. He had intended to say that women in the garrisons rendered them unsafe—for the necessity to protect women made men vulnerable.

When Colin returned to Cottington Crest, she was downstairs in the dining room, toying with a blueberry muffin, ignoring eggs, fresh fruit, and a glazed ham, set out especially because of Sir Cottington's return. Colin couldn't understand why she wasn't still lazing abed if she were not hungry. But here she was, down so early and with no rag curls in her hair.

Hungry again after his ride, Colin filled his plate at the sideboard, poured himself a cup of strong, black tea, and sat across from her. Her presence made him uneasy, although he did not want to think why that might be.

At least Sir Cottington wasn't about. Colin did not want to indulge him in another long chat about India. The longing in Sir Cottington's eyes as they spoke of fabled places both had known had unsettled Colin. He had felt as though he were looking into the mirror of the future. If he did not return to India, would he become like Sir Cottington?

I'll be gone from here today, he thought with relief. Sir Cottington would spend the morning penning an answer to Colonel Todd, and then Colin would be on his way to London to see the reply posted from the East India Company offices—whatever the answer might be.

After that, Colin had not decided where he would go. He might go to his family estates, but there he would be toasted as the Sword of Pandeish, and he was weary of that. Perhaps he would find some far-flung outpost of British India to disappear to. The Sword of Pandeish would not be heard of for years. Perhaps never again, he thought. The idea pleased him.

"re up early, Miss Cottington," he observed, feeling
make conversation.

pang of disappointment without knowing
called her Miss Cottington, instead of
someone," she said distantly.

"A visitor? This is not the proper hour for anyone to pay a call."

"No matter. He will be here."

She had an air of nervous expectancy about her that intrigued him. She pursed her lips delicately over the rim of her steaming tea cup, and suddenly memories of the night before washed over him and he felt inundated with desire to kiss her. He was startled, for he thought that his heart had gone with Tamila forever—to the death, if that was where she had gone.

"Who are you waiting for?" he asked gently.

As he watched, a tear slid from the corner of her eye and, tracing the fine, high line of her cheek as he wished his fingers might, it slid over the edge of her mouth to merge with the beverage.

"Lord Rutherford. He's coming to ask Papa for my hand. It's your fault. You've spoiled everything!"

"My fault! How can it be my doing that a man I scarcely know is proposing to marry you? Anyway, I should think you'd be happy. He's a perfect match."

"It's your fault because you let it be known that I was on the moor. It was William I was meeting there, and the gossips have put it together. You are—no gentleman!" she cried angrily.

"I beg your pardon, Miss Cottington. It's you who are no lady. You were on the moor. That is only the truth. Anyway, if Lord Rutherford loves you——"

"He does not!" she declared, weeping openly and furiously. "He is only afraid that Papa will kill him in a duel. I want to marry Colonel Todd, but I will never be allowed to if William speaks to Papa!"

Colin felt a wave of relief. Perhaps she would not marry Maxwell Todd. But Colin did not analyze the reason for his relief. Was he glad simply that his friend was not going to wed a troublesome, immoral woman? Or did he sense that he himself had narrowly escaped some untold destiny of passion and grief?

"It is not my fault, but you'll do better to marry Lord Rutherford and remain safely in England," he told her gravely.

Her chin lifted proudly. "I am not afraid to go to India. I love Colonel Todd. What a privilege it would be to be his wife! It is everything I have ever dreamed of! I know you do not think I am worthy."

"No, I do not," he said harshly. "Dreams. That is all it is,

Miss Cottington. You are nothing but a silly romantic. You are spoiled and willful and determined to have your own way. How could you possibly handle India, when you have made such a muddle of your coddled little life!"

She rose from her chair, the color of her eyes darkening to the blue of fire's hottest flame. Her hand fastened about a silver bread server, and he thought she might hurl it at him. He was all at once aware of how much he had underestimated her and of how much she hated him.

Claire did not throw the bread server, for just then a man's footsteps sounded on the stair. And in the driveway the wheels of a carriage crunched.

"It's Lord Rutherford!" cried Claire. "And Papa is coming down! Oh, if only I could have intercepted William and told him I am engaged to Colonel Todd. It's too late now!"

Claire ran from the room. In a moment he saw her running from the side door to the summerhouse. From the windows on the other side of the room, he could see Lord Rutherford alighting from his carriage.

Sir Cottington's boots ceased to thud as he paused on the landing, then thumped nearer. In a moment the two would meet in the front hall, and that simple happenstance would decide Claire's destiny. But destiny had been changed before because of Colin Whitecavage. He had taken victory where defeat was meant to be, led men to safety over mountains there had seemed no way to cross, loved a woman who had been intended to see only her husband's face.

Now Colin felt the urge to change Claire Cottington's fate. There had been something in her eyes that had seemed to restore him, rushing over him like a spring breeze, lifting the heaviness he had felt inside. He was convinced that Claire loved Maxwell Todd with the same depth and passion that Maxwell loved Claire. The idea filled him with amazement and somehow with hope. He had only seconds to decide, and thinking of her questionable morality and penchant for trouble, he hesitated.

Then, looking at William stepping down from his carriage, in his Newmarket jacket and brightly-colored nankin trousers with a stripe down the side, Colin was suddenly aware of how little he liked him. All at once he was determined that Lord Rutherford would not marry Claire.

He stepped casually out the terrace door and, having glanced appreciatively about at the beautiful morning, greeted William as he came up the steps.

"Ah, Whitecavage, good morning!" William called in return. "Is Sir Cottington at breakfast yet?"

"He's still abed," said Colin, "but Miss Cottington is waiting for you in the summerhouse."

4

Claire Cottington stood gazing out at the sunlit Mediterranean, oblivious of spray that splashed over the ship's rail onto her short velvet polka jacket and her traveling skirt of green merino. Her wide-brimmed bonnet had blown off her head and cavorted behind her, held by broad ribbons about her neck. Mama would have conniptions if she were to see Claire exposing her pink and white complexion to the sun, but Mama had been shut in her cabin with seasickness ever since they had run past the rocks of St. Elmo, out of the harbor of Malta.

At Malta, Claire had been nervous and impatient, while Mama had reveled in purchases of gloves and Maltese crapes and laces. Now their roles were reversed. The tiresome shopping was over, and Claire felt as if her own excitement made the ship fly over the water toward Alexandria, where an emissary from Colonel Todd would wait to escort her across Egypt to Suez and from there across the Red Sea to Calcutta.

She was to arrive during Christmas Week, the most gala time of the year, when all the most important personages of the British Raj, and in fact all who could get leave from their posts, gathered to celebrate. Amid the glitter of Calcutta society, Claire would be united in wedlock with Colonel Todd, who was journeying down from Delhi for the event. Afterward, there would be a reception in the palace of the Governor-General, where she would be feted as the bride of one of the most respected and influential men in all India.

As she thought of it, as she did every moment, even asleep in her dreams, Claire seemed to feel herself float over the ship's rail and go flying ahead of the boat, borne like a gull on the loose velvet sleeves of her jacket.

The time since that autumn day when Papa had returned from London and opened the letter had been filled with happy preparations. Claire's trousseau had come with her in innumerable trunks and boxes. The wedding gown itself had taken the whole of one Saratoga trunk.

Claire's only regret was that Jenny Bainbridge would not be at her wedding to see her triumph. But Claire did not really mind the absence of Jenny and the London tongue-waggers. Claire was too happy to mind anything. She did not even mind the steamer with its orgies of food, wine, and cigar smoke. The smell of liver and bacon, roast goose, duck, and pea soup did not disturb her, even on the warmest day. But Mama was indisposed by the time the breakfast bell rang at nine, while Claire hurried to consume a plate of hot rolls, eggs, and chops.

A stroll on the deck gave Claire a voracious appetite for cheese and buttered biscuits at noon, and by five she was ready for dinner. At any other time Claire might be found as she was now, staring off with rapt expression toward the east, where rose the sun of all her girlish hopes and expectations.

Claire had no idea that she owed the realization of her dream to Major Colin Whitecavage. She did not know that he had changed the course of William Rutherford's footsteps away from the front hall toward the summerhouse, thereby altering the course of her life as well. Had Claire known, she would have been as much at a loss as to why he had done it as was Colin himself.

But Claire only supposed that a kind fate had caused William to see her as she ran toward the summerhouse. She had been sobbing, face down on a potting bench, when he had entered, and the expression of joy that had shone through her tears had warmed his heart. In fact he had felt warm all over, and though the hour was so early he had seized her in his arms and kissed her. Memories of the cottage had overwhelmed him, and he had dared to exceed the bounds of propriety, thrusting his hand into her bodice, where it had immediately become entangled with a grosgrain ribbon hung around her neck. Instead of the soft nipple he had hoped to grasp, he found a hard ring pushed into his hand. Claire was removing the ribbon from her neck and his hand from her bosom. He was baffled to hear her say, "I'm sorry, William. I can't marry you."

Claire's rejection had unnerved Lord Rutherford. For a few days he thought it only an attack of feminine jitters. But when he had called upon her again, he had found her wearing another man's ring, a large diamond that had come in a silk-covered box in Colin's dispatch. As for the Major, he had long since left to post Claire's acceptance of Colonel Todd's proposal. There had been wonderful light in Claire's eyes. . . .

William had been demoralized. He had moped and cherished the notion that his heart was broken. In such condition he had been an easy mark for Jenny Bainbridge, who had ministered to his grief. At length the ring William had intended to give to Claire had found a home on Jenny's proud finger, and less than a month before Claire had left for Calcutta, Jenny and William had been married.

Jenny had still been so grateful to Claire for not marrying William that she had asked her to be maid of honor. This duty Claire had performed, to William's consternation—for while he was pledging himself to Jenny, he kept looking at Claire, and she was aware that his feelings about her had not changed at all. When they had danced afterward at the reception, he had held her too closely, his face flushed with the wine he had consumed. He had seemed almost dangerous, and Claire, her stomach knotting with revulsion, had not envied Jenny her wedding night.

Mama had cried prodigiously at Jenny's wedding, not out of any feeling for Jenny, but because Claire might have been the bride. In the end it had seemed that nothing would restore her except to go to Calcutta to be present at her daughter's wedding. How could she miss it? Her desire to witness the great event had at last overcome her fear of uncivilized lands, and in spite of much trepidation on the part of her husband, who was unable to go along, Claire's travel plans had been arranged to include her mother.

All the way from England—across the Channel, to Paris, to Malta—Mama had moaned of the rigors of the land to which they were headed. "Oh, I don't see why Colonel Todd couldn't have returned to England, if he wished to marry you, Claire," she would remark a dozen times a day. "Your father was much more considerate. *He* did not want his bride to subject herself to an atrocious climate and terrible living conditions."

"It will not be like that," Claire would repeat a thousand times. "Colonel Todd is building a house for us at Simla, and he has promised that we'll spend all our summers there, where it is cool."

Mrs. Cottington never was quite convinced. Perhaps she understood how little it mattered to Claire where Colonel Todd built them a house. Mrs. Cottington guessed that Claire would have gone to marry the Colonel in the meanest residency in British India.

Claire tried to spend most of her time away from the cabin and her mother's laments. So doing, she found herself often in the company of British officials returning to their posts and was included in rubbers of whist and strident discussions. An officer from the Punjab argued endlessly that the democratic methods of the area must be applied throughout India, while a clerk from Mysore insisted it would mean chaos. A third was given to decrying the treacherous Mohammedans, while a fourth thought that Mohammedans could be civilized but that Hindus were hopeless savages. Claire listened to all, utterly confused in the welter of opinions.

This morning, Claire had refused all offers of company. Today, Claire would not move from the rail, for this was the day that they were to sight the port of Alexandria. Everyone else was at the noon meal when Claire glimpsed the yellow dunes of the sandy shore, studded with little windmills, whirling like silver jewels in the sun. Through a glass she made out Pompey's Pillar and the great obelisks of Cleopatra's Needles.

Before long an Egyptian pilot came aboard, wearing a fez cap, a vest with many metal buttons, a silk sash, and baggy breeches. His naked legs were covered with festering bites, and he had only one eye to guide them to their berth close to a double line of men-of-war, a three-decker, and five frigates bearing red flags with a crescent moon. To Claire's surprise, all the crew of the pilot's boat were one-eyed, too.

She scarcely had time to think about it. A swarm of boats had come alongside ready to transport them to shore. She was heaved into one with Mama, who was certain the clumsy vessel would sink.

"Oh, do make them be careful!" Mrs. Cottington cried to her daughter as they approached the shore driven by a big lug sail.

A pair of Claire's acquaintances in the same boat tried to communicate the lady's fears to the Egyptians and immediately the boatsmen began to solicit baksheesh, the cry for money trailing over the water like the wail of some peculiar water bird.

One of the Englishmen tossed some coins, and in the ensuing scramble a dirty crewman trod upon Mama's foot and crawled across her silk skirt in pursuit of a shilling. Grasping the coin in a skinny hand, the man lost his footing and tumbled backward against the helmsman, giving the rudder a violent jar. The boat jibed crazily, the sudden shift of the boom sweeping several natives into the water before the boat fetched up with a thunk against the side of a clipper ship.

Mama shrieked as her pretty rice straw hat went flying. Claire clutched a gunwale. She wasn't afraid of drowning, but she'd been told there were sharks. The captain of the clipper bellowed a string of outrageous curses, while the Egyptians hurled back a standard insult, "You, Johnny, no good!" The vessel regained its course and whacked the pier. People already ashore cheered. The boatsmen, pleased with the accomplishment, demanded baksheesh once more, and one put a filthy hand in front of Claire's face. Without thinking she poked him with the point of her white lace parasol.

"Come on, Mama!" Claire cried. But Mrs. Cottington seemed rooted to her place, her eyes staring and her mouth moving wordlessly. Claire tried to pull her up and was aided by another English passenger in trying to heave her mother ashore.

"I am not coming, Claire," said her mother with sudden strength.

"Oh, of course you are," said Claire. "You won't see my wedding if you don't." Claire braced her Balmoral boots on the pier and pulled. Her cheeks turned rosy. People were beginning to watch and laugh. They were creating a spectacle.

"I will never see England or Henry again, if I come!" Mama wailed, beginning to weep.

"Then do stay right where you are and let these fine fellows take you back to the ship," said a new voice.

Claire felt herself relieved of her burden as a masculine hand seized the arm she had been tugging. She turned and looked into the face of Major Colin Whitecavage. His usually sharp, censorious eyes were full of merriment, and his mouth kept twitching as if he could scarcely keep from breaking into laughter. Nonetheless, his voice, as always, had a ring of authority; and Mrs. Cottington, considering the alternative he had pointed out to her, ceased to resist. As if mesmerized, she gave him her hand to help her out of the boat.

For a moment Claire was so grateful she could have thrown her arms around him. The burst of joy she had felt on seeing him had been only natural. He had been a familiar face in a strange place. She had begun to tremble, but that was only because of the situation, too.

She remembered how much she disliked him. He had told her she was spoiled, a foolish dreamer, unequal to the East, and here he was to laugh and feel vindicated by her poor management at the very pier! She remembered that he did not think her worthy of his wonderful Colonel Todd. But why on earth should his opinion count for so much? Why should it reinforce her own doubts of her worthiness until she was almost as jittery as Mama?

Gasping from her exertions, Claire gathered her wits and said, as coolly as though they were at a garden party, "Why Major Whitecavage! Imagine meeting *you* here! Are you on your way back to your regiment?"

"No." A cloud passed over his face. "I'm heading south to Madras."

She saw his expression of infinite sadness and for the instant before it was gone, wondered what it meant. "This is a pleasure, Major," she went on. "We did not ever expect to see you again."

The twist of his mouth told her that he did not really believe she thought it a pleasure. "I have the advantage, Miss Cottington," he said. "I knew I should meet you here."

"You knew! But how would you know I was to arrive today and on the Oriental and Peninsular Line?"

"Because I was ordered to meet you. Colonel Todd wishes me to escort you to Calcutta before I go south."

"You!"

"Yes. I apologize for the Colonel's unfortunate choice. He thought it would be appropriate because we are acquainted, and I, of course, could not tell him how inappropriate our very acquaintance makes it. We're stuck with each other, Miss Cottington. Hurry up now. We've no time to stand about chitchatting. The train is leaving, and we've only a few minutes to catch it."

"Leaving! But we have to rest. We've been on the ship for three days."

"Oh, that's nothing, Miss Cottington. You will be on shipboard longer across the Red Sea. Come along or we won't get a seat."

He flailed about him with a walking stick, making a path

for them among the unwashed horde. Claire, dazed by the strange sights, tried to assess her feelings at finding him her escort, but all thought was swept away in the confusion. She could only follow him numbly through the swarm of Nubians, Copts, and Arabic mixtures. Some wore nothing but short breeches. Others had only a shirt and a pipe. There were those who wore nothing at all except long beards. Claire expected Mama to faint dead away, but Mrs. Cottington held on, her reliable bottle of smelling salts pressed to her nose. Camels jerked their heads and brayed at the foot of the pier. Women were veiled, but dangling nose ornaments were visible beneath. Major Whitecavage pushed his way through, seeming oblivious to everything—the women, the boisterous animals, the pleas for baksheesh, the clouds of flies that circled the people as though they had been horses or cows. Claire was appalled to see many more one-eyed men and others with eyes made putrid with disease.

By the time they reached the big white railway station Claire was reeling from exertion in heat that had reached nearly ninety degrees despite the season. Her jacket had been discarded and her bodice was wilted and damp with perspiration. She suspected that at least her crinoline, which allowed air to circulate beneath it, was cooler than the Major's tight trousers.

"Can't we at least have a cool drink before we start?" Claire pleaded as he handed them into a rattletrap railway carriage. For answer he reached out the window and bought a basket of oranges from a vendor. Egyptian police flayed about with whips, making way for the passengers, and then the train jolted and chugged off, while young blades inside the coaches pelted the crowd with oranges.

The train ran past a large lake covered with ducks and teal, while Colin peeled oranges for Claire and her mother. Claire looked about at the first-class compartment they occupied. The floors were bare and none too clean, the leather seats oozed stuffing, and the violet-paned windows gave the interior a strange gray light. The roadbed was anything but smooth, and a lurch tossed Claire off her seat and right into Colin's lap. She looked at him with shock and he at her with equal consternation. The physical contact had caused them both to think of the intimate moment they had shared in the Bainbridges' garden.

An image of Claire as she had been then, glorious with abandon, came unbidden to Colin's mind. As for Claire, the contact of his thighs with hers charged her with the same overwhelming sense of being swept into a thrall beyond her understanding as she had felt then. Mrs. Cottington's orange rolled beneath their feet, and as they hastily parted, each tried to cover feelings of agitation by bending to retrieve it.

Tears trickled down Mama's cheeks as she beheld the remnants of the juicy orange, enveloped in dust and grime."

"Don't worry, dear," Claire said comfortingly. "We have plenty more."

"Oh, it's not that," sobbed Mama. "I am sure that I am going to die in this heathen place. I shall not even have a nice funeral at home.."

"Nonsense. You are going to a wedding, not a funeral. We will be the toast of Calcutta, you and I. And in a few hours we will see the pyramids. What a tale you'll have to tell at the Bainbridges' when you get home. You must remember everything and make a good story of it."

"Yes," mumbled Mrs. Cottington.

"Tell us about Calcutta, Major. They say it's very glamorous this time of year."

"Indeed it is, Miss Cottington," Colin said, answering the look of appeal in her eyes. So far she was showing spunk, but this was only the beginning. The very beginning, he thought wearily. She was young, so eager, so grateful to him for his help in distracting her mother from her fit of hysterics. Colin was very nearly touched by her as he chose the words he thought would soothe Mrs. Cottington.

"The Governor's Cup is the great racing event of the week, and everyone comes in hats and gowns from London and Paris. There are rajahs and nabobs in jeweled turbans and flowered frockcoats, and thousands of natives in white and turbans of every hue—they look like a vast tulip bed. All the world goes driving down the Red Road, along the Strand and on the Esplanade by the Eden Gardens, where bands play at sunset. The native royalty parades on elephants more finely decked with jewels than the Lady Sahib, the Governor-General's wife. Every evening there are balls and dinners. . . ."

Major Whitecavage talked on, extolling a part of British India that he did not especially enjoy, until at last Mrs. Cottington relaxed and fell into a fitful sleep, snoring gently. Claire smiled at him to reward him, and he felt ridiculously happy.

Colin did not feel happy often these days. He had not been able to shake the dust of India from his feet, but he was going south to dry deserts that would not remind him of the pine-clad hills where he had loved Tamila. Darkness fell and the train stopped in the emptiness.

"Why are we waiting?" she asked.

"Oh, we are crossing the territory of a pasha, and it is his right to come and pass us," he replied. "You should sleep."

"No. I'll wait until we get to Cairo. We will have a hotel there, won't we?"

"Yes, the Shepherd's Hotel."

"Thank heaven," she said, smoothing skirts too crushed to be improved by it. She was afraid to sleep; she could not allow herself to trust Colin to watch over her and her mother. She did not want to surrender to him in even such an innocent way. Colin, feeling oddly rebuffed, discomforted her with an explanation of the one-eyed Egyptians.

"It's ophthalmia," he told her. "They say that the flies cause it. They light on infected matter and then on the eyes." He produced two pairs of gauze spectacles for her and her mother. The flies had departed with darkness, but in the morning they would return. Then, Colin said, Claire and her mother should wear the spectacles.

"But they will ruin my appearance," said Claire with distaste. She had seen people wearing these goggles already. The effect was ludicrous.

"Ophthalmia will not enhance your loveliness either," he said in his infuriatingly righteous way.

"Then why aren't you wearing a pair?" she demanded.

He took out a cigar and showed it to her. "Tobacco smoke keeps the flies away."

"Perhaps I'll smoke a cigar, too," she threatened.

Such was the effect she had already had on him that Colin did not put it past her. "If you're not going to sleep, then I will," he said. He stretched his lean, graceful limbs on the railway seat opposite her and was instantly slumbering.

She studied his unguarded face. In repose it softened only a little. His mouth, his taut cheeks, still held their military expression. It was only around the eyes that she noticed a difference and sensed his anguish and his vulnerability. He was a warrior, she thought, but a warrior engaged in a battle from which, even in sleep, there was no surcease. Colin Whitecavage was at war with himself.

She wondered why. Whatever could make Major Whitecavage question himself? He seemed too arrogant to be self-searching. But no doubt he had done many corrupt and immoral things. Think of how he had kissed her! Think of how he had tried to ruin her by setting in motion the story about her and William! Had he done that in hopes that her shattered reputation would prevent her from becoming Colonel Todd's bride?

Claire slept anyway, too exhausted to keep her vigil any longer. A man's hand, tugging at her fingers, jerked her awake. Her eyes flew open, and she looked into the dark face of a fez-wearing Egyptian who was trying to remove her engagement ring. Claire screamed. The fellow tried to dart away, but not quickly enough. Colin was upon him, and the man drew a jeweled dagger to defend himself. Colin reached for his service revolver, and then, seeming to reconsider, twisted the Egyptian's knife away and heaved him over his shoulders, right out the window.

At that moment the train started again. Mrs. Cottington was awake, bewailing her fate once more as Claire leaned out to see what had become of the thief. "Oh, make them stop!" she cried. "It's a desert out there!"

"I can't make them stop. We'd be miles away by the time I did. Anyway, the fellow's probably hopped onto the last car. We'll see him in Cairo, no doubt. You are tempting more than one with that ring of yours. You might wear it somewhere out of sight—on a ribbon, for instance."

She blushed angrily as though he might be referring to William's ring, but he had never known about that ring. Colin wondered what her reaction meant. He had ceased to think about William at all. Lord Rutherford seemed as long ago as he was far away. That was the nature of things out here. Colin was annoyed at her concern for someone who had nearly stolen her prize possession. He wanted to think that she was self-centered. She was wasting her sympathy on a worthless ruffian, he found himself thinking. He wished she would, just once, show as much concern for *him*.

At midnight they arrived at Cairo, disembarking into a confusion of donkeys and hackney coachmen. He tried to hurry her aboard a hackney, but she stood bemused, staring off toward the river in the moonlight and murmuring in a tone of wonder, "Oh, it's the Nile! It is really the Nile!" Her voice was so soft he knew she was not speaking to him; perhaps she did not even know she had spoken aloud. Colin became lost in reflection himself, seeing the sacred yellow river through her eyes.

Mrs. Cottington's complaints roused him. Most of the hackneys had already raced off, but Colin managed to acquire one of the last and pile his charges into it. "To the Shepherd," he commanded.

"No good, it's full," said the driver. Colin ordered the hackney there anyway, suspecting the driver had been paid by another establishment to give that information. But early arrivals from the train had taken the last rooms. Colin cursed to himself and allowed them to be driven to a place among the quarries and lime kilns. Here, at the Hotel du Nil, they ate a meal of tough chicken, cheese, and wine. The drink made Claire hotter than ever.

Having slumbered beneath mosquito netting she awakened badly bitten anyway. But she was rested again, and an intensity of excitement took hold of her. She was really in Egypt. But she couldn't believe it until she had rushed to the window to have her first glimpse of Cairo by day.

Beyond the yellow Nile stretched reddish-gray desert. Closer was the green oasis of Cairo, lush with sycamores that reminded her of the trees at Cottington Crest. For an instant she was homesick, but then she caught sight of the pyramids and the dome of a mosque. Minarets were covered with flocks of white storks, camel bells rang, and herds of black goats were being driven through the streets. It was hardly past dawn. No use trying to wake Mama. No use trying to go back to sleep either.

As she was debating what to do a soft knock came on the door. "Miss Cottington, are you awake?" came the Major's voice. "I have two horses. Would you like to go riding and see the bazaar before it opens?"

Claire was delighted and dressed hurriedly in her riding outfit of a dark blue skirt, cambric shirt, and small straw hat. Before running down to join him, she took his advice and put her engagement ring on a ribbon about her neck.

The air was still cool and the clouds of flies had not yet appeared. Mist hung in golden veils over the domes of Coptic churches. Sunlight glimmered on white walls, a monkey playing in the feathery branches of a mimosa scolded her, and a pair of ostriches strutted about scratching at fleas with their beaks.

They found the bazaar deserted except for vendors setting up their wares of latakia, little marble eggs, tarbooshes and Egyptian whips. The filigreed jewelry of the goldsmith's bazaar was unlike anything she had ever seen, and although the perfume bazaar wasn't open officially she insisted on selecting one of the scents of the East. Passing over the musky ones she settled on a lighter jasmine, dabbing it at her wrists and behind her little ear lobes and lifting her hand to Colin for his approval.

"Do you think the Colonel will like it?" she asked.

"I would hardly know his taste in perfume," Colin said with a laugh, but he lifted her wrist to his nostrils. Immediately he was sorry, for on her warm, soft skin the aroma was a thousand times more provocative than in the bottles.

To take his mind off her desirability, he suggested breakfast and ushered her to a Turkish restaurant he knew where dining room and kitchen were one. At Colin's knowledgeable command the turbaned cook produced delicacy after delicacy from pots cooking over a huge fireplace.

They could not help being pleased with each other this morning. Colin had been in Cairo perhaps a dozen times, but he had never had anyone with whom to share the early morning hours. Always his comrades had been snoring away after nights of debauchery.

Colin had shared the company of beautiful women in Cairo, but always after dark. It seemed pleasantly strange to be sharing dawn in Cairo with a woman. The guarded expression dropped from his eyes, and the depth of his love for the East shone through to mingle with the ecstasy of discovery in hers.

They began to talk to each other as they never had before, as neither had ever talked before to a member of the opposite sex. Claire certainly had never shared confidences with William Rutherford. Colin had come closer with Tamila.

Tamila had spent her life in the company of women, and at first had had no idea of how to talk to him. In the beginning she had had no notion of how to communicate her devotion except by the very effective offering of her body. But she had had natural spirit and intelligence and had been a willing student. When he had talked to her about the future of Pandeish, she had listened worshipfully; and she had urged her ill and aged husband to adopt the Sahib's reforms. The Rana had deferred to her; he would do anything to please her. Eventually Tamila had had power. But in the long run what Tamila had needed was courage.

Colin Whitecavage did not speak to Claire of Tamila. She was hidden too deeply in his heart. Colin supposed no one would ever know—no one but Maxwell Todd, his dearest friend.

Colin spoke instead of the infinite possibility he saw in India, the mystery of the Eastern mind, the beauty of its art. After he had come to India he had begun to listen to scholars and holy men. He had felt set down on a different planet, for even his punkah coolie had seen life in ways dissimilar from the British. Colin had been awed by the dignity of Eastern thought. The affinity he felt for the Indian mind, the great freedom he experienced in a land where palm-treed desert and pine-covered hills were open alike for adventure, had convinced him early on that his life would be devoted to that country.

Claire listened eagerly, full of interest and questions. But when her questions came close to the time when he had represented John Company in Pandeish, he turned the conversation to her. Claire found herself telling him about her love of Maxwell Todd—how she had danced with him, and even how he had kissed her, how she had never forgotten him. In another mood Colin might have laughed at her and called her a foolish romantic as he had on other occasions.

"I'm frightened," she confessed. "How shall I ever be an adequate wife to a man like Colonel Todd?"

"You will be more than adequate, Claire," he said softly, though in England he had espoused the opposite view.

Her heart sang, as much because he had used her name again as because of what he had said. But somehow the talk of her approaching marriage seemed to displease the Major. He suggested abruptly that they visit a certain mosque from which there was a splendid view.

Having ridden through winding streets, they dismounted in a central court planted with cypress trees. Climbing the worn steps of the minaret, they passed the bones of birds that had flown there to die, soaring to the highest spot possible, to end as they had lived, in the air. Beneath them lay the soft clouds of green, the brilliant whites and golds of Cairo. To the right was the desert where camels glided by, seemingly in pairs, the dark shadows moving in unison with their buff-colored companions. Beyond the Nile, the pyramids rose, while the Nile itself was dotted with white sails, looking like butterflies at rest on the sulphurous water. The mist had lifted, and the sky was utterly blue.

She turned to him to share the moment and as though the wind had blown the clouds from the sky of their passion, they were suddenly in each other's arms. Colin was kissing her as though he could never stop, murmuring words of endearment.

"Oh Claire, oh my darling, my beloved!" He heard himself in amazement, not knowing how these words came from his lips. She could not be his beloved, for all the love he had been capable of had died with his loss of Tamila. She could not be his darling, for she was the betrothed of Maxwell Todd, the one man in all the world he must not betray, the man who had stood by him and believed in him when there was no reason to believe in him any longer.

She clung to him helplessly, pressed against the buttons of his scarlet cavalry uniform. Her knees seemed to melt; she felt as though she might be one of the birds that had flown there to die. Below her there seemed to be nothing; her being seemed to ebb away into his. There was only Colin, Colin. His name floated on the breeze. She was aware that she was whispering it as he kissed her eyes and cheeks and throat. His name was like the cry of a muezzin from the top of the mosque.

Gradually sanity began to return. She looked long into his eyes and was frightened by the raw hunger she saw in them. She found a tottering footing and fled away from him down the steps.

Claire spent the rest of the day with her mother. She didn't protest when Mama wanted to stay indoors with the shutters drawn over the bay window against the heat and the wonders of Cairo. Mama had made a mid-morning foray into the city, and where Claire had seen Romanesque arches and minarets, Mama had noticed the slave market, the wolflike dogs that roamed the streets, and the peculiar state of dress or undress of the inhabitants. Mrs. Cottington decided that the city wasn't for her. She was gratified that for once her daughter agreed with her, and they sat together playing cards through the long afternoon.

"It will be different in Calcutta," Mrs. Cottington said. "There is real society there." She was glad to have the opportunity to comfort her daughter. She was aware that she had been a trial to Claire during the trip and that had upset her as much as the trip itself. She and Claire had always been close. Now Claire had become almost a stranger. She seemed to live in a different world, which her mother could not understand or penetrate. Mrs. Cottington was afraid that she was losing her only child, not simply for the few years that they must be separated, but in some more profound manner.

But unaccountably Claire had reverted. She seemed almost like a child again, seeking her mother's skirts. Mrs. Cottington thought that Claire must be thinking of the wedding night, and she wondered how much Claire knew.

Perhaps we should discuss it, Mrs. Cottington thought, but she was at a loss as to how to begin. Better, maybe, for Claire to be in ignorance. It was something that women simply must get through.

Claire thought that Mama must be right about Calcutta. Everything would be all right when she reached the capital and saw Maxwell Todd again. She worked the matter over until she decided that the Major had taken advantage of her while she was exhausted and confused from heat and travel. Everything was strange here; she simply could not get her bearings, but one thing at least was no different. Colin Whitecavage was no more a gentleman here than in England!

Claire dealt another hand of cards. The room was full of flies, and she and her mother presented weird countenances to each other wearing the spectacles Colin had provided.

I love Maxwell Todd, Claire thought. *I always have.*

5

Colin Whitecavage, too restless to remain in his room, spent the time walking along the Pharaoh's aqueduct with the avowed purpose of shooting game birds. The Turkish cook would roast them for him, and they would be assured of having a good meal on the train to Suez tonight. But Colin wasn't in the mood for serious shooting. He walked morosely along, now and then loosing a few rounds at kites, for the dubious reward of seeing them fly off screaming. Colin was an excellent marksman, but today he was too engrossed in his problems to care about hitting anything.

Colin was furious with himself. How had he let her bewitch him? Had it been the sunlight on her hair, making it shine like polished jet? Had it been her porcelain features, the pastel tones of her skin like the glow of dawn? Her eyes, so brilliant and alive, reflecting her own wonder? She had the natural grace that so many English girls lacked. When he watched her from a distance he felt hypnotized by the gentle dance of her crinolines and curls.

Hypnotized! Yes, that was it, a trick she must have with all men. How else could it have happened to him? He had thought better of himself, had believed himself above such temptations since Tamila. He had thought himself above such behavior with the fiancée of his friend. She had taught him that he was no better than ordinary men.

The first time he had kissed her had been only a game. But today! Today she had been Maxwell Todd's fiancée! And the kiss, though Colin would not admit it, had been far more than the mere indulgence of animal appetite.

But though he would not admit it, she bothered him still, her image seeming to shimmer in the heat waves rising from the stones of the aqueduct. He understood at last just how compelling Claire Cottington was, and why, in spite of his protests, Max had insisted that no one but Colin could be entrusted to escort her to Calcutta.

Colin had betrayed that trust, but now that he was aware of his weakness, he swore he never would again.

She was a woman any man might fall in love with; he supposed many already had. Maxwell must know that. But what Max could not realize was the way that Claire responded.

If it had not been for Colin, she would have remained Lord Rutherford's fiancée and probably cuckolded him a dozen times over. If only he had not delivered the letter!

Colin cursed himself for a fool. *I ought to tell Max*, he thought. But he knew he couldn't. Max was obsessed with the girl. He would only destroy the one friendship in the world he valued above all others.

Whatever the kiss had meant to Colin, it meant nothing to Claire, he was sure. She had merely been toying with him. Why had he kissed her? God, he despised her!

Colin thought he knew what he needed, and as darkness fell, he made his way through little streets where cloth lanterns glimmered like fireflies and pasha's grooms flooded the night with the gleam of torches. A single lantern glowed quietly at the door where Colin knocked, as though guests were expected. He was greeted effusively. He had been here before and had always paid well, but that wasn't the reason that the girls vied for him.

They sat him on a divan in a bay window that overhung the cobblestones below. Two glassless windows brought in the night air, and the sweet aromas of the soft Eastern night mixed with the sandalwood incense in brass burners. One girl poured him a glass of raki. Another played a *darabukeh*, and a third danced, rolling her girdle low on her hips. The one who had poured him the drink sat on his lap, laughing, and opened her jacket to allow him to stroke her breasts.

Colin frowned. "Where is Hadely?" he said. She was the one he had had the last time he'd been in Cairo. He had enjoyed himself with her. That was the problem; he didn't have the right girl.

"She's dead," they answered, speaking French. "She died with childbirth fever. The baby died, too."

He wondered vaguely whose baby it had been. He hoped not his.

"I am as pretty as she," said the girl on his lap. She kissed him, darting her tongue like a serpent's between his teeth. He knew immediately that he did not want to sleep with her. Her kiss was nothing like Claire's.

"You," he said to the dancer.

She smiled in triumph and led him off to a bedchamber. She undressed by torchlight, the light of the flame playing over her firm, bronze stomach and her admirable breasts, which peeked boldly through cascades of shining black hair. The special place between her legs shone with the same golden sheen as her hips and thighs, for it was cleanly shaven. Lying on the bed she raised her legs and parted them, placing his hand on the smooth mound between. He cupped his fingers over it. Once Colin had though the custom of shaving was erotic; now he found that he was simply relieved that he would not acquire crabs or fleas from intimate contact.

His fingers were skillful; the girl began to squirm and cry her appreciation in gasps of Arabic which he only half understood. Sitting up, he opened his breeches. The girl seemed eager, guiding him to her, wrapping slender, ringed fingers about him as he thrust violently into the ready channel of her body. Sensing his mood she twisted her hands in his hair and pushed upward, her hips leaving the bed. He caught her buttocks in his hands and dug into her flesh, as he held her firmly and used her.

Her back arched suddenly higher, and she gave a moan of release. Then, noticing that he wasn't satisfied, she tried to pull him back. Colin shook his head and took out money.

"No, pay later, when you have gotten your money's worth," she said. "I'm not a cheap soldier's prostitute. I won't cheat you."

He smiled and refastened his breeches. "I'm not being cheated." Feeling irritable, he headed back to the Hotel du Nil to retrieve his charges.

In the moonlight the desert beyond Cairo resembled the bed of a sea, corrugated and thrown into mountains and reefs, seamed with shallow ravines. Great plains were dotted with oval stones that shone in the moonlight, the beams catching them so that they seemed to be rushing like frothing waves toward the train. A date palm stood alone on the horizon.

Claire and Colin treated each other with cold politeness. Colin reminded himself of his duty to deliver her to Maxwell Todd. Though he did not imagine it possible to deliver her as a virgin, her lack of that condition must have nothing to do with him. He must not fail his duty again because of a woman!

Scenes of the Battle of Pandeish filled his mind as the train lurched through the desert. But Tamila had been pure and courageous while this woman might have been one of the sirens whose song lured men to the reefs. Colin almost thought he heard eerie music as the train rumbled along. It was only a squeaking in the wheels, of course; but she, in the rear seat of their compartment, seemed to be pursuing him; while he, no matter how fast he traveled, could not escape.

Claire, also, wished she could get away from Colin. She had never been so frightened by a man. In fact, she had never really been frightened of a man. Even when Lord Rutherford had had her almost naked on the bed in the peasant cottage, Claire had not been frightened as she was now. Then she had been able to count on her own considerable resources to save her. Now Claire seemed able to count on nothing. Lord Rutherford, with his instinct for judging women, had tried to show her what kind of woman she was. But he had not been the man to do it. Colin Whitecavage was, and Claire's journey of discovery was just beginning. Claire felt lost in a land as devoid of signposts as the desert, the moonlit sand a weird violet beyond the colored glass of the train window. Her mother, chattering on about the wedding and getting little response from Claire, worried.

Hours later the train jerked to a halt. Claire, having dozed, blinked in confusion. "Where are we? Are we waiting for another pasha?"

"This is the end of the line," said Colin brusquely. "Out you go."

She stepped down into sand, which, still hot from the day, filtered over the top of her short boots. Mama gave a shriek at seeing a bleached camel skeleton almost in her path, and Colin, glad to be distracted from Claire, murmured soothing words.

Colin understood Mrs. Cottington. He'd seen plenty like her at the Bengal Club in Calcutta. There were hundreds of such women in India, leading insular lives, which tended to reinforce their dependence and shallowness of mind but which did not really protect them from the harshness of India. It was a mere conceit of men to think that they could shield their women out here. Many were only robbed of the self-reliance they might have used to defend themselves. Others played an unconscious game, battling heat, insects, and childbirth with calm bravery while seeming to rely on their husbands.

Colin wondered if Claire would ever fit into either category. Her image shimmered in front of him like a moonlit mirage as she walked to a wooden shed in the center of a cluster of tents. Here a late supper was being laid. It reminded Colin of their repast at the Hotel du Nil, and he wished he had taken more care on the aqueduct with his gun.

Claire took one look and announced she wasn't hungry. "Then we'll go right to the vans and get good seats," said Colin with relief. The vans were usually crowded, but this time they'd have an advantage.

She followed him out of the shed and saw the vehicles sitting ready, seven or eight little contrivances that looked like Brighton bathing boxes lying on their backs. Shaggy, vicious-looking horses were attached to pull them.

Claire hurried toward the first van.

"The second is better," Colin advised. "The lead horses resist command. You'd have a wild ride."

"What? Go in the second and eat all the dust that the first will throw up? My clothes will be ruined. We'll go in the first. I'm not afraid of the horses. You'd go in the first if you were alone, wouldn't you?"

"Well, yes, but——"

"Then we'll go in the first." Claire climbed aboard and took a seat. It was almost the last seat available, since during the time they had been talking, other passengers, having reached a similar decision about the food, had poured out of the shed to the vans.

The Major was taken aback and paused for a moment to throw her a furious look. In that moment the last seats disappeared. "Will you please get down from there, Miss Cottington?" he commanded.

"No," she said.

"We will all go in the same van, Miss Cottington," he said furiously. "It is my job to look after you, and I will do it!"

"No doubt you intend to, Major," she said, her voice laden with double meaning, "but I do not need your kind of taking care. I don't find your company enjoyable enough to breathe dust all the way to Suez, not even if I were certain of a cool bath when I arrived. I will ride in the first van and take care of myself perfectly well!"

Claire was aware of her mother making little gestures of distress below and was touched by remorse. Poor Mama! She couldn't possibly understand what Claire was doing. But the Major could.

His face burning with rage, he reached to lift her down forcibly. She struck at him with her parasol, just as she had struck at the native boatman in Alexandria. She glared at him as though to say, *You're no more to me than they! You're as low as a flea-bitten beggar!*

She recoiled as he lunged toward her, leaping onto the wheel of the van, the wild temper he had never shown before utterly released. But just then the van started, and Colin was forced to leap back to avoid being thrown into the sand. She looked back at him, racing foolishly for the second van with her mother in tow as the first rumbled off.

There! She had done what she had needed to all day—showed him that he did not rule her. Better yet, she had showed herself that she could defy him. It had been easy, even enjoyable.

The horses stretched out their necks and began to run. Claire had to grab the edge of the seat to avoid being thrown about, but she was in the mood for an exhilarating ride.

"Was that your husband?" asked a wondering voice.

Claire looked around and saw that she was sitting next to a slender blond woman in a plain skirt without flounces. Her jacket bodice closed up to the neck and was finished with a small white collar.

"No, he's not," said Claire. "Certainly not! Aren't you melting in that outfit?"

"Yes, but I'm traveling alone. I have to project a certain appearance. I need to look like a stiff, dowdy spinster."

Claire studied her companion. She wasn't quite dowdy, though her skin looked rough and had been exposed to the sun. Her hair was soft and thick, but it seemed limp, as though its owner didn't care. In a very few years, if she continued her present mode, she would not have to try to look dowdy. She didn't really look stiff either, but there was something about her that Claire thought would make men lose interest. She seemed indifferent to her womanliness.

"*Are* you a spinster?" asked Claire.

The woman smiled. "No. I was married once, to a captain. But he was killed fighting the Sikhs at Chilanwala."

Claire shivered, thinking of the battle on the river Jhelum in which the British had lost twenty-five hundred men. "And you haven't remarried? I thought a woman had all sorts of chances out here."

"Oh, I had all sorts of chances. I received a proposal from the Lieutenant who brought me word of my husband's death. He begged my forgiveness, but he didn't want anyone to get ahead of him. That's the way of things in the cantonments. I felt like a fox chased by a pack of hounds, so I decided not to remarry at all. Anyway, I might only have been widowed again. I've known some women who've had three or four husbands that way."

"So what did you do?" asked Claire. It was amazing how quickly confidences were arrived at here in the desert.

"Well, the company would have sent me home if I'd insisted; but the resident made it difficult. He kept urging me to consider various officers. I was company property, going to waste. I decided to devote myself to the church instead."

"The church. Are you a missionary?" Claire looked at her with renewed curiosity. She had never known a woman who wanted anything other than marriage.

"I teach in a mission school at Cawnpore. My name's Jo Baker, by the way."

"Claire Cottington." Claire let go of the bucking seat with one hand, her fingers in Maltese gloves grasping Jo's rough, bare ones.

"I suppose you've come husband-hunting," Jo said.

"No. I'm engaged to marry Colonel Maxwell Todd. I'm on my way to meet him in Calcutta. That obnoxious Major is my escort."

"Colonel Todd." Jo repeated the name with an appreciation that made Claire glow.

"You've heard of him."

"I know him. He visited the school last year and saw to it that we got the books we needed. He's remarkable, for all his being a company man."

"You don't like John Company, do you?" Claire asked.

"I hate John Company."

Claire, who had always been taught the highest regard for the mighty East India Company, was astounded. "But why?"

"Because the Company shouldn't be in India at all. It is plundering the country. The lowest clerk is likely to go home rich."

"But surely India is better for the Western presence there!"

Jo smirked. "You are speaking of the white man's burden, Claire. That's a lot of poppycock to justify overrunning a country and all its inhabitants."

"Then why did you stay? Why didn't you make them send you back to England?"

"Because of the children, I suppose. So many were hungry and in need of affection. I suppose it makes up to me for the two I lost. Maybe I just can't leave their graves. Anyway, that's what I thought in the beginning. Some people just become obsessed with India, you know."

"Yes," said Claire. A vision of Colonel Todd should have risen to her mind, but instead she thought of Colin Whitecavage. She had been thinking of him all along. She had shown him! But now she had begun to wonder what would happen when they reached Suez and he caught up with her again. The shaggy horses could not outrun Major Whitecavage in the long run, even with the bit in their teeth. The explosiveness of his temper had unnerved her; but somehow she was also filled with excitement, and she thought of their next meeting with an emotion that was not quite dread.

Jo Baker had not forgotten the Major either, for now she said musingly, as though reading Claire's thoughts, "Funny, I was certain he was your husband."

The way led between boulders, and Claire, daring to twist her head around, could see no trace of the second van coming behind them. "We've lost the others," she said, feeling a trace of disappointment.

"No, there they come," Jo said, pointing out a cloud of dust in the moongleam.

"It can't be. That's the wrong direction."

"Oh, it must be. The horses must have taken some turn that they shouldn't, but we'll be back on course soon."

The cloud of dust gained on the van, and they could see that it was raised by horsemen, not by any vehicle. Jo conjectured that the horsemen were some of the Arab workmen who were camped in the desert to finish laying the railroad.

"Don't be alarmed, Claire," she said with a gentleness that was disquieting.

The driver cracked his whip, and the horses went even faster. The van went over a large rock and leaned dangerously. Claire was thrown against Jo, their foreheads banging together as they slid down the wooden seat. Claire's whalebone cage flew up in her face.

"Ow!" said Claire, touching her forehead.

"I wonder which of us will have the bigger bump in the morning," Jo said, doing the same.

"Thieves!" a man suggested in the rear of the van, as speculation grew over the pursuing party. Women began to scream.

Claire looked at Jo for confirmation. The missionary nodded. "Most likely it's so, but there's always the chance they aren't robbers. We'll know soon enough. If only we hadn't got separated from the others!"

"Oh, how can you be so calm?" Claire cried.

"Why shouldn't I be? I've no valuables."

"What about your life?"

"I have put my trust in God, Claire. Try to do the same."

"I would sooner depend on Major Whitecavage," said Claire, surprising herself, though she knew how sadly lacking she was in faith. Claire sometimes called on the Almighty in times of crisis, but she never quite expected an answer. If only God would send the Major, she thought, or maybe prayed. Why was it that everything, even her prayers, came down to Colin Whitecavage? If only she had not been so willful, she wouldn't be in this van at all.

The horsemen surrounded them suddenly, taking a short cut across the path of the van. Dust from the horses choked her and nearly obliterated her vision. For a frantic moment van and horsemen raced along together; then one of the horsemen sprang onto the seat of the van and knocked the driver to the ground with a rifle butt. The van squeaked to a halt as the bandit pulled on the reins. They were all made to get down and stand in a line.

The thieves walked along taking watches and jewelry. One of the robbers became frustrated with Jo. Unable to find any jewelry, he spilled out her valise on the sand. It yielded only a Bible, a muslin nightgown, and an assortment of tortoiseshell combs.

"Bah!" The thief turned to Claire, who tried to emulate Jo's composure. But her attempt was doomed as his eyes gleamed into hers, and she recognized the man who had tried to steal her ring on the train. So Colin had been right about his having gotten back on board! She wondered how many thieves had ridden the train with them, before joining up with their desert fellows.

He grabbed her hand and tore off her expensive glove. At the sight of her bare finger, he muttered a string of what sounded like Arabic curses, stripped off her other glove, then thrust his hand arrogantly into the pocket of her skirt.

Claire remained impassive. She did not intend to part with her treasure. She did not intend to arrive for her wedding minus the ring Colonel Todd had sent her. The ring, the only tangible manifestation she had of the Colonel's love, rested deep within her bosom, the ribbon partly obscured by the lace of her round-necked bodice. She hoped he wouldn't notice.

He spat a question at her. She knew he was asking about the ring. She shook her head and would not answer. If he couldn't find it, he would have to assume that she didn't have it with her anymore. He would think that she had packed it in a trunk for safekeeping or even that someone else had already had better luck at stealing it.

The robbers were loading bags of loot onto their horses. They wouldn't want to remain long. They'd been lucky to catch the van apart from the others, but soon the rest would catch up. There had been enough soldiers among the passengers to rout the brigands, Claire thought; but only one had been aboard this van, and he had easily been relieved of his weapon.

Claire cocked an ear, thinking she heard the distant sound of hoofbeats somewhere on the desert. The Arab seemed to listen, too; then suddenly he seized her about the waist, lifted her, and tossed her onto his horse. She beat her heels into the animal's flanks and whipped it with her parasol in a wild effort to get it to gallop away with her before he could mount behind.

He was the leader, it was plain. He shouted orders, and as he hit the animal's flank, she saw Jo jerked up by another of the thieves. Then they dashed off into the night. The Arab kept his arm tightly around her, and though Claire had not partaken of the meal at the desert station, she felt her stomach churn with disgust and thought she might vomit.

She lost all sense of direction. Before five minutes had passed, she would not have been able to find the van again had her captor set her free. Between her breasts the ring bounced with the galloping of the horse. He had not got it yet, at least there was that. He would not get it! But why had she and Jo been abducted instead of any others? And how would Colin ever be able to find her, as completely as the night had swallowed them?

The waning moon vanished over the horizon as they

reached an encampment of white tents among the dunes.
Their arrival was sudden and bewildering, since from fifty
feet away the tents were invisible. A horseman might have
ridden into the side of one without seeing it, except for the
tiny fires that glowed here and there, like rubies lying on the
sand. Claire and Jo were shoved into one of the tents, which
shone like a peculiar, triangular ghost from a lamp inside.

"What's going to happen to us?" whispered Claire when
their captors had secured the tent flaps and left them alone.

"We've become plunder," said the missionary, her voice
cold. "They couldn't steal jewelry from you or me, so they've
decided to rob us of something else instead."

"They won't rob me!" said Claire. "I'll never let them get
my ring!"

"You have a ring? You should have given it to them.
They'll rob you of something far more precious."

"Nothing is more precious to me than my ring. Colonel
Todd gave it to me!" Claire thought her new friend was talking very strangely. Perhaps she'd gone mad. Claire had heard
her mother talk of women who had become insane out here.
Certainly Jo was behaving oddly, but something about her
face, ghastly and colorless in the lamplight, frightened Claire
more than the Arabs.

"What are we to do, Jo?" she asked. The missionary was
older and more experienced than Claire. It seemed reasonable
that she would have an idea.

But Jo gave a shrieking laugh. "Do? There is nothing we
can do about it! Pray for the courage to endure it, that's all."

"Are they going to kill us?"

"No, but you may beg them to kill you before they are
done."

"We must think of some way to escape!" said Claire. She
did not know what Jo was talking about, but an instinctive
dread, as old as life itself, chilled her.

"Escape? There's no way. They have guards outside. Can't
you see their shadows against the tent? The best we can hope
is that they abandon us to wander about the desert and perhaps die of thirst after they've finished with us."

"Major Whitecavage will find us, Jo. I'm certain of it!"

"You set great store by your Major, Claire. No one could
find us—not in time."

The flap of the tent opened, and two Arabs beckoned to
Claire to come outside. She obeyed, not realizing that Jo was
being left behind. They were separated, and even the comfort

that she had felt from the mere presence of the missionary was gone.

The lamplight cast Jo's silhouette on the white wall of the tent as she stood alone. Then a half a dozen Arabs entered the tent, and Claire saw Jo throw up her arms wildly as if in supplication. The Arabs surrounded her, seeming to tear at her like dogs. Claire started senselessly to run to help her, but strong hands held her back. It was her clothes that the men were tearing at, Claire saw now. Pieces of cloth flew up against the light like leaves blown from a tree. Jo struggled, her body writhing and gyrating. None of it seemed real to Claire. It reminded her of when she had been a child and Papa had made shadow animals on the wall to amuse her. But then a soul-rending scream shattered the illusion of unreality.

Jo wasn't standing anymore. She had fallen to the ground, and the men had fallen atop her one after the other. The screams stopped, and the silence was more horrifying than the screams. The tent flaps opened, and the men dragged Jo out onto the sand. Only a few shreds of clothing clung about her. A cuff of a sleeve hung around her wrist like a bracelet. Her body looked bruised, and an expression of horror was painted lifelessly on her face. Was she dead?

Again Claire tried to run to her, but the Arabs began to pull her to the tent. It was going to be her turn now! Claire had only vague ideas about sex, but she sensed what had happened to Jo and what was about to happen to her. She struggled to get free, aiming a kick behind her at the groin of one of her captors. He howled and let go, but there were others to take his place. She felt her skirts rip and drop from her. Then her bodice was torn away. She was entirely naked, except for the ring swinging about her neck.

The sight of the magnificent ring seemed to confuse her captors, distracting them from the wonders of her body. Twisting the ribbon in their fingers, they tried to pull it from her neck. But the ribbon was strong, and they began to fight among themselves over who should have the ring. While she watched Jo raped, Claire had almost forgotten her vow to protect the ring, but now she remembered she had sworn the bandits should not have it. Jo had succumbed to the inevitable, but Claire would not! They would not have the ring, and they would not have her body. But how was she to prevent it?

Her skirt and petticoats lay in a pile near one of the little fires. If she could get them . . . but even if she could put them on, her assailants would only rip them off again. With a sense of futility Claire reached for the clothes, ducking among the squabbling Arabs, dragging along one who had his fingers tangled in her hair. As the material of her skirt came into her hand, she was inspired and pulled the garment through the fire. The thin organdy caught instantly and flames shot skyward. Quickly she added the muslin petticoats.

The fire that had been no more than a pile of coals would be visible for a long way now across the desert where anything on the vacant horizon would be noticed. If only Colin would see it and rush to her aid!

The outlaws began to beat at the fire and hurl sand onto it. It would be out in a minute or so, she thought with despair. But for that minute or two her tormentors were preoccupied with the beacon that could give away their location; and inspired again, Claire dashed toward a cream-colored mare and, grabbing its silky mane, flung herself onto it. Whispering urgently to the beast, she nudged it with her knees; responding to her need, it galloped off. Several Arabs, seeing her escape, rode after her, their burnooses sailing out.

She would have to outrun them all! But she could, she must. The animal she rode was larger and more powerful than the mares she had used to race along the beach below Cottington Crest. She spoke gently to it, and it stretched its able limbs over the sand. The dark air seemed to rush by too rapidly for her to draw it into her lungs.

But they were coming at her from different angles to cut her off. She hardly knew which way to guide the willing horse. Suddenly horsemen were in front of her. She reined in abruptly with a sob, and the mare stumbled. The accident gave her pursuers an advantage, and they gained on her from the rear. But then she made out that the horsemen before her wore Western clothes. Shouts in English came across the sand. She galloped toward them joyfully. Spotting the Englishmen, all but two of the Arabs turned back to warn the others. With a whoop the Britishers rode after them. One horseman continued toward her, all alone. She knew who it was even before she heard the shout, "Can you take that pair, Whitecavage?"

"With pleasure," came the answering yell. "Find the other woman!"

Then she could see his face, his fierce eyes burning away the darkness as his pistol barked and his sword shrieked. The mare, spooked at the commotion, reared. Claire lost her grip and began to slide head first to the sand. But in midair strong hands caught her, and she was lifted onto Colin's horse, set in front of him on the saddle.

There were more gunshots, more howls of pursuit, and the mare galloped away as another band of the Arabs came after them. Colin was hopelessly outnumbered, and the gleeful shouts of the thieves told of their delight. Colin cursed. How could he outrun them, riding double? It occurred to him to jump off the horse and let her ride on alone, but he rejected the notion. Neither of them would have a chance that way. She would not be able to manage his spirited mount; he would face certain death. He would have to use his wits.

He set off at a dead run, clutching her tightly to keep her from falling. So intent was he that her condition of nudity barely registered on his consciousness, and yet a powerful desire began to build inside him, while he was still unaware of it. The Arabs gained on him, and he pushed the horse even harder, pressing his heels into its flanks and leaning into Claire as he bent closer to the animal's neck. The beast went faster, but it had no more to give; and mentally Colin measured the rate at which the distance was being closed.

Then suddenly a field of boulders was before him. Ordinarily he would have skirted it, especially in the dark, for there was many a danger of misstep or falling rock. But tonight he welcomed the hazards, feeling the gamble was a godsend. Soon they were in a maze of twisting paths, and sand hills blocked them from the view of their pursuers. The boulders diminished to small, glistening, oval gems, and Claire sighed with relief that they had made it safely through. Colin's daring speed had given them an advantage.

Colin urged the horse to a full gallop again, and she was aware of a strange exhilaration, of a sensation blossoming inside her, as urgent as their flight, as mysterious as death at their heels. The emotion she had felt riding with him through the moor had been a mere harbinger of this, a zephyr beside a tempest. She shivered; and he, mistaking the reason, remembered to throw his military cloak around her. But Claire was not shivering from cold or fear or shame as she ought to have been. What she felt was entirely different. She wished he would kiss her again as he had in Cairo. Then she had been afraid; now she was not. A primal instinct had taken control of her; it was beyond comprehension and beyond denial.

"Are you all right," he asked her. "Did they. . . ."

"I wasn't harmed," she said, and felt a certain tension in him subside.

"Did we lose them?" she asked.

"Yes, but I lost my bearing in the boulder field. I do not know how to go to return to the caravan."

"The stars. . . ." she suggested.

"Yes, they will help to guide us to Suez."

"But?" she asked, sensing it in his voice.

"The horse is almost exhausted, and we cannot last long in the desert," he said gruffly.

"Is there no waterhole where we can stop to rest?"

"Perhaps we will find one. But we can stay only a short time. They are bound to look for us there. I am sorry, Claire."

"I am the one who should be sorry. I was headstrong and stubborn about the van."

"You have learned."

She leaned against him wearily, realizing that he was telling her that they would probably die despite their escape. She was close to death, but never had she felt so alive; every inch of her body seemed to throb with life, with desire for a depth of life she had never experienced.

Date palms loomed in the starlight as they approached a tiny oasis. He dismounted and held out his arms to her. She slid down, and his hands slipped unintentionally beneath the cape and touched the rise of her breasts. She gasped and sank against him.

He kissed her, and she drank in his kiss, feeling more refreshed than by a dipper of water from the well. His hands moved again and moved the universe. She knew that something momentous was about to happen, but she had no thought of preventing it. She knew that he ought not to be touching her, that his touch ought not to provoke her to such ecstasy, but *ought* was a word for the drawing room of Cottington Crest. Ought did not seem to apply.

But instead it was he who demurred. "Claire, we must not. You are engaged to Colonel Todd."

Was this, then, the marriage act? The thing Mama had tried to tell her about? No, surely it couldn't be, for Mama had told her that it was to be endured, not longed for.

"I will never see Colonel Todd now, Colin," she sighed; and as she embraced him about the neck, his cape slipped from her shoulders.

Colin groaned as he ran his hands over her. The need that had been growing in him exploded, and the intensity of his feeling overwhelmed him. It was true that she would never see Maxwell Todd again, true that a torturous death might wait for them on the morrow, and he needed the solace of her love to face it.

She had hypnotized him, but now he did not care where that mesmerization would lead him. He supposed he was only one of many who had fallen in love with her—admitting now that he belonged to this club and did not care that it had a legion of members.

He pushed her back in the soft grass, and suddenly she was frightened after all at the strange, wonderful things that began to happen to her. She began to understand just how profoundly this ought not to happen and tried to protest. But his lips were sealed against hers. His tunic was unbuttoned, and the springy hair of his chest caressed her nipples. Then came a touch she had never before experienced, a touch too profound to be denied, and she threw herself open to him beneath the starry palms.

A moment of pain, and then their bodies melded. She shuddered with wave after wave of helpless transport, struggling toward some unknown goal. At last she felt herself dissolve, and the essence of her being flowed incredibly into his.

Slowly the reeling desert stilled. They lay together, aware of their unbounded love, its horizons reaching as broadly as those of the desert, silhouetted finally in the pearl and pink of growing dawn. She had been a virgin, and he knew that he had been a fool to think she might not be. He knew no other man would ever experience her love as he had done. He thought of Pandeish and wondered if he had been healed.

But then he realized he wasn't healed at all, but the victim of a new and serious illness. Between them, Maxwell Todd's ring nestled in the valley of her naked breasts.

A cloud of dust appeared on the horizon, and they thought the time had come to die. He kissed her and pledged his love, and she responded with a promise of her own.

"Death cannot end our love, my darling," he swore.

"I will love you forever," she vowed, sensing the immortality of her love, even when the bodies that had burgeoned it were ashes.

He placed her inside the well, lowering her to an interior lip where she might hide; and then he turned to meet the oncoming threat, hoping that the Arabs might be convinced that he was not the same soldier who had ridden off with their prize, hoping that somehow at least his own death might save his beloved from a fate like Jo Baker's.

But then someone hallooed him, and he stood hands on his lips laughing. For it was his own party that had found them.

6

Claire and Colin would never be the same. Their lives had changed in the desert. But the world they re-entered had not changed. Claire had her mother to deal with, clinging to her, petting her, and sobbing hysterically.

Claire longed to pour out her heart to her mother, but she could not, of course. It was the first time in her life that she had not been able to share her problems with Mama. She had even managed to confess her escapade with Lord Rutherford. But this she could not confess, and she knew she had become a woman. She was no longer merely her mother's child, and she felt isolated and helpless.

She had returned to the caravan wearing Colin's army tunic, which covered her to the knees. Thankfully, one of her trunks had been on the baggage wagon, so she had been able to make herself presentable. Poor Jo would not look herself for some time. Her face was covered with bruises, and she lay where a place had been made for her, not speaking, her eyes blank.

The soldiers had routed the bandits and recovered most of the passengers' valuables, but they were faced with crossing the desert in daytime, and water, running low, had to be rationed. Colin gave most of his share to children. The act of atonement soothed him, and his tormenting thirst helped blot out the agony of his love for Claire, from which he would never be able to escape.

When they reached Suez, the sun was shining fiercely over the town. Light reflected blindingly from houses built of little stones, held together by wooden frames; and glassless windows were covered with lattices to keep out the glare. The traffic of horses and gondola-shaped slippers had pulverized the sand streets into a gold powder that blew like glitter in the air. The hotel, located near the consul's house and several other residences, was built of soft, ragged oölite.

There the travelers rested, reveling in food and coolness. Claire had not thought she could eat, but having missed supper at the desert station, she was ravenous. Sleep, however, eluded her at this hour, and she went foolishly out into the heat, threading her way through crowds of Nubians and threadbare Egyptian soldiers to the bazaar to purchase a bolt of gaudy mulhouse calico for which she had no use. The cheerful material improved her mood for no more than a few minutes. The sights of Suez were wasted on Claire. In her mind she saw nothing but Colin, Colin.

Toward evening a string of camels came in from the desert, carrying most of the travelers' luggage, and an enormous pile of trunks, portmanteaus, and guncases was deposited at the wharf.

Claire and Colin walked down the dock together to check on her luggage. Shadows were growing long, and the heat was diminishing. A sort of calm had settled over the town, and in that peaceful atmosphere it seemed impossible that the events of the previous nights had occurred. Yet even now currents ran between them; love pulled at them as they walked the sandy streets. But Colin fought against that natural tide with all his strength. It did not matter that heaven might have created them for each other. Colin remembered only that he had loved once before, disastrously, where he should not have loved. His betrayal of Maxwell Todd sickened him. He was angry with Claire simply because he loved her. He was angry with her because *she* loved him. It would not have happened, he thought miserably, if she had loved Max as she should have. He had thought she loved Max; well, by God, he would see that she married Max. Then he'd bury himself in the south in the exclusively male life of a soldier.

Unlike Colin, Claire had never loved before, and though she was bewildered, she could not quite fathom the immensity of what had happened. She wanted nothing more than to run away with him across the desert or across the sea, wherever he would take her. But Claire, for once, thought of duty. She remembered her many transgressions—her banishment from London, her near ruin in the matter of William Rutherford.

Can I do nothing right? she wondered. She felt doomed to self-destruction and determined it would not be so. What a laughingstock she would make of Maxwell Todd—and her parents—if she ran away with Major Whitecavage! Just this once, when it really mattered, she would do as she ought and be a credit to her parents, to her fiancé and to herself. As for Colin Whitecavage, she was too proud to love him, surely!

He had taken his devastating pleasure with her as though she had been a harlot, not the fiancée of his superior officer! Because of him she would go to her marriage bed in an impure condition. Colonel Todd would assume she had been raped by the Arabs and take pity on her. Claire sighed. She had compromised herself once with Colin. The unspoken lie would compromise her again.

Suppose she told Colonel Todd the truth—that Colin had taken advantage while she had been hysterical with gratitude? Colonel Todd would make him pay for his misdeeds. But Claire had told herself the same lie in Cairo, and she was no longer able to believe it. If she could not lie to herself, how could she successfully lie to Maxwell Todd? Claire was in a terrible mood as they reached the dock and began to count her trunks.

One was missing.

"That's not unusual," he said. "They'll find it sooner or later. You've eight others; surely you can make do."

"Make do!" she wailed. "That trunk contained my wedding gown!" She flew into a fury, blaming the mishap on his carelessness. "My wedding is ruined, and it's all your fault!" she stormed.

"You women! You bring three times as much as you need, and then you're surprised when some of it is lost. Max will have to hire half a dozen coolies to carry it when you leave Calcutta!"

Each knew the other was speaking of more than the wedding gown. Pent-up feelings gave way, and they shouted accusations.

"You'll be rid of me in Calcutta!"

"It can't be soon enough. I'm sick of this petticoat errand!"

"Imagine. I shall have to tell Colonel Todd that the wonderful Sword of Pandeish cannot even manage a woman's luggage!"

"Do not call me that! Not ever again!" His face was so thunderous she thought he might strike her; and she subsided, letting him have the last word, wondering at his intense hatred of his hero's sobriquet.

They walked back to the hotel in cold silence. For the rest of the time in Suez, they did not speak to each other except when absolutely necessary. Each one tried to think it was because of their quarrel, but the quarrel had been essential. If the gown had not been missing, they would have made another excuse to fight. For if they had not been quarreling, they would have been loving, and loving was what they knew they must never do again.

Colin sent telegrams to Alexandria and Cairo to try to locate the errant trunk, and a day later the steamer that was to take them to Calcutta arrived, seeming suspended in blue sky as it lay at anchor, white awning stretched over its decks as protection from the sun. The thermometer hovered at ninety-three despite the winter month. In the evening some of the passengers gathered in the salon of the hotel and sang. Claire, unable to catch the spirit, spent her time with Jo, who was going on with them on the steamer. She might have turned back and gone home to England after the catastrophe, but she had decided not to.

"I would have to cross that desert again if I went back," Jo shuddered. And then added more calmly, "It wouldn't fix anything if I went back. I have important work to do in Cawnpore."

"Oh, to think it could have been you!" Mrs. Cottington moaned each time they left Jo's presence. "How can I go home and leave you in this dreadful part of the world? Who knows what may happen to *you*, Claire! You are prettier than she. Oh, why couldn't you have married Lord Rutherford? I will never be able to understand why he didn't ask you."

Claire never ceased to feel guilty at the pain she caused her mother. Nevertheless, she sometimes thought she would be glad when Mama returned to England and was no longer there to doomsay. Claire had enough somber thoughts herself. She *was* prettier than Jo; and Jo, who had tried to save herself by being plain, had managed just the opposite effect. Claire was sure that Jo had been raped first because they had been saving the choicest morsel for last.

Mrs. Cottington pestered Claire constantly about her attitude toward Colin. She liked the company of handsome young men. What a shame to have this one going to waste! "My dear child, he saved you from a terrible fate," she said.

"I don't see why you cannot even be civil to him," she would say.

"Oh, that was merely his duty," Claire would snap. "He couldn't have done anything less. He's lost my wedding dress, and what shall I be married in without it?"

At the mention of the wedding dress, Mama would look on the verge of tears. "They will find it, Claire; they must!" Mama had a kind of faith when the occasion demanded it. Jo had faith, too. Only Claire did not, and she felt herself in need of it. How could she believe that anything would ever go right again? Her gown might be returned from the desert, but her virginity could not be!

Claire was unable to talk to her mother, but she unburdened herself at last to Jo, when they were several days out, aboard the steamer. They had passed Mt. Sinai, on a strip of blue sea hemmed in by mountains and sand. The temperature was still high, and the only amusement was to watch the flying fish as they played around the ship. Dolphins followed the flying fish to make meals of them.

"Ah, I knew it wasn't the wedding gown all along," said Jo. "What will you do?"

"Do? I am not going to allow one foolish night to spoil the dream I've had for years! I'll make up to Colonel Todd for what happened, though he doesn't even know what did."

"But if you and the Major have really fallen in love, perhaps you should break your engagement," Jo suggested.

"Oh no! I've learned my lesson!"

"Poor Claire," Jo sighed. "Maybe it will be easier for me to get over what happened to me that night than for you to recover from what happened to you. It's hard to be a woman, but harder in the East than elsewhere."

"But I will succeed at it, Jo! I am determined. I will forget him. I've forgotten him already!"

Though the cabin was fiercely hot, Claire slept better that night. Some of the ladies found cooler spots on deck, sleeping, crinolines and all, in lifeboats under guard of British soldiers. But Claire chose to remain below. She would not admit to herself that the reason was her fear of the combination of night, moonlight, and Major Whitecavage; but she had far from forgotten him.

She had, though, as she had told Jo, learned her lesson. It was the lesson that William Rutherford had not been man enough to teach her. She had acquired the knowledge she must live with for the rest of her days. She had learned what kind of woman she was.

A day or so later, they caught sight of Aden, at the mouth of the Red Sea. "It's the hottest place in the world," said Jo, who had made the trip before.

Claire stared at the island in despair. Not a tree grew on the barren mountains, not even a blade of grass. The sea seemed to fizz at the edge, as if it were ready to boil. Hoping to be a little cool at least on land, they went ashore to spend the night at the Prince of Wales Hotel while the ship coaled.

Mama was terrified from the moment of their landing, for the island was inhabited by Simalees, a tribe of African descent with painted faces and huge wigs of hideous red hair. The islanders danced about the group from the ship, offering wares of ostrich feathers, sea shells, and leopard skins. Claire bought an ostrich feather muff, but Mrs. Cottington took no delight in shopping. Leaning on the Major, she kept her smelling salts pressed to her nostrils. But for once the faithful little bottle failed her, and she collapsed in a faint as they entered the hotel. A glass of water, poured from a long-necked pitcher, was lifted to her lips. Mrs. Cottington recovered in time to see a black creature wriggle to the surface. At the sight of its large mouth, black eyes, and palpitating gills, Mrs. Cottington fainted again.

Colin barked angry words at the half-naked waiter, who cringed away with orders to bring bottled soda water. Colin was vaguely ashamed of himself. He was still in a foul mood and wanted to shout at Claire. But since the wedding gown, she had given him no excuse. Shouting at the waiter had given him no satisfaction at all. Claire would have been better, but it was really himself he wanted to shout at. How could he have been so careless as to fall in love with Claire? Trying to fall out of love was hopeless. He kept trying to remember her as he had seen her with rag curls in her hair—a spoiled aristocratic twit.

But he could think of her no way but riding toward him in the desert, her body naked and glowing.

Mrs. Cottington regained herself and was taken to a room screened from the outdoors with coconut mats. Here she lay gasping, fanned by Claire, Jo, and a punkah coolie who sat outside and pulled a fan attached to a string. The Major, deciding his charges were safe enough, went off to drink ale with some acquaintances from the garrison.

Claire, for once, was not thinking about Colin. Her

mother's experiences had reawakened her guilt, which had taken a back seat to her preoccupation with the Major. "We should go back to the ship," she sighed.

"Oh, no, dear," said her mother bravely. "The ship's even hotter, and you need exercise. You're looking peaked, and you must look your best when we reach Calcutta. Take Jo with you and get some of the others to go for a walk with you."

"But there will be no one to look after you," Claire objected.

"No matter," said her mother. She was afraid of many things, including being left alone in the hotel, but she wasn't a coward. There was nothing at all Mrs. Cottington wouldn't endure to see her daughter happy and successfully married. Mama saw no difference in the two.

"All right." Claire was bursting to walk about after the long confinement on the ship. She was interested in seeing more of the peculiar natives.

"Don't forget to keep your parasol tilted," said her mother. "I'm afraid your nose is starting to brown. Oh, this miserable sun!"

Claire promised, but before long she had found another use for her trusty parasol. She joined some others from the steamer who were attempting to stroll around town; but the painted Simalees impeded their progress, the scrawny, barrel-chested natives hopping in circles around the Europeans.

Finally one of the travelers gave a native a thunk with his umbrella. The fellow toppled to the ground, his head bleeding profusely.

Claire jumped into the thick of it and whacked the traveler with the parasol, smashing the crown of his straw brimmer. "How dare you hit that man! Do you think he's not a human being like you? How do you expect these people to learn to be civilized if we don't set an example?" Claire had quite forgotten that she had found it necessary to use the same parasol on the Egyptian boatsman at Alexandria. She was spoiling for trouble, like Colin; and she had no opportunity to hit *Colin* over the head.

"Hang it!" cried the astonished traveler. "I only tapped him!"

"Oh, you did!" said Claire furiously. "It took more than a tap to do that." Gathering her embroidered skirts, Claire took a step toward the repugnant man she had been defending. Jo, showing no distaste, was bent over him, bathing his hideous face with her handkerchief. Arab police arrived and demanded money of the traveler, whom Claire was quick to point out as the assailant. The European took out his wallet, while his companions protested and the natives cried approval.

In the midst of it Claire felt her arm seized, and she was pulled aside in no uncertain way. She looked up into Colin's angry face and felt a wave of excitement. They were going to fight!

"You imbecile!" he began.

"Are you addressing me?" she said coldly.

"Yes. You are the stupidest one here! Defending that rascally savage!"

"I suppose you'd defend the one who hit him, you greedy Imperialist!"

"Look!" He pointed out a bloody shell lying unnoticed in the sand.

She looked uncomprehendingly.

"It's an old trick. That savage hid the shell in his hand and cut his own scalp with it. And now the poor traveler has had to pay."

"Oh!" she cried. "Are you quite sure? I thought——"

"That is the problem with you! You are always jumping into things without thinking them through! No doubt you are jumping into marriage without thinking that through either. Have you any idea the furors you could cause with that impulsive behavior of yours? No, of course you haven't! Max must be losing his mind! Of all the women he might have picked, you must be the most unsuitable!"

Tears stung Claire's eyes. He could hardly have been more cruel. She was hot, exhausted, and unsure of herself.

"In Cairo you said I would be more than adequate as Colonel Todd's wife," she reminded him.

"Then I must have been as mad as poor Max!" Colin returned. He was trying to forget that he understood exactly why Colonel Todd had chosen her—because she was capable of sharing his dreams and working beside him, because she was the sort of woman who wasn't content to turn her back on the world and leave the running of it to men.

But were those good reasons? Tamila had learned to share Colin's dreams and look what had happened! She had acquired power far beyond what was natural for one of her sex—even a rani—and then some spy had told her secret to the Rana to undo her. Women belonged in parlors and nurseries, he thought. Seclusion in the zenana was not such a bad idea.

"I will make Colonel Todd a good wife," she said, with a determined tilt of her chin.

"You had better!"

He took her back to the hotel, leaving her there until the ship sailed the next morning. The winds of the southwest monsoon sped them toward India now. Silver skipjacks frolicked around the steamer, making fountains of green water as they fell back. At Ceylon, where they stopped to coal again, cool coconut trees hung over yellow sand, but here, to her mother's distress, Claire would not go ashore. She did not want to risk an encounter with Major Whitecavage on that idyllic island.

A week later they reach the mouth of the Hooghly, a desolate expanse of yellow water up which they must travel to Calcutta. Toward evening, Saugor Island, inhabited by tigers, was on the starboard. They passed great Indiamen, heading out to sea; and fleets of native boats worked the river's many channels. Villages of mud-and-bamboo huts were scattered along the creeks.

Claire was stifled by the air in her cabin, and long after midnight she wandered out onto the deck to breathe the fresh air and look at the stars. "How far I have come from Cottington Crest!" she thought, remembering how blithely she had set upon her journey. Tomorrow she would meet her bridegroom. The features of the man whose image she had kept so long in her heart blurred in memory. She shivered, realizing that she could not even expect to recognize the man she had promised to marry. Would *he* recognize *her*? Would he be disappointed?

Beneath the bright constellations another sleepless traveler wandered. They came upon each other suddenly, each rounding a smokestack from a different angle. Each was stunned by the abruptness of the encounter.

"It's tomorrow, then," Colin said at last, breaking the silence in a pained voice.

"Will I ever see you again?"

"Never. Oh, my beloved, you must make him happy! You must make him a good wife, for my sake!"

"I will try—my darling!"

She was swept into his arms, and her soul was lost in his kiss. Then he was gone, and she sank to the deck weeping.

He was so much stronger than she. She would have run

away with him, had he but said the word. But in terms of pain and passion Colin had lived a thousand times as long as Claire. The agonies he had suffered were just beginning for her, and he had become staunch in ways beyond her comprehension.

She must try to make his strength hers as well, she thought. But even yet she did not know that the strength of love was beyond honor, beyond duty, beyond death.

7

In the morning the white cupola of a Hindu temple rose amid the trees. The river churned into buttery foam along the banks, and beyond the sun glistened from the half-naked bodies of men and women working in the fields. Trunks and bags began to be lifted out of the hold, amid noise and confusion.

"Claire," wailed her mother. "Just look at my hat box! It's utterly ruined. It's the one Papa bought for me in Paris."

By noon they were passing pretty, two-storied houses, shaded by deep verandas and painted white, buff, or blue-gray. There were gardens and plantations, and European women on balconies waved to the newcomers as they sailed past. The houses became more closely set and ran into streets fringed with trees. A wide walk was lined with natives and carriages. Around a bend a wharf appeared, lined with many ships, and a cheer went up from the passengers as they passed a Union Jack, fluttering from a green bank. The spires of the city were indistinct, hidden in mist created by the heat.

"You see, Mama; Calcutta's quite beautiful," cried Claire.

Mrs. Cottington was almost weeping with relief. "So civilized! Isn't it wonderful, Claire! We'll have hot baths and drink from crystal soon! Egad! What is that smell?"

A dreadful thing came down the river as they rowed toward the landing place from the steamer. "It's a human body," Colin elucidated grimly.

The corpse swirled toward them, arms outstretched, bleached white, serving as banquet table and boat for crows and buzzards. Even Claire was glad for a whiff of her mother's smelling salts.

"Most of the dead are cremated and their ashes scattered on the sacred water; but some are too poor to afford cremation, so they set their dead adrift," Colin explained. He looked at Claire to see how she was taking it, his expression challenging her. *There will be worse. Are you equal to it?*

If not for him Claire would have been safely and dully married to Lord Rutherford, but Claire did not know that. She could not know that he was still wondering just how large a mistake he had made when he had stepped out the door at Cottington Crest and directed her eager suitor away from her father toward the summerhouse.

Claire was looking ahead to the shore, trying already to make out the faces of men there, hoping to recognize Colonel Todd simply by his bearing, praying for a moment to take stock of him before he had seen her.

But then they were on the wharf; and no one came forward except a white-garmented coolie, who handed a note to Colin. Reading it, the Major gave a grunt of dismay.

"What's wrong?" asked Claire.

"Colonel Todd has injured his leg and cannot ride. He'll be here by the end of the week, but in the meantime I'm to continue as your escort."

Claire looked at him dumbstruck. She had thought to bid him farewell and had imagined nothing could be worse; but now, although she could not help rejoicing at the reprieve from parting, she wondered how they could go into Calcutta society together and show nothing of their feelings for each other. Each of them knew that there must be no whispering about them. There must be no breath of scandal. It would not be easy, for they were in love and each attracted scandal as tall trees did lightning.

The city seemed crowded as they drove to the Great Eastern Hotel, where Colonel Todd had reserved a suite. Tents were pitched on the lawns of great houses. If not for the Colonel's influence, she'd be staying in one of those herself; for she learned that there was not a room left in Calcutta. The rooms Claire's fiancé had reserved were a delight, the best in the city. Attached to the bedroom was a dark, latticed room where stood a bathtub and many red earthen pitchers filled with fresh, clear water. After Colin had left to find accommodations at the Bengal Club, a knock came on the door; and opening it, they found poor Jo, adrift with no place to stay. After the close accommodations of the ship it seemed easy to make space for her in the luxurious suite, and they arranged for a couch to be her bed.

"I'll only trouble you for a day or so," Jo said. "I'm going on to Cawnpore."

"Do you mean you're not staying for Christmas Week?"

"No. I've money to spend for presents for the children and then I'll leave. Cawnpore is where I want to be for Christmas."

"But Jo—after all you've been through! You can't just start out again! Stay here——" Claire had an inspiration. "You could be matron of honor at my wedding. I haven't one, and I can't think of anyone I'd sooner have, even if I had been able to bring someone all the way from England."

"What a lovely idea, Claire!" Jo laughed and kissed her friend. "But I couldn't. Just look at me. I'd be out of place."

"You'll have a new gown, and someone could dress your hair. . . ." Claire protested eagerly.

"No, no. I wouldn't do even then. And Cawnpore is where I need to be. You'll have to manage by yourself, Claire. I'm sorry I can't help you."

"I suppose you're right," Claire sighed. Jo, with her weather-roughed skin, would not fit into Claire's society wedding. But it would have been wonderful to have had Jo beside her for courage as the wedding march started to play. Claire admitted that she had wanted Jo to stay more for her own sake than for Jo's. In England, marriage had not frightened her, but then she had not known Colin's love. Could she ever feel for her husband what she felt for Colin? Could her girlish admiration be transmuted into a woman's love?

In the evening there was a grand turnout of carriages filled with ladies in flounced silk skirts and drawn bonnets of taffeta or tulle. Beside them resplendent gentlemen, many in dress uniform, took the air. Claire, Jo, and Mrs. Cottington went driving on the Race Course with Major Whitecavage. Turbaned drivers and black footmen abounded, and high-capped Parsees drove about in fine broughams. Among the European spectators were sprinkled young baboos in knee-length robes and sockless patent leather shoes. Though there was no sign of rain, they carried umbrellas under their arms.

As darkness fell the carriage lamps were lighted, and vehicles passed each other in the twilight, feathers and plumes and finery catching the twinkling gleam. A carriage with four white prancing horses came past, surrounded by outriders and a crowd of servants. The occupant was Indian, dressed in shawls and rich silks, jewels sparkling in his turban and on his ringed fingers. A lazy posture and a flush to his sienna skin gave him the look of a sybarite, but his handsome face was hard and formidable as a soldier's. Canny eyes darted with surprise at the sight of the carriage containing Mrs. Cottington, Claire, Jo, and the Major.

"Ho!" cried the Indian, rising in his seat with an expression of mockery. "You're back, Whitecavage! I salute you!"

Colin stared ahead and ordered the driver to go faster.

"Who was that extraordinary man?" Mrs. Cottington wanted to know.

"The Rajah of Rambad," said Colin shortly.

"A rajah! Oh, my! Isn't he superb, Claire?" Mrs. Cottington leaned out to gaze after him. "You didn't return his greeting, Major, but I suppose that's because one doesn't want to be too intimate with any of *them*, even the rajahs."

"I'd sooner be friends with a sepoy than the Rajah of Rambad," snapped Colin.

Claire was frightened by the hatred she saw on Colin's face. She was glad that the Rajah's carriage was disappearing into the darkness. She had almost expected Colin to draw his service revolver and put a bullet through the Rajah's heart.

Mama lost interest in the Rajah and returned her attention to the costumes of the ladies. Claire, however, stuck doggedly to a subject that Colin obviously did not want to pursue.

"Why do you dislike the Rajah so?" she asked. "Has he done something to you?"

"Nothing that I'm certain of, Miss Cottington. It's that I did him a favor without meaning to."

"What favor?" she persisted.

Colin grimaced. He was learning that Claire always went for the heart of the matter. She could not be put off with masculine generalities like other women. He wondered how Max would manage her and tried to be glad that the problem would not be his for long.

"When I fought the old Rana of Pandeish, he was injured and finally died. Because of the Doctrine of Lapse, he could not adopt a son, and he had no heir. That pleased the Rajah."

"What is the Doctrine of Lapse?" she wanted to know.

"A rather new policy of Lord Dalhousie's, and one I take exception to. When the ruler of a British-created state dies heirless, the territory is ceded to the British Raj. But Indians hate the doctrine especially because it interferes with the sacred Hindu right of adoption. Any Hindu who doesn't have a son adopts one—to say prayers and make sacrifices to save him from suffering in the next world. Lord Dalhousie's plan was to get rid of tyranical governments and help the people, but like so many English ideas, it has backfired."

"Was the Rana of Pandeish a tyrant?"

"Yes. He became fat and debauched on the throne, but he was a bloodthirsty militarist. He had fought with the British to defeat the Rajah of Rambad. He knew the mountain passes as no European could, and because of him, we were victorious. Pandeish was carved away from Rambad and given to him as reward. Now that the Rana has died heirless, the Rajah will try to regain Pandeish. It will be almost impossible for the British to defend, and there is no one its people can rally to. Pandeish is as good as his. He salutes me for having delivered it to him, but I am not pleased with having added to his territory. He is vile, where the old Rana was only debauched."

"Is that why you are not going north again?" she asked.

"A small part of the reason," he hedged, and ordered the carriage back to the hotel. "It's almost dinnertime," he explained, but they both knew that they had been together as long as they dared. He felt the strength of her presence too keenly and knew that she was resisting the pull of her love. These conversations did not help, for he would begin to imagine how it would be if she were his, if he could bare his soul to her and seek solace in her arms.

"The Governor's Cup is tomorrow," he said.

"Yes. I suppose we must go."

"Everyone is expecting to see Colonel Todd's bride. There would be talk if you didn't appear."

She went back to the hotel to her first meal in India. The menu was totally British—beef and cheese, boiled potatoes and cauliflower, orange marmalade and soda water. But it was hard to get used to having a personal servant stand behind the chair to seize the plate and compete with other servants to heap it with delectables.

The morning dawned fair, and the mists blew quickly away. The air was almost cool, a rarity even in December. Claire dressed to greet Calcutta society in a gown of blue moire with pagoda sleeves that fit tightly at the shoulder then expanded, fluttering out like butterfly wings behind, while her dainty arms were exposed through slits in the front. A little bonnet, perched on the back of her head, accented her exquisite features, while a domed parasol of fringed silk kept off the sun. Her mother wore a gown of the newest fashion—stripes of violently contrasting colors. Hers were green and purple. Even Jo had come along, wearing a gown of Claire's.

Major Whitecavage presented Claire dutifully to dignitary after dignitary. Everyone was enchanted by her beauty and the sincerity of her smile. Governor Dalhousie, in white satin, covered with orders and ribbons, kissed her hand and murmured that he expected to see her at his wife's reception on Thursday.

"I shall look forward to it," she murmured. "And shall I see you at my wedding next Sunday?"

"I would not miss it," he said, charmed at her ingenuousness. "Let us hope your bridegroom arrives quickly. Poor Max!"

Colin wished that Claire had not worn the dress that reminded him of butterflies. A white butterfly, he thought, thinking of the swallows he had watched near Cottington Crest. An innocent white butterfly—but Claire wasn't a white butterfly. She was wearing blue, and she wasn't innocent.

On Sunday she would wear white. But the Major tried not to think of Sunday. Colin frowned, distracted by the grand entrance of the Rajah of Rambad, riding an elephant decked in jewels. The Rajah wore emeralds on his turban and a necklace outside his flowered satin frockcoat. His tight-fitting trousers were trimmed with tinsel braid and French passementerie. He paused to speak to Colin, and Colin was obliged to introduce him to Claire.

"Why don't you share my box?" the Rajah suggested as he bent over her hand. "There's shade and a wonderful view of the course."

"My mother and I are sitting in the Governor-General's box," Claire demurred. She was aware that he lingered over her hand too long; she knew that he looked at her with lustful eyes. But she could not help being excited by attention from such an exotic man.

"She's delightful, Major," the Rajah said. "What a pity you can't keep her."

"He knew! How could he?" Claire gasped beneath her breath as the Rajah moved on.

"He was only guessing, but now he knows," said Colin ruefully. "The Rajah doesn't miss much, and the expression on your face told him everything."

"Oh, I must be more careful!" She had an impulse to run after the Rajah and try to correct the impression, but of course that was impossible. Looking up into the boxes, she accidentally caught his glance, and he leered down at her, his smoldering eyes telling her that he knew she was the mistress of Colin Whitecavage.

"Will he tell anyone?"

"Probably not. The Rajah's not a gossip. He'll prefer to file it away for his own use. A secret's no good if everyone knows."

"Oh." Claire did not know whether or not to be relieved.

Colin was angry with her again. He should have expected she would give them away. Hadn't she given herself away when she had misbehaved with Lord Rutherford? No doubt she had shared her secret with that drab little missionary, too; just as she must have shared her adventures with William Rutherford with some friend. Women, he thought, excepting Tamila, had no sense of honor. Was it some derangement of grief from losing Tamila that had made him so vulnerable to Claire?

Colin had not missed Claire's excitement when the Rajah had asked her to share his box. The Rajah even reminded Colin somewhat of William Rutherford. He looked at beautiful women with the same salacious expression. But the Rajah wouldn't dare to make a play for Claire now, under Colin's nose. He knew how short Colin's temper could be. But Max was more sanguine—who knew what might happen? Simla, where Max had built a new home, was not as far from Rambad as Colin might have wished.

"Who are the little boys in the Rajah's box?" Claire asked, trying to penetrate his dark mood. Her unguarded moment had left her weak in the knees and fearful. If only they could speak of mundanities, perhaps she could regain her composure.

Colin's expression changed. He gave her a searching look and began to talk to her gently, so that she would not lose control. "The children are the princes of Rambad, the Rajah's sons. The elder will be the rajah himself someday. The princesses are not allowed to appear in public."

"I suppose the Rajah's wife is kept in seclusion, too," Claire said.

"No. She died last year in childbirth. The poor girl was

only fourteen. He has many concubines, of course." And then Colin turned the conversation away from the Rajah entirely, pointing out the horse that was the favorite as the animals were lined up for the race to begin.

Claire was able to fall into the mood, cheering on the winner, and afterward at a ball at the Government House, she was in triumph. Everyone turned to look at her as she mounted the steps, between rows of lancers, treading the red carpet that had been laid for guests. Colin was foolishly proud to have her on his arm. How he wished he could own her as his! Perhaps he did announce his devotion with his eyes. And perhaps some of the ladies who were looking at the handsome Major noticed and envied her his love. How unfair it seemed that she should have the love of two such men as Maxwell Todd and Colin Whitecavage!

But the men only noticed the radiant Claire. She waltzed the night away in the arms of Lord Dalhousie, lieutenant-governors, and commissioners. At last the Rajah of Rambad begged a dance. She gave him her hand hesitantly, but he proved an excellent dancer and behaved as a perfect gentleman, his dark hand resting lightly at her waist.

Claire fought back her blushes and talked to him about his children, glad that Colin had provided her with a topic of conversation. The Rajah's eyes lighted with fatherly pride, and Claire was pleased. It was hard to think that this was the same man who had leered at her from his racing box.

"They are the children of my first wife," he told her. "I've had three wives, all dead. All of them left me children, but the other two, only girls. The older of my sons, Aleka, is ten. Sona is eight and terribly spoiled, I'm afraid. He was only a baby when his mother died, and the women of the zenana pampered him. But I've taken him away from the women now and put him in the charge of men, like Aleka. Aleka has never given me a moment's trouble. What a fine horseman he is, at his age! Ah, Miss Cottington, you've come to Calcutta at the best time of year. Have you seen the gardens yet? And the Ochterlony Monument?"

He charmed and fascinated her. His swarthy, turbaned presence lent an air of fantasy to the night. A woman might step into another world with such a man, a world boundless with adventure.

But Colin was at her side, leading her away. "You said we must not dance too often together," she objected. It had been a relief to dance with the Rajah. Though she found him romantic in his exotic way, the idea of any liaison between them was absurd; while with Colin she must worry every instant about revealing the wild emotions that leaped within her at his mere presence.

Mrs. Cottington was in ecstasy over the day's events and at the sensation Claire had made. "Oh, do think, Claire, how envious Jenny's mother will be!" she said, and stayed up until dawn writing down all the details in her journal and pausing only to shudder at the howls of jackals in the streets.

In the morning, while Mrs. Cottington still slept, Jo packed her boxes and bade Claire farewell. Claire almost wept. Now she had only Mama, whom she could not confide in. "Perhaps you'll come to Cawnpore sometime," Jo said, upset as well. It was Claire who had helped her recover from her experience in the bandits' camp. For the space of several weeks they had been closer than most sisters.

"I suppose Colonel Todd will take me to our new home at Simla," Claire said, the words sounding strange.

That evening there was another dinner, this one at the Bengal Club. Again each diner had a servant to stand behind him and do battle at filling his plate. There were other servants to wait the shining mahogany table and punkah coolies to operate the fans. The fare included iced wine, cooled from the cargo of a New England ice ship, dry champagne, mutton, and chicken curry. A controversy ensued over the prawns, which some of the diners devoured, declaring that they came from a lovely salt lake into which the Hooghly did not flow.

"Is there such a lake, Major Whitecavage?" Mrs. Cottington wanted to know.

"I have never seen it," he returned; and Claire pushed her prawns to the far corner of her plate, the remembrance of the filthy Hooghly with its concourse of bleached bodies making her nauseous, even amid the gleaming mirrors and shining crystal of the club. Her mother pronounced the prawns delicious; for she was in her element now and had decided that India was a wonderful place, so long as one remained as one should with one's kind.

"If only your wedding gown would arrive, Claire," she said. It was her biggest worry. The missing trunk had been located still in Cairo and was being sent after them with all the haste that could be mustered.

"If only Colonel Todd would arrive!" Claire would fret. How was she to have a wedding without bridegroom or gown?

On the day of the Governor-General's wife's tea, Mrs. Cottington rose early to arrange her hair and choose her jewels. But before the breakfast hour at ten, Colin arrived wearing an expression so grave that both women knew that something had gone seriously wrong.

"Is it the gown?" cried Mrs. Cottington, imagining that the ship bringing it had sunk.

"Colonel Todd?" Claire gasped, thinking he might have died of his injury.

"It's black cholera. There were a few cases yesterday, and this morning people are dying by the hundreds. Pack at once. We must leave Calcutta. I've hired a gharry."

"Leave Calcutta!" The two women were stunned. "What of the wedding?" Claire asked.

"You cannot be married if you are dead," said Colin impatiently. "I've seen the work of black cholera. Sometimes it takes no more than three hours to die."

Mrs. Cottington wrung her hands. "Oh, but the tea. Can't we at least go to that?"

"Perhaps it's been canceled," Claire suggested.

"No. I suppose that the Governor-General feels that a semblance of order ought to be maintained. He thinks that it would be unseemly for him and his family to run at the first sign of trouble and cheat everyone out of their Christmas festivities. But I am sure he'll send his lady away in a day or so, if the disease continues to spread. And it will. But the British seem to wait for casualties among their own kind before they flee. It's as if the dying of the natives doesn't count."

"Then we will wait, too," said Mrs. Cottington.

Claire for once agreed with her mother. "I am to be the bride of Maxwell Todd, and it doesn't suit me to run like a frightened rabbit. We will attend the reception. We are expected."

Colin ranted. He paced the halls and debated whether he ought to throw her over his shoulder and carry her bodily away from the Great Eastern Hotel. But he knew, too, that she was staying because of him. She was staying to prove to him that she could be all that the wife of Maxwell Todd ought to be. He dared not break her determination, for if he did, might not he break his own along with hers? He cursed the fate that had kept Max away from Calcutta and brought the cholera instead.

Claire and her mother went to the reception, climbing a white staircase lined with red-coated, white-turbaned servants, and curtseying to the Lady Sahib, who wore a diamond tiara and sat in a silver arm chair. Claire was striking in a moire gown she had worn at Queen Victoria's court, and Mrs. Cottington created a stir with her little spotted veil, a fashion that had not yet been seen in Calcutta.

The Governor's lady herself asked where such an item could be acquired, and Mrs. Cottington was rapturous. Everyone seemed to have a wonderful time, a determinedly wonderful time, Claire thought. The ladies downed wine and sherry more rapidly than Claire had ever seen women do in England, and laughter hit falsetto notes. Everyone was thinking of the cholera and trying not to think of it. Each woman seemed to think the reception worth the risk of her life, and more than one had disobeyed her husband to remain in Calcutta for the event.

"My dear, I've been planning this all year," she heard one tell another.

"Of course, we've all been dreaming of Christmas Week for months. Anyway, the cholera is among the natives; they care nothing for sanitation. It won't come here."

"Have you heard? The L. G. is going to open his villa at Belvedere. Some lucky ones will be able to get out of the city at least."

Claire did not have a good time. Instead, a sense of panic began to tear at her. It was not merely fear of the cholera. Here in this lavish palace, she began to understand for the first time what a woman's life must be like in India. How bleak it must be for these women to care so much about this event!

For the first time, Claire was truly frightened by the prospect of her future. She was afraid of becoming like these sisters in womanhood and living her life for Christmas Week.

"We are leaving in the morning," she told her mother when they were once again in their rooms at the Great Eastern Hotel. On the drive back to the hotel they had seen people stagger in the street, and now, even inside their rooms, they could smell the reek of charred human flesh from the burning ghats along the river, where the dead were cremated and sometimes murder was committed.

"Claire, your wedding!" wailed Mrs. Cottington.

"I will marry Colonel Todd in Delhi or Simla or wherever he wishes," said Claire firmly. "But we will not wait here."

"We'll go to the Lieutenant-Governor's estate at Belvedere," Mama suggested. "The ladies say it's quite beautiful."

"No, no, no! We are going to Delhi! I am not going to be like these women, willing to risk my life for a tea party!"

"But Claire, dear, your life will never be like theirs. Most of them are from isolated little stations. No wonder some of them are desperate! Oh, why must you spoil everything? The cholera hasn't struck any British."

"But it will! Major Whitecavage says so. And I am not spoiling anything. My wedding gown is not here and neither is my bridegroom."

Mrs. Cottington wept. Claire had always been headstrong, but she had never so completely defied her mother. Claire packed to keep her mind off her mother's tears.

"I'm not leaving Calcutta," Mama sobbed. "I will not go until you are married!"

And she didn't.

Deep in the night, amid the cries of jackals, Claire heard a moan close at hand. Lighting a lamp, she crept close to her mother's bed and found her thrashing amid the covers, her body burning with fever. "It is so infernally hot here," her mother said.

Terrified, Claire roused a servant in the hall and sent him running to the Bengal Club with orders to fetch Major Whitecavage and a doctor.

Mrs. Cottington clung to her daughter, gasping. "I cannot die, Claire, and leave you in this godforsaken place!"

"You won't die; you mustn't!" wept Claire.

But Mrs. Cottington felt the awful thing working inside her. She knew why they called it black cholera, she thought. Her very soul seemed to be filling with impenetrable night. She ceased even to whimper, and Claire caught her breath, thinking her dead. But then her mother opened her eyes again and whispered, "Claire, promise me that there will be no more scandals. I will not be here to help you out of your fixes."

"I promise," said Claire.

"And there's to be no period of mourning. Have your wedding at once and all in white, just as it would have been. Oh, how I wish I could be there to see it!"

"You will be there, Mama! You must!" cried Claire.

But her mother sighed, and her eyes closed, and though Claire shook the bed, her mother did not move again.

Claire was all alone in Calcutta now, except for Colin, in whose arms she wept with abandon. He held her, trembling at the privilege, wanting to soothe her grief, yet not wanting her to remember herself and withdraw from him.

But though he did not want her to move from his arms, he could not forget the threat that loomed larger over them every moment they stayed. Mrs. Cottington was not the only European who had been stricken during the night. A dozen who yesterday had sipped wine in their organdies and lace were corpses today. Colin was aware of gharries being loaded outside the hotel as the British rushed to flee the city.

He set her away from him, holding her by her arms. "Claire, you must be brave now. We must bury your mother, and then we must head for Delhi."

She looked at him confusedly. "Have you found some lady who will chaperone us?"

"Don't be a fool, Claire!" he almost shouted. "There isn't time!"

"But we must have a chaperone," she insisted hysterically. "We will be a scandal if we arrive in Delhi alone together. I promised my mother there would be no more scandals!"

"It cannot be helped!" he said. Why was she always improper when she ought to be proper and now proper when improper would be better. God, how she perplexed him!

"Oh, Colin, you know what will happen if we are alone that way," she said desperately.

"No," he said, "it will be all right. We will be strong, and we will find some group of travelers to join on the way."

But Colin tingled with excitement. Never before had she made a direct reference to what had happened in the desert. Never before had she suggested the possibility that it might happen again.

She tried to move into his arms again for comfort, but needing to fight his emotions, he held her back and began to talk quietly of the funeral. It must be immediately, he told her. He would arrange for a chaplain to say prayers.

Claire was stunned. Somehow it seemed indecent—death and burial all in one day. But Colin knew time was of the essence, and before noon Mrs. Cottington was buried in the Park Street Cemetery, wearing the spotted veil the Governor's lady had admired to hide the ravages of the disease.

Spiky pyramids rose all over the graveyard, reminding Claire of their journey through Egypt, and sacred cows wandered among the domed crypts and palm trees, lowing as the brief service was read. Dazedly she let Colin lead her away from her mother's resting place in the burial ground of the Raj. "It's time to go, Claire," he said.

"No," she murmured, thinking of her promise to her mother. But this time he did as he should have done before and, lifting her off her feet, tossed her bodily into the waiting gharry.

The first hours out of Calcutta, Claire wept brokenly, wedged dejectedly into a corner of the little van. Colin, in the opposite corner, watched woodenly. He might have tried to comfort her, but like Claire, he was afraid. They were alone now, except for a driver who had come with the gharry when he had hired it. The journey along the Grand Trunk Road, would be long, arduous, and intimate, without the buffering presence of Mrs. Cottington, who had unknowingly protected them from their passions. Mrs. Cottington had often irritated Colin, but now he missed her. She had been an asbestos shield to prevent the heat of his desire from escaping its confines and exploding into disaster. Her garrulous silliness had distracted him from Claire. He found he had almost liked her. Certainly, on one level of his consciousness, he had been grateful.

Mrs. Cottington, with her talent for dissolving anything romantic into something commonplace, was gone. Now something else occupied what should have been her place in the gharry—a sense of inevitability.

Colin fought against that presence with all the strength he could muster. He was a man of great fortitude and courage. He believed in duty and in honor. How could it be possible that he would not win this battle, he who had defeated the mighty army of the Rana of Pandeish with his smaller number of men? He had held sway over his soldiers, inspiring them to feats beyond their capabilities. Why did he fear that he could not even hold sway over himself? But Colin had already surrendered his two finest weapons—his heart and his soul. His powers were decimated.

He was pleased at least with the gharry. Sliding panels in its sides opened for doors or window, and the shelves and lockers at the ends of the vehicle had been well loaded with provisions. A spare cushion, which fit between the two seats would convert them into a bed for Claire. He would sleep with the driver beside the van. He was lucky to have acquired the gharry early, the day before the epidemic spread into the British community. Now there were none to be had in Calcutta, but Claire could travel in relative comfort, living in the van as Indians did on journeys. Such was Colin's well-intentioned plan.

But toward evening clouds formed on the horizon. Colin watched apprehensively, realizing they were in for a blow. He was not surprised when the gharry halted; and the driver, in the tattered blue caftan of a mail driver, poked his head inside and announced, "Sahib, we must stop at the next dak bungalow."

"No," said Colin. "There is a river ahead. I want to get across before it is too high."

"That would be dangerous, Sahib. Look at the clouds. It is already raining ahead of us. We will stop and wait a day or so for the water to go down."

But Colin ordered the gharry on. The danger of high water seemed nothing to the danger of adding another day or two to the length of their journey. Soon rain pounded down on the roof, and gusts of wind shook the gharry. Claire ceased weeping and stared at him, white-faced but wordless. She had committed herself into his keeping unquestioning of whatever he might do.

The gharry lurched to a halt at the edge of the river, and the driver, dripping water inside, appeared to announce that he would not cross. "Too high, Sahib," he said.

Colin got out to look. "It can be done," he decided. "I will drive."

"Am I dismissed, then, Sahib?"

"Yes," said Colin, and took out rupees. "Is there somewhere you can go?"

"A village over there. I would not wander the road. Three nights ago a man was taken by a tiger near here."

Colin climbed onto the driver's seat and yelled to the horses. The gharry plunged into the current. Inside, Claire sat in darkness as the van leaned and water trickled inside the door. Instinctively she drew up her feet to save her silk slippers. At last she became disoriented as the gharry seemed to spin in the water, and she wondered whether the van was still attached to the horses or whether it had broken loose and was careening downstream. Colin's voice was far away; she wondered if it were a trick of the wind. Should she try to open the sliding door and swim toward the voice? Were there crocodiles? She had heard that there were in the Hooghly.

The thought of the Hooghly reminded her of the white corpse she had seen drifting toward the ocean, and she imagined she would soon be such a corpse herself. Ill with the horrors she had encountered since reaching India, she murmured to herself, "Mama was right. She said we should never survive, and already she is dead. I'll be next, and I deserve it! All this is my fault. If only I had married Lord Rutherford!"

William's face, smug and accusing, rose before her, then suddenly she felt the wheels crunch onto land. They were across! But now a bolt of lightning frightened the horses. They began to run. Colin urged them on through the night and she felt in the power of a madman as they jolted along the stormy road.

At last the gharry came to a halt. Colin slid the door open and looked in. His face was strained, his dark hair dripping. He stared at her as though he hoped he had only dreamed her presence, as though he hoped that some demon had been outrun.

"Are you all right, Claire?" he asked.

"I am perfectly all right," she said, though she was badly shaken. Colin Whitecavage had thought she had not the stuff for India, and now she herself was beginning to doubt that she did. The desperation of the ladies of Calcutta had alarmed her, and the death of her mother had thrown her into panic. But Colin must not know. She had wept and been done with tears, since there was little room for the luxury of grief here; but she was awash with self-doubt and terror—terror of India, of the future, but most of all, terror of the present and the man with whom she was so alone.

"We'll stop here for the night," said Colin. He placed the spare cushion between the seats so that she could lie down.

"But where will you sleep?" she asked.

"Beneath the wagon."

He unhitched the horses and tethered them away from the gharry so that they could not run away with it during the night. Then he settled himself beneath the van with his rifle. But the rifle had been hung atop the gharry and the ammunition was wet. The spot beneath the gharry was far from dry, too. Water ran in streams and collected in puddles under it.

Several hours later the horses whinnied and jerked at their tethers. Colin, half dozing, came alert. Something was nearby, perhaps no more than a pack of jackals. But the driver had mentioned a tiger, and three days was enough for the beast to be hungry again.

Colin cursed and opened the door to the gharry.

Claire screamed.

"It's only I," said Colin.

"What do you mean, only you?"

"I mean I'm not a robber or a brigand."

"You might as well have been the other night," Claire observed.

"Well, I cannot sleep under the wagon anymore. There's some animal outside. Imagine what would happen to you if I were dragged off and you were left alone."

Claire tried not to imagine what might happen to her if he were inside instead of out, but she ceased protesting; and he closed the door, plunging them into utter darkness, with even the dim nightglow shut away. But the coach shook as he busied himself with some activity, and she asked in alarm, "What are you doing?"

"Undressing."

"Undressing! You cannot do that, sir!"

"If I don't, everything in this gharry will be as soaked as my clothes, and we have far to go in it, Miss Cottington. Don't be concerned. I am not going to touch you."

They lay as far apart as was possible, each intensely aware of the other, each with nerves taut, wishing for morning to release them; but at the same time savoring the sweet intimacy of the van, swaying like a cradle in the wind while rain hammered on the roof.

Certainly Colin's intentions were the best. Surely Claire did not mean to give in to temptation. But in the predawn, thunder cracked and a tree fell across the road with a devastating roar.

Claire shrieked, and as though a spring inside her had been released, plunged across the van to the safety of his arms.

She found not safety, but new danger, as his powerful arm wrapped around her. Where her ear lay against his chest she heard a moan of agonized bliss rise softly. Her being melted into his.

And they were lost.

8

They were unaware of the passage of time, drifting in the dimensionless heaven of their love. But at last the terrified whinnying of the horses and the awful commotion of attack returned them to reality.

"Colin!" she pleaded.

"I can do nothing, love. The gun is wet. Lie quiet and it will go away."

She clung to him, her face pressed to his chest, her fingers digging into his flesh, until at last it was quiet outside.

They opened the door on a clear blue day. Jays and shrikes perched on telegraph wires, and where two horses had been, there was only one and the gory evidence of the savagery she was becoming so familiar with as the mark of India.

They no longer tried to deny themselves as they journeyed on. Each felt that the journey could never end, for that end would be too painful to endure. They were on another journey as well, a journey beyond the limits of civilized morality, beyond duty, beyond honor. They existed in a space apart from their earthly universe, where no value bound them except love.

The country rose into broken hills covered with brush and scrub. Villages were scattered away from the road in distant groves, but water tanks were frequent, and striped squirrels scolded them from the trees there, as if they knew the immensity of Colin's and Claire's transgressions. Sometimes at night they lay together in the gharry, sharing the bed, leaving the door open to the stars and the breeze on their unfettered bodies. At other times they came upon dak bungalows with high-pitched roofs of thatch or tile and shady verandas or porticos. The inns were always uncrowded, for they had a head start on the others who had been leaving Calcutta; and in these overnight resting places they would take a suite of rooms to enjoy what luxury was offered.

Some had only a few forks with broken tines, a table of rough deal, and windows with broken panes. Others had linen table clothes, soda water, and ice. But always there was the bath with its earthenware jars of cool water. They would bathe together, delighting in the sensuous flow of refreshing water as they poured it over each other. She was becoming accomplished in the ways of love. She was learning to please him as he pleased her, taking the initiative of lovemaking upon herself, astounding him into insanities of desire.

He had never known a woman in such a way, a woman who had broken every taboo of her upbringing and so was no longer held by any inhibition. She had become utterly natural, completely free; her soul and being existed only in the soul of his love.

Tamila had submitted herself to him as though he were her god. Claire did not submit; she transcended herself. She became an incarnation of love, a sacred river of wide, incredible currents.

They spent a night at Benares, where pilgrims journeyed to be cured, but neither Colin nor Claire sought or found remedy for their malady among its minaretted and spired temples.

Soon the countryside became a dry plain with bushes growing out of sand. Blue cow, deer, and antelopes fled as the gharry rumbled past. Here and there they met other travelers who had fled Calcutta. Although most British were behind them, wealthy Indians were in evidence, traveling with entourages. Cooks made curry paste and chupatties in the open air, goats had been brought along for milking, and there were special tents for grasscutters and camel men.

Colin and Claire camped beside them in topes of green trees and noisy parrots, sometimes buying their supper from the chef. The Indians called Claire, Major Memsahib. It was perfectly obvious that she was his wife.

But one morning they awakened to find themselves in the company of someone who was aware they were not husband and wife. Sometime during the night the tope had been invaded by the Rajah of Rambad and his entourage. Trumpeting elephants, braying camels, and rambunctious goats created pandemonium, while innumerable retainers hurried about the business of seeing to the Rajah's comfort. Breakfast cooked over open fires around which at least a dozen tents had been thrown up. Smaller tents housed grasscutters and syces; others were for domestic servants. A fringed silken tent contained women, favorite concubines and their attendants, all wearing the loose trousers of hill women.

The Rajah himself had the largest tent of all, and sat before it, smoking his hookah in the morning air. Colin's face registered displeasure when he stepped from the gharry where he and Claire slept and recognized the Rajah.

The Rajah was smugly amused. "Ah, good morning, Miss Cottington, Major. It's a beautiful day, isn't it?"

It *had* been a beautiful day, but now it wasn't. Bright parrots flashing among palm and pipul trees were only garish. Golden sunlight glittering on diamonds in the Rajah's turban was only glaring. The smutty gleam of his eye had transformed her world. Claire was furious that it should be so.

He could not know, of course, what had transpired inside the gharry during the soft night. He could only guess, but guess he did; and his gaze upon her idyl spoiled it, making her see it as others would, making her see herself not in the glow of love but in a tawdry beam of immorality.

"So, Whitecavage, still minding petticoats, eh?" said the Rajah.

Colin bristled under the taunt. Claire saw him fight for control, his lean cheeks growing tight as he set his jaw. Dislike flared in his eyes before he covered it with bland calm, and said easily, "We are bound for Delhi, though I hope Colonel Todd may meet us in Cawnpore. It is irregular, of course, but it could not be helped. Mrs. Cottington died from the cholera, and we were forced to go on alone."

"Ah, yes. Some things cannot be helped," said the Rajah, his voice gentle with hidden meaning. "My condolences, Miss Cottington. Can I be of any service? Perhaps you would feel more comfortable traveling with my retinue, Miss Cottington."

She shook her head vehemently, only to hear Colin accepting the offer. "There are many dangers in traveling alone, your highness. We will be grateful to have your protection." His voice had an almost imperceptible edge, but she was certain the Rajah heard it, too.

Claire almost wept. Why should he want to travel with the Rajah, whom he hated? Was he willing to endure the Rajah's

company simply so that he could not be tempted by Claire
again? Had the arrival of the Rajah affected him in the same
way as it had affected her? Was Colin seeing her on the
plains of India in the same way he had on the moor—as a
reckless wanton?

Perhaps he had awakened from the dream. Perhaps the
black mist had cleared at last from his mind, and she, the
demon spirit sent to lead him to destruction—as to the
haunted bridge—had lost her power. She knew she should
hope that he was no longer possessed by love for her. Then
she might manage to marry Colonel Todd, as she had
promised her mother, without scandal.

Surely it was only the nightmare of her journey that had
caused her to surrender to the compelling Major. He had
taken advantage of her on the Egyptian desert when she was
vulnerable from her experience with the Arab thieves. And
he had taken advantage again, when her mother had died and
they had begun the frantic trek toward Delhi.

Would she never learn to defend herself from the treachery
of Colin Whitecavage?

He rode with the Rajah today, leaving a native driver supplied by their host to manage the gharry. Aleka, the Rajah's
older son, was captivated by the addition of the Britishers to
the entourage. Mounted on a fine black mare, he sometimes
rode proudly beside his father, but now and again, fell back
to circle the gharry, showing off for Claire, making the horse
prance and rear on its hind legs. He was a handsome boy,
lithe and arrogant in the saddle, and for some reason, determined to make an impression on her. Claire smiled at him as
she watched his antics. He would grow up to be like his father, she supposed. Already he demanded—and received—
unquestioning obeisance from everyone in the retinue. He
was the crown prince and could do no wrong—he was all a
prince should be and knew it. His self-esteem was natural and
almost innocent.

Aleka bullied everyone—the women, the camel men, and
especially his younger brother, Sona, who was in the care of
the women. At midday the caravan stopped in a tope where a
troupe of monkeys played by the water tank and swung in
the trees. Sona was delighted and enticed one of them to
come and take bread from his hand. Claire watched the little
boy's pleasure as his face lighted and he clapped his hands
softly at his success. She smiled at the child, and he gestured
for her to look at the monkey, which had scurried up a ban-

yan with its prize and was grinning and chattering at them from a high branch.

Suddenly a whistling sound came though the air. She thought at first it was bird wings, a shrike or parrot. She could not imagine why the monkey toppled from the tree or why little Sona began to shriek, his face contorted with rage and agony. She turned to see Aleka looking self-important, leaning on a bow from which an arrow had just been spent and receiving congratulations from courtiers on his excellent shot. The animal, not dead, emitted loud human sobs as it writhed on the ground, trying to remove the arrow with its hands. Sona ran to help, but the terrified monkey, forgetting their recent friendship, bared its teeth. Sona was pulled away by servants, while the Rajah, arriving on the scene, took out his revolver and fired to end the creature's suffering.

Tossing the dead monkey to one of the cooks, the Rajah spoke to Aleka harshly. Humiliated at being chastised before servants, Aleka dared to protest and was silenced with a fierce word that sounded like a warning.

Then the Rajah spoke to his younger son with even more anger, an expression of contempt on his haughty features. Sona tried to stop weeping and failed, his sobs becoming only more audible and gasping for his attempts to hold them back.

After the Rajah had gone, Aleka began to strut about, trying to show how little his reprimand affected him. He jeered at his brother, and suddenly Sona broke from restraining arms and, putting out a foot, managed to trip his antagonist. The pair went down in a heap, hitting and kicking, screaming insults, pulling hair. Howls filled the air, jackets ripped, turbans rolled and were rolled upon. They did not fight like an ordinary pair of brothers, but as though their lives depended on it. Sona, being smaller, took the worst beating, but hung on with bulldog tenacity, clasping Aleka's leg or coattail as the older boy tried to fling him aside.

Nobody separated them. Nobody seemed to care. Claire looked for Colin, but he was nowhere in sight, and unable to stand the sight any longer, she waded in to do the job herself. The startled children ceased their fisticuffs almost immediately. Sona clung to her, sobbing, and instinctively she began to comfort him. At her kind words, which he could understand only in tone, he pressed himself more tightly against her and let her take him away to her gharry.

Sona rode in the gharry all afternoon. When he was finished with his tears he fell asleep with his head in her lap, and waking, looked up at her adoringly and basked in her smiles. Claire herself felt comforted. She had not had a friend since Jo had gone. Night came quickly as they camped by a reedy jheel. The plain became a dark monochrome against the sky; and sounds of domestic activity echoed—pots clattering, tents being raised against the silvery sky, women whispering and laughing, gliding through the twilight like soft clouds across the moon.

Neither Claire nor Sona was able to partake of the evening meal, a goatchop to which both were certain the monkey had been added. She ate dried fruit from the stores of the gharry and gave some to Sona, who took it away to eat alone, so as not to become impure by eating with a casteless person.

As the stars came out she stood alone with her thoughts, longing for Colin's company. A footstep crunched beside her, making her turn sharply, but it wasn't he. "Good evening, Miss Cottington," said the Rajah.

"Good evening, your highness." Claire took a step away. He was not really standing too close to her, but he seemed to be. He projected an atmosphere about him, like the magnetic field of a planet. She sensed something feral, an uncanny sense of splendid danger.

"You are spoiling my son, Miss Cottington," he said conversationally.

"Do you mean Sona? He seems in need of love and attention."

"Bah! He is eight, and soon it will be time for him to live with men and not with the zenana. What am I to do with him? He behaves like a baby."

"There is nothing wrong with Sona," she said, her fondness making her defensive. "He is filled with compassion and love."

"That is exactly what is wrong with him. Someday I will set a crown on his head, and he cannot rule with love and compassion."

"Why not?" she asked.

The Rajah was amused. "Because he will need to be ruthless. You can have no idea what the court of an Indian state is like, Miss Cottington. It is not Buckingham Palace!"

"I suppose not." Claire thought of her last audience with the Queen and thought that the London court was not without its pitfalls. "I suppose it is different," she sighed.

"In India a ruler must keep his subjects in fear. There is not a court in the land that is not full of intrigue and plots to depose or assassinate the sovereign or those in his favor. Can you imagine anyone being afraid of Sona?"

Claire thought, remembering the ferocity with which the child had attacked his larger brother. "Sona is not lacking in courage, your highness."

"Perhaps not. But to weep over a mere monkey! And he will not handle a weapon. Aleka! What a man he'll be! No one will dare to cross him in battle! He'll be a warrior. Did you see the shot he made today? And he is only ten!"

"You mean you approved of his shooting the monkey?"

"Certainly. I only objected to his not killing it at once. Many men will not kill monkeys because they seem to be human. But that is illusion. They are not human and are reasonably good to eat. Aleka will never be swayed by sentimentality. He'll wear his crown well."

"The crown of Pandeish?" she guessed.

"Your Major told you that."

"He is not my Major."

"Ah, I thought that he was. But if he is not, then he must be someone's, a man like that." His eyes narrowed and seemed to intensify in the nightglow. She felt as though a beam of light were being focused upon her. He was attracted to her as a man to a woman, but he had not sought her out tonight to make advances. It was something else he wanted. She was not certain what, and she felt uneasy.

"Will Major Whitecavage leave you in Cawnpore?" he asked. It seemed an innocuous question.

"If my fiancé meets me there."

"And if not?"

"Then I imagine he will take me all the way to Delhi."

"Ladies' escort is a peculiar assignment for a man of the Major's caliber," the Rajah mused. "I had heard he was going to Madras."

"So he planned. But the cholera changed that."

"Ah, I thought there might have been some other reason. Delhi is a long way north."

"No," she said, and after a moment he bade her good night and went abruptly away.

She found that she was trembling. She was afraid of him, though he had given her no reason to be. She was afraid of him because she loved Colin Whitecavage.

It was because of him that he had sought her out. But she could make little sense of the things that he had said. *He must belong to someone—a man like that.* What had the Rajah meant? He had had something specific in mind, had hoped to elicit some unguarded reaction. *A peculiar assignment—a long way north*—as though Colin might be traveling toward Delhi with some other intent than merely delivering her to Colonel Todd. Was he? As though some other woman—she found she could not bear the thought. But why should the Rajah care?

Exhausted from the day's travel and the emotions tumbling within her, she went to bed in the gharry, but not to sleep. She was too tired to sleep, or she missed his warmth beside her; and as the chill of the night crept through the sides of the van, she thought of how it would be to sleep without him forever. There was no question, of course, of his sharing her bed while they were in the Rajah's camp. The Rajah had many sharp eyes.

Later on, Colin knocked on the door and asked her to throw out a roll of bedding so that he could sleep beneath the gharry. He was definitely out of sorts and remonstrated with her about the Rajah's visit. "You want to be careful," he said shortly. "The Rajah has a reputation with women."

"I suppose you haven't," she replied, still angry about his acceptance of the Rajah's invitation, still smarting from the Rajah's insinuations.

"It's *your* reputation we're concerned with," he shot back.

Claire was furious. He was intimating that she was encouraging the Rajah in dishonorable attentions, when in fact she would be receiving Colin's dishonorable attentions had he not decided they would travel with the entourage.

But he was right, of course. It *was* her reputation that counted, and she swallowed her anger without making a scene. If he were jealous of the Rajah, it served him right, both for joining the caravan and for thinking her an easy woman. To punish him she was friendlier to the Rajah the next day.

That night Colin slept beneath the van again, but long after the camp had quieted, she heard him rise and walk away. On an impulse she followed, leaving her crinolines behind as she dressed rapidly.

She caught up with him the edge of a dahl field beyond the camp. Footpaths led here and there through the deep green leaves of the crop, which stood impenetrably seven or eight feet high. Colin was crouched behind a gray mud wall which once had been part of a farmer's house.

"Colin!" she whispered. She did not stop to think what reasons he might have for being there. She thought only that here was a chance for them to be together, to share their mindless, engulfing love.

He muttered a curse as he saw her and pulled her down beside him, but not to kiss her. "Be still," he hissed. She obeyed, for his tone told her she could not do otherwise. They stayed that way for what seemed a long while. His nearness made her want to weep. She wanted merely to touch his face, so smooth and hard in the starlight. She longed to bury her head against his chest and breathe in the male aromas she had come to associate with him—aromas not of the tobacco and cologne which had perfumed her London beaux, but of boot polish, rifle oil, and leather.

But Colin paid no attention to her, his body tensed, his concentration all on the quiet dahl field. He had, for the moment, forgotten her, and her mind screamed with resentment that there should be anything in the world that could occupy him as profoundly as their love. And what was it? What could it be?

The crops swayed gently in the breeze, and once a deer came crashing through the stalks, leaping the crumbling wall only yards away. Shivering in the cool night, she waited beside him, not knowing why they waited, waiting only to be with him.

Then at last he caught her arm and gestured urgently. The tops of the dahl had begun to move in a pattern. Someone was walking along one of the footpaths, causing the stalks to shake. As they pressed themselves against the wall, a figure emerged from the dahl. Claire had never seen the man before. He could not be a member of the entourage, for he was too dark, and his turban was tied in a different way.

"Who——" Claire began, when he had vanished into the night.

But Colin placed his fingers against her lips to command her to be silent. She might have swooned at the ecstasy of his mere touch, but another figure came out of the dahl, chilling her desire.

The Rajah of Rambad. He looked about him cautiously, scanning the countryside as if to make sure that he was not being observed. Claire willed her body to immobility, and in a moment, the Rajah blew a breath of satisfaction and set off toward the tope.

Colin relaxed somewhat; the tenseness left his limbs, but

his face was still held tight. He told her, without waiting for her to ask. He had learned that she would.

"The messenger came from the Nana Sahib, the deposed king of Oude. I was not close enough to overhear the conversation, but I am sure that the Nana Sahib is trying to recruit the Rajah's aid for a plot against the Raj."

"A plot against the Raj! Are you quite certain?"

"It's in the air—like the aroma of bread baking. But who knows when the loaf will be taken from the oven. The Nana Sahib has lost his title and his pension. Annexation is an issue which will unite the religions. The King of Oude is a Moslem, but Hindus are outraged at the abolition of the pension of the Peshwa, the head of the Martha Confederacy. Everyone hates the doctrine of lapse."

"But that has worked in the Rajah's favor," she said, remembering that he had told her in Calcutta that Pandeish would be easy for the Rajah to invade since the dead Rana had not been able to adopt a son.

"Nonetheless, I think he will stand with the Nana Sahib," Colin said. "Don't forget that the Raj took Pandeish away from the Rajah of Rambad to begin with."

"Is that why we are traveling with his retinue?" she guessed suddenly. "So that you can keep an eye on him?"

He nodded. "The Rajah is up to something. I suspected as much in Calcutta, but now I'm sure. None of his military advisers are with him and only a few soldiers. Ordinarily he would have taken them for show. They are somewhere else—Pandeish, most likely. He's trying to fool the British with this trip! But why do you think we were invited to join him?"

Claire's cheeks heated, and Colin laughed ruefully. "You thought it was because the Rajah finds you attractive, I suppose. He does, obviously; but the Rajah has never ordered his life around women. Indians seldom do. Women mean no more to them than their horses, and perhaps they are right. Life is simpler that way."

He looked at her with displeasure, as if wishing she were no more to him than his favorite mare. He hated himself for loving her, and she wondered if he hated her for being the cause of his hating himself. "Why, then, did the Rajah invite us to join his retinue? It wasn't out of friendship for *you!*" she said.

He laughed softly, liking her incisiveness in spite of himself. He had been angry that she had jeopardized his secrecy, but now he was glad to have her with him at the edge of the dahl field. He wished that he were not glad, but he could not seem to help it. Indeed, her presence seemed as natural and welcome as the brass lota of cool water that he hung on his saddle.

"The Rajah asked us to join him so that *he* could keep watch on me," he said. "Each of us is keeping track of the other."

"But why is the Rajah interested in you?"

"He's afraid I may go back to Pandeish to defend it against him. He would kill me and have done with it if he thought he could get by with it. But you complicate the matter."

"I?"

"Suppose I met with an accident, and you took exception to the manner of my demise. It would make an incredible uproar. But if you did not live to object to my death, the uproar over the loss of Colonel Todd's fiancée would be even worse. So you see, I am hiding behind your skirts. I am safe so long as I am with you."

"And afterward?" she murmured.

"Afterward is another matter. But I am not going back to Pandeish."

He looked off across the moonlit dahl and saw things that she did not see. She read grief and regret and knew that it was not fear of the Rajah that kept him from Pandeish.

But it seemed that he had gone there after all, so far away had he traveled from her. He was only the mysterious shadow of her lover; she was alone. She touched his arm to bring him back to her. He shuddered and laid his head against her bosom as though he were glad to return. His arm slid behind her neck, and he drew her down to kiss her gently and deeply. It was a kiss unlike any he had ever given her before; and while it thrilled her, it frightened her—more than the Rajah. It was a kiss bittersweet with need and resignation.

Her body throbbed with longing to be touched as a man touches a woman; her soul ached to be lost in the vastness of love, caught in release wider and deeper than the expanse of silvery plain that spread to the horizon and beyond. But Colin disentangled himself and rose.

"We have made commitments, Claire," he said. "You, yours, and I, mine."

"Colin——"

He silenced her again, with his fingers against her lips, as he had done when she had first found him beside the wall. She spoke no more, but a sob rose in her throat that could not be silenced. She scarcely knew what she had been about to say. Perhaps that they might break all commitments and disappear from the Grand Trunk Road, never to be heard of again, as if they had indeed met with a fatal accident. But Colin was thinking along other lines.

"The Indians know the weakness of the *Angrezi* for their women, and when the time comes, they will make the most of that weakness to cause us to be foolhardy. There will be mayhem and atrocity to prevent on both sides, and I must not be vulnerable. There must be no woman to interfere with my commitment to my men and to India."

He was vehement, but she could not know why. She could not know that because of a woman, because of the Rani Tamila, he had failed his duty—as he saw it—once already. He signaled her to cross to the gharry, while he watched to see her safely there. Inside the van, she lay restless and unsatisfied, after a time hearing his footsteps and the sounds of his settling himself for the night beneath the wagon.

The next day Sona was nearly trampled by an elephant. He had been riding in a howdah, when Aleka had challenged him to jump across to another. Aleka had bridged the gap easily, but Sona, trying to match his brother's feat, had fallen between the two beasts.

Dazed and bruised the boy had been pulled from beneath the elephants by Colin, who had scarcely averted being kicked himself. Sona had begged to be taken to the memsahib, and when put into her arms, had sworn that someone had caused the elephant to move as he had been about to cross. His father demanded to know who, but the boy had not seen a face, only a figure.

The Rajah had decided to be disgusted with the entire incident. "The child is only making excuses," he told Claire. "You will make things worse by coddling him. He should learn to accept the consequences of his own actions like a man."

"He is far from a man, your highness."

"Not as far as you think, Miss Cottington. Children grow up quickly in India." He grumbled, but he left Sona with her.

Claire wondered if the Rajah had been right about the boy's making excuses. It was a reasonable explanation. But Claire remembered what the Rajah himself had told her about court intrigues, and speculated. Poor Sona would never be ruthless. Had the time come so soon when he needed to be?

Aleka seemed furious at the attention Sona received. Perhaps he had hoped to win Claire's admiration with his skillful exchange of the elephants. But clumsy Sona had been the winner where Claire was concerned, and every time Aleka rode past the gharry that afternoon, he scowled.

The morning after that, they parted company with the Rajah's entourage, having encountered a middle-aged bookkeeper and his wife, who when told the circumstances of their flight from Calcutta agreed to travel on to Cawnpore with them and let it be thought they had been together all the way. They began to pretend again and, reaching Cawnpore on Christmas Eve, were jolted by the return to grand society, not unlike that of Calcutta though on a smaller scale. The Resident provided a fine room for Maxwell Todd's intended bride, but to Claire the marble-topped tables and tester bed were sorry accommodations compared to the makeshift bed she had shared with Colin in the gharry.

He struggled to make his expression dispassionate as they met in the dining room for a holiday feast. How beautiful she was in her evening gown of shot silk, her little hands encased in gloves trimmed round the top with ribbon ruching! But how much more beautiful she had been amid the parrots of the topes, in the bathing rooms of the dak bungalows!

Along the vast road they had lived in a world of their own making, and they had forgotten they owed allegiance to anything but the monarch of their love. Now each remembered duty, and the agony was worsened by the atmosphere of gaiety and Christmas carols that drifted into the warm air.

Afraid her sham would falter, Claire arranged for a carriage and, leaving the cantonment, went out to the edge of the native town to find the mission where Jo taught. Her friend was working inside the school bungalow, a low building with unglazed windows, large doors, a tiled roof, and earthen floor covered with mats.

The pupils, all girls, were decorating the room for a Christmas pageant, and the pretty children wore caste marks with their angels' halos. The smaller girls wore only a simple dress of figured calico tied at the waist. Older ones had jacket bodices over light, white robes. Black hair was worn in braids or clustered at one side and adorned with flowers. Their eyes glowed with the excitement of the holiday, and so did Jo's. Claire could not imagine that she had ever thought of Jo as faded. Here she bloomed, needing no cosmetic but the calling she had found.

The girls clustered around Claire, asking permission to touch her skirts and to handle her parasol. They had rarely been so close to anyone like her. Jo was not so grand a lady, and the women of the cantonment they saw rarely. Usually the ladies were inside their carriages as they drove past. Claire passed out sweets she had had the forethought to bring and made a Christmas present of one of her paired bracelets to a small girl who was so ill with dropsy that she could barely rise from her mat.

"You should get some of the officers' wives to come and help you out here," Claire said.

"Yes. There is plenty of work, but they don't want to do it," her friend sighed. "They don't approve of the mixing of the races."

Claire did not understand, so Jo had to explain. "Families only send their daughters here so that they can learn English, the language of the conquerors. Then perhaps they will marry some low-ranking British soldier. There was much marrying once, but there's less now that English women have come out. But many officers keep an Indian mistress, and their families benefit, of course; for he always provides for her in better style than she's accustomed to and gives her relatives gifts of food and cloth."

"Do you mean the mission school is actually a training ground for concubines?" Claire asked, amazed.

"That is it, exactly," sighed Jo. "We shall not have the girls for long. Their parents will take them away by the age of twelve. You can understand why the British women do not rush to help. They would only be educating rivals to climb into bed with their husbands. But it is where we must start. The only other Hindu girls who are taught to read are the temple girls, and they are prostitutes. It will take many generations to raise the women of India, Claire. But we can begin to give them some idea of Christianity. If we teach them their worth in God's eyes, someday they will make men value them, too, as they should be valued. They will show men they are not moths in candlelight."

"Moths in candlelight?"

"That is a common wisdom of Indian men. That women are like moths in candlelight. Unless they are kept restrained they will fly and be burned in the flame."

"Perhaps there is some truth to it. I have flown into the flame already, if the flame is love."

They had left the children and gone into Jo's private quarters, simply furnished with rattan settees, rush mats, and coconut-oil lamps. A punkah fan swung from the center of the ceiling, but it was still. Jo had given her servants the holiday off, though most were unconverted.

"You are speaking of the Major, of course," said Jo, pouring tea from a pot on the deal table.

"Of course! Oh, Jo, what has happened to me? I loved Colonel Todd so well! I was in ecstasy to marry him! How can I have surrendered myself to Colin Whitecavage? I promised my mother on her deathbed that there would be no more scandal, and she had not been in her grave an entire night before I betrayed my promise! I have become a woman of appetite; a glutton who cannot get her fill!"

"Dear Claire! Love and death come quickly in India. I withdrew from that world because I could not stand it. But that will not do for you."

"I must give all my devotion to the man who is to be my husband. But what if I cannot? I have been weak so far. And Colin, for all his strength, has done no better. We will end by destroying ourselves and the man we so admire."

"There is a way to prevent that from happing," Jo said, gazing out a window at a pipul tree in the courtyard.

"Tell me how! I shall be forever grateful!"

"It's simple. You must confess to Colonel Todd that you have fallen in love with Major Whitecavage and marry him instead."

Claire was stunned. "But I am betrothed to Colonel Todd. I've come all the way from England to marry him."

"That is going a long way to make such a mistake. Tell him, Claire. If he is the man you think he is, he'll understand and forgive you. The feelings you had for him were only girlish infatuation. And now you love someone else. You have become a woman, Claire!"

"Yes," she said, suddenly aware of it. She had changed since she had left England. She supposed William Rutherford would hardly recognize her as the flighty girl who had induced him to meet her in the moor cottage. Hope rose inside her. Maybe Jo was right. Maybe she should tell her fiancé she had fallen in love with another man.

How could she have known what could happen to her out here? In England there would have been no vicious Arabs to steal her off from the caravan to Suez. There would have been no cholera to set her adrift, totally alone with a man whom she desired. Out here passion grew and flowered as rapidly as jasmine and oleander in the hot sun.

Suddenly she understood more clearly why her father had not allowed her mother to come to India to marry him. She herself had come in good faith to marry Colonel Todd, but now everything was different. If she had known!

But Claire knew she was fooling herself. Even in England she had been falling in love with Colin Whitecavage. From the first moment she had seen him, he had set her heart pounding. She had thought it was because he reminded her of Maxwell Todd in his uniform. But it had not been that! His first kiss behind the bush at Jenny Bainbridge's should have told her. But she had not wanted to know. She had covered the truth by hating him, but that would not do any longer. Out here, she had had to face the truth, though in England she might have escaped it.

She spent the night with Jo, helping her lay out presents for the orphans who lived at the mission. The Christmas play was especially touching, with a dark-eyed Indian as Mary and a pair of live, recalcitrant goats as the stable animals. Claire had to excuse herself to wander weeping into the courtyard. She was thinking of Cottington Crest as if had always been at Christmas, the chill weather shutting the family away in the cozy house where a fire burned brightly, always with an apple log added on Christmas Eve to add special colors and fragrance to the flames.

What was Cottington Crest like this Christmas Eve? Her father had not had time to receive word of his wife's death. Would he blame Claire, or feel to blame himself? He had allowed her to come to India, but there was nothing he would have denied his only daughter. She had always had her way. It was no problem for Claire to get her way with men.

Having dealt her father one blow, she must deal another. Soon he would find out that she was not going to marry Colonel Todd.

Christmas morning passed with exclamations of joy and shyly beaming faces. The child to whom Claire had given her bracelet made Claire a gift of flowers. Claire understood why Jo had given up the glamour of the season at Calcutta to return.

"I couldn't have stood it at the cantonment, Jo," she told her friend. "This has been the saving of me."

"I know. I felt the same way after my husband died," Jo agreed.

But before noon, Colin came in, telling her to make ready to travel again. A telegram from Colonel Todd had come, urging them to press on to Delhi. A group was leaving the following morning, Colin said. They could have chaperones. "The British representative to the Court of Delhi has offered to host your wedding," he said. "You'll find his home magnificent, Miss Cottington."

She drew a deep breath and gave him her news. "We won't need chaperones."

He was astounded. "Why not?"

"Because I am not going to marry Colonel Todd after all. I am going to marry whom I love."

She hoped her decision, resolving their intolerable situation, would make him happy, but his face, already strained, darkened. "You promised to make Colonel Todd a good wife," he reminded her. "Have you forgotten your promise?"

"No, no, I haven't forgotten it, but better to break a promise than wedding vows. I know now that I cannot make anyone a good wife but you!"

"Then you will never make anyone a good wife, Claire. I will never marry you!"

She was stunned by the finality of his words. "Don't think I don't understand your game, Major," she said. "You think that if you refuse to marry me, I will have no choice except to wed Colonel Todd. I have decided not to marry him because I don't love him. My decision doesn't depend on what you do."

"What will you do, then—stay here and become a teacher like your friend?"

Claire had not thought what she would do. Going back to England was out of the question. Why not stay here? "Maybe I will," she said.

"Maybe you won't!" he replied. "Such a life would never satisfy a woman like you!" She found herself again in the gharry, deposited there in the same precipitous manner as when she had refused to leave Calcutta. He would haul her all over India without a by-your-leave!

Claire's blood heated as she remembered what had ensued before, but when they were on the road again, he slept beneath the wagon. Claire, feverish with desire, tossed on the mattress above. How humiliating to know that every movement of hers was transmitted to him by the creak of the gharry's springs! In the predawn he found her standing beside the van, shivering, her hair tumbled from its pinnings.

"Are you ill?" he asked anxiously, for he still feared the cholera.

"Yes, I am ill!" she cried. "I am ill with love for you. It is a disease for which there is no cure."

"It *can* be cured, Claire, with fortitude."

"Are *you* cured so quickly?" she cried. She flung herself at him, her pride and self-control swept to insignificance in the flood of her love. He unwound her arms from around his neck, his strong hands impersonal. "You will be cured in Delhi, Claire. When you have seen Max, you will know you should marry him."

"Oh! Do you think I am as flighty as that? Do you think I don't know whom I love? Do you think that I love one man one day and another the next?"

Her passion boiled into rage. Colin had never seen Claire's temper fully unleashed and he was unnerved by a quality in it not unlike his own. But Claire's anger was not the cold fury of a man. It was the volcanic wrath of a woman. She began to unload the gharry by hurling things at him. He dodged a fusilade of ripened oranges and tins of food.

He thought her an easy woman! He had always thought her that! It was her own fault that he had received first impression, but in spite of everything that had passed between them, he had not changed his opinion. She had been having a great love affair, and he had been having a mere fling. She had thought he was as agonized as she over their betrayal of Colonel Todd. But it seemed he could make peace with himself simply by ceasing to love her now.

Claire exhausted herself and went to sit stonily away from him at the edge of the tope, while Indian servants impassively obeyed Colin's orders to clean up the mess she had made.

Breakfast cooked, the rich smell of salt pork and chupatties floating through the air. But Claire wouldn't eat. She thought of unhitching one of the horses and riding back along the road to Cawnpore and the mission, but she knew that Colin would only ride after her and bring her back. There was nothing to do but go on to Delhi and confess the whole thing to Colonel Todd. She would tell him that she had lost heart for the marriage, and she would not omit the reason. She did not mind involving Colin in the story. He deserved it.

Colonel Todd would release her from her promise and she hoped allow her to return to Cawnpore. She would only shame her father by returning to England. She herself did not want to go to face Jenny Bainbridge, now Lady Rutherford, and her acquaintances. What a fool they would all think her! Claire thought of her mother and grieved, mourning the high hopes they had had as well as Mrs. Cottington's death. She had not kept her promise to stay free of scandal long! She could not seem to keep any promise. Perhaps Colin had been right about her. It would not be the first lesson he had taught her.

Claire little guessed at the lessons she had taught Colin. She was too naive to know that he knew he was the first man she had allowed to love her.

They treated each other with a stony politeness, as they traveled on to Dlehi. A lieutenant's young bride whom Claire had met at Government House in Calcutta insinuated herself into Claire's friendship, chattering on about the loss of the week of activities and clucking only briefly about the death of Claire's mother. "If cholera must come, let it be in the summer!" she would say resentfully, as though the thing were a matter of poor planning.

Near Delhi, cattle grazed in wide meadows among the remains of mortuary kilns. Then they glimpsed the Jumna River. Beyond it on a high ridge, shone the minarets and domes of Delhi. Soon the red walls of the town were visible.

They passed over the river on a bridge of boats lined with lampposts, and Sikh sentries waved them on toward the castle keep, looming over the river. The sterns of the boats were covered with matting to provide shelter for the natives who worked there, managing the ropes and anchors by which the huge bridge was secured.

At the far end of the bridge there were more guards, then passing under an arch, they entered Delhi, the city of the great Mogul rulers.

The Chandi Chauk, the Silver Square, was crowded with natives, and a line of marketplaces sold jade and diamonds, sheepskins, bangles, and raw meat. White-clothed merchants in tiny jewelers' turbans hawked temple jewels and Queen's ornaments in rusty tin boxes. Chickens squawked from two-storied camel wagons at the steps of the gateway to the Jama Masjid, the most imposing mosque in India, and troops of sacred apes roamed the surrounding park in quest of devout Hindus to feed them rice.

Most impressive of all were the red sandstone facades of the palace of the King of Delhi, but Claire hardly saw any of it. Somewhere in this fabulous city the man she had once dreamed of marrying waited to make her his wife. She glanced at Colin, wondering what he was feeling. Was he glad that he was soon to see the last of her? That he would be free to travel alone at last to whatever destiny awaited him? But Colin's wooden expression told her nothing.

Several miles upriver they came to a mansion with turrets and clock towers in the style of a French chateau. The gharry drew up under a pillared portico, and Colin jumped down to speak to the salaaming servant who met them.

With a suddenness that was dizzying after her interminable journey, she found herself ushered between lines of cypress and rose trees, across a veranda, and into a damask-draped drawing room. Footsteps, slightly irregular, hurried toward the glass-paned double doors; and she waited, eyes riveted on the porcelain knobs.

The doors opened, and Claire gasped, unable to compose herself quickly enough to hide her shock; and she seemed to see it mirrored in his eyes.

She remembered him. Yes, he was the same man she had fallen in love with, but it was as if he had been drawn by a different artist. The hair, which had been graying, was entirely white. The eyes, remembered for their intensity, were tired, but not hopeless, and glowed with the same light she remembered in her dreams. The skin of his face had sagged over a profile still sharp and uncompromised.

He came toward her, limping a bit on his injured leg. "Claire, my dear!"

"Colonel Todd!"

He smiled at her, and the gentle warmth of his smile made her want to weep. He was different; not the Maxwell Todd she had fallen in love with; and yet he was the same after all. But then she wasn't the same person he had fallen in love with either. She saw him appraise the bloom of her womanhood, his eyes admiring. If he were to learn just how fully she had bloomed, what would happen?

She trembled as he came toward her and lifted her hand to his lips. He, quite naturally, mistook the reason. He had gripped her hand too tightly or his kiss had been too fervent. Quickly he released her. She was young and motherless and had come halfway around the world to marry a man who was almost a stranger.

"Dearest Claire, you must be tired," he said. "I'll have someone show you to your rooms at once." Turning to Colin, he added, "How are you, Whitecavage? I'm much obliged to you for the care you've taken of my bride."

"It was—a privilege to be of service, sir," Colin replied. Only the momentary flicker of his eyes in her direction betrayed his soldierly mien. In that glance she read the shame and passion their journey had made them heir to. She thought he had almost said it had been a pleasure.

"Are my orders ready, Colonel? Has my transfer been completed?"

"Yes, but you'll spend some time in Delhi to rest before you go. Will you be my guest here?"

"Thank you, sir; but I prefer my bungalow," said Colin.

The Colonel nodded, but a flicker of worry passed over his face, seeming to illuminate the depth of the concerns already etched there. Colin took his leave, bowing over Claire's hand. The chaste kiss he left there burned as her intended's had not.

9

Colin made his way through the cantonment toward the huts of the native soldiers. Aromas of dahl, rice, and frying chupatties wafted into the air. Once he whiffed opium. Colin felt an ache of familiarity. He was home. In these houses of bamboo matting and mud lived men who had followed him with trust and devotion. In front of one little house he stopped to admire a baby that had been born since he had left. The mother offered him the child to hold and told him, "I offer prayers that he may be a great soldier someday. Like you, Sahib."

"Like his father," Colin said, remembering that the man had died in Pandeish. So many huts were empty of husbands and fathers! His men had been Kshatriyas—warrior caste—and to them theirs was a calling of honor, like the calling of poets. They had followed him like a god of destiny, and now word of his return leaped among the dwellings. He was surrounded by sepoys, wearing not the uncomfortable red jackets and shakos of their uniforms, but shirts to their knees fastened by cumberbunds, which they donned to take their ease.

"Sahib," they clamored, "when are we going to fight again?"

"We will go to Pandeish with you again, Sahib!" someone shouted, and a cheer went up.

"There is no more Pandeish. The Rana had no heir for its people to rally around, and we cannot defend Pandeish without those who know the hills."

"You can defend Pandeish, Sahib!" they cried. "You know the hills!"

Suddenly aware of his weariness Colin headed toward his bungalow. Behind him the sepoys raised a cry, "Pandeish! Pandeish!" Colin's stride lengthened. He almost ran from the sound of the chant. He had wished never to hear that word again.

Colin entered his quarters, breathing a faint smell of watered cow dung with which the packed earth floor was shellacked to repel flies. Windows gave onto a veranda. The place was deserted except for a lieutenant who shared the house with him. Colin sighed. He had hoped to be entirely alone.

"You're here, eh, Whitecavage?" said the Lieutenant, looking up from oiling his rifle. "I thought so, by the sound of that ruckus. You've been expected. Is the Colonel's bride beautiful?"

"You'll see for yourself," said Colin brusquely. "I'm sure there'll be a party before the wedding to introduce her to everyone."

"Oh, don't be cagey, give us a hint! Is she a morsel? Have you given her a taste of the loving of a Bengal soldier? It's more than that bridgegroom of hers will be able to do, I'll wager!"

Colin's face went dark with fury, and with one stride, he crossed the distance to lift the Lieutenant out of his chair. But the Lieutenant pushed him away, laughing. "Take it easy. I was only joking. You've been away so long I'd forgotten what a serious chap you are."

Colin regained his control and helped himself to a glass of whisky from a bottle on a shelf. "Why are the sepoys talking about Pandeish?" he asked, downing it in a swallow. "Hasn't the Rajah of Rambad recaptured it yet?"

"No."

"Why not? We cannot defend it."

"Pandeish remains a state, Whitecavage, and its own people defend it."

"Remains a state! But that's impossible. There was no heir."

"No visible heir. But here's the thing. No sooner was the old Rana dead than the Rani escaped from the zenana, running away from those who wished her to die a suttee. She sought protection from the political officer there and what do you think she had to say, eh?"

"What?"

"Why, she claimed to be with child!"

"The Rani Tamila is alive and with child!"

"I see you're surprised," said the Lieutenant. "Everyone was. The political officer was inclined to disbelieve it, but before long it was impossible to doubt. She claims the throne for her child, of course."

"It was a boy?" Colin was more than surprised. He was thunderstruck. At the news that she was alive his heart had seemed to burst his chest with its pounding. Then, hearing of her pregnancy, he had endured an opposite sensation, a weightlessness, as if he had really exploded and was adrift in the atmosphere.

"No one knows whether it will be a boy," the soldier answered. "We are waiting to hear. Word travels slowly from the mountains. The Rajah of Rambad waits to hear, too. If it is a girl, the inhabitants will cease to defend the border, and he will take Pandeish with very little trouble. But if it is a boy, then there will be a bloodbath!"

"The Rajah was in Calcutta for Christmas Week. I saw him," said Colin, still stunned. "I sensed a trick."

"A ruse," said the Lieutenant. "Our spies say his troops are assembled in every pass between Rambad and Pandeish."

"And the Rani?"

"Her men are willing to die for her, but they are ill-equipped and have no one to lead them."

"Will this regiment march to Pandeish to aid her?"

"Rumor is it will, if the child is a boy. They will be ordered to go, most likely, but whether they will obey is another question."

Colin nodded. Mutiny would not be out of the question. The Bengalis were the finest of Indian soldiers, but their high caste made them difficult to handle. The mere idea that they might be required to travel by water, for instance, could stop them in their tracks. Wise leadership was needed.

"They say they will go with you, Whitecavage. How about it? Will you lead them? Ah, who would have thought the old Rana would get himself a son?"

Colin made no reply. He knew what the Lieutenant could not. The Rana of Pandeish would not have a son. It was he, Colin Whitecavage, who was about to be a father; he, whose son, if it were a son, would be born a prince. Over his son's kingdom there would be mayhem, and there would be many enemies to wish his child dead. Tamila was alive. For the sake of his child, she stood against armies that would sweep down through the mountain passes to annihilate her and it.

"Well, how about it, Whitecavage?" the Lieutenant asked again, but in Colin's heart the question of whether he would lead needed no answer. All his being had begun to throb in chorus with the chant beyond the barracks walls:

Pandeish! Pandeish! Pandeish!

Until tiffin, Claire was alone in the Colonel's mansion—or rather she felt herself alone. Actually she wasn't alone at all. Not by herself, was more the truth. Servants scurried around her, filling a bathtub for her, unpacking her clothing. No one spoke; they were there only to serve, to anticipate her every need. One rushed to bring a bar of scented soap, another stood holding her towel, while a third gently scrubbed her back with a soft brush. Her hair was washed and rinsed in lemon juice to make it shine. Then, sitting in a wicker chair, she dried it in the winter sun streaming in through the window. The whisper of saris faded, and Claire almost dozed off. Her problems were many, but she was exhausted. A sense of presence cut short her rest, and she sat up with a start. Across the room a dark-eyed girl stood waiting patiently, her hands clasped as if in prayer.

"It's all right, you can go," Claire said, but the servant bowed and stood waiting. There was nothing to do except to dress, while the Indian girl hurried about, expertly arranging crinoline and petticoats.

"What's your name?" Claire asked.

"Sevaley, Memsahib," said the girl, and smiled shyly. "I have learned English. That is why the Burra Sahib permits me to serve you."

Claire was glad to have someone to talk to. But Sevaley's knowledge of English proved far from complete. She told Claire she was twelve years old and would marry a sowar when she was fourteen. She didn't go to school, but why should she? She wasn't a boy. Her knowledge of the conqueror's language and the money she earned would secure her a fine match. She did Claire's hair in a chignon and having adorned it with a fresh white rose, settled down again to wait.

Sevaley's presence did nothing for Claire's nerves. She expected to see Colonel Todd again at tiffin, and she knew she must tell him without delay that she had changed her mind about marrying him. But now Claire knew what Colin had meant when he had said it would be different when she had seen the Colonel. Standing before her, even tired and worn as he was, he had had the same godlike quality she had sensed as a young girl. She had felt the same wave of awe and admiration she had felt then, but now she knew that awe and admiration were not love.

Was it possible that these strong emotions could take the place of love? Why not? Colin Whitecavage was the love of her life. She had never loved any man as she had loved him, and she would never love another as profoundly. But she was convinced that he would never marry her. In fact, she thought that he hated her as much as he loved her, for she had been the cause of his betraying his friend. Even more than that, she had caused him to betray himself, turning his back on honor, which he held so dear. No wonder he could hardly wait to head south, where they would never be likely to meet again!

Once she had promised to make Colonel Todd a good wife for Colin's sake. She had abandoned that idea as nights of passion beneath the Indian moon had brought home to her all that could be between a man and a woman. But might she not after all cleanse herself with devotion to the Colonel? For all his grandeur, he had such a look of need. He needed what only a woman could give. He needed the comfort and surcease that only she could give because he loved her.

His face had shone with new light when he had seen her. Would marriage to Colonel Todd not result in a life of noble self-abnegation? The vision of herself as a mission teacher faded, along with the advice Jo had given her. She was a woman who needed a man to love, if not in one way, then in another.

Yes, yes. It could be done. He would adore her; she would devote herself to him singlemindedly. It made a pretty picture. She would live in the beautiful house he had built for them at Simla. She would wear wonderful clothes from Paris and be the Colonel's lady, who sustained him in all his accomplishments. People would remark that they were a fond couple.

She would show Colin Whitecavage.

That was best of all. Let him think that she had ceased to love him. Let him imagine that she had used him as a toy to ease the boredom of her journey, instead of he her! She knew she would not stop loving him, but that only added a suitable poignancy to the future she was imagining. In time he'd become only a memory, dry and lifeless as a flower pressed between pages. And the pain would become a thing of the past.

She would keep her promise to her mother—there would be no more scandals. And her father would be proud of her.

Claire went down to tiffin, eager to see her intended, but he had been called away by some emergency. Several junior officers who had been invited to take meals at the Colonel's house gave her their attention, but even they seemed distracted by a confusing conversation that ran about the table.

"A baby boy—the telegram came from Simla not an hour ago."

"The Rani?"

"Well, apparently. She's asked for troops."

"What will Colonel Todd do? It's a bad business, I tell you!"

"It will be a disaster. But we are pledged to protect our subsidiary states."

Each time Claire entered the discussion, the topic was changed to suit her imagined interests. "Do you like theatricals, Miss Cottington? We did *Midsummer Night's Dream* last year. Nichols, here, was a marvelous Puck."

A burst of laughter, with Nichols laughing the loudest. "Do save me a dance, tonight, Miss Cottington!" he pleaded. "The ladies will be wild with envy when they see how beautiful you are; and of course, being betrothed, you'll break all the bachelors' hearts. Ah, me! I think mine's broken already!"

Nichols smiled at her warmly and speared another chop. Claire made properly coy replies and nervously ate too much of the heavy meal. No one would tell her what was going on; nobody thought she was, or ought to be, concerned. All Claire could decipher was that a party was to take place tonight in her honor. The Colonel had sent coolies about the cantonment with invitations this morning after her arrival; but the emergency, whatever it was, must have prevented his telling *her* what was about to occur. She began to see what she would have to deal with as his wife. She went to her room with a stomachache and set Sevaley to steaming wrinkles from a ball gown.

Her mind on the evening ahead, Claire had forgotten the officers' strange conversation as she came downstairs in her peach-colored silk dress, trimmed with a silvery lace to match the silver hair net that covered her chignon. Large hooped earrings made her dainty face even more delicate, and two coral bracelets adorned her arm. She was aware of the sighs of admiration that arose as the gathering caught sight of her, and there, at the foot of the stairs, her fiancé waited to offer her his arm.

Claire charmed everyone. It was like Calcutta again, but this time Max was there to enjoy it. He beamed as scarlet-tunicued officers began to beg for dances. "No, no, she's mine first, gentlemen. You'll have to wait your turn."

Then she was in his arms, dancing with him as she had so many years ago, when, little more than a child, she had fallen in love with him. His thoughtful gray eyes told her that he remembered, too. And suddenly, as if in a dream, Claire felt as she had then. She felt the power of his convictions in the decisive touch of his hand at her waist and, as before, she felt swept into his visions. It was enough, she thought with relief. Surely it was more than enough. It was more than most women had.

She gave him a dazzling smile as he danced her out into the garden where hibiscus, jasmine and perfumed creepers overhung an artifical pond. Frogs jumped with shrill sounds of alarm as he led her by the hand to a wrought-iron bench beneath an overhanging pipul tree. Then there was silence and they were completely alone.

"You don't mind if we don't dance anymore, do you, Claire?" he asked. "My poor leg will not take it. I thought it would be healed by now."

"I don't mind," said Claire.

His eyes held hers. "Have things changed for you, Claire? Are you willing to marry an old man? Tell me honestly if you are not. I will release you from your promise. I am not the same, and perhaps I am a shock to you."

"I will be honored to marry you, Colonel," she said evenly.

He smiled at her, his tense features relaxing in infinite relief. "Then, my dear, you cannot go on calling me Colonel. You must call me Max."

"Yes, Max," she murmured. He moved closer to her on the bench and, sliding his arm around her shoulder, kissed her. A sob rose in her throat and slipped from her lips.

"Dear child, I apologize!" he said at once. "I've been too thoughtless. Too hasty. Your poor mother—it's only that I've waited so long—longer than you can imagine. I've loved you since the first time we met. I forgot how you must feel."

"No, Max—it's quite all right," she stammered. He thought her innocent, of course. He could not guess that she had allowed a man to be far more familiar with her than he. His lips had been cool and dry, his kiss hard and fervent. Unlike Colin's fiery kisses, his had seemed empty, as though his spirit had hollowed with the years, as though the Indian heat had shriveled his soul. It was that comparison that had made her sob.

She shivered, trying to deny how profoundly different he was, trying to recapture the moment on the dance floor when he had seemed his former self. "How soon can we be married, Max?" she cried, afraid of losing her resolve.

He seemed surprised. "Why, Claire, there's no hurry. You'll need time to recover from your mother's death. You shall have your own apartments and a chaperone, until we are wed."

"That's not necessary," she babbled. "This is India, not England. I know that everything happens more quickly here. I want to do things the Indian way. Besides, Mama would like it. Mama always did say that mourning was a bother. Mama liked parties; she liked people to be happy."

"Yes, I remember," he said. "Do you know, I was at your mama's wedding. She danced all night, and your papa could not get her to come away with him."

"Exactly," said Claire, familiar with the story. "So it's settled then. We'll be married soon. Perhaps on New Year's Day?"

"Ah, Claire, it cannot be just now. There is trouble in the north. I am preparing to send most of my troops to war."

"War? Where?"

"Pandeish. You may have heard of it from Major Whitecavage. We'll be married as soon as the crisis is over, if you like. There are so many problems, Claire. But everything will be easier now that I'm to have you by my side."

A peculiar light came into Maxwell Todd's eyes. Claire felt frightened, although she knew no reason she should be. "Claire," he said, "did your mama tell you—ah—what to expect from the wedding night?"

"I know what to expect," she said softly, blushing.

He gave a long, shuddering sigh. "Thank heaven for that!" he murmured. She wondered what he would have said if she had led him to believe that she knew nothing of the marriage act. Would he have assigned some officer's wife to educate her? Or would he have made the attempt himself? He leaned toward her again, and she fought not to recoil, for she realized that he was going to kiss her again. But the second kiss was not like the first. He clung to her, almost weeping, his tongue pushing between her teeth while his quivering hands moved beneath her bodice seeking her soft nipples.

Frantically she tried to disengage him, but he was beside himself and would not cease his activities. "Oh, Claire, dear," he moaned, "I've suffered so much; so many of my plans have gone wrong! But you will give me new strength. You'll make me young again! Just let me touch your breasts, dearest—for only a moment! I am sending men into battle, and I need courage! I am sending more men to die in Pandeish. I must! But only you can give me courage! I could not have gone on if you had not come! Oh, please, darling; we'll be married soon. What we do together now can't matter!"

She wept, aghast. He was not the man she had so admired anymore. The magnificence she had so esteemed had slipped away. Having seen him this unnerved, she would never be able to see in him what she had before. He pleaded with her as she pulled away and ran, looking for some rear entrance to the house which she might use to avoid being seen in her disheveled state. But suddenly, rounding a piece of statuary, she ran right into another wayfarer in the garden.

"Colin!" The shock of seeing him at all was enormous. Perhaps she managed not to faint only because he did not really seem to notice her. When he did acknowledge her, it was in a distracted way.

"So, Miss Cottington, you've not wasted any time in making yourself at home. This reminds me of the first time we met."

Pain filled her. Beginning in the pit of her stomach, it spread outward in throbbing circles until she thought she would die of it. "For godssake, show me the way inside," she whispered.

Roughly he took her arm and steered her on a safe course. Had she not been in agony, Claire might have noticed an expression of hurt on his face that almost equalled her own.

Colin walked back through the garden thinking that he should be pleased at the way things were turning out. He had imagined she would not be able to abandon Colonel Todd when she realized the depth of his need for her, but he had not expected her to begin to fulfill it with such alacrity. He should be glad, even so, he thought. She was no more than he had taken her for when he'd first encountered her with William Rutherford. She was a woman who had game for any man. Colin had been the first to know the full explosiveness of her passions; but had it not been he, it soon would have been another. What a fool he'd been! And what a fool was Maxwell Todd!

Colin found his mentor still sitting on the bench where Claire had left him, chin resting on his hands, staring out dejectedly over the water at the lights of Delhi in the distance.

"Max," he said, "you will have to defend Pandeish."

Maxwell Todd did not look around to see who was there. He knew. "Pandeish will be defended," he promised. "The Rani's request will be honored, and troops sent. The British Raj cannot seem to tremble before the likes of the Rajah of Rambad. I've telegraphed the Governor-General for authorization to deploy men from the Delhi garrison."

"What of me, Max? Put me in command, and I will bring home a victory!"

"You know I can't do that, Whitecavage!"

"You must! We can't win otherwise! I have lived and fought in Pandeish, and I know every trick of the border. I know the mountains!"

"We cannot afford another victory like the last one in Pandeish," said Colonel Todd. "It was a personal fight, Major; and you fought it as such. You advanced when a more prudent officer would have retreated. You wasted lives."

"A soldier's duty is to win, sir! No one can say I was careless or mismanaged the battle. I expended only those lives necessary to carry the day. You are losing your nerve, Colonel. That is the problem!"

Maxwell Todd leaped to his feet, fury burning his tired face. "Can you deny that there would never have been a battle in Pandeish if you had not gone there? If you had not gone to Pandeish, can you deny that the present situation would not be as it is?"

Colin quivered, red-faced. He could not deny that he had been the cause of the old Rana's having turned on the British troops in Pandeish. Neither could he deny that he had precipitated the present problem in Pandeish. But for Colin, the old Rana might still live. And obviously Colonel Todd was aware that it was Colin's son to whom the Rani Tamila had given birth.

"It will be another personal objective you'll be pursuing if you go to Pandeish. No, Major. You must go south as we agreed before, and stay out of affairs in Pandeish."

"I cannot turn my back on Pandeish now!" Colin burst out. "I can't abandon it to the tyranny of the Rajah of Rambad! He has his spies in Pandeish. He dares to invade it because he thinks I will not be allowed to come. You should have seen how he laughed at me in Calcutta!"

"So he knows, Colin," said the Colonel more gently. "Why doesn't he tell the world, then? The people of Pandeish would not fight to keep a half-caste heir on the throne. There would be a multitude of potential assassins to threaten the lives of Tamila and her child. It is a miracle that the Rani has escaped death thus far—either at the hands of the Rana or as a suttee. But if it becomes known that you are the father of the new prince, she and he will have no chance at all. And that is why the Rajah will not tell anyone what he knows. He hopes that the secret will keep you out of Pandeish. Once you are there, he will have no reason to remain silent. She and the child—and you—will be marked for murder on both sides of the battle line."

"But I cannot turn my back on the Rani and my son!" cried Colin in anguish. "The Rajah will have them put to death most certainly if he conquers Pandeish!"

Colonel Todd placed a hand on each of Colin's shoulders. "You must trust that the war can be won without you. Many good men will be fighting for the Raj."

"Many good men who will die without proper leadership," said Colin bitterly.

"Go on to Madras, Major," Maxwell Todd advised. "Pandeish is the past. The Rani Tamila is the past. Go south and try to forget. You can do nothing else."

"If I cannot go to Pandeish, then I will stay here at least," said Colin.

"As you wish," sighed the Colonel. "You are on leave, and your time is your own."

10

The days passed slowly for Claire. An early morning ride about the cantonment was the best part of the day; when she could catch glimpses of Indian home life as women drew water from the well and sepoys hurried to parade. Later she might walk seashell paths to inspect the vegetable patch or the flower gardens of roses, jasmine, and oleander. Then, with the sun high, there was little to occupy her except writing letters and needlework.

Each morning she looked for Colonel Todd, but usually he was already in his office, working before the sun was up. Servants hurried through the French doors to carry his breakfast to his desk. Often as not the food came back, cold and untouched. Sometimes Claire took in his mid-morning tea herself. Often he was so distracted that he hardly noticed her; and these times Claire came to prefer, for at other times he looked at her in ways that terrified her. His eyes had a lustful, desperate shine that never failed to remind her of the night he had lost control with her. He had never repeated his untoward behavior, but Claire could not forget.

What was it he wanted of her?

She had an uneasy feeling that it was something more than a wife and helpmeet. It was even something more than access to her bed and her body. It was as though he were starving and had found sustenance in her. He seemed to expect her to save him from all that was destroying him, both physically and in spirit. She was not even married yet, but already burdens not fully understood weighed upon her.

He wanted to milk her of her youth and her enthusiasm.

He wanted to see his faded visions new and fresh through her eyes. He seemed to think that loving her could renew the vigor of which he had been sapped, and Claire thought he was ravenous with desire for their wedding night. When they were together, he sometimes seemed almost beside himself, his hands clutching the carved arms of his chair, as though that were the only way he could keep himself from lunging across the room at her.

He had not yet acquired a chaperone for her. Although he had asked about, other matters had kept him from pursuing that quest. Claire did not mind. She did not want the company of some obnoxious old lady, who certainly would not be able to deter Max if Max were unable to deter himself from overfamiliarity.

He had pleaded with her to give him courage that night in the garden, and she thought that courage was what he needed more than anything else. But how could she give him courage when she did not have enough even for herself?

A chaperone would make running away more difficult, and at times Claire seriously considered it. But there was no easy place to run to. There was Jo and the mission school in Cawnpore, but as Colin had predicted, Claire was unable to make the break. She was awed to be needed as Colonel Todd needed her. How could she leave him to be destroyed without her? She had her memories of Maxwell Todd; if she could not love him now, she respected him for what he had been. Since she was doomed never to marry for love, why not marry Max? As for Colin, she did not see him at all and did not know whether to be glad of it. She would have given anything for a glimpse of him, but that glimpse might have increased her agony beyond endurance. She thought of him day and night, her mind fevered with memories of his embrace.

The war was heating in Pandeish. Claire was sure that Colin would be in the fight; but when the troops marched off, it was with another officer in command. Colonel Todd would talk about Pandeish in the evening as they sat in the drawing room with a coal fire lighted on the grate. The weather was not always dank enough to require the fire, but Max always seemed cold. He would relax a little when the wine was brought—in goblets with silver covers to keep insects out—and he would tell her wearily the problems of the day.

"So little of the good that was intended has come of reform," he would say. "There was the policy of subsidiary alliances that was meant to allow native rule, but in effect gave Indian rulers the right to oppress their people with the protection of the Crown. Whenever the Raj dethroned offenders, hordes of princes were done out of their titles by the closing of the court, and ambitious Indians were done out of honorable posts. We tried to open the civil service; but many did not have the needed skills, and wherever education is begun, we are accused of trying to convert the students to Christianity—often with justification, I'm afraid. It's the same with the land barons, the talukdars. They mistreat their tenant farmers by the thousands, but when they are divested of their holdings, no one is happy. And now there is Pandeish, where we lost so many men in last year's rebellion."

"Tell me about Pandeish, Max," she urged, and heard at last the story of the beautiful Rani Tamila, who had obtained power through her ailing husband, and who, beloved by her countrymen, had turned her country's face toward the future. She heard of the infant Rana, whose birth had saved Pandeish as a state and in whose name the Rani now fought for its survival.

"Can the Rajah of Rambad really be so cruel, Max?" she asked. "He seemed quite pleasant when I met him in Calcutta."

"He is a cultivated man, Claire, but ruthless. He gobbles up whatever territories he can around him, and his subjects go hungry from paying taxes to support his expensive tastes and grand palaces. They say he never travels without a hundred elephants, and all the howdahs are set with precious jewels. The Rajah is power mad."

"Dear me, Max. Can't you put a stop to it?"

"Rambad is independent, Claire. The best we can hope for is to save Pandeish from such exploitation."

But the news from Pandeish was grim. East India Company troops had been cornered in a pass blocked with snow. Reinforcements were difficult to come by, for at least half of the garrison refused to go to Pandeish. Colonel Todd might have had them all court-martialed and shot, but he had not heart for it. Besides, the British were only a handful, should the sepoys decide to turn on their masters. Although most Britishers scoffed at such an idea, Colonel Todd thought it a possibility in time of growing discontent. Major Whitecavage agreed with him. Colonel Todd had settled for offering promotions and bonuses to those who would go, but the problem wasn't solved.

"I have heard it said that the men would follow Major Whitecavage," Claire said.

"Yes, yes, my dear, they would. They would follow him in spite of the sort of win-or-die battle they know he would fight. Ah, perhaps they would follow him because of it. But I cannot send Whitecavage. There are reasons, Claire, that you would never understand."

He refused to take her into his confidence, but Claire felt a chill. Something about the way Maxwell Todd spoke of Colin and Pandeish filled her with foreboding. But she did not know why.

Claire had imagined that life in India would be exciting, but to her dismay she grew more bored with every passing day. Often she had no one to talk to but her maid Sevaley, and at last she found herself confessing her boredom to the girl.

"Oh, memsahibs are all bored," the child said matter-of-factly. "You must start a butterfly collection. That is what the other memsahibs do."

Claire was delighted with the suggestion and immediately sent out for a butterfly net and a pith helmet. But her pleasure was short-lived. The sight of her dressed in riding gear and armed with jars brought Maxwell from his office.

"What are you doing, Claire?"

"Oh, I am going out to hunt butterflies, Max."

"But you can't do that. I can't allow you to go alone. Not outside the cantonment."

"But other ladies have collections," she pouted. "Sevaley says so."

"Of course, my dear. Have your collection."

"How?" she wondered.

"Send the servants to procure your specimens. That's what the other women do."

So Claire sent coolies on her errand. They greeted the task with enthusiasm, glad to be able to please their new mistress. But the specimens they brought her were not lovely butterflies. Instead, the servants came smiling and eager for praise, presenting horrid cockroaches and varieties of beetles. Claire gave up the idea of a collection and spent more time at tea parties and gossipy card games among the ladies.

Claire had expected better. Was she to spend the rest of her life this way? She might endure the loss of her true love and the prospect of marriage to Max, but Claire had never been able to endure boredom. Though the cantonment was blissfully unaware of it, she was still the troublesome minx who had caused Queen Victoria to banish her from London.

Claire was utterly bored one morning when Sevaley came to attend her wearing a green silk sari, a gift from her sister who was a temple dancer. Admiring it, Claire playfully borrowed the jeweled veil and draped it over her head.

"Memsahib looks pretty," Sevaley ventured.

"It is rather becoming," Claire agreed, excited by her exotic appearance in the mirror. "I wish I could see how I would look in the sari. Your clothes must be so much more comfortable than my crinolines. Sevaley—would you like to see yourself as a European lady? Let's trade clothes, and I'll pretend to be you and you'll pretend to be me."

Sevaley was perplexed by the unorthodox request, but it didn't occur to her to refuse her mistress; and soon, with the door bolted against surprise visitors, the two were disrobing and giggling together at their unaccustomed apparel. Sevaley cried out with real fear that she could not breathe in her lacings; and when she tried to sit down, the whalebone hoop of her skirt blew up and hit her in the nose. It was really necessary to loosen her garments then, for Sevaley was beginning to go purple with laughter. Regaining her breath, she announced in awe, "Oh, how do you ever manage, Memsahib?"

"I suppose I'm used to it. It's so important to have a narrow waist, you know."

"Why?" said Sevaley.

"Why, so that men will think one beautiful," said Claire, astonished at such a question. "When you're old enough, you'll want men to think you are beautiful."

"I'm old enough to be a man's wife already," said Sevaley proudly. "My parents celebrated with a feast when I attained by womanhood not six months ago. They will chose a husband for me soon, and I will never have to flaunt myself as Englishwomen do."

"But what if you don't love him, Sevaley?"

"Love is not important. He will be my god, and I will serve him. I will love my children when I have them. I will have many children, for nothing brings honor to a woman like giving her husband children."

Claire observed herself in the mirror clad in the green sari, worn over a gold brocade bodice, a *choli*. Her feet sparkled in Sevaley's gold shoes with pyramidal heels and upturned toes. Sevaley's Hindu philosophy interested her. How simple it would be if she could approach her own marriage in such a manner.

"One would think you an Indian woman, Memsahib," Sevaley said, gazing at the transformation.

"But I have blue eyes."

"So do many hill people. Blue eyes would cause no comment on the streets of Delhi."

"My skin is too fair. I haven't even been in the sun," Claire obejcted, feeling a demon stir inside her nonetheless.

"Many women paint their skin a saffron color," Sevaley offered.

Claire laughed at the idea of yellow skin and began to remove the sari. "It's almost time for tiffin, Sevaley, and neither of us can be seen as we are. Hurry now."

They became themselves again, but the matter stayed on Claire's mind. Several days later she told her servant she would like to have a sari of her own. "Will you buy one for me? And sandals, too? Larger than yours by a size or two, if you can."

Sevaley did as she was asked, and Claire became the owner of a costume of blue kincob trimmed with silver bangles. Trying it on became one of her favorite distractions.

The news from Pandeish continued to be distressing, and Max continued to be preoccupied. Sometimes Claire awoke at night, shivering with fear. But it wasn't the howls of jackals or pariah dogs that frightened her, though these reminded her that she was in an alien and dangerous land. Claire was frightened because she could not get her bearings. She felt adrift and deserted—by Mama, who had died; by Jo, who had returned to her own life; and especially by Colin Whitecavage, who had placed honor before love. If only the wedding would take place, she would have a safe anchorage. She could begin to make a life. Then, surely her awful discontent would cease to haunt her. If she married Max, she could begin to become the grand lady and devoted wife whom everyone would admire. She could begin to have her revenge on Colin Whitecavage, making him miserable with her illustrious marriage.

"Max, can't we go ahead with our wedding?" she would ask. "This business in Pandeish is going on forever. We don't have to have a grand affair, you know."

Max would smile and pat her hand gently. "No, no. It must be done the right way, so that you will always have it to remember. We'll be wed beneath a marquee of Kashmir shawls with silver poles and Persian carpets. A fountain of champagne will flow in the gardens for a day and a night. Bands will play, and the officers will form an arch of swords for us to walk through. I cannot marry the daughter of my dear friend in an off-hand way. Honor will not permit it."

"Oh, honor! I am sick of honor!" cried Claire. "I would like to hear of love!"

Maxwell Todd stared at her, open-mouthed. He was unused to such outbursts from women. He had been a bachelor all his life; and since Claire had arrived, it had occurred to him that he might be inept as a husband. The idea had never entered his mind before. He was a man and she, a woman; each knew what was expected, and nature would take care of the rest. Oh, how he loved and needed her! But Claire was not like the other young women who came out to India. It was not only that she was vibrant and eager for life. She was frank and impatient. He had seen her throw down her embroidery in the evening and frown at the clock. He knew she longed to be dancing, but he was always too tired for a social evening.

She wanted to be helpful. She would come to his office and ask to answer dispatches for him. Told he had male secretaries for such work, she would try to be a good companion, curling into a chair with a novel to read. But in such a situation, Max was better served by the company of his cat. Claire fidgeted and shifted her position and kept looking at him hopefully to see if he were done. She made him nervous, and a sense of uneasiness permeated his being.

He had chosen her exactly because she had such spark. An empty-headed woman would not have eased his burden at all; but he had not realized that from sparks came flames. He had chosen her for her beauty, too, imagining her as a sanctuary of surcease and rest. Instead, there was nothing restful about Claire, and Max had begun to entertain a terrible fear. Suppose he were inadequate in the bedchamber? Suppose he couldn't satisfy her? He was touched at her eagerness to marry him, but could it be that this innocent girl was longing for passion? Suppose he were incapable of possessing her at all? If he could not, he thought he would die of desire to do so. Only the awful fear kept him from losing control of himself again, as he had done on the night she had arrived. Sleeping, he dreamed of her; waking, thoughts of her intruded into his work.

Max regretted that first night, but not because of his ungentlemanly behavior. Rather, he regretted he had not pushed things further. Had he managed better, he might have overwhelmed her with his own tremendous passion and laid claim to her in a way that would have settled forever the doubts that plagued him. Once she was his in that way, he would feel himself in control of her; but even then, might she not be his ruin instead of his salvation?

When Max had proposed marriage, he had not guessed the possibility of the consuming passion he now felt. He had not been a celibate, of course. A number of clean, attractive, native girls were attached to the regiment for the benefit of the men, and Max had not failed to make use of them. But this was so different that it seemed strange that the means to satisfying the need should be the same.

Max knew that Claire had worshiped him in England in her schoolgirl way. And he guessed that that image had been shattered for her now. His aging need not have caused it, but the weakness he had shown on their first night together had made it inevitable. Had he mastered her then, perhaps he would have earned her deathless devotion. But would he ever be capable of truly mastering Claire? Even as he dreamed of reducing her to helpless ecstasy, he feared it would never happen. Max was afraid of marrying her.

The situation in Pandeish had become as much excuse as reason to delay the wedding. Max thought how easily Claire had put aside her period of mourning for her mother and admired her single-minded resolve.

I am sick of honor. I would like to hear of love!

Her words struck him to the core. She was right. It was time to put love to the test. And still he hesitated. Did she love him in the ripeness of her womanhood as when she had been only a girl? He had sustained himself with dreams of her for a long while. How would he go on if her love for him faded?

Colonel Todd wrestled his demons, and Claire hers. Claire's was a demon that had been dormant for some time—ever since she had met William on the moor. Claire, of course, did not recognize the demon as such. She never did. When Claire's demon tempted her, it was always in the guise of a good idea; an idea that others were not likely to approve of, but a good idea nonetheless. Claire always had more confidence in her own opinions than in those of anyone else. As usual, there seemed no flaw in the plan. A slight risk, perhaps, but nothing worth bothering over. It had occurred to

Claire that it would be enjoyable to go to the Hindu temple where Sevaley's sister danced.

And this idea Max had not approved.

"I would like to get to know the customs of the country," Claire had said.

"Not Hindu customs, dear. There are too many vile ones."

"But those are forbidden, now that the Company governs India," she said innocently. "Suttee and thuggee are against the law."

"There may be things Westerners can admire in the Hindu religion, Claire; but the things that are disgusting are far more. These temple girls, for instance. They are lewd women who sell their bodies to men. Ah, I should not be discussing such things with you. You should not know about them."

Claire was horrified. "But Sevaley's mother consecrated her sister to the gods while she was still in the womb. I do not see how anoyne's mother could——"

"You are speaking of a Western mother like yours, Claire. Here, babies are put out for tigers' meals, just because they are born under unlucky stars—or because they are girls."

Claire was appalled, but intrigued. "I would still like to see the dancing," she said. "My friend Jo told me that the temple girls used to be the only women who were allowed to learn to read and write."

"Since you are interested in learning about India, my dear, one thing you must learn is that mixing in native life is out of the question. Even if I would allow you to go to the temple, *they* would not."

Westerners did not go to the Hindu temples, but Claire had a lovely blue kincob sari; and one day, with her face and arms painted with saffron brought by Sevaley and with a round, red *pottu* smeared on her forehead to show that she had made her ablutions, Claire crept out of the mansion and went with her maid to see the dancers.

The gate of the great pagoda opened through a pyramidal tower, its summit topped by a crescent moon. Beyond the tower they walked through a large court. It was time for the morning sacrifice, and water was brought from the river on an elephant, preceded by dancing girls. The women whirled to the beat of skin drums, wearing skirts of crinkled red cotton. Yellow shawls, patterned in red, went over their heads, and their bodices were covered like breastplates with necklaces of silver. The jingle of foot bracelets accented the shocking dance. Claire could not imagine ever moving her body in such indecent ways, but Sevaley smiled and proudly pointed out the dancer who was her sister.

They entered another court, and behind that was the shrine where the idol was kept. Here it was dim, and Claire felt no fear of discovery. Behind a screen, priests washed the idol in the sacred water and dressed it. Then, wearing a sugar loaf cap, the ugly thing was set in its niche. The low room was heavy with the smell of sandalwood as bits of the sacrifice was distributed to the worshipers. Today the idol had been offered hibiscus blossoms, which women thrust into their hair and men attached to their clothing. An orchestra of clarinets, trumpets, and cymbals produced harsh music and a chorus of Brahmans sang ragas in Sanskrit, while the dancing girls performed the ceremony of *aratti* to avert the influence of evil persons, from which even the gods were not exempt. The whole thing ended with a procession around the temple.

Claire and Sevaley walked back to the Colonel's house and scrubbed the saffron from Claire's face and arms. The adventure was accomplished without incident, though Claire was in a rush not to be late for tiffin and had to leave her hair arranged in the Indian way, coiled into a chignon at the left side of her head. She looked especially beautiful, flushed and happy from her experience, and her fiancé remarked on it.

"Your hair is lovely like that, Claire," said Max, who was unstylishly fond of Indian things. "But I would be careful to change it before you go to tea with the officers' wives. Ah, I did not know we had any red hibiscus blooming in the garden."

"You've been too busy to notice, Max," she chided, her heartbeat quickening.

"Yes," he agreed. "But I will always be aware of any flower that you wear. Then its beauty becomes too great to be missed."

Claire's world broadened. It was too much to expect that she would be satisfied with one foray into a city of such fascination. When the chill mists and frost hazes of winter mornings burned away, the sunshine refracted into human rainbows on the Chandi Chauk, the Silver Square. Sepoys lounged on charpoys before the palace of the King of Delhi, with tunics unbuttoned and turbans awry. Claire wished she could see the King himself or at least the room where the Peacock Throne had stood before it had been carried away as plunder over a hundred years before. But Sevaley said that the King was old and fat and a king in name only anyway.

Instead, they wandered through the marketplace, where mangoes and parrots and red bananas were sold along with brass and copperwork, lacquers, and embroideries. Especially there were silver and jade merchants. Claire bought jade, after weeks of looking, acquiring quality no European shopping there would have been able to uncover. She bought silver ankle ornaments, but not the rings made for each toe. Above her elbows she wore hollow silver bracelets. There were gold bracelets and necklaces as well, but Sevaley told her she must never put gold on her ankles or feet, for gold was sacred and must not be defiled. The merchants took Claire for a Brahman lady, one with a wealthy and very indulgent husband. Perhaps they whispered to themselves that he was a foolish man to give her so much money to spend and repeated the proverb about women being like moths drawn toward the candle flames.

Claire was having a wonderful time, discovering India as she had dreamed it would be. She needed only a few words of the language to get by, for Sevaley was on hand to make transactions for her seemingly modest mistress. Her world was full of color and tapestry, of the rich smell of the spicy new foods she was learning to savor. She loved to watch clouds of birds whirling down from nowhere at the sound of the pigeon caller's lonely cry, as he waved his yak tail from the rooftops.

But Claire fit the proverb of the moths, and each step she took brought her closer to the flame. Her situation was even more dangerous because she used her excursions as escape. When Claire put on the sari, she forgot about her approaching marriage. She could even put the memory of Colin Whitecavage from her mind.

She was living a secret life, and she knew it was unwise. But perhaps all that happened could not have been prevented. Claire was not destined to lead the sedate life of an officer's wife. Sevaley, being Hindu, might have said it was preordained. *It is written on her forehead,* Sevaley might have said.

11

Maxwell Todd was preparing to send more troops to Pandeish. The men were tribesmen from the hills, recruited especially for the purpose. They were a rascally lot, resistant to discipline, Max said. They had been offered rewards to join the expedition, and knowing the hills, should prove fine soldiers, except that they were barbarous and independent.

Even the departure was causing problems. The recruits wanted to hold an *avuda-puja*, a soldiers' feast, which all faiths would join indiscriminately. Swords and rifles would be brought to a priest, who would sprinkle them with holy water and turn them into divinities. Then a ram would be sacrificed in honor of the weapons. The idea of the feast worried Max.

"But why not let them?" asked Claire. "What can it matter? I suppose it will make them feel invincible in battle."

Max sighed. "I will allow the ceremony, Claire. Indeed, I would not dare prevent it. But I have heard a rumor that other ceremonies are being planned in conjunction with the *avuda-puja*. Indecent ceremonies which have been forbidden."

"What indecent ceremonies, Max?" Claire wanted to know.

"It is not the sort of thing a gentleman discusses with a lady, Claire."

"Oh, Max!" she laughed. But he insisted that they could not discuss the matter. He felt protective of her innocence and did not realize how far from innocence she really was. Claire thought him fusty. And she was consumed with curiosity.

"What do you know of these ceremonies, Sevaley?" she asked. Her little servant was an endless source of information, her window on India. But this time the girl shook her head.

"It is a ceremony that exists only far in the mountains," she said. "The *Angrezi* have put a stop to it everywhere else. It is the power sacrifice, the *sakti-puji*, offered to the wife of Siva."

"Then perhaps no English woman has ever seen it," Claire mused. "Shall we attend?"

"Oh, no, Memsahib!" said the servant, horrified. "Unmarried ladies never go to the *sakti-puji*."

"Married women do?"

"Yes, if their husbands take them."

"Have you ever known anyone who went?"

"My mother had a friend long ago who had been to the *sakti-puji*. She would not go again even though her husband beat her. Her husband went alone and later died in battle. It was her own fault she was a widow, her relatives said. He had lost power because she would not go. The rest of her life was miserable, of course. But she told my mother that some women do not find the *sakti-puji* disgusting at all."

Claire repeated Sevaley's remarks to her acquaintances at tea, where the tribesmen roaming the city were the subject of excited conversation.

"Thank heaven they are camping outside the cantonment!" said a plump little lieutenant's wife who had brought a servant to fan her in the heat of the afternoon. With her bulk she needed it in addition to the punkah.

"There's going to be trouble," said another with a shudder.

"No, no, dear, don't worry," said a third. "These rumors are always cropping up." She had been in India for some years, which gave her a position of seniority in the group. As they talked, she worked on a scarf depicting a British country scene. When finished it would adorn a sideboard; but it was so long that it might never be finished, and the end dragged on the floor. She had been engaged in the project for over a year, and sometimes she told her friends that the task of bringing color and life to each tree and flower was all that kept her from going mad.

"Our husbands wouldn't tell us!" said the lieutenant's wife. "Humph! They never tell us anything important."

"I think it's gallant of them to spare us worry," put in a young bride, pregnant with her first child.

Her remark caused an animated debate which threatened to erupt into an argument, until finally the lady with the needlepoint interrupted with, "Tell us what *you've* heard, Claire."

Everyone stopped to listen then, for they had already learned that Colonel Todd made Claire his confidant. Claire hesitated. She had to be careful what she made common knowledge, since often what Max told her was for her ears alone. When a new officer was to be assigned to the regiment or an entertainment planned, Claire could be counted upon for the details. But sometimes she was as close with her information as though she were a man herself. She seemed almost as much in their camp as in her own natural female one, and it gave the women a peculiar feeling about her.

Today, however, Claire had nothing to keep to herself, since Max had refused to discuss the tribal ceremonies. She told what little she had learned from Sevaley and added that Max thought it would be indecent. The women shivered to think what *they* might be capable of.

"They hate us, you know, and they outnumber us. We'll all be murdered in our beds someday," said the lieutenant's wife, as her coolie impassively fanned her.

"No, quite the opposite!" cried the wife who was making the scarf. "Last summer a syce risked his life to save me when the horses ran away with my carriage. Surely most of them are grateful and devoted to us."

There was more spirited discussion, interrupted by a servant with a tea tray. The matter was forgotten as everyone exclaimed over the pretty cakes.

The city seemed to overflow with the fierce-looking new recruits wearing flat black caps ornamented with yellow flowers. Inhabitants stepped aside for them as they paced the streets in shoes of knitted whipcord, tulwars and daggers glinting at the waists of their voluminous trousers. Many were deadly with the bow and arrow, Max said. They seemed more fearsome than the sepoys who paraded with rifles and red jackets; and to Claire, if not to the other women, they were as thrilling as they were frightening.

Small wonder that on the day of the *avuda-puja* Claire painted her arms and face with saffron and, putting on the blue sari and her silver bracelets, went outside the cantonment to join those who were attending the feast of the weapons. When it was over, she was disappointed, for there had not been much to see. But a caravan was moving off to the encampment of the hill men, a mile or so distant. Sevaley would not join it, shaking her head and saying that the power sacrifice, the *sakti-puji*, was about to occur.

Claire hesitated. The sky was blue, and the sun glittered on kettle drums and silver cymbals, beating their eerie, compelling summons.

"Please, Memsahib," Sevaley whispered. "You are not married. You are not even one of them."

"But I may never have another chance," Claire replied, and felt release sweep her as the old familiar demon gained control. Today would never come again. That was reason enough to use it to the utmost and damn the consequences. But there would be no consequences. "Tell Max that I have a headache and cannot join him for dinner this evening," she commanded, and raced off to join the gay procession.

The presence of many other women reassured her as she crossed the sunlit plain in the wake of howdahed elephants. Some were the wives of sepoys; others were hill women, camp followers with finely-cut features and coronets of silver filigree across their foreheads. Their thick black hair was drawn up in wreaths and varicolored streamers fluttered from behind their heads. Skirts were bunched and fell in long folds to the ground, while amber and turquoise, in contrast to the silver and jade of Delhi, decorated their arms, necks, and ears. An air of expectancy pervaded the procession. Claire did not doubt that the *sakti-puji* would be worth the walk.

In less than an hour they arrived at the encampment, a collection of tents beneath a tope of mangoes and banyans. Carpets and fringed cushions had been thrown on the ground for the chiefs, and platters of fruits and roast mutton were being passed. A huge vessel of native raki was brought, and a priest chanted over it, offering it sacrifices of flowers, incense, sandalwood, and colored rice.

Then a girl stepped forward and, to Claire's astonishment, removed her clothing. As the rum was passed among the celebrants, the priest made the same incantations over the girl and laid the same offerings at her ringed feet. Claire whiffed opium, mingling with the scent of the sandalwood incense the priest had lighted. Someone handed her a cup of raki. She drank and felt her throat fill with flame. With a gasp she dropped the cup, but someone caught it and quaffed the contents. Around her other women were drinking, their expressions intense but varied. Some drank exultantly, as though the act allied them with the god that had been evoked to reside in the liquor. Others drank with desperation, as if to drug themselves stuporous.

The Indian night fell with the suddenness that still surprised her, a flash of fire on the Western horizon that was quickly transmuted to the gleam of bonfires. The darkness seemed a signal for the revelry to intensify. The drums and cymbals beat again, but in a different, disturbing way. The mountain liquor was potent; to a man, the hill soldiers were intoxicated.

The women were at least as inebriated as the men. Some danced wildly, and others staggered as they walked, crashing into trees and causing the collapse of tents. Camels and elephants brayed and trumpeted. Horses whinnied and pulled at their hitchings. The darkness brought a chill; and Claire, who had not drunk any more raki, pulled her sari more tightly around her. She had seen the power sacrifice, and she wanted to go back to the cantonment. But no one was going yet, and Claire was afraid of losing her way in the emptiness beyond the firelight. The scene was disgusting, but suddenly it became infinitely more disgusting. The naked girl who had received the sacrifices appeared on a platform, screaming and gyrating, her body thrust in a grotesque attitude. The throng of revelers gave a cry. The goddess had at last taken residence in the body of the drugged, drunken girl; and as she spun hysterically on the platform, her hair unwinding to veil her breasts, a man leaped from the crowd and flung her over his shoulders.

Just as Claire had thought the *sakti-puji* was coming to an end, it began in earnest. All over the tope, men began to take women in their arms. Some moaned and limply acquiesced. Others, less drunken, were dragged shrieking into tents. Here and there a woman's laughter rang among the mango trees as a man's hand thrust roughly into her clothing.

Reminded of her night with the Arab thieves, Claire was panic-stricken. A bearded hill man lunged for her, but Claire, with her wits about her, jumped free, leaving only a corner of her blue sari ripped away in his grasp. She retreated to the edge of the camp, huddling in the shadow of a thornbush, held there by the cries of wolves and jackals in the night beyond. If another found her, she might not be so lucky. She knew at last what Max had meant by indecent. If only he had told her! She would not have come, then, she thought, trying to blame her predicament on her fiancé.

Then, in the distance, she saw flares and heard the sound of a bugle. Her heart lifted. Max had ordered out the regulars to stop the unlawful ceremony. She should have known that Maxwell Todd was not one to allow his authority to be compromised.

A cry went up from the camp. The hill men had seen the flares, too, and knew what it meant. Wild and drunken, furious at being interrupted in their debauchery, they ran for their weapons and their horses. Claire was terrified anew. The regulars were depleted by the men sent to Pandeish. The hill men would have the advantage.

They all hate us. It had seemed a silly female idea when Claire had first heard it at tea. But now it was real. She saw that hatred written on their faces. They hated the British for gulping up their country and dismantling their governments, but interfering with intimate customs was the worst offense of all. There was going to be a mutiny. *We'll all be murdered in our beds someday.* Would someday be now? Claire, of course, was not in her bed to be murdered, but she was not sure that was any consolation. What horrible thing could not happen to her out here, whether her masquerade were discovered or not?

As long as she lived Claire would never forget the savage anger of the faces around her. For years she would awake screaming, having dreamed of it. And finally it would be the nightmare from which all British India could not awaken. But tonight, as the two groups approached each other, a single figure rode out from the British line. The soldier carried a flag of truce and held up his hand in a gesture of peace. She thought at first that the maddened tribesmen would trample him in their rush, and she closed her eyes, not wanting to open them again, for she knew that the daring figure had been none other than Colin Whitecavage. She was certain, too, that he would be massacred; but when at last she looked, he was still astride his horse, surrounded now by the hill men, among whom he was riding to the tope.

Hordes of shouting tribesmen gathered around as the group galloped into the camp. She could not see Colin, and she imagined that he had been knocked from his saddle, his body pierced by spears. Climbing quickly into the crotch of a pipul tree, she saw him alight of his own accord, looking composed, and allow himself to be shoved into a large tent in the center of the camp. Guards took up stations around the tent. Colin was a prisoner.

Far off, on a hillock, the dusky silhouettes of loyal sowars stood against the moon. Horses whinnied as though sensing a charge, but the line held. Outrage flared in Claire's breast. Colin had been captured under a flag of truce, but now the sowars dared not attack, for that might condemn him to death. Torches leaped into flame in the hill-men's camp, and the cool night seemed suddenly sweltering. The hot orange of the torches washed out the pale moonglow; and sweat, from bawdy exertion and the imbibing of raw rum, trickled down men's faces. Bare torsos gleamed on some who had removed their tunics. Nearby she heard a woman sob in the shadow, and the half-smothered sound made her press herself flatter against the tree limbs. Somewhere beneath Claire's arboreal perch lay a woman who did not like the power sacrifice, a woman who had not managed to swallow enough raki to numb her mind and body. Claire had not the courage to try to help her and give herself away in the process, and silent tears streamed down her cheeks. Most likely the man who was possessing her wasn't her husband, for Claire had seen one woman call out to her husband for aid as she was being roughly fondled by another. He, bent on his own quest, had ignored her. Tonight there were no rules, except that every rule was to be broken. Colin had saved her from the camp of the Arabs, but he could not help her tonight. Tonight Colin himself needed saving.

From her perch beyond the campfires, she watched as chieftains with shining swords entered the tent where Colin had been taken. In a few minutes they came out again and stood together talking. She wondered what they were saying, but it would have done her no good to be close enough to hear. She had learned only a few words of Hindustani from Sevaley, and the hill men spoke a different dialect. Whatever they were planning, no one could save Colin. No one could even get into the camp to attempt his rescue.

Clifflike clouds along the ridge dissolved into silver banners as it came to her slowly that the responsibility was hers. At first she resisted the idea. She knew nothing of warfare; she was not even a man. But she was already in the camp; and rescuing him might be all the easier because she was a woman, she thought, her stomach tightening with fear.

She slipped out of the tree and walked purposefully to the central fire, where platters of food were spread on rugs. Men sprawled on the edges of the rugs, so that she had to reach over them to the serving dishes. She might have leaned, but then her breasts would have been in easy grasp, so she stepped across instead and felt a hand tighten about her ankle. The man jerked to pull her off balance, but Claire kicked and heard him curse as her silver ankle bracelet made violent contact with his teeth. Putting a joint of mutton and some fruit onto a brass Benares tray, she fled before further indignity could occur.

At the door to the tent where Colin was, a guard blocked her way, but Claire gestured at the food, indicating she had been sent to feed the prisoner. The guard shrugged and let her pass.

Little bells on the tent flap alerted Colin to her entrance as he sat on a goatskin rug, his head resting against drawn-up knees. Chains of glass beads swung from the high ceiling creating diffused circles of multicolored glow as they caught the gleam of a lamp on an inlaid ivory table. Her figure swam in the rainbow haze as he lifted his eyes and saw her. Her heart pounded, and it seemed to her that her love would sear away her disguise. But Colin did not appear to recognize her.

She knelt before him, offering the food. He waved it impatiently away. She rearranged the mutton and fruit and showed him a dagger she had concealed beneath it. It had been easy to take the weapon from the belt of a snoring hill man.

But Colin showed no interest in the dagger, and seemed lost in thought. Why didn't he take it? Surely he could see the possibilities. The tent was obiviously that of a chieftain, and plentiful clothing hung from pegs for a costume. The dagger could slit the rear of the tent, and if necessary, the throats of his guard. What was she to do? She could not converse with him. With her poor command of Hindustani, he was certain to uncover her identity if she spoke.

She sat silently, holding her veil to cover part of her face. Perhaps she should reveal herself to him. But she dreaded his anger, and she was afraid he would risk too much to include her in the escape. Maybe he thought that the gift of the dagger was a trick. He might think that the hill men wanted an excuse to kill him, claiming he himself had violated the flag of truce.

He seemed withdrawn, as though she had disturbed him at some sort of meditation. She could almost have thought that he did not see her, for he seemed to drift away as she sat there, his face hardening. She thought of the caterpillar of the monarch butterfly, which she had seen metamorphose into a waxy green chrysalis, so changed did he seem to her. Some instinct told her that his mind was not on escape and that it would unwise to speak to him in any case. But as she rose to go he spoke to her in Hindustani, his voice soft and even. She did not understand most of it, but she thought he said, "Don't worry."

Among the words that she did not understand was the term by which he addressed her. *Larla,* he called her, knowing it was safe to do so to her, knowing she did not know it meant "darling."

When Claire had gone, Colin Whitecavage tried to return his attention to the matter at hand. He had known who his visitor was the moment she had lifted the tent flap. She might as well have been naked for all that her saffron skin and blue sari did to conceal her identity from him.

Colin loved her, and the memory of her perfume had so permeated his heart that he knew it instantly. Another man might scarcely have been aware of the faint flowery scent, so different from the sandalwood of the incense burners or even the insipid lavender water favored by the ladies of the cantonment. The jasmine scent, so different on her skin than on that of an Eastern woman, swept him back to the day he had helped her purchase it at the Cairo bazaar. She had been wearing it when he had kissed her at the top of the mosque where the birds came to die, and the memory filled him and constricted his throat.

Somehow Colin was not astonished to think that the woman behind this jasmine veil was Claire. Others might have thought her eyes the blue of a hill woman's, but even in the dim light, Colin recognized those turquoise eyes, agleam like a deep sunlit lake. No hill woman had ever had such eyes! His heart had sunk with the realization; for he knew what danger she was in, and he knew that he could not risk the lives of many others to save her. He could not do as she wanted him—take the dagger and escape with her. It made him all the sadder to see her courage, which was the other side of the coin of her foolhardy venturesomeness. She had not brought him the dagger so that he might spirit her out of the camp. She had been thinking only of him. He refused to allow himself to think what she perhaps had suffered in her attempt to free him. She could not have known that he had come to the camp of his own will. He was not a prisoner, and he must stay to do the thing he had come to do.

He had tried not to look at her. If he looked at her, he might have held her and kissed her; and with that, he might have lost his nerve and all that depended on his keeping it now.

Colin had been concerned about the hill troops from the time that Maxwell Todd had begun to recruit them. With misgivings he had watched group after group join the encampment beyond the cantonment, until its numbers had exceeded that of the garrison itself.

"There is nothing else to do, Whitecavage," Max had always answered to Colin's protests.

"Send me!" Colin had said. "The regulars will follow me, though they will follow no one else." But Colonel Todd had refused, and Colin had well known the reasons. These weeks in Delhi, he had been fretful as a caged lion.

Now the worst had happened. Colonel Todd was not a man of compromise, and the law had been broken. The *sakti-puji* was forbidden and all India must learn that the prohibitions of the British Raj were not to be ignored. Colin had advised against sending the regulars tonight, but he had been placed in command. The Colonel had thought a mere show of force would quiet things, but Colin had understood it would not. There might be a full-fledged mutiny. God knew how far it would spread. Certainly to the walls of the cantonment, where innocent women and children slumbered. Colin did not think he could put the rebellion down without paying a high price, and so even before he had topped the hillock with his men, Colin had formulated a plan.

He had decided to place his own life in jeopardy first, hoping to save bloodshed. Colin had not been betrayed beneath the flag of truce. He had come to the camp to resolve their differences according to ancient custom.

The chieftains had agreed to settle the matter by ordeal, though it was an odd suggestion to come from an *Angrezi*. The English usually wanted to take disputes to some court or tribunal. But to the Indian, words settled nothing. Actions were more natural, expecially the actions of the gods. It was not to be expected that an Englishman would understand, but they had heard that this particular officer was different.

Sitting among the rugs and cushions of the tent, they discussed with Colin the various possibilities. There was ordeal by fire, during which he must hold red-hot tongs, or ordeal by water, during which he would have to remain submerged a certain amount of time.

Colin shook his head at both of these. He wanted to be sure that if he succeeded, the hill men would be impressed enough to keep their word. "Give me an ordeal that is truly dangerous," he said.

"There are those that might cost you your life, Sahib," they said.

"Yes. Speak of those."

"The ordeal of poison. You swallow arsenic and butter, and if you live, you are judged successful."

"That would take too long," Colin objected.

"The ordeal of snakes, then. There is nothing as swift and deadly as the *krait*."

So it was agreed, and men were sent among the rocks armed with poles and heavy gloves to seek out the little brown snakes.

For more than an hour after Claire had gone, Colin waited. The tent grew darker, losing its translucent shine, and he thought that the moon had set. The wait was not easy, and now and again he shook all over as though suffering the chills of malaria. But why shouldn't he surrender his life in this manner if he must? He could not go to the aid of Tamila and his son, and the agony of that was worse than any the snakes could deliver.

And there was his betrayal of his dear friend Colonel Todd, who had advised him and saved him from court-martial after the Battle of Pandeish. Colin knew he could trust Maxwell Todd like no one else on earth, and what had he given in return! Why was it he could never lose wisely? Might not his love for Claire cause a tragedy someday, too, just as his love for Tamila had resulted in the Battle of Pandeish?

If he died tonight, he might save many lives and atone for those that had been lost in the battle. He had been more composed before Claire had come in with the knife, for her presence, the jasmine scent, her deep, pleading eyes, had been almost enough to make him forsake his duty. He might almost have run away with her, not back to the cantonment but away forever. Because of her he had put honor aside once. Might it not happen again? But had he gone with her, he would have been as good as dead, without the participation of the small brown snake. Everything he valued in himself would have succumbed.

At last a delegation of hill men entered to tell him that three of the *kraits* had been captured. One of the chieftains took a ruby ring from his finger. "This will be in the bottom of the basket of snakes, Sahib. You must reach inside and fetch it out. If you are bitten, you must ride back to your troops and order them back to the cantonment. But if you are not bitten, we will withdraw."

"That is fair," said Colin.

"If you are bitten, ride quickly, for the poison works rapidly. Perhaps your own doctors may be able to save you, though ours could not."

Colin and the chiefs exchanged salaams and went outside to the basket of snakes. A cheer went up from the hill men at the sight of Major Whitecavage. Colin was nearly undone again at the sight of Claire near the fire, her face frozen with fright. She had been watching the preparations, he supposed. He hoped she did not understand what was about to occur and that she would not give herself away by screaming or trying to rush to his aid in the event of his being bitten.

Incense and flowers were put into a circle drawn on the ground, and the *purochita*, the person directing the proceeding, presented these offerings to the gods, turning to the eight points of the globe. Then the *purochita* addressed the basket of snakes.

"Snakes, you are deadly and meant to kill. Behold this man, and if he finds favor, then be harmless to him."

The snakes, coiled in the deep basket, looked anything but harmless as the ruby ring was dropped among them. But Colin had chosen the ordeal of snakes not only for its impressiveness, but because he had had some training in the art of snake handling. One of Colin's native lieutenants had known the secrets of snakes and had instructed his superior during long marches when it had been too hot to travel for most of the day.

It had been merely an amusement then, but now Colin thanked his stars as he put his hand into the basket. Moving slowly, he slipped his fingers past the heads of two of the snakes. But the third shifted, and a murmur went up from those who could see. The snake had settled on the ring itself!

Colin's breath came shallowly. There was nothing to do but lift the snake off the ring. He did so gently, his stomach contracting at the touch of the dry lethal thing squirming in his grasp. With a flip of his wrist, he threw the snake out of the basket and closed his fingers around the ring. The nearest snake, disturbed, struck as he withdrew with his prize, its fangs striking the straw side of the basket so close to him that he seemed to feel a stab of pain and thought he had been struck himself.

Dropping the precious ring carelessly on the ground, he turned his hand over dazedly as cries of admiration rang out. Colin Whitecavage went weak in the knees. He had averted a battle, and no blood would be shed this night. His horse was brought for him, and he mounted it, lifting his triumphantly-undamaged hand to the throng of hill men.

A bearded chief with an enormous white turban like a monstrous dinner roll offered Colin the ruby ring. "Take this, Sahib. It's a gift for a brave man."

"No," said Colin.

"If not the ring, name something more magnificent, Sahib. We would like to give you a token of our esteem."

"Then I shall require the most magnificent thing in the camp," said Colin with a grin. "I require a woman to warm my bed. I've an appetite this night!"

A cry of approval went up at his words. The hill men were delighted to learn that this Englishman had desires like their own. Several debauched women crowded up beside his horse, lifting braceleted arms and catching hold of his stirrups.

"Not any of these," said Colin. "That one." He indicated Claire, who stood a little apart, not understanding what was said.

"Very well, Sahib."

Claire screamed as she was heaved into the air and flung across his saddle. Colin placed an insolent hand on her rump to hold her in place; and then, to the cheers and calls of good wishes, he galloped away with her into the darkness.

All in all, he was pleased with the night's work. The fires of the hill men's camp lay behind him, burning lower now. He had prevented rioting and saved Claire neatly in the bargain. In the middle of the plain, he stopped and signaled to his men, telling them to withdraw.

Suddenly Colin was exhilarated. The tensions of the last hours had vanished, and instead of feeling drained, he was in high siprits. He was alive! The plain had never looked more beautiful. A deer leaped ahead of him, dancing off in danceful leaps over tussocks of grass. Even the howl of jackals seemed musical. He started to speak to Claire and realized that she did not know that he was aware of her identity.

Devilment seized him. She must really think that he had taken her from the camp to have his way with her. He wondered if she were frightened, supposing he would make love to an Indian wanton in ways more savage than to an English lady. He imagined that she was excited. Hadn't she longed for him to love her even after he had found strength to stop? He remembered how the springs of the gharry had creaked as he lay beneath it, betraying her restlessness within.

He was alive, and she was alive, when neither might have been! Why, after all, shouldn't they have this moment. Neither of them would ever have to acknowledge it, even to each other. So thinking, he turned the horse down the side of a nullah and, stopping at the bottom, dismounted, pulling her off after him. He closed his arms about her and kissed her deeply on her yearning lips. With an ardent sigh he slid his hands under her clothing, felt the warm breasts that were home to him and yet never should be.

"*Larla*," he said again, laying her beneath him on the ground.

Eagerly he began to unwrap her from her sari, the bangles twinkling like fallen stars on the grass. Caressing her, he moved to spread her braceleted ankles. But inexplicably she began to struggle.

"Colin," she whispered, "it is I. It's Claire. We cannot. . . ."

He cursed to himself, for now she had found more sense of honor than he. She had spoiled the idyl they might have had, but Colin found he could not stop himself, and his caresses became more insistent. He trespassed in intimate places, touching her in ways which he knew would drive her wild with desire.

In a moment or two he knew triumph for the second time that night, for Claire gave a helpless moan and flung herself flat on the earth. Her arms clutched his neck and her bare breasts went taut as she wept and begged him to take her, take her quickly.

The very earth seemed to quiver under them. Claire imagined it only part of her rapture, but Colin's more practical soldier's mind recognized hoofbeats.

Yanking the sari about her, he looked up. Colonel Maxwell Todd, mounted on his fine bay horse, stared down at them from the top of the nullah, his face fire-white with fury.

12

Colin Whitecavage was sent to Pandeish at last. His assignment to lead the reinforcements shattered all Claire's illusions about her fiancé.

She flew at him and beat upon his chest. "You're a coward, Max! You're sending him to his death because of me! You're sending him because we've been lovers!"

There had been no use in trying to conceal the relationship anymore, and Claire was glad, glad! Yes, unpleasant as it had been, it had been worth the humiliation not to have to lie. And now she knew the truth about the man she had been about to marry. Not only did she not love him; she hated him!

Max was disillusioned about Claire, too, of course. In his dreams he had idealized her as much as she had idealized him. He must be getting foolish with age, he thought sadly. She was perhaps the last of his youthful illusions to be lost, and he felt desperately tired.

He had been blind. He had imagined her an angel; but she was only a woman and full of spirit. Small wonder that she had fallen in love with Colin Whitecavage. He should have known. Why else had Colin refused all invitations to dinner and entertainments since her arrival. Max had thought it was because he was angry at not being sent to Pandeish, but it had not been that. Colin had been trying to uphold his honor and hers; and he had learned how little force honor held against love.

When word had come that the hill men were rampaging,

Colonel Todd had ordered the gates of the garrison drawn shut and a check made to see that everyone was inside. Claire could not be accounted for, and her little maid had broken under the questioning of the imposing Colonel. Believing her mistress in grave danger, Sevaley had told Max the truth, including a description of the blue sari, so that he would recognize her.

Max had set out at once to look for her, but when he had reached the line of British troops, he had learned of Colin's ploy. It had been impossible for him to go closer to the camp, and he had spent hours pacing anxiously. Finally, celebrants from the garrison had begun to make their way back. Max had seen Colin's signal to the soldiers; and taking a small detachment, had begun to search for Claire among the groups scattered on the plain.

Max had felt sick when he had stumbled upon her and Colin so intimately entwined at the bottom of the nullah. The hope she had brought him had drained away, and he had felt himself ready for the grave. Colin had offered him the satisfaction of a duel, but Max had refused. Instead, in a private conversation in his study, he had given Colin command of the relief force bound for Pandeish.

"I might as well let you go. The latest dispatches make it clear that Pandeish will fall—your presence cannot make matters worse. Take the regulars and those of the hill men you think will be loyal. It's obvious after tonight that they cannot be disciplined. The Army is falling apart, what with the abolition of capital punishment and the enlistment of so many Brahmans, who care more about their caste than their commission. What an abomination it is to continually find some officer groveling before a Brahman who is a mere private!

"What you averted tonight cannot be averted forever, I'm afraid. This annexation of Oude may prove our undoing. The Rajah of Rambad is far from the only powerful leader who wishes to annihilate us. He is one of the most unprincipled. There is dissatisfaction and disdain for the British everywhere in India. Most Britishers are too pig-headed to admit it."

"I'm grateful for the command, sir," said Colin, unable to look his superior in the eye.

"Don't be," said Max. "You will probably lose your life. But at least it will not be a senseless death as it would have been should I have had the luck to kill you in a duel."

"I'm grateful anyway," said Colin.

"Good luck, my boy," said Max.

And so Colin was disposed of in a gentlemanly and utterly necessary manner. But had they dueled, Colin, younger and quicker, would have had the advantage and most likely would have ended the Colonel's life. And that was all Claire saw to the matter.

"He would have killed you, Max," said Claire scornfully. "That's why you've sent him to Pandeish."

"It had to be done," he replied. "You're a woman and don't understand all this. We must forget what's happened and plan our wedding."

"Our wedding!" she cried.

"Yes, my dear. I'll honor my commitment. I won't send you home to your father in disgrace. I know that you don't love me and that you are not virtuous; but it doesn't matter, God help me! We'll dispense with formalities and be married right away."

"But Max, I won't marry you now!"

"What else can you possibly do?" he said in amazement. He felt icy inside, for he still desired her insanely, and he wanted to possess her however he could. Whatever the cost to his pride, he could not give her up.

"I'll do what I should have done all along. If Major White-cavage returns, I'll marry him."

Max gave a pitying laugh. "My dear, he will never come back!"

"Because you've sent him to his death!"

"Because I've sent him where he longed with all his heart and soul to go. He only seemed to love you, Claire. It was because he believed he could never have *her* again. Because he thought he could never go to Pandeish again. He has gone to what would be hell to any other man, but is paradise to him. If he dies in her arms, he will be in heaven before his soul has fled his body."

"*Her*, Max?" Claire whispered.

"The Rani Tamila," he told her cruelly. "He rides like the lough winds to her. And to his son—the infant Rana."

She was stunned. The room, with its *chik* blinds drawn against the spring heat, spun. When it returned to focus, she saw him looking at her in that hungry way of his, waiting for her to capitulate, waiting to take her sobbing into his arms and comfort her and forgive her for the fool she had been. She steadied herself and said evenly. "I cannot stay here under the circumstances. I will go to the mission school at

Cawnpore. I've a friend there; and if the Major doesn't return, I'll teach. I was always good in the schoolroom."

She had shocked him again, since in his mind a well-bred
young lady had no alternative but marriage. He shuddered to
think of the hardships that might wait for her in such a place
as she described.

"I cannot allow it, Claire," he said coldly. He was beginning to feel that she was beating him. Although he held the
better hand, she was determined and obstinate. "I am responsible for you to your father, and you will have to obtain his
permission to go to the mission school. Until then, you'll remain here."

She wrote to her father, well knowing that he would be bewildered by her request. He adored her, but he had no idea
of what went on in her mind. He would be amazed at her
having any other idea than to make a good match. That
done, Claire had little to occupy her except to wait and deal
with the increasing heat as summer approached. By mid-May
she had given up even her early morning ride. She sipped
iced drinks and went without as many petticoats as she dared.
Red ants and other insects climbed the insides of her skirts
and stung her on the stomach and thighs.

By eight every morning the blinds were drawn and tatties
of scented grass roots were pulled across the doors. Servants
with horse tails stood behind each dinner at mealtimes to flick
away the flies.

After five the weather cooled enough to go outside, and everyone tried to make up for the boredom of the day with
parties that were tedious themselves. It was too hot for dancing, and gossip was scarce. Claire herself was the subject of
the best of it, since everyone was wishing that the wedding
date would be set. A lavish wedding would be something to
look forward to. It was given out, however, that Claire was
observing a period of mourning for her mother. Some idle
minds thought that Claire simply could not bear to be married without the superb wedding dress that had never yet
caught up to her, and Claire did nothing to discourage that
theory. So long as they did not guess the truth, Claire did not
mind if they thought her frivolous.

Immediately after her debacle at the *sakti-puji*, Max had acquired a chaperone for her at last, in the person of an
unmarried sister of one of his high-ranking officers. One
might have thought that Abigail needed a chaperone herself;
but she was past thirty, and so stiffly proper that the entire

cantonment accepted her as a suitable companion for the Colonel's intended.

Abigail's spinsterhood interested Claire, since she was planning the same for herself, and she would question her endlessly on the subject.

"Were you never in love, Abby?"

"When I was quite young," said Abigail with a blush, "but a dozen other girls were in love with him. I, of course, was shy and not very pretty; but I was destroyed when he married the belle of the season. After that, I persuaded my parents to let me join my brother out here. He was glad to have me to keep his household running smoothly, and I had heard that every girl has plenty of chances in India."

"And didn't you have chances, Abby?"

Abigail was a retiring woman burdened with an overly large nose and a figure that was too slight to fill out the cleavage of her gown, but she had soft brown hair and eyes to match. Although Claire never knew her to flirt or use her fan for other than cooling herself, she was a woman; and unattached British women were scarce in every cantonment in India.

"I had plenty of suitors the first few years," sighed Abby. "But my brother found them all unsatisfactory. So many couldn't provide a fortune, you know. I suppose, too, that as long as I stayed with him, it saved him the trouble of marrying himself to have a hostess. It was only as a special favor to the Colonel that he allowed me to come here."

"But didn't you mind, Abby? Didn't you care?"

"Oh, yes. I would cry every time. But I suppose he knew best."

Claire was aghast. She could not imagine surrendering *her* future so calmly. "What about now, Abby?" she asked gently. "Don't you have needs?"

That was a matter that bothered Claire, especially about the idea of remaining unwed. She had not been eager for the marriage act with Max, even before he had proved himself a cowardly scoundrel. But how would she survive without even a mildly pleasant facsimile of the rapturous nights she had known with Colin? Once she might have submitted to Maxwell Todd with duty and reverence at least.

Abigail looked at her strangely. "Needs? I have none. I have an income of my own, and my brother provides my room and board."

With nothing better to do, Claire set about finding a suitor for Abby, interesting men in herself and then innocently transferring them to her companion. Abigail would be with her only for the summer. Then her brother would be transferred to Cawnpore, and Abby would go along.

"You must meet my friend, Jo, there," said Claire, and told her all about the mission school.

Early in June they removed to Simla, making the last of the journey into the hills in jampans carried by native bearers. The trip, through pine-covered hills and valleys and up and down deep ravines, brought them to Mt. Jacko, covered with white English bungalows.

Here was the house that Max had built for their main residence, and he watched with delight as she explored it. This, at least, had turned out well. It was a large one-story dwelling, surrounded by verandas. Every room had a majestic view. The sitting room looked out on a zig-zag path, suitable for jampans but not for carriages. The path led down to the valley, or cud, with ridges and spurs jutting here and there, set with bunaglows. Behind the house a pine forest rose to a wall of rock, and from her bedroom Claire could see the upper rides of the Himalayas, and the white, cool lines of the Snowy Range.

She had the luck to see the mountains first on a sunlit day, light and shadow making a patchwork of gold and velvet green. On and on the forest of fir and pine rolled, until it merged into the white of snow and the Delft blue of sky. Fresh breezes wafted around the rhododendron beside the veranda. The pines were full of little aberdavats, flitting among the branches, and inside the house a costurah, a thrushlike bird with an orange bill, sang sweetly in a cage.

Claire loved the house. She loved the idea that Max had had it designed in tribute to her. It showed her the soul of the man, as she had seen it long ago at Cottington Crest; and that night she wore her engagement ring, which she had been keeping in its box with the excuse that it was loose on her finger.

Max began to hope that Claire was mellowing. He felt invigorated himself in the cool air. By heaven, everything would be all right now that they had come to Simla! He was doubly pleased when, a week later, she received a letter from her father forbidding her to go to Cawnpore. The death of her mother had been upsetting, but of course Claire must get over this girlish fit of nerves and marry Max, who would take care of her. The answer was what Claire had expected, but with the letter actually in hand, she plunged into despair. Whatever she might find to admire about Colonel Todd, he would always be the man who had condemned her lover to death in battle, rather than duel him.

They were closer to Pandeish here, and the news reached them more quickly. It was all bad news, and at last came word of the final defeat of the British forces. Colin Whitecavage had fought bravely, but had arrived too late to make the difference. Max was secretly relieved that at least the Rajah had not chosen to make public the parentage of the little Rana. Apparently there had been no need, and the Rajah had never been one to waste weapons. Having captured Allapore, the capital of Pandeish, the Rajah had installed himself in the palace and put his young son Aleka on the throne. Company troops fled from mountain ridges and passes; many battled to the death in hand to hand combat on rocky promontories. Only one question remained. Where were Colin Whitecavage, the beautiful Rani Tamila, and the infant Rana?

All had vanished as though the mountain mists had swallowed them. Had they slipped through the net laid for them? Without them the Rajah could not be satisfied with his victory.

Were they dead or alive?

It hardly mattered if Colin Whitecavage were alive or not, Claire thought. He was dead to her either way—in his grave or in the arms of the Rani Tamila. She felt dull and wooden. There seemed nothing to do but marry Max and try to forget.

The Rajah of Rambad arrived to effect a treaty, arriving with a grand retinue mounted on richly caparisoned horses and waving banners of gold-encrusted satin as they came up the road into Simla. The Rajah himself rode an elephant outfitted with a silver howdah decked with hangings of red velvet and lace. Followers of the court, some afoot and some on horses, carried wands of silver, and a band with instruments in the shape of silver serpents played discordant Eastern music, while dancers in bearskins and masks leaped to the sound. Braceleted, earringed courtiers paced on their chargers; and fierce sowars flaunted matchlocks, curved tulwars, and large, deadly bows. Camels, wearing the Rajah's colors of orange and blue, carried swivel guns mounted on their backs, with an artilleryman to each.

"He's trying to frighten us," Max said.

"But Max, he's already beaten us," Claire protested.

"Yes. But he is not satisfied. He will make the treaty and

immediately begin to think of ways to violate it. Probably there will be nothing we can do about it. Victory does not quiet men like the Rajah; it makes them hungry for more. Look at him smirk! He is telling us that we are few, and there are many of him. Ah, Claire, I wish more of our men were as dedicated as the Rajah of Rambad!"

Claire repeated Max's remarks to Abigail, who laughed and said that her brother disagreed with that sort of thinking entirely. "We are perfectly in control of India, Claire. Look at all we have done for the country! There are a few rotten apples in every barrel, and the Rajah is one of them. Pandeish is a small matter after all. My brother says that Colonel Todd has lost his nerve. He's afraid of that silly prophecy, that's all!"

"What silly prophecy?"

"That the Raj will stand for a hundred years and no more. The hundred years will be up in eighteen fifty-seven."

"Two years from now," mused Claire.

"Yes, how utterly foolish."

They were women and did not have to worry their heads about the British Raj; but as they prepared for the balls that would accompany the Rajah's visit, Claire reflected that if British were not superstitious, Indians were. Might not the mere belief that the time was ripe make it so?

Claire had decided to remake her chaperone; and in spite of Abigail's protests, she arranged her hair in the stylish Marie Stuart fashion, rolled back from the face. The coiffure gave height to Abigail's forehead, and her nose fell into proportion. The soft hair made a flattering framing for her face; and suddenly in a gown of rose glacé, chosen by Claire, and jade from Claire's own collection, Abigail became not dowdy, but elegant. From the first waltz she had partners; and Claire smiled with satisfaction, not only at Abigail's pleasure, but because Abigail's sober presence as a chaperone had been confining.

Max noticed the transformation and was correspondingly displeased. He was learning about his fiancée, and he recognized her hand in the change. With admirers of her own, Abigail neglected her duties; in fact, her duties now seemed ridiculous. Max groaned. His spirited fiancée was causing him trouble again. How was he to handle this delicate matter? Where would he get another companion if Abigail were dismissed?

The Rajah of Rambad danced often with Claire. It was

difficult for her to refuse him, for he was to be treated with courtesy since the treaty was being negotiated. He was taller than most Indians and seemed even taller in his gold tissue turban, adorned by a tall aigrette and a clasp of diamonds. His three-quarter-length coat, his *ackkan*, was embroidered and trimmed with chips of emerald; and his jeweled belt held a gold-handled sword.

He danced as wonderfully as he had in Calcutta and made as dazzling a figure, but now Claire noticed that she did not like the way his black eyes assessed her. It was almost as if he were estimating how valuable a possession she would be if he owned her. Thank heaven he did not! She was aloof; and during a soiree at the summer residence of the Lieutenant-Governor of Bengal, he guessed somewhat accurately at the reason.

"My dear Miss Cottington, you do not like me because you think I may be responsible for the death of your lover," he said, smiling insolently, fine teeth white in his swarthy face.

"Sir! she said, so startled that she thought she had not heard him correctly.

"I mean, of course, Major Colin Whitecavage."

She would have pulled away from him and run out to the veranda, but he held her in a masterful grip, so that to separate herself from him, she would have had to create a disturbance. She stumbled in the dance, and the Rajah said easily, his double meaning apparent, "Dear me, I'm afraid I've trod on your toes. Don't be surprised, Miss Cottington; you gave yourself away in Calcutta by the way you looked at him. Most would not have noticed, but I am interested in everything about Colin Whitecavage. It is wise to know one's adversary. But I assure you, I do not believe that Whitecavage is dead. I offered a reward, you see, and no one has come forth to claim it. Do you think me bloodthirsty? I am simply being prudent. No *Angrezi* knows the hills like Major Whitecavage."

"But the hostilities are over."

"True. But the people of Pandeish adore the Rani and respect Whitecavage. Even now they might rally to the new Rana if Whitecavage were to lead."

The music stopped, but the Rajah still did not release her, and led her out into another waltz. Abigail caught her eye and gestured, for dancing twice in a row with the same man was not approved.

"Who do you think is the father of the young Rana, Miss Cottington?" he asked.

She blushed and tried to pull away, but he held her, laughing. "That is what my spies think, too. What an upheaval there would be in Pandeish if it were proven! The Rani and her child would be burned alive—if they were found. And as for Whitecavage, I would not want to die such a death as he would be dealt. But I am not so evil as you English think. There is no reason for me to implement the death of the woman and child as long as my son Aleka, not the son of an *Angrezi*, sits on the throne of Pandeish. But perhaps you hate Colin Whitecavage as much as I, since you have learned how he deceived you."

Feeling sick, she trembled in his arms; and reading her confused face, he laughed again. "So you love him more than you hate him! What will you do, Miss Cottington? Your heart cannot be in this marriage to Colonel Todd."

"I had hoped to teach in Cawnpore," she confessed.

"Ah, but they will not allow it!" he guessed. "But if you fancy yourself a teacher, you might join my retinue. My sons should be instructed in English. It is well to be able to converse with the conqueror."

"Join your retinue!" It was Claire's turn to laugh. "When I am not even allowed to go to Cawnpore?"

"Only think—if you love Whitecavage so, you might find him someday and vie with the Rani for his affections. Persuade him to return to England with you, and then there would be no reason for him to die." The Rajah spoke lightly but he saw that the idea took hold.

"But how——" she began.

"You need not ask for permission, my dear. It would please me to confound Colonel Todd by kidnapping his fiancée."

He let her go then, and she ran outside where the cool air fanned her burning cheeks. From a tree nearby, a little hill monkey scolded her, and she felt she was being warned against even thinking about what the Rajah had proposed.

It was outrageous, of course; but perhaps no more outrageous than was to be expected of the young woman whom Queen Victoria had banished from her court. It was impossible, for Abigail still slept in the adjoining room and would hear her leave.

Claire was aware of the Rajah's attraction to her, and she remembered that Colin had told her in Calcutta that the Rajah would use his knowledge of their affair to his own gain. The Rajah wanted more of her than instruction in English for his sons. If she went, perhaps she would not be able to keep him out of her bed.

But she knew that she wanted to go. More than anything in the world, she wanted to find Colin and fight for his love. She would have to go to him, for Max had said Colin would not come back. He had returned to a world of which she was not part, and to win him again, she must follow him there. She wondered how she would find him and how she would compete with the exotic Rani. But if fate brought her to Pandeish, then surely it would carry her on until she was in his arms once more.

But it was impossible. . . .

And then, as if it were meant to be, it was not impossible. One evening Abigail was caught kissing a young officer and was sent back to her brother. Claire slept alone, with no one to hear her escape.

The next night Claire awakened with a start to find Maxwell Todd in her bedroom. He had been drinking too much, and he wept as he bent over her and kissed her, begging her to be as generous with him as she had been with Major Whitecavage.

She pushed him away in pity and disgust, but Max had at last taken leave of his senses and he flung her back on the bed, ripping the bodice of her simple cambric nightgown. Tears and kisses mingled on her naked breasts, and her stomach convulsed as the skirt of her gown gave way. She was utterly unclothed, her inviting body helpless on the cool sheets. Ribbons of moonglow from the half-open blinds adorned her like a mysterious gift as he murmured words of wonder and hope.

Claire wept, too. He must not profane her! He must not! He must not sully her memory of nights with Colin with his unsanctified lust! She was far more adamant than when she had had her maidenhood to lose. Struggling up at last, dragging bedclothes around her, she dashed for the door.

He caught up with her and fought to take her face in his hands to kiss. But Max wavered, unsteady on his feet, and she had an instant to shove him beyond the doorway and latch the door behind him.

She heard his voice softly pleading outside and fell asleep after he had long gone, sitting with her back against the door to brace it.

In the morning nothing was said, and Max seemed relieved. But Claire knew finally and forever that she could not marry him and share a bed with him. *It is as though I am already wed to Colin*, she thought, and that day she sent word to the Rajah of her decision to accept his offer to join his retinue.

A few days after the Rajah left Simla, he deserted his entourage and turned back with a small party and an extra horse. It seemed a perfect solution to Claire that she should be kidnapped, carried away convincingly in her nightdress and in no way to blame.

Indeed, when the Rajah appeared in her bedroom, he had to put a hand over her mouth to stifle her instinctive scream. She rode away with him into the pine-scented night, little guessing that he intended to use her not only for his pleasure, but to effect the death of her beloved; or that Colin Whitecavage, wherever he was, would soon learn that she was hostage to his life.

13

They traveled all night, picking their way along the steep road from Simla. Claire dozed in her jampan, fatigue overcoming her fear that her bearer would stumble and allow the contraption to go sailing down into the cud below. In the morning the road banks were covered with bright wild flowers. The upward slope was a tangle of pines and rhododendron, clematis and creepers, while on the other a sheer descent led down to broad sheets of fir trees, their tapering tops like blankets of sharp pins. In the afternoon they passed a settlement of people who had emigrated from Tibet, and women with Chinese features came out to look at them. Their hair, worn in many little plaits, fell to their waists and was adorned with gold and silver coins and turquoise.

The Rajah dispensed gifts of tobacco, and the party moved on hastily. Claire wondered if the Rajah were usually so generous or if he were buying silence with his largesse.

By now Max must have discovered that she was missing. She was sure, too, that the Rajah had left some clue behind to take credit for having spirited her away. Max would be in pursuit with soldiers. Claire shuddered. If the two groups met, there would be bloodshed, and it would be her fault. She thought of the tulwars and the camel-mounted guns of the Rajah's main entourage and wondered if the British would be a match for the Rajah in these hills, should it come to it.

What a disaster she might cause, she thought, and remembered how Colin had advised her to marry Lord Rutherford because she had made a muddle of even her coddled little life. Claire had chosen to blame not herself but the confines of that life. No, it seemed she could stay within no boundary that did not include Colin Whitecavage.

As they moved rapidly on, the Rajah seemed in high spirits. His beaters flushed some *coqplas* pheasant from the woods, and the Rajah brought down a brace. The prospect of roast pheasant with the usual curry for dinner made him even more ebullient. Often he rode beside her, making light conversation, telling her what he hoped to have her accomplish as his sons' tutor.

"I expect to send Aleka to England someday to see how the *Angrezi* live in their own country. He will need to know the language well. And the customs, Miss Cottington. Can you teach him the quadrille and the waltz?"

"I will try," sighed Claire. She had not thought of being a dance instructor, but as long as no more intimate role was required of her, she was willing to do her best.

She was nervous as the evening shadows of the mountains darkened the road, and the Rajah called a halt. A small silken tent was erected for her use, and she slept there with her maid Sevaley, whom Claire had had abducted with her and who thought in truth they had been kidnapped. Sevaley, knowing only one reason a man would make away with a woman, did not undress, imagining that she would be aroused and sent out during the night.

Claire did not want to undress, either; but Sevaley, wiser in spite of her inferior years, advised her to make herself inviting for the visitor. "It will go easier with you if you do, Memsahib. All the stays and buttons will delay him only a little while, but he will be angry and more brutal because he has been delayed."

Claire saw the wisdom of it and reluctantly acquiesced. She had put herself in the Rajah's power, and she had not a friend in the camp to protect her. Escape was not practical, either, but Claire did not want to escape. She wanted to travel on to Pandeish, where she might reclaim the love of Colin Whitecavage. If it were necessary for her to submit to the Rajah, then submit she must. She dressed in a thin night dress and wrapped herself in rugs against the chill mountain air. But even in the rugs she shivered, with tremors that had little to do with the cold.

Nightglow came in through the sides of the tent, and Claire heard footsteps; the shadow of a man, standing outside the tent fell across her. But it was only a syce, who had been assigned to sit at the door of the tent and keep watch. Daybreak came, and there had been no visitor. Claire wanted to shout with relief. Was it possible that the Rajah did not want to share her bed? Perhaps she had imagined his attraction to her. But she had felt so certain. . . .

By the end of the day they had joined the main body of the entourage. They traveled more slowly now, not only because of the size of the retinue, but because the Rajah felt safer. The next morning, coolies were sent ahead to prepare the night's campsite while the Rajah lazed about, smoking his hookah on a rug laid over an expanse of pale blue snapdragons in a little meadow. Before the noon meal, she was called to sit beside him.

"There is a letter you must write, Miss Cottington," he said.

"What letter?"

"Why, a letter to Colonel Todd, of course. You must tell him that you are happy with me and do not wish to be rescued."

Claire flushed indignantly. "I will write no such letter." It was obvious that he meant her missive to imply that she had become his mistress.

The Rajah puffed on his hookah. "Well, then, I will have to send you back, Miss Cottington."

"Send me back."

"Yes. You are not worth fighting over, and there will surely be fighting if you do not write the letter."

He had tricked her neatly, she saw. She had expected him to outwit Max in stealing away with her, but she had not expected him to use her in his outwitting. She had thought to remain unblemished, vanishing without a trace into the mountains. It was not to be so easy.

"Colonel Todd will not believe I have written such a letter of my own free will," she protested.

He leered at her. "Oh, I am sure you can make him believe it, Miss Cottington." He motioned to a servant, who brought writing materials and set them before her. An ugly laugh told her that he knew all the reasons that Colonel Todd was likely to believe it.

Max knew she had been Colin's mistress. Was he so unlikely to accept the idea that the glamorous Rajah had not also awakened her lust? Claire wondered if the Rajah even knew that she had repulsed Max from her bed. She was sure that his network of spies extended to the Colonel's residence. There was nothing to do but follow the Rajah's instructions. Claire was humiliated, and she thought that the Rajah enjoyed humiliating her, an Englishwoman.

She wondered if there were a chance that Max would continue on from pride after receiving the letter, and decided there was not. He would not risk lives to soothe his own vanity, for he was a decent and honorable man, worthy of her respect.

Max deserves better than I, she thought. If only I could have loved him! She constructed her letter carefully, so that nothing in it would give him reason to hope, and took solace in thinking that no violence would occur. As they prepared to move on, she watched the messenger begin his trek back over the way they had come and pictured the mortification Max would suffer as he returned to Simla without her.

Poor Max! He had trusted her to save him. Had she destroyed him instead?

The entourage moved on, through forests of deodar, yew, fir and oak, rising from an undergrowth of creepers and wild roses, humming with bees. Day by day they came nearer to Pandeish. Now and then they entered some small principality and were greeted with great ceremony by its ruler, who would visit the encampment accompanied by bands and sometimes dancing girls. Occasionally the Rajah accepted an invitation to pass the night in one of the turreted castles. Claire, though she was curious to see the insides, was never invited and was left to slumber, as usual, undisturbed.

One afternoon, emerging from a spot where hills had run close to both sides of the road, they came upon a view of the whole of the Snowy Range. The serrated lines of its ridges seemed so close that Claire imagined they would soon travel into the snow, but the Rajah, laughing, said they were many days away. He gave her time to stare at the magnificent line of eternal snow, rising above village and forest, and at plateaus of granite and mica, shimmering in the sunlight.

Then he called her attention to what lay below: china-patterned lands, dotted with fairy-tale stone houses built with slate roofs and balconies.

"There," he said, "is Pandeish."

It was easy to understand the pride in his voice, easy to understand why he hated the British for having sliced the territory from his ancestral domain. She had never seen a prettier spot. As they rode down the cud, flocks of parakeets flitted through the trees. Wild strawberries grew in the meadow grass. The air was warm and scented with flowers; Pandeish washed like a balm over all her senses. Watching her, the Rajah smiled. He knew that Pandeish was so beautiful to her not only for itself, but because Colin Whitecavage was somewhere within its boundaries.

The Rajah was well-pleased with the plan he had engineered. He had studied his man and found only one weakness. Major Whitecavage was not interested in wealth or in power; he was not susceptible to drink or opium. Whitecavage was weak only when it came to women. He had been foolhardy enough to love the Rani Tamila in the palace, under the very nose of the Rana. And he had thought himself privileged to return to Pandeish in a hopeless effort to save her and a baby whose fathering he could never acknowledge.

He had been Miss Cottington's lover while he had thought the Rani dead, and the Rajah did not think him indifferent to her now. It hardly mattered which woman Colin loved more or which would have had him in the end. The Rajah was determined that Colin Whitecavage would not live long enough for it to matter. The Rajah studied Claire's well-formed figure as she rode happily in front of him. The way she jounced in the saddle made his smile even broader. The Rajah congratulated himself on his cleverness. It wasn't often that a man could deal with an enemy in a manner that afforded such enjoyment.

The next day they entered Allapore, the capital of Pandeish. Courtiers decked themselves in gold bracelets and earrings for the occasion. Harlequins donned masks and bearskins. The band played, and wands and batons of silver gilt waved in the sun. Heralds with *blazons* shouted the Rajah's titles in chorus and invoked blessings on him.

It was the same procession that Claire had witnessed at the side of Maxwell Todd when the Rajah had entered Simla. But how long ago that seemed! And now she was part of the procession herself, riding an elephant adorned with a silver howdah and trappings of crimson velvet and lace. Claire felt dizzy to be up so high, but Sevaley, who had come along to hold a gold-fringed umbrella over her head, seemed perfectly unconcerned on what seemed to Claire a precarious perch.

All along the route people turned out to greet the Rajah, but Claire noticed that in spite of much salaaming, expressions were impassive. Some people chewed betel and pawn and others squatted casually on their haunches. They had been conquered; they were not patriots who had been reunited with the homeland. It was obvious that the populace of Pandeish was not glad to be once again in the domain of the Rajah of Rambad.

The great man did not appear to notice their disaffection. In fact, he paid them no notice at all. He sat in his howdah, adorned by jewels, armlets of emeralds and pearls twining around and around from elbow to wrist. Rings set with brilliants covered every finger, and his feet were bare so that his toes could be decorated as royally as his fingers. A plaque of diamonds hung from his turban, and he wore a breastplate covered with carved emeralds the size of pigeons' eggs.

Looking him over critically, Claire decided that the Rajah must have worn the breastplate as much to protect himself from some assassin's bullet as for its sartorial grandeur, The position of his elephant—in the center of a regiment of his troops, dressed in blue coatees, shakos, and white cross belts—gave weight to her opinion that the Rajah feared for his life as he rode among his subjects.

The procession arrived at the palace, entering the courtyard through a richly-colored, ornamented gateway flanked by two turrets of jalousied windows. Inside was a garden and a kiosk, long-winged, in a sort of Hindu style, but with frescoes that gave it an Italian air. A guard of honor drew up, and the elephants knelt. Claire clung to her howdah as it jolted disconcertingly.

When she recovered herself, she discovered towers of fretwork, marble and ivory. The air was cool from fountains tinkling into lily-pad-covered ponds, and cockatoos and parrots flitted among courtyards planted with walnut and chenar trees. The great hall—the divan—was covered with thick carpet and vividly colored in arabesque. A line of glass chandeliers reflected the colors from their long prisms and threw them against walls, catching them again and tossing them in a ball game of light, until the entire room seemed bathed in rainbows.

Following the example of the courtiers, Claire removed her shoes to tread the luxurious spring green carpet with a weave of gold thread. She had the sensation of walking in a field of buttercups after a spring shower. Even the scent was there, a flowery aroma emanating from brass incense burners.

"A lovely room, eh, Miss Cottington?" the Rajah said.

"It is incredible."

"It's because of the divan that the palace is called the Palace of the Rainbows."

"The Palace of the Rainbows. How lovely!" She seemed to sense Colin's presence in the room, perhaps simply because he seemed part of all things beautiful, perhaps because to her, her arrival in Pandeish seemed the end of the rainbow indeed. She had not thought that Colin must have sat on these very cushions when he had come for audiences with the Rana.

"They say the Rani Tamila is responsible for the charm of this room," the Rajah said, shattering her reverie. "She is supposed to have persuaded the Rana to have the chandeliers hung."

The Rani Tamila! It was her palace, of course. Claire had not thought of it. Later, when she was shown to her chamber, she wondered if it had belonged to the Rani herself.

It, too, was thickly carpeted, equipped with charpoys and sofas and a door onto a little courtyard. A dressing room and a private bath adjoined it; and though it was located near the zenana, it was not a part of it. From her windows she had a view of the Snowy Range, which fascinated her with its many moods. In the morning the distant whiteness blazed pink and gold, the crystals glittering, seeming to dance, as though the mountains were alive. She looked there on awakening and felt alive with hope herself. At midday there was serenity; and toward evening as sapphire shadows fell over the slopes, the mountains reminded her of their eternity. She was comforted that they would remain unchanging through the night.

Claire wondered if the Rani had stood at these very windows and been comforted in the same way. There was a roof some distance below, and a series of irregularities in the fretted wall which suggested that an enterprizing lover might climb it. If so, then Tamila must have spent many hours here, gazing at the mountains and waiting anxiously to savor her perilous, unsanctioned love.

The Rani Tamila in her gossamer veils, her exotic scents, with her skills in loving. She would have been trained early by courtesans to please her man in every possible way. He was her god, whom she was put on earth to satisfy. How could Claire ever compete with the Rani for Colin's love?

If the Rani still lived, she thought. If Colin still lived.

On mornings when the mist obliterated the mountains,

Claire felt bereft and adrift, as though she needed to see the shining peaks to keep her bearings. He must be there, in some secret hideaway, in some remote cud or col. How would she ever find him, when every gun and tulwar in the Rajah's army strained for the honor of his murder? But perhaps the deed had been achieved already. Perhaps it was only the spirit of Colin Whitecavage that she sensed among the mountains.

Her reunion with Sona was joyous. He threw himself into her arms and salaamed time after time to his father, thanking him for having brought home such a wonderful gift as his new tutor. Their hours together in the sunny classroom were a delight to both. His desire to please her made him a quick student, and she became a pupil as well as teacher, learning and then mastering the dialect of the region on the chance that it might be useful.

Aleka was more reserved than Sona, but Claire grew to understand that the older boy valued her good opinion as much as the younger. It was only that he was trying to imitate his father, and he had been taught that it was unmanly to show a need for affection. All his natural affection, which should have flowed openly to a mother, father, brothers and sisters, would undoubtedly be twisted into the brutal assaults he would make on his concubines when he was older.

As time went by, he unbent slowly, talking to her of his excursions with the Rajah and bringing her his hunting falcon to admire, a creature which Sona considered disgusting. Aleka was a little boy who had scarcely known a mother, a child deprived of love, confused by his feelings for the memsahib his father had brought into the palace. When he carelessly cut his finger on his knife, it was she who bandaged it, while he, manfully, tried to pull away. But when she was done, she looked up to see him staring at her with adoration in his eyes. When she enticed a marmoset into the classroom and began to sport with it with Sona, Aleka was unable to refrain at last from joining in.

He was the ruler, and when he was not in the schoolroom or riding out to hunt, he held court on a cushion-covered dais that served as the throne. It was unseemly that he should have lessons—he who wore the crown of Pandeish and was heir to all Rambad. Yet every day his feet moved faster on the stairs that led to the schoolroom.

Once there, Aleka did not forget that he ruled. He fought

endlessly with Sona and sometimes tried to bully Claire as well. Here, too, he was confused. How was it that Claire, a mere woman, did not defer to him? His father's concubines leaped to obey his command. Unable to have his way, he relaxed gradually and began to be a child.

The two princes and Sevaley were Claire's only friends in the palace. Her rooms were near the zenana, and Claire had hoped to become acquainted with those of her sex who lived there. But to her dismay, the women seemed hostile, even though she was able to address them in their own language when she encountered them in the halls or courtyards.

"They have led very sheltered lives and are afraid of foreigners, I suppose," Claire guessed to Sevaley.

"No, that is not the reason," her maid laughed.

"Why, then? Surely I have done nothing to make them hate me."

"They are jealous. The Rajah has not given any of them much attention since his return. They think it is because of you."

"Because of me?" she said surprised.

Sevaley lowered her eyes. "They think you are the Rajah's favored one."

"That is ridiculous. He has never come to my room, and I have never gone to his."

"But he walks with you in the gardens, and once he picked a hibiscus blossoms and put it in your hair. He has kissed your hand as though he wished to devour it. These are the things they say in the zenana, Memsahib. He would not be so kind to any of them. They think you go to him secretly, and that you have bewitched him with foreign pleasures."

Claire was aghast. It had occurred to her that the Rajah might want to bed her, but never that his mere pleasantries would arouse the passions of the zenana against her.

"You had better watch out for the tall one, Memsahib. She is carrying a child of the Rajah's and hopes that if it is a son, he may marry her as a reward. She had been his special woman since the death of his last wife. If she prepares food for you, don't eat it!"

After that, Claire tried diligently to avoid being in the presence of the Rajah. It was impossible. He sought her out almost every day and would order refreshment brought while he chatted agreeably and inquired about his sons' progress. He was so charming that Claire sometimes almost forgot that he was Colin's enemy. She found herself animated and laughing with him and told herself it was because she had no other adult to talk to.

But she noticed now that eyes watched from behind fretwork or chik blinds. And she was especially aware of the woman Sevaley had warned her about—a beauty whose butter-colored skin seemed at odds with a rigid chin and sharp nose with thin-rimmed nostrils. Sometimes she saw the woman unveiled, but she was always glad when she covered her face. The glare of her eyes, only partly alleviated by shadowing lashes, was unnerving.

Claire remembered what the Rajah had told her about plots in the palace and began to think that she should not delay too long in finding Colin. But how? She had left Colonel Todd's house without considering how she would contact him. Would Colin even be glad to see her? She must be careful that she did not lead the Rajah's men to his refuge. She must locate some friend of Colin's who would be willing to shelter her in secret until some better arrangement might be made. Perhaps she could become a tutor in some more suitable household until things became safer and she had some notion of his whereabouts.

She was frightened that he was consumed with the Rani and their child and had forgotten about her, that his love for her had been only an insane reaction to his grief over the presumed loss of Tamila. If that were so, she must leave him in peace; but she must find out.

She began by sending Sevaley into the city on trumped-up errands, to learn what she could. It was only a week or so before the maid had news to report, for although Colin had been forced to fight against the army of Pandeish, before the death of the old Rana he had been well liked. Many in Pandeish were fiercely loyal to him, since he had returned to the country to risk his life in attempting to save it from the Rajah.

"There is a certain silk merchant who can arrange for secret accommodations for you," she said. "Tomorrow we will visit his shop to talk about it."

Claire was elated and sent word to the stables that a horse should be saddled for her the next morning; but before she was due to leave the Rajah sent for her. Claire was annoyed. She would be delayed and miss the appointment.

"I thought we might stroll in the gardens," he suggested pleasantly.

"No thank you, not this morning. I am going to the city to buy some silk for a new dress."

"There's no need; I will have the finest materials brought for your inspection. It would be my pleasure to make you a gift of whatever parcel you chose."

"Oh, but. . . ."

Claire was unable to hide her dismay. She must go to the silk shop! And as for his giving her a piece of silk—the resentful eyes of the tall concubine flashed into her mind and made her shiver.

The Rajah laughed at her obvious discomfiture and made her privy to his long-formed plan. "There'll be no need for you to leave the palace, Miss Cottington—Claire. You will find all your wants provided. As for Colin Whitecavage, even he will be provided. Didn't it occur to you to wonder why you were given an elephant to ride into Allapore? It was so that everyone would see you and wonder who you were. And then I allowed the rumor to spread through the city that you were the fiancée of Colonel Todd, the Burra Sahib, kidnapped from under his very nose and brought home as spoils to Pandeish.

"The Major will hear of it, and he will risk himself to save you, as he risked himself for the Rani. He knows my reputation with women, and he will not be able to stay away. But he will come alone, so as not to endanger anyone else, and he will not be so lucky as to escape me again. You shall have the silk, my dear, and anything else you like. I shall even give you the reward I have offered for his death. Come now, there's nothing like jewels to restore a woman's spirits."

He took a necklace of rubies and pearls meant for Colin's murderer's reward and, seizing her from behind, tried to fasten it around her throat. She fought him, clawing at his hands and choking as she tried to pull away. Catching sight of a gold-handled knife he had carelessly left on his table, she reached for it desperately and raised it to her own throat, cutting loose the string of rubies with a violent thrust.

The Rajah gave a grunt of surprise as gems clattered everywhere, rolling under the charpoys, bouncing on tables, ricocheting from walls. In the midst of the hailstorm of jewels, she turned the knife on him as though to kill him.

Had he been less quick to react, perhaps she might have done so; but Claire, hating bloodshed of any sort, hesitated the barest instant and he twisted the blade from her hand.

She tried to cling to the knife and cut her palm. Blood spurted from the wound onto her riding habit and onto the Rajah's velvet jacket. The wound was near her wrist; she thought wildly of trying to cut the other so that she could die.

Intuiting her thought, the Rajah put the knife inside his vest and said calmly, "Neither your death nor mine will solve anything, my dear. Should you die, no word of your death will escape the palace, and so you will endanger Major Whitecavage as much in death as in life. Should I die, it would change nothing. Aleka is ruler of Pandeish and technically it is he who has offered the reward for the life of Colin Whitecavage. Come along, and I will have someone bandage your hand."

Dazed and sick, Claire went meekly. She knew she should try to gather herself and think what should be done, but she was in despair and could not bring order to her numbed mind. How could she have been so stupid! She had played right into the Rajah's hands with her wild, impulsive behavior. It was a small consolation that Mama wasn't here to see it. Claire was utterly beside herself. She gave no lessons that day, and when she tried to eat to keep up her strength, she vomited what she had eaten. Sona found her at last, weeping hysterically in her room.

It was he who finally comforted her, talking to her tenderly and bathing her face with a towel wrung in cold water.

"What is wrong, Memsahib?" he asked. "Please tell me."

She did not see at first how she could divulge such a terrible plot to a young boy, especially since his father was involved in it. But perhaps it was wrong to shield him. The Rajah had said that Sona would need to learn to be ruthless. Exposing him to the reality of the plot against Colin might begin to prepare him. She found herself pouring out everything, while Sona listened intently. She remembered that he had been fond of Colin when they had traveled with the Rajah on the Grand Trunk Road and that it had been Colin who had pulled him from beneath the elephants.

Sona's lip quivered as he listened, and she expected him to break into tears. But when she was finished, he startled her by saying, "Yes, I suspected something like this. But there is a simple solution, Memsahib. We must get you out of the palace. Then those who know where the Major is hiding can take him word that you are no longer the Rajah's prisoner. Then he will not come to save you."

She blinked at him, amazed at how simple he made it

seem. "But how can that be done, Sona? I will be watched. I will not be allowed to leave."

He gave her his sweet smile. "I am the one to help you. I know a way out of the palace that is never watched. I have only to get the keys to the doors. You can leave just before dawn. My own horse will be waiting for you, as if I myself wish to ride out. No one will suspect."

"But you are not allowed to ride out alone, Sona. What of the syce?"

"I will tell him that a friend will come to ride. He can be trusted. He is devoted to me."

Claire wept again, this time from gratitude. Sona, becoming eight years old again, climbed into her lap and cried too, drinking in, perhaps for the last time, the same scent of jasmine perfume that Colin recognized as hers. He loved her more than he could remember loving anyone. He was man enough to save her and child enough to weep because he might never see her again.

In an hour he returned with two ornate keys in an embroidered bag and showed her the way to go through the labyrinth of the palace. The first door was not far and led into an unused portion of the palace. The rooms beyond the great carved door were hung with magnificent but dusty-looking tapestries, and Sona told her that this had been closed off since the old Rana's death.

"Aleka is going to open it again," he said, pointing out an area where his brother would have a sword collection hung and another where he would place the mounted heads of animals he had shot. "He has only deer and a mountain ram, so far, but after the monsoon comes, our father will take him to the jungle to bag a tiger." Sona spoke of his brother with awe.

"And you, Sona? Are you going to the jungle?"

Sona looked abashed. "No. I have not even killed a little squirrel. And if I cannot shoot animals, how shall I fight my enemies? That is what my father says. I don't know how I shall ever become a man."

"Why, Sona, you will be a fine man!" she said fervently. She wondered how he had acquired the keys and at the nerve it must take to lead her so expertly through these murky passages. Alone, Claire would have been apprehensive, but with him she felt protected. He looked at her and shook his head wistfully, as if he wished he could believe what she had said.

"Sona, I think I'm lost," she confessed. "I shall never find my way here again.

He grinned, pleased with himself. He had lived in the palace only a short time, but he had explored everything with the inquisitiveness of a young boy. "Don't worry, Memsahib. It would not be safe for me to escort you tonight, since someone might see me leave my bed, but I have marked the route on the walls." He showed her scratches he had made with a piece of stone at each turning.

The second key unlocked a door that opened outside the palace wall. From there he showed her where the horse would wait near a little-used gate.

She packed her valise—all she had been able to carry away from the house in Simla—and having hidden it, lay awake, watching for the morning star above a certain mountain peak. Sona had told her that it would be time to go when it stood there. She hated leaving Sevaley behind, but Sona could provide only one horse, and Claire thought the Rajah would return Sevaley to her family in Delhi. In Claire's pocket was a map, showing her the way to the silk merchant's house.

She must have dozed, for when she awoke with a start, the star shone in its appointed place, beckoning her to follow it to freedom and to love. She had only to slip on her riding boots, since she already wore the cambric shirt and rifle-cloth skirt of her habit. Finding her way to the first door she opened it easily. Beyond, the little marks on the walls guided her. After a little while she felt as though she were somewhere she had never been before. Screens and tapestries she had thought to use as guideposts were nowhere as she remembered them.

Thank heaven for the faithful marks to depend upon! Arriving at the outside door, she imagined that even it looked different. But it was the right door, certainly, for her key fitted into the lock.

But when the door swung open, Claire thought she was dreaming. Surely she had never left her bed! But in nightmares the impossible seemed possible, and this could not be! She had followed the marks. She had opened the door with the correct key. How could it be that she was not outside the palace wall?

Instead, she was in an enormous bedchamber, the royal apartment of the old Rana, she suspected. Canopies of gold brocade were suspended from the ceiling, forming a peak over a grand bed, piled everywhere with tassled, silk-covered cushions. A sweet aroma of opium scented the air, emanating from a little pipe.

Smoking it, the Rajah sat in the middle of the bed, wearing a velvet skull cap, his dressing gown, baggy trousers, and shoes with curled-over toes. The memory of Lord Rutherford in the peatcutter's cottage was nothing to compare with the naked lust in his eyes.

During the night he had had the signpost marks rearranged and the lock moved to the bedchamber door. She knew a flash of fear for Sona, who would surely be punished for his part in her attempted escape; then that was forgotten in terror for herself. The Rajah's expression told her that he knew he had taught her at last just how completely she was in his power.

It was the moment he had been waiting for. He saw the horror fill her eyes as she realized how irrevocably her life—and her lover's—were in his hands. He had not wanted to take her to bed on the trek to Pandeish or even, after that, until she realized the extent of his sovereignty.

She regained herself enough to try to flee, but he had anticipated her and leaped quickly to bolt the door. "Come, my dear, I've been waiting," he said gently.

Claire remembered Sevaley's advice about submitting and tried to remain quiet. *I will command my body to feel nothing,* she thought. *I will humiliate him by not deigning to make any response.*

But at the first touch of his hand on her bodice, she began to struggle, trying to claw him and succeeding only in ripping his dressing gown and exposing his fine mahogany chest. It looked strong and hard, and in a moment she had occasion to know first hand, for her own naked torso was pressed against it. In another instant, her skirt seemed to fall away of its own accord. His baggy trousers followed, and lean hips and ready manhood appeared, as though a drapery had been removed from an exquisite painting.

She sobbed and fought on the bed beneath him, not knowing quite how he had got her there so effortlessly. Could it still be a dream after all? The thick fumes of opium filled her lungs, making her dizzy, making the colors of the bedhangings go fuzzy.

But then her body began to experience that which was not the stuff of dreams, and it was not against him but against herself that she needed to struggle. She screamed with outrage as she delivered him the triumph of her release. His hot seed inside her seemed to burn into her very soul.

And then, unable to abide the degradation longer, she fainted, aware in her last moments of consciousness that he had placed the blood-red rubies like a chain of bondage about her neck.

14

She awakened lying naked among the twisted silk covers of
the immense bed. Sunlight filtered through the bamboo chik,
making a pattern of gold threads on the tile floor. Something
hard and rocklike was pressing into her, hurting her breasts.
She rolled over, saw the coil of rubies on her bosom, and
remembered.

In an instant she was off the bed, rushing to the door to try
to tug it open. It was late, but perhaps the horse was still
waiting if she could find her way. But the door did not give.
It had been bolted from the outside, and she was a prisoner.

She looked for her clothing and did not find it. It seemed
as much as anything symbolic that her garments were gone.
The Rajah had stripped her of every vestige of dignity and
honor. She had nothing with which to clothe her body, and
nothing to clothe her soul. Nothing but the rubies, which he
had had restrung after she had cut them apart. It seemed to
her she had never severed that cord, that her life was a
thread of dishonor to which stone after blood-red stone was
added. She thought of her mother, who had died because of
her whim to marry Colonel Todd; of Colonel Todd himself,
whose spirit she had helped to shatter; and most of all of
Colin, who would surely lose his life if he tried to save her.

Perhaps, she thought, he would not try. Again and again
he had shown her what kind of woman he thought she was.
The last time had been in the nullah beyond Delhi after the
sakti-puji. "We cannot," she had protested. "It is Claire." And
it had made no difference. He had dishonored her, just as he
had dishonored her in the Egyptian desert, as he had dishon-

191

ored her in every tope and dak bungalow along the Grand
Trunk Road.

He had never understood that she had been undone time
after time because she loved him so overwhelmingly. She had
been, to him, only a substitute for the beautiful Rani Tamila,
who had looked to him as her god and borne him a
princeling.

Claire was sure that she had loved him no less than the
Rani, but he had thought her an easy woman. It was a judg-
ment he must have made that night on the moor; or if not
then, when he had seen her in Lord Rutherford's arms. If he
had thought her sincere as they crossed India together, he
must have cursed himself for a fool when he had seen her
come disheveled from Maxwell Todd's embrace on her very
first night in Delhi.

Now that Colin was with Tamila again, surely he would
not come to help her. He would think her capable of dealing
with the Rajah in the manner of her kind of woman. And
wasn't she capable of it? Hadn't she proved it last night? It
was true that his first caresses had filled her with revulsion.
But finally another emotion had ruled her. It had not been
love; it had been closer to hate. But it had been passion nonetheless. Whatever had taken possession of her had been raw
and primitive and angry. She had responded to him with the
frustration and fury of a woman who knew she had no control over her fate. She had clawed and kicked and tried to
hurt him, but her very helplessness had produced an abandon
of a very different sort than she had known with Colin. But
she had not hurt him, she had only inflamed him, and that
flame, a spark of the age-old fire of conquest, had jumped between them. The explosion she had felt had been common to
centuries of subjugated women, a kindness of nature to dissi-
pate an insupportable rage and sense of violation.

This Claire did not understand, and she felt unutterably
soiled. She felt she had made a discovery about herself a
thousand times worse than the one she had made in loving
Colin. The Rajah had been skillful—she shuddered to remember the way he had touched her, his intimate kisses
transmitting fever to her skin. Ah, but skill was no excuse!
She had responded to Colin's mortal enemy. Surely Colin
would hate her if he knew. He would hate her as she hated
herself.

Draping a silk coverlet about her she explored her surroundings, finding a door that led to a roomy bath and an-

other into a courtyard enclosed in high stone walls. There was no gate, no possible way to escape. Claire suspected that the old Rana had preferred the gateless garden for security.

Returning to the bath, she dropped the coverlet and began to scrub herself in a frenzy, pouring jar after jar of water over herself as her body turned pink from her merciless rubbing with the bath sponge. But Claire felt no cleaner. It seemed to her that she could still feel him burning inside her, but in truth she was only burning with shame. She would feel no cleaner if she scrubbed her skin off, she thought. He had made her dirty to the core of her being.

Claire wept, the tears trickling down with the wash water toward the drain in the floor. She could not convince herself that Colin Whitecavage would not come to save her. If he loved her, he would. Maybe even if he didn't. He was an Englishman and subject to an Englishman's feelings about the sanctity of womanhood. Obviously, danger was of no consequence in his decisions. It had been virtual suicide to return to Pandeish to assist the Rani, but Colin had done it. He had begged Max to allow him to do it. It would be only a matter of time before his hideaway was discovered, and there was a fortune riding on his head. It would be like Colin to double the risk by coming into the open to rescue her.

She, like the Rani Tamila, had brought him the near certainty of death.

She was still in the bath when she heard the door open in the room beyond. Her heart pounded, and the jar she was holding dropped from her quivering hand and shattered on the floor. Could he have returned so soon? But a familiar female voice called to her. It was only Sevaley, who had been let in by a guard. She had brought food and clothing—not Claire's Western apparel, but kincob saris and turned-up Indian shoes.

The graceful clothes, which would once have enchanted Claire, were a mockery now. She dressed listlessly, not even bothering to look at herself in the mirror. Sevaley proved of little comfort, although she was to be allowed to remain with Claire.

Sevaley saw little to complain about in their situation. "Jana, the Rajah's favorite, thinks you are gone," she told Claire, "and as long as the women of the zenana believe you are not in the palace, you'll be safe."

"Not from the Rajah!"

"One is never safe from men," Sevaley said wisely.

"He will come again tonight, I'm sure of it," Claire said with a shiver.

"That is good," replied the little maid. "You've nothing to worry about so long as you please him."

"On the contrary, I have a great deal to worry about," said Claire in exasperation. "Major Whitecavage, for one thing. He mustn't come here for me, Sevaley!"

"But why should he come?" Sevaley could not conceive of a man's endangering himself so profoundly for the sake of a mere woman. It seemed unnatural. One did not risk one's life to save a goat or dog or a woman. A man might sigh over losing a woman, but he acquired a new one. In Claire's case it was especially confounding. Claire had not belonged to Major Whitecavage; she had belonged to Colonel Todd. Sevaley would never understand the *Angrezi*.

After a while Claire ceased trying to talk to her servant. She sat in the courtyard, her dark hair brushed straight down her back like a thunderstorm against the sunny yellow of her sari. Doves cooed in the afternoon, while Sevaley made a curry on a brazier. The spicy aromas mingled with the sweet scent of blooming jasmine, and when Claire sighed, the sigh came back to her in the whisper of the leaves of the lemon trees.

"You must eat, Memsahib," said Sevaley.

"No," said Claire, "I'm not hungry."

But Sevaley proffered a tempting bowl, and Claire considered the idea that she would have no chance to right her wrongs or to help Colin if she became weak or starved herself to death. She tried a bite of the curry and felt her stomach contract and bile rise in her throat. It was as though she needed to punish herself for what had happened during the night, for all that had transpired after the morning star had stood above the mountains. She could not see the mountains here and felt they no longer protected her.

And in fact, they didn't. For when night fell, what had occurred the night before occurred again.

Sevaley took a mat out to the courtyard to sleep beneath the moon. Claire wanted to join her, but she knew it was no use. He would find her. She had nowhere to hide, and Sevaley was right. One was never safe from men.

She fell asleep on the low string bed, worn out by grief and shame and dread. He came in noiselessly and dropped his clothes. She did not know of his presence until she felt the bed sink with his weight. Resigned to what must follow, she gave only a mild cry of alarm. And if Sevaley, in the courtyard, heard it, she did not rush to her mistress's aid. Beyond her cry there was only silence, like the silence of a battlefield when the guns have stopped firing at last, an eerie silence broken suddenly by the shriek of an owl as the Rajah took her in his arms.

And then, as though the bird had signaled the end of the universe, nothing existed but the man and the woman, locked as one in the eternal struggle of passion. She had felt herself drained of feeling, but now anger coursed through her, as though he had injected it into her body along with himself. Her nipples tightened, and her breath came sharply as she flew at him, cursing and screaming, her hips jerking upward in awful arousal.

His hands moved everywhere, and everywhere they touched she recoiled and burned until the tension in her body could no longer be endured. But even then she fought against that final surrender that would end this session of degradation. She would not—would not. . . . She heard her strangled moan from a distance, as though it were someone else who cried out—in a way it was, she thought. And then again came the uncanny silence.

He came the next night and the next. Claire lived in a daze, scarcely noticing the rising of the sun and its setting beyond the garden wall. In the morning the pinkening sky seemed to blush for her, as though she had disgraced the Creation itself. But in the evening the purple twilight was lush with promise. Claire was unaware of the sounds of the city—the creaking of carts, the baaing of a flock of sheep being herded toward the bazaar, the cry of the muezzin from some mosque. She was imprisoned in another world, in which there was nothing to listen for but the soft sound of the Rajah's gold leather slippers. She listened with dread and with a sort of fascination. It was as though she constantly stood at the edge of a precipice, hypnotized by the distance of the fall, the unreasoning urge to hurl herself into the void.

She had ceased to weep, but her eyes grew overly bright and seemed too large for her hollowing face. She continued to eat little and slept only in exhaustion after the Rajah's visit ended the tension that had grown through the day. She grew to feel something akin to gratitude on his arrival, for it meant a temporary release from her ongoing ordeal. And her ordeal was far more than simply the violation of her body. It was her ultimate recognition of the consequences of her string of impulsive actions. From the turfcutter's cottage to the Rajah's bedchamber, events had been moving on a steady course. From the moment that she had climbed up behind Colin on his horse and pressed against his strong back, she had been on the road to destroying him.

Colin would die.

And only in the Rajah's assaults could she lose herself or punish herself for her wickedness. That strange punishment was, in a way, her only comfort.

He did not rape her, for she did not resist. He only took her in the manner of an Indian man, as a matter of course. But the Rajah of Rambad had never had a woman like Claire.

He had had many women who had simply submitted. And when he had been a young man, that had been enough. The voluptuousness of the female flesh had served to satisfy. In those days he had chosen women for the zenana on the basis of the size of their breasts, the richness of their hair, and the turn of their hips. But at twenty he had been married to a Princess, and afterward his desires had never been the same.

She had been younger than he, little more than a child, but infinitely more sophisticated, for she had been elaborately schooled in her function in life—to please her man. The Rajah had felt as though he had never known copulation before. He had spent every night with her; and before she had died, she had given him his son, Aleka.

She had died because he had used her up, worn her out, as he might have one of his silk robes. He had done only what had been expected of him, and never felt to blame. But too late he realized that he had loved her and was lost without her. In bewilderment he had married other young girls to try to replace her. Sona's mother had been the last of those—but she had given no satisfaction at all. She had simply screamed for her mother and languished and taken the occasion of childbirth to escape her bondage, by dying as the others had.

The Rajah had given up on marriage and had stocked the zenana in a new way. He had learned to notice a certain aura about a woman, a certain pride, a certain sway of her body; and he had found women to please in every way. There was no pleasure available to a man that the Rajah did not possess. Save one.

The Rajah had never bedded a woman who dared to strive for her own gratification, and indeed to put it before the satisfaction of her lord. And that was what Claire did. The Rajah was more excited by her than he had imagined it possible for him to be ever again. Ravenous new appetites assailed his jaded palate.

He laughed gleefully as she flailed at him, his arousal heightening as he gazed on the raw passion in her face, as he felt her stomach coil tighter upon itself, seeming to clutch like an iron fist beneath him, a fist of pure hatred, wanting to lash at him, but able to strike only in one special way. Her convulsions, when they came at last, were so strong they seemed to beat inside him, setting loose a wild drumming of his own unleashed ecstasy.

Afterward, he was filled with a need to be tender toward her, and would lie stroking her dark hair, beneath which she lay crying or sleeping. Her hair was as long and shining as any Indian woman's, but it seemed softer to him. It was like an impenetrable forest in the depths of which she hid, like a rare bird among the mountain spruce. And he felt a peculiar longing as he lay beside her, a longing he could not satisfy by taking her.

It was as though he wanted the bird of her spirit to fly out and sing for him as did the parakeets in the palace gardens. He did not understand himself at all, and yet it was simple enough. The Rajah of Rambad had fallen helplessly in love. He had intended making love to her simply because it was convenient. He had never had an *Angrezi* woman, and she had been marvelously beautiful. Moreover, it had amused him to triumph over Colin Whitecavage in such a way. He could humiliate his enemy while waiting to have his head on a platter.

But the Rajah had outwitted himself. It wasn't working out as he had intended. He had intended to release the woman and send her packing to her own people when the Sword of Pandeish was finally vanquished. Now he realized that would not do at all. He could not bear to part with Clair Cottington.

Perhaps he had felt that even after the first night. Perhaps that was why he had sent her a wardrobe of exquisite saris. He had wanted to make her seem a part of the palace life—as though she belonged here.

He had not the slightest doubt that Colin Whitecavage

would attempt to remove his one-time mistress from the Rainbow Palace or that Colin would lose his life in the attempt. After that, what would Claire be like? She might sink into lethargy or she might try to take revenge by killing him. If not, she might kill herself, since no reason left would prevent her. She had shown such inclinations when she had discovered that she was part of his plot against her lover. The Rajah wished that he could believe he had conquered Claire and was her master, to whom she owed allegiance. But he knew he could not. She was a Western woman in spite of the saris and flowing kurtas, a Westerner in spite of her dark hair and her eyes, more vivid than any hill woman's. She had not been raised in a zenana, and in her soul she had not submitted to him. The Rajah knew that Claire still loved only Colin Whitecavage. He possessed her physically, but that was only a beginning. The Rajah would not feel that he had triumphed until he saw worship in her eyes.

But Claire did not give him that pleasure, at least. Instead, she began to regather her wits. She was made of sturdy stuff, and she would not give up, no matter how hopeless it seemed. She must not give up and consign her beloved to death before the bullets and tulwars had ripped away his life. But Claire had no idea how she might help him.

Then one afternoon a little monkey climbed over the wall and dropped down into the branches of the lemon tree. Claire, lost in desperate thought, did not notice it at first. Then it chattered at her, begging for a handout. With a quick leap it hopped onto her shoulder and reached for a piece of mango on the table beside her. It was the marmoset that had been the pet of the classroom, and Claire almost wept with joy to see it. She spoiled it with treats, and the next day it returned.

"If only you could tell Sona that I am here!" she told it.

The monkey chattered, and Claire suddenly clapped her hands as though the animal had actually spoken.

"But you could. Of course you could! I could tie a note around your neck, and when you go back to Sona he would find it!"

Then she fell silent, considering. What good would it do, she thought. Sona believed she had escaped. It would only make him unhappy to think her still a prisoner. She shut the animal in the bath until her plan was complete. She would send a letter to the silk merchant through Sona. The silk merchant in turn would be directed to send it to Colin. The letter would be the same sort as the one the Rajah had made her write to Max to prevent his following her.

Claire wondered what Sona would make of the letter. Had she taught him enough English to read it? She hoped she hadn't or that he was too young to understand it. Then he, at least, would not be disillusioned with her. A note to Sona would accompany the letter to Colin, containing instructions and assurances of her well-being. She wondered if Sona would be able to read even this, for it was written in English, too. English was safer, and Claire could write very little in Hindustani. Sevaley, who could not read or write, was no help at all in constructing a message in her native language.

Having attached the letters, Claire set the monkey free, but for the longest time it showed no wish to leave her courtyard. At dusk, it went at last, having made up its mind that she would feed it no more, and scolding resentfully as it clambered over the wall.

She had something to think of as night fell, something other than the Rajah's impending visit. Would Sona send her a reply by the monkey and tell her that her wishes had been accomplished?

The moon rose and filled the courtyard with soft light. The paving stones, having soaked up the heat of the day, emitted gentle warmth, and the scent of bougainvillea was carried on the breath of night. Birds twittered, kept awake by the light, and then the moon sank out of sight beyond the wall, vanishing like a silver dish dipped into a suds of clouds. The Rajah was late. Perhaps he wasn't coming.

She fell into a doze, dreaming in the peaceful night of Cottington Crest, of fields of harebells and daisies; and she smiled in her sleep, believing she had returned to that simpler time when the most serious problems in her life had been scandals over bloomers and which gown to wear to please Lord Rutherford. She felt a presence and thought that it was Mama, coming to wake her. Sitting up, she saw the Rajah's shadowy form beside her. Alarm swept through her, for tonight something was different. A heavy atmosphere had enveloped the room, as though a low-hanging cloud had slipped down from the mountains to shroud them.

She blinked as he lighted a lamp. Yes, tonight was different. The Rajah had never before put on a lamp. And tonight he had not removed his clothes. The sight of him fully dressed should have reassured her, but it did nothing of the sort. For a moment she did not know why. And then she realized that the marmoset was perched on the Rajah's shoulder.

Claire wept, and for a while he let her, waiting until she subsided into dry, quivering sobs. And then he did not speak of the monkey or the message it had carried. He did not threaten her. Instead he said the most amazing thing she could have imagined. "My dear Claire," the Rajah said, "I've come to ask you to marry me."

"Marry you! Never!" she cried dumbfounded.

"You must!" he replied quietly, with fervor. His blazing eyes commanded more strongly than his voice. He was the Rajah, and all his life he had had what he wanted, especially from women.

But Claire had had the same sort of experience of men. In her girlhood they had danced attendance on her, and she had ordered them about imperiously, with little more thought for their feelings than the Rajah had had for the women of the zenana.

"You may take my body, and I cannot stop you," she told him defiantly. "But you can never force me to marry you. If I had been going to marry anyone, it would have been Colonel Todd, who was worthy of me, not a vile despot such as you!"

"You don't think me so vile, my love," he said gently, a smirk beginning. "Why, I am sure that my manners are quite perfect—"

"Your manners, sir! You have none!" she spat at him.

"In bed, you mean. But then, neither have you! Ah, Miss Cottington, you are the only woman I have ever met who had no bedroom manners at all. You are a match for me, and I did not think that any woman was. I did not believe that nature made them so. Claire, we are perfect for each other!"

"I hate you!"

"I know. You hate me now. But that hate is close to love, admit it. When you are beneath me in bed, you cannot separate them!"

"You are an arrogant fool!" she cried.

He laughed. It was a laugh he used when he had her trapped. A laugh she had come to know and hate. A short, sharp, two-syllable laugh, like the cry of a bird swooping for prey. "Claire, I must have you! You must be my wife. The

had ended her hopes by announcing their engagement. No wonder Jana hated her. She would have been surprised to know that Claire wished that Jana could have her way and become the next rani, but Claire contented herself that Colin's life would be spared and felt almost happy. The Rajah's priest had selected an auspicious day, and on that evening, when the first of the wedding ceremonies had been completed, the Rajah had promised to send messengers through Pandeish with word that Major Whitecavage was not to be harmed.

Colin, Tamila, and their son would be allowed to leave Pandeish together, the Rajah had promised. All three would be exiled forever from Paneish, but surely the Rani would not mind losing her kingdom when she had acquired what was so much more valuable. Claire herself would have traded anything for such a prize. They would be safe together—Colin, the woman he loved, and their child.

It could not have happened without me, Claire thought with satisfaction. If I had not come to Pandeish, they would have hunted him down and killed him—and the Rani and her baby, too.

With this single act of atonement, Claire would make up for all her transgressions. She would give Colin and those he loved their lives and their future, and for once Claire felt good about herself. Her attitude toward the Rajah softened. It had been no small thing after all for him to grant clemency to his enemies for the sake of a woman. He was, after all, to be her husband, and she worked at finding things about him to like.

He treated her more like a Western wife than a woman of the zenana—or perhaps more like a Western mistress. He showered her with gifts, presenting her a beautiful white mare to ride with him in the mornings. The horse stood sixteen hands, and its tail, mane, and fetlocks were dyed red. The saddle cloth was gold brocade set with pearls, and the saddle was heavy gilded silver. Each day brought new jewels and perfumes, fresh blossoms for her hair and for her flower vases.

At midday he would join her for a feast of mangoes and jackfruit, wines and bread, partridge or pheasant—this though it was not the custom for men and women to eat together. It was the custom that the bride ate with her husband only on the wedding day, to show closeness of spirit; afterward she could eat what he left behind on his plate if she wished. The Rajah laughed as he told her this, for he knew how hopeless it would be to subjugate Claire as Indian women were subjugated.

As for the nights, Claire no longer dreaded them, and indeed found herself looking forward to the time he would come to her bedchamber. Their wild lovemaking had mellowed with her acceptance of him, and had, incredibly, become even more sensual. He utilized her body with a strange Eastern mystery, touching her in secret ways that must have come down through the centuries, ways that he had not been taught but seemed to have been bred into him along with his elegant masculinity. Their union became as silken as the sheets on which they lay, their passion a breathless whisper in the summer nights.

Claire knew it was not love. And yet it took care of unspoken needs. In the Rajah's arms, Claire could deny for a while her ineffable longing for Colin Whitecavage. She gave herself to the Rajah with utter abandon, and in her wanton debauchery she denied that there was some depth of her that his probing manhood could not touch. While he occupied her bed and body, she was totally immersed in the sensations he provoked. Her very toes strained toward ecstasy, stretching, curling under to grip the slippery sheet. But afterward, when the explosion had come and gone, when the moments of floating nirvana had passed, she would feel an emptiness, a chill; and no number of coverlets or rugs wrapped about her could end it.

Her stormy, forbidden lovemaking with Colin had touched her soul as the Rajah did not. The simple force of Colin's own being was more than silks and incense, more than the thousand mysteries of the East. She knew that the mere sight of his face would set her atremble, and that with his intense eyes, he could penetrate her heart more profoundly than the Rajah could penetrate her amid the cusions of her bedchamber.

But she would never see those eyes again, never see that face, and she must make peace with that fact. Colin had known her to be a carnal woman, and it was fortunate that she was. If she were not a carnal woman, she would not have the comforts of the Rajah to sustain her. If she had not been a carnal woman, the Rajah would not have cared to marry her at all. This very quality, which had so nearly undone her, had been the means to save her beloved's life.

So fate had decreed that she become a rani. Perhaps this was what life had held in store for her all along. From the ballrooms of London, and the desolate moors, across the deserts of Egypt, up the corpse-strewn Hooghly, along the Grand Trunk Road, she had been journeying toward a marriage, not with Lord Rutherford or Colonel Todd, or even Colin Whitecavage, but with the Rajah of Rambad, who was perhaps the best match after all. She remembered that she had been told that he was unprincipled, but what matter? Hadn't she been unprincipled as well? Hadn't she devastated Colonel Todd by breaking her promises to him? Hadn't she been the reason that Colin had betrayed his own sense of honor?

Perhaps she might have found the right place for herself at last. Certainly there were compensations—in the bedroom and beyond. There was the Rainbow Palace itself. She adored the lattices, fountains, and courtyards, the tame birds and monkeys and mongooses. She loved the pools full of enormous gold fish, as though treasure chests of long red coins had been spilled there. She relished the smell of flowers and of incense, the rooftops from which one could look out over Allapore and see children playing in the twisting, dusty streets, women on their way to the well, and the crowded bazaar where tin and brass pots and Manchester cotton were on sale, along with sweetmeats, grain, sugar and ghee.

In the evenings, Claire always went to the rooftops to view the mountains. Then, as the smoke of dung fires and the scent of baked stone rose into the dusk, the breath of the mountain wind brought her the memory of Colin. He was there in the mountains, looming about her soul as their peaks loomed over the city, and when she turned to the mountains, which spoke of strength, purity, and eternity, it was Colin to whom she turned. He, for whom her love was strong, pure, and eternal. And to the mountains she offered wordless prayers that he was safe, and that her sacrifice would not be in vain.

She had begun already to forget that she was an Englishwoman. Cottington Crest seemed like a story her ayah had told her, instead of a story that she told herself to the young princes and to Sevaley. Her existence in the Rainbow Palace had become unfettered in every way. She went where she liked, bedded the Rajah without modesty, wore not crinolines but saris or the kurta and loose trousers. Earrings of gold coins dangled from her veils, and she rimmed her sapphire eyes with kohl, making the color deeper and more startling.

The result was so effective that the Rajah suggested she should cover the splendor of her face during the wedding ceremonies.

"You wish me to be demure?" she asked. "It is a bit late for that, and I warn you, I've never been very successful at it."

Her husband-to-be rocked with laughter and gave up the idea. "My love, we are perfectly matched. You will be the Queen and behave however you choose. But you must never be demure with *me!*"

And constantly and joyously he made her keep that vow as their wedding approached. Now and then he would press his hand against her stomach and gaze at her speculatively. "Have you nothing to tell me yet? Well, it may be too soon to know. But perhaps he's there, even now—my son."

Claire wondered herself if she were pregnant. She was still ignorant in such matters and, unlike a young English bride, she had no mother or aunt from whom to acquire such delicate information. Sevaley did not know, and the women of the zenana were, of course, hostile, for the Rajah was making plans to send them away. Some would go back to their families with gifts of clothing and jewels. Others were to be taken to a certain house in Allapore where their talents might be put to good use. The youngest and most beautiful were to suffer this fate, and Claire was horrified to discover it.

"I will not allow it," she told the Rajah. "It is utterly barbaric."

He grinned at her, his teeth sugar-white against his lips, which could by turn be sensuous or cruel. "You will not allow it, my dear? How are you to stop it? And you are quite right, of course. It is barbaric. Didn't the women at the cantonments in Delhi teach you that we are a barbaric race?"

"Yes. And they were right!" she blazed.

"It is a matter of practicality, my dear. Hindus are more particular than the *Angrezi*. Hindus do not marry used women. Even a widow may not remarry, so it is easy to see why sometimes she is eager to die a suttee and acquire the honor she can have no other way. The older women, who return to their families, go to be ayahs or servants. And the younger to serve men, as God intended."

"It is horrible!" said Claire, knowing that she was to blame for their fate. "I never thought—I never intended. . . ."

"Then perhaps you want me to keep them?" he suggested.

Claire thought it over. These women would not be grateful

and loyal to her if she saved them. The jealousies and intrigues of the zenana would not evaporate. They would not love her for her benevolence. She would still be the enemy, and they would think her a weak enemy at that. "Let the ones who have children stay," she said, reaching a compromise.

"Very well. Then, since you insist that they remain, I will avail myself of them, of course, if I wish."

"That will be your decision," she told him coldly. And she shuddered to think that she herself would be little more than a slave when she had married him, a brood mare for the sons he seemed to want of her. Oh, he might adore her, he might treat her with the respect due an Englishwoman. He might grant her whims; but when her wishes differed from his, his rule would be absolute. She had had only one prize to give him, and that she had exchanged for the lives of Colin, Tamila, and the baby. For the future, for the rest of her days, her life would be as he chose to make it. And she was sure that she did not trust him.

Perhaps I will acquire power over him as the Rani Tamila did over the old Rana, she thought, wondering what charms the Rani had worked on her ailing husband in this very room. But the Rajah wasn't old and ailing, and it would not be an easy task. She was beginning to think like an Indian, in terms of power and survival. But not enough like an Indian.

Her European values still worked against her. Her humanity concerning the Rajah's concubines meant she would still have enemies in the palace. It meant that Jana, whom she considered the most dangerous, would stay.

The preliminary ceremonies seemed endless. Allapore was thronged with wedding guests. Each day some new chieftain rode into the city with his contingent of warriors and camp followers, and the howdahed elephants of the rulers of neighboring states made grand entrances with horns and banners.

On one day the god Vigneshwara was carried beneath the marriage canopy and sacrifices of darbha grass and wood from seven sacred trees were offered. On another day a sacrifice of sacred fire was made to honor the planets, and both of these occasions were followed with feasts.

The third day Claire sat with the Rajah beneath the marriage canopy and faced the East while their heads were anointed with oil and the unclothed parts of their bodies smeared with powdered saffron. Finally they were doused with huge quantities of water. Claire was perplexed, and her patience was tried. *Imagine if Mama were here*, she thought. Mrs. Cottington could never have dreamed of this when she had set out to see her daughter married in India. There was no need for the wedding gown that had become separated from them during the trip. Instead, her marriage dress was of green and gold, and tiny gems hung from the tassels of her veil to glimmer in the light. The nights had become long and lonely, for the Rajah did not come to her bed. He was taken up with the feasting and entertainments, and Claire could hear the laughter and the sounds of the instruments that accompanied the dancing girls. In the stillness of her quarters, without the wild distraction of his nightly visits, Claire had time to think about the bargain she had made and to wonder how she would fare. Always she wished that somehow she might have married Colin, but barring that, that she might have married Colonel Todd or even William Rutherford. William Rutherford would have ignored her after a time and gone back to his affairs, perhaps leaving her to hers. Colonel Todd would, in the long run, have been as gentle as her old collie dog. But the Rajah of Rambad! He of all the men she had known, might exhaust her, even drive her insane with with his unutterable lust.

She would tell herself that it didn't matter, so long as Colin Whitecavage went free. And then she would wonder about her children—how many she would have and what would become of them when one day she died from the bearing of many infants. Would her daughters be subjected to arranged marriages at early ages? Would her sons use their women brutally and without love?

Sometimes Claire wept. It seemed everything she did affected so many lives.

The day of the *muhurta* approached, the first of the five days of the wedding ceremony itself. This was the auspicious day that had been chosen, and by the end of it, she would be his wife. At the end of this day, too, it would be announced throughout Pandeish that the Rajah, in celebration of his marriage, granted safety to the Rani and to the leader of the resistance, Major Colin Whitecavage.

Before dawn on her wedding day she was awakened and dressed in the green and gold sari and the little gold-heeled slippers that were part of the ensemble. Roses and orange blossoms were tied in her hair, and the veil was draped over her dark hair.

Then, to Claire's amazement, Jana entered and ordered all

Claire's servants away. Claire called out to them to stay, but they all obeyed Jana, scurrying away as if frightened. Faithful Sevaley had been sent to oversee the arangement of the wedding canopy.

"Come with me," Jana said.

Claire sensed treachery and stayed where she was.

"The Rajah sent me to bring you to your wedding," said Jana. "You will have him to answer to."

Claire considered. What Jana said was possible, and she did not want to anger her bridegroom. Jana was taller than Claire, but slow and clumsy in her condition. Surely she could be no danger. Cautiously Claire followed her into the corridor.

"We are not going in the right direction," she said as Jana turned a murky corner.

"It is the right way," said Jana.

But Claire knew it was not, and turned on her heel. The point of a knife against her ribs and an arm about her neck brought her up short. "The Rajah will have you put to death if you kill me, Jana," Claire said, finding the words in Hindustani.

"He will never know it," the concubine replied. "You will vanish. And he will think you lost your nerve and run away to your *Angrezi* lover." Jana pressed the jade-handled knife more firmly against Claire's back.

The wedding sari tore as Claire struggled. Surely it was possible to get away from Jana, who had the handicap of pregnancy. But Jana's pregnancy was advantage as well as handicap. It gave her mission a sacred purpose. What she did was for her child, and that gave her a desperate strength beyond what was normal. She pulled Claire deeper into the unused portion of the palace. Claire wondered if Jana had found a burial place—an ancient well or a forgotten courtyard where a grave might be made and never discovered. She would perhaps become a legend of the Rainbow Palace, the English bride who had disappeared in her wedding gown. Future generations would imagine that she haunted the halls, searching for her bridegroom or for Colin Whitecavage.

The thoughts raced dizzily through her mind as she turned suddenly and grabbed at the knife. But even as she felt Jana's hand give on the handle, another hand covered hers. Not a man's hand, though it seemed as firm. The hand belonged to a stout servant of the zenana, and it was not to be trifled with.

Claire released the knife with a cry. The woman's leathery face grinned at her, and she realized that other women had come to join her. She was surrounded, and each face bore the same determined look. Some were very young and beautiful, girls with fine features and well-turned bodies that gave them every reason to hope for the Rajah's favor. Some wore veils, as though to hide their identity should they be discovered. And most of them, veiled or not, seemed frightened. Their very fear deepened Claire's alarm. Their terror transmitted the seriousness of the crime they were about to commit.

How ironic that she should be undone at last, not by the likes of Arab thieves, but by members of her own sex! She had been taught to think of women as the gentle sex, the nurturers of life, but these women were capable of violence. They had been driven to their unnatural condition by the subjugation and brutalization of men. Even in this awful moment, Claire could not blame them for the murder she was sure they intended to do. Because of her marriage to the Rajah, they would be sent from the comfortable zenana to lives of servitude or degradation. No wonder they wished her dead!

"Please! It will do no good!" she pleaded. "If the Rajah finds my body, it will go hard with you!"

But her words had no effect. She realized that now she had begun to speak in English, and that all the words of their language had fled her panic-stricken mind. And then, losing the power to speak altogether, she emitted only hopeless sobs.

The women's eyes were pitiless as they shoved her into a small room and bound her hand and foot with silk scarves. She waited, scarcely able to breathe with fear, trying to remember some prayer to say. But back in England she had been more interested in eyeing such eligibles as William Rutherford over the edge of her prayerbook, and the memory of its contents had vanished.

Suddenly she was alone. Claire shivered helplessly. She was certain that they were not finished with her, and she would as soon not have had time to contemplate her fate. The room was bare except for a charpoy with a rug thrown over it. Light entered through a small window high in the wall and, glancing up, she glimpsed the mountains which had so often comforted her. Even now the sight of them steadied her, and she began to compose herself to die with dignity, if die she must.

She seemed to be high in the palace, perhaps in one of the turrets, she thought. Guards used these towers to watch for the approach of an enemy, but this room was dusty and disused. It might have been years since anyone had been here. She supposed this was the reason that it had been chosen, but she wondered for exactly what purpose. Sooner or later someone would think of looking here.

She could hear the hubbub in the streets surrounding the palace as guests arrived with much braying of camels and trumpeting of elephants. And the townspeople were gathering outside the palace in hopes that they would be treated to a glimpse of the bride. Had she been missed yet? Surely they would begin to look for her soon. She twisted vainly against her pretty bindings.

Then she was aware of a different sound, a soft crunching on the nearby rooftop. Pigeons, she thought, but there was no cooing.

A shadow dropped across the window, and Claire felt a chill as the patch of sunlight disappeared from the stone floor. It was not that the lack of sun made the air cool; indeed, the air was stifling. But she felt bereft without mountains; her last friend, her last comfort, had been taken and she knew what was coming.

The man entered, thrusting one leg over the sill, his foot clad in whipcord sandals. She screamed, for they had not thought to gag her, and the sound reverberated from the cramped walls. But her scream was as much a prisoner as she, the thick stone containing the cry and muffling it so that only a thin echo escaped the window, which the man had just vacated. He dropped down into the room and clamped a hand over her mouth. Vainly she tried to bite his tough, calloused palm as he heaved her to her feet, slipping his other arm tightly about her waist. She recoiled, seeing him in a blur.

She understood that the ladies of the zenana had hoped to claim innocence by hiring this badmash and paying him with their jewels. Better for them not to actually have her blood on their hands! Dimly she saw the dark bearded face beneath the turban, and the knife in her attacker's hand. For the second time that day she expected her throat to be slit, and she swayed in his grip, hoping to faint before the atrocity occurred.

The room swam and colors exploded before her eyes as she heard someone call her name. "Claire! Don't have a fit of vapors! Not now, for godsake!" The voice was familiar. It was even beloved. It called forth an image—the beautiful, impossible image of the man for whose sake she now died. She clung to the impression, trying to take courage from it.

"Claire!" the voice insisted. "Don't you know me?"

The scarf binding her hands parted with a sudden snap. Her arms fell to her sides, rousing her from her near oblivion. Oddly, the face of Colin Whitecavage did not disappear. Only now it resided on the swarthy Indian, who, kneeling to cut her ankles apart, gave the impression of bending in the supplication of a lover.

Could it really be he?

He took her in his arms and kissed her, and she knew without question that it was Colin—sunburned, weary, thinner, but Colin nonetheless. She wept in relief, and then with renewed terror.

"Why have you come here? There is a price on your head! And there must be hundreds in the palace itself who would like to collect it! And the women of the zenana——"

"Are my friends. They are expecting me to carry you away to someplace where you will cause them no more trouble. There is an ekka waiting outside."

"No! It's too dangerous! I am going to marry the Rajah!"

"Never. That was a stupid idea of yours. I cannot imagine how it came about. I left you safe with Max. I realize that the Rajah is compelling to women, but even if you disgrace yourself with this marriage, Jana would soon have your life for it!"

"Ooh! He is not——" she began, and recognizing the lie, broke off in shame. "The Rajah will have *your* life if you are discovered! Do you actually believe you can escape from the palace with the bride?"

"I am going to try. And I am not in the mood for arguments." Before she could protest, he lifted her and, having thrown a long shawl over her to cover her exquisite sari, he set her out on the roof.

She gasped as he swung her into the air, but she obeyed him as he led her down over the roofs. The perilous descent made her glad for the tors of Dartmoor, which had given her practice at heights as a girl. They reached the ground safely, but now the way led through throngs of wedding guests. Colin did not try to evade the crowd, but pushed among them rudely, sometimes shouting impolitely for them to make way. She scurried in the wake of his belligerence; and nobody noticed her, though angry glances abounded in Colin's direction. Each time anyone looked at him, she felt a blast of paralyzing fear. Voices seemed far away, as they passed columns and statues decorated for the nuptials with wreaths of mango leaves.

The aromas of roasting goat and chunna for the wedding feast filled the air, and everyone's mind was too much on the festivities to take note of a humbly-dressed hill man. They moved out of his way, aware of nothing but his rudeness, thinking him the pompous retainer of some outlying chieftain. Why should anyone see what Claire hadn't seen herself—the features of Colin Whitecavage beneath the turban and beard? The sun had weathered his skin to a rich sienna so that he no longer looked European, but he had an aura about him that didn't fit his disguise. He seemed as fierce as the coarse hill men she had seen in Delhi at the *sakti-puji*, but something about him seemed too sharp, too fine. Perhaps it was the determination of his step or the set of his jaw. Who could not recognize the Sword of Pandeish? Once she herself had done so, it seemed to her that his identity could not be missed. She herself was in much less danger, for she kept her veil over her face.

Then, just as they reached the gate, she saw the flash of recognition she had been dreading. She expected that a cry would be raised, but the camel driver, who had been holding the reins of one of his animals, passed them swiftly to his subordinate and, reaching into his sash, took out his knife and hurled it. No use alerting others to the prize so near at hand, the driver must have thought; but Claire jerked Colin aside, and the knife merely grazed his shoulder, fetching up against the flank of a donkey, which reared and fought at its tether to raise the alarm.

As they reached the light, two-wheeled ekka, she heard the commotion erupting behind them. The sound of his name rang on the air, and the trumpets began to blow, summoning the Rajah's men to the chase. She expected to see Colin jerked from the trap and murdered before her eyes, but instead the crowd seemed to part for him. Miraculously the path in front of them was clear. He yelled to the horses and grinned at her as they sped away.

Claire looked back fearfully and saw that the crowd had closed across the street again, milling aimlessly as the soldiers of the palace guard tried to pass among them. "The women of the zenana aren't your only friends in Pandeish," she observed.

"No. I have many friends and need them all. If only I

could have deserved their friendship by saving Pandeish. If only I deserved. . . ."

Colin did not finish his thought, but she knew what he was thinking. He was thinking that his love for the Rani Tamila was a betrayal of that friendship. He was a man whose heart could never find its way on acceptable paths. Like Claire, he loved without honor.

Over her shoulder she saw the guards break through the crowd. On they came with bloodthirsty shrieks. Gunfire spattered and arrows whizzed about the ekka. "Get down," shouted Colin—needlessly, for she was already huddling on the floor of the trap.

The streets emptied now, but not quite. Where the ekka had passed lay heaps of what looked like discarded bed linen. Each heap was a bystander who had come into the line of fire in the hysteria over Colin. Shots were fired wildly, some pinging off stone walls or shattering chiks. There were many who wanted the Rajah's reward, the string of rubies, and did not mind the cost of pursuing it. The people of Allapore were patriots of Pandeish, and the Rajah's wedding guests were willing that they be shot like parish dogs should they get in the way of the death of Colin Whitecavage. One of the fallen closest to the ekka's path was a child, whose short legs had not carried it speedily enough to shelter and whose agonized cries reached Claire's ears.

"Colin!" she screamed and instinctively tried to climb out of the racing cart to save it. He turned his head and saw for the first time the carnage in his wake. For an instant the ekka lost momentum as he shoved Claire back, deterring her from her hopeless endeavor; and in that instant the bullet struck, and he collapsed wordlessly, falling across her with his head in her lap.

"Colin!" she shrieked again, but this time there was no response. She did not know if he were dead, as she reached for the reins. If he lived, his life was in her hands, and she did not even know the way to the city gate! It would be easy for her to save herself. She had only to stop the cart and allow herself to be returned to the palace for her wedding. But if he were alive, he would be executed for his crimes, including the audacious crime of kidnapping the Rajah's bride on her wedding day.

His face was so gray that Claire was certain he was dead, but even so, the alternative of stopping did not really occur to her. The reason for her marriage to the Rajah no longer existed; and she knew she would never be his wife, just as when she had fled Simla she had known she would never marry Maxwell Todd.

On impulse, she turned the ekka down a side street. The cart slowed with the twists and turns, but perhaps she could lose the soldiers in the maze. She ached with exhaustion. It seemed that the chase had been going on for hours, instead of only a few minutes. Colin's head jounced heavily in her lap and cries of pursuit rang and echoed as the palace guard spread out to search. It was hopeless. How could she ever escape the city?

A man stepped from the shadows and, leaping aboard, took control of the horses. She relinquished the reins without a thought. It was simply inevitable. She was in his power and she lolled back with relief that her fate and Colin's had passed from her hands. The new driver was a huge man with a thunderous black beard. A rope of pearls hung in his bright gauze turban, and his three-quarter length *ackan* and his trousers were made of fine linen. He was someone wealthy and important, obviously, but she had never seen him at the Rainbow Palace.

Dark eyes looked at her as though to understand what manner of woman a man might give his life for. She stared back numbed, seeing no light in the coaly irises, no indication of friendship or hostility, only infinite lightlessness as incomprehensible as the future.

The eyes fell on Colin's unmoving form, and when they looked at her again, they gleamed with purpose. "I am Ala Ram, the silk merchant," he told her as he guided the horses skillfully behind the gates of a courtyard filled with orange and lemon trees.

Claire sat where she was, still holding Colin, too stunned to protest when the big Indian lifted him tenderly from her lap.

"Is he——?" Her throat seemed suddenly choked with the dust stirred up in their flight.

"He's alive," said the silk merhcant with satisfaction.

"Then we must get a doctor. Can you send for one?"

"That is impossible, Miss Cottington." And now the fathomless eyes were definitely inimical. It was apparent that he blamed her for what had happened. His expression told her that she had caused Colin's grave injury, but Claire did not need to be told. "There is no time for a doctor. They will begin to search house to house before long, and mine will be first on their list."

"Why?"

"Because I am known to be the Rajah's special enemy. The regiment I led against him was the last to retreat. We kept fighting for a week after all other help had gone. And then we were saved from total annihilation only because Major Whitecavage and his men held the pass above us. Most likely I was not executed after the war because the Rajah hoped something like this would happen. He hoped I might lead him to Major Whitecavage. I am watched all the time, but today the spies have paid with their lives for the little time we have."

"The Rajah will learn of it and have you executed," Claire gasped.

"No. The Rajah will only send more spies. I am safe so long as I am a link to Colin Whitecavage."

All the time Ala Ram talked, his fingers gently explored the wound at the side of Colin's head. "I will have to dress this myself, and then we must get him out of Allapore."

"But surely they will block the roads!"

Ala Ram nodded. "There is a way that might work. But someone will have to go with him, and this is not a thing for a memsahib."

"It is for me, if it may save him!" she said fervently, and saw the expression shift in his eyes as he reappraised her.

"There is barely a chance in a hundred that either of you would survive. I will arrange for someone to go with him, and you will go back to the palace."

"I am going with him," she said flatly.

"The way lies on the river," he told her.

"I can row a boat, and I am a good swimmer."

"I am not speaking of boats, and even swimming will not be easy, should you need to," said Ala Ram.

He had called a servant to bring water and bandages, and his big hands moved as expertly as they might unrolling a bolt of his fine merchandise. "The soldiers will be watching for boats on the river."

"What do you mean, then?"

"The corpses. At least a dozen people must have died in Allapore this afternoon. And those whose families cannot afford the ghat will set them adrift in the river. No one will pay any attention to two more corpses, floating on a raft."

"A raft!"

"A very simple raft, the sort some use in hopes that the bodies of their loved ones will not be dragged under by a mugger or an alligator before they reach the sacred waters of the Ganges. Of course, the raft doesn't guarantee safety. Many a raft has been overturned by a hungry mugger. And there are rapids—rocks. The Major is badly hurt, and it's likely that he is only being sent down the river a few hours before his time. But at least his head shall not hang before the palace gate. And no one shall have the pleasure of collecting the reward. Do you still wish to go with him?"

"Yes."

Ala Ram actually smiled at her. "Twenty koss below Allapore there is a bridge, and there you must try to bring the raft to shore. It may be dark when you pass it, but you must be alert and not miss it. Hide him by the river and take the road east. Go two koss to the village and ask someone to point you to the Reverend Wester."

"The Reverend Wester!" she said in wonder.

"He is a dedicated missionary who would not leave Pandeish, even though he is here without the Rajah's permission. Ah, without the Rajah's knowledge. He runs a small mission school, and the villagers would never betray him. If the Major is still alive, he can recuperate there, and if not, he will have burial according to his own religion."

A short time later, Claire found herself wrapped in a linen shroud, side by side with the still-unconscious Colin in an open cart. It was a disguise which in a short time might be no disguise at all, but appropriate apparel. She longed to be able to take his hand at least as the cart jolted along the streets, but she could not, wrapped as she was. She was aware that Ala Ram was not one of the attendants who lashed them to the raft. His presence would have only alerted their pursuers, but she missed him. Already she had come to depend on him, though she had known him for less than two hours.

Colin was bound tightly so that he would not slip off, while she was tied more loosely so that when the time came, she could free herself. The sweet smell of flower garlands draped over them mingled with the stench of the river as they were set into the current. Colin moaned as the cold water splashed onto the flimsy pole raft, and gray terror spiraled behind her closed eyes. Voices of soldiers echoed near the water, checking boats, and someone laughed at the sound of the moan. Claire did not know that it wasn't unusual for a person to be set afloat not quite dead or to be hurried through the streets gasping his last breaths to be cremated at the ghat before noon. The soldiers didn't care about some poor villager sent down the river half dead by an enemy or greedy relatives. The soldiers were interested only in the Sword of Pandeish, and so the pair of them drifted away undisturbed, as Ala Ram had predicted.

They were undisturbed, but not alone on the river. Other rafts were adrift there, carrying white, still companions for her journey. And some merely drifted, winding cloths unfurling to the flood like the chunks of ice that had used to float in Dartmoor's streams in December. Allapore slid away to the gurgles of the swift current, but now and then there were people fishing from the banks or poling small boats. She could hear their voices as the raft slipped past, and she hoped they offered prayers for the souls of the unfortunate sojourners. Each corpse seemed to drift with quiet faith, certain of its sacred destination. But Claire was bound, not for holiness, but only to a bridge, which she might miss in the night. She sought to pray herself and could find no one to pray to. The stuffy God of the church at Cottington Crest seemed ridiculous here. And yet the Eastern idols could not claim her allegiance. She was alone, removed from humanity and God, with only her enormous love to sustain her. She was drifting on the river of death, but she drifted with *him*. And she would sooner have been on the river with Colin Whitecavage than feasting with the Rajah beneath the marriage canopy. Once she saw a party of horsemen galloping along the bank and wondered if they were looking for her. It must be common knowledge by now that the Rajah's bride had been stolen by the Sword of Pandeish. Ah, but it was no more than he deserved, she mused.

The Rajah had stolen her himself from Colonel Todd. And even Colonel Todd, in a way, had stolen her—from the very embrace of William Rutherford. It was all so long ago— Dartmoor, Delhi, Simla, even the exotic nights of the Rainbow Palace. All was reduced to the eternal sigh of the water as it ran forever to the sea.

Once a corpse hung up on a rock, and the raft bumped it as it went past in an eddy. Cold and yielding, it made her shudder, seeming less merely inert than possessed of some eerie antilife. The sun glared on the water as the evening approached. Claire's eyes ached, but she was afraid to close them, afraid she might miss the bridge, afraid that if she closed them, she, too, would be lifeless. She was so cold and exhausted that it would not be hard for her to imagine herself no different from the rest.

And Colin? Once or twice he had groaned, and she had been grateful to know that he was alive. But now he had been silent for a long while. The odds were that he was dead from the wound and exposure. But Claire would not allow herself to think it.

Suddenly one of the other floating bodies seemed to come to life. Claire watched in fascinated horror as it writhed in the water, thinking that the person had regained consciousness after the trip downriver. She must help, she thought, trying to slip out of her wrappings. There was little danger of being seen now, in the heavy dusk, as she unfastened the pole that had been tied to the raft for her use and reached out toward the thrashing bundle. Its arm came free and shot into the air as if grasping for the pole. Then the body went under slowly, the arm visible to the last, as if pleading.

Claire shuddered with a violent chill, her head swimming. A mugger! Were there others? And then ahead of her was the dark shape of the bridge.

New strength swept over her as she poled toward the shore. The current pulled her half a mile farther downstream before she could maneuver the raft into the shallows, and finally she swam behind it in her sari. She felt it touch rocks at the water's edge and dragged herself to the edge of the river, her fingers clutching the roots of a pine overhanging a cut in the bank.

"Reverend Wester. . . ." Her mouth formed the words, but she did not speak them aloud. It was only in a dream that Claire walked back to the bridge and into the village to ask the way to the mission. And while she dreamed, she lay in the mud, her wedding sari lapped by the water, the gardenias in her hair leaving the impression of their petals in the muck. Her spirit willed her to go on, but only in her delirium could she comply, for her energy was totally spent.

16

She saw a face and was certain that it was the face of Jesus. Then the face vanished as a shadow passed between her and it. *I may be dead, but I am not in hell,* thought Claire, vaguely surprised that it should be so.

A tear crept down her cheek. She had tried so hard to keep Colin from harm, to keep him from venturing into Allapore. It did not seem fair to her that she had failed, when she had struggled so hard, when her concern had been not for herself, as in most of her misadventures, but for Colin.

"John, I think she is coming around," said a voice.

"It's not fair," Claire said loudly, and the shadow moved, and she saw that the face of Jesus was only a picture on the wall. She wasn't dead after all! She tried to sit up and fell back dizzily. The shadow beside her moved again, and she felt a cool cloth on her forehead. Looking up, she focused on the kindly features of a middle-aged Englishwoman.

"John!" called the woman. "There dear, you're safe now. You're with your own kind, though one could hardly tell you're English to look at you. And your companion—I would swear he was Indian if he did not rave in English. I'm the Reverend Wester's wife."

"Reverend Wester!"

"Some of our converts found you by the river and brought you here. Whatever are you doing in Pandeish, dear? I haven't seen another Englishwoman since the old Rana died, though seeing you doesn't seem much like seeing another of my kind! Is he your husband?"

"No, he is Major Colin Whitecavage of the Army of Bengal."

"That's what John thought," said Mrs. Wester, seeming to shiver. "And you are the Rajah's intended bride. The soldiers are looking for you."

"I am putting you in danger—you must arrange. . . ." Claire began.

"Nonsense," said a voice from the door. The Reverend Wester stood there, an insignificant-looking man wearing tight black trousers and an alpaca waistcoat. He was bespectacled and balding, and his hair was a length no longer fashionable back home. But something in his manner told her that he was not insignificant at all. She felt comforted, much as she had been by the great bearded presence of Ala Ram. "You aren't putting us in danger. We are quite well hidden—unless, of course, you wish to go back to your wedding."

"No," said Claire, but in the days that followed, she wondered where she *was* going to go. Colin began to recover rapidly from his wound, a circumstance which almost made her sad. When he was able to stand, he went to the balcony of the little house and gazed out over the mountains as if he could will himself to see the Rani Tamila and know that she was well. The house itself was as well concealed as the Reverend Wester had said. It was situated on a little spur of a mountain with thick rows of trees between it and the path into the village. The chiks had been painted green at the front of the house, so it was almost impossible to see it from below. Yet every day, children found their way from the village and sat on mats while Mrs. Wester taught hymn singing and embroidery to the girls and her husband instructed the boys in religion and Latin.

Colin took a dim view of these proceedings, which Claire thought charming. "The Westers are fine people, but they aren't giving these people anything they need, Claire," he would say. "It's a waste."

Claire disagreed, watching through the door as Mrs. Wester cooed to a little girl dandled on her knee. "Why do they come then? There is trust here between East and West. That cannot be bad."

"No, but it will amount to nothing. It's Mrs. Wester's sweets the children come to get."

"Oh!" she said scornfully. But it was true that Mrs. Wester was a fine cook. She made Indian vegetables taste as though they had just been picked from some Yorkshire garden, and somehow her roast mutton, from mountain sheep, was tender. She even managed jam cake that rivaled that from the kitchens of Cottington Crest. Claire, like Colin, ate ravenously and grew stronger day by day. And in time she helped Mrs. Wester in the classroom.

Colin spent endless hours pacing the balcony, and she supposed he wondered what to do with her. Soon he would be well enough to leave, and it was obvious that he was eager to return to the Rani's hideaway, the love nest from which he had been driven to save her from the Rajah's palace.

Was it simply pride that had made it impossible for him to accept the idea of her as the Rani of Rambad? The Rajah might have hoped that the marriage would draw Colin out after all, for the Rajah was very clever. Cleverer than I, Claire thought.

Claire wondered if Colin realized what her relationship with the Rajah had come to, even without the benefit of marriage. She hoped he did not, but she supposed it did not matter. He would go away in either case.

"I wish I had a calling like yours," she sighed to Mrs. Wester one day, helping a small girl untangle her stitches. The mission school reminded her of her wish to teach with Jo at Cawnpore.

"You will find it one day," the older woman said sagely.

"But how? I have no faith, no dedication. Colin once said that I was spoiled and willful and determined to have my own way. And he was quite right."

"My dear, that must have been long ago," laughed Mrs. Wester. "That doesn't describe you at all."

"It doesn't?"

"No. You have had faith all along. You came to India searching for love and would not settle for less. When you found it, you followed it to Pandeish, where no ordinary woman would have; and you tried to sacrifice yourself to it by marrying the Rajah. Can't you see that love is your calling, just as this school is mine? Colin Whitecavage is your calling, Claire."

"Then I have a useless calling. Could I stay here and help you with the school when he leaves?"

Mrs. Wester laughed. "It would be wonderful to have another woman here, but I don't think that you'll stay, Claire."

"I don't know why not. It's the perfect solution."

Reverend Wester approved the idea. The children were delighted, for Claire unbent to play games as Mrs. Wester didn't. Even Colin liked the plan.

"You'll be safe enough here," he said.

"You didn't think I could fill a teacher's calling at Cawnpore," she reminded him.

Colin grimaced. "That was when I was still determined that you would marry Colonel Todd. That was before I knew that you would not marry Colonel Todd. That was before I knew that you couldn't be made to do anything."

"And you have learned that now?"

"Yes. I've learned you are stubborn and completely impossible. You might as well have your way about this. The border will be guarded; it would be difficult to take you back to Simla."

"I would never go! And I would never allow you to escort me there, with a price on your head."

"Tell me, are the stones very large on that string of rubies?" he asked.

"They are monstrous in size!"

"Good," he said with a grin. "I wouldn't want to be hunted over a trifle."

"Oh! How can you joke about it?" she cried, and tears came to her eyes as she remembered the journey downriver with him more dead than alive beside her. "I cannot bear to think that it isn't over—that it could happen again."

Colin made no move to comfort her. Instead, he became thoughtful, heeding her command not to joke. "In the long run it would be less dangerous for you if I took you back to Simla. I ought to insist you return to England."

"There is nothing for me there. I'd become a dried-up old spinster."

That vision struck him as ludicrous, and he laughed again. Again he saw that she wanted to be serious. "You might still marry."

"Someone I did not care about," she said stiffly. "If you wished me to do that, you ought to have let me marry the Rajah."

She saw the look of fury that flashed over his face before he controlled it. "Can't you understand, Claire! You should leave India. There will be a price on all our heads in the long run. Not even the Westers will be excluded."

"You will stay in India," she accused. She noticed that he had never asked her about her relationship with the Rajah—never inquired whether he had made advances or forced her to bed with him. Perhaps he thought that if nothing had happened, she would have told him. Perhaps he thought he already knew the answer.

"I am needed in India," he told her. "India is my life. And I have made a commitment to the Rani and her child."

"Your son," she said, casting her eyes down at the rough rail of the balcony as they stood in the evening breeze. Yellow buntings and reed sparrows flitted among the pines, settling for the night. Mist already filled the valley below, vapors rising above it like steam from a cup.

"My son," he acknowledged, his voice like an echo of the pines.

"What is the commitment you made to the Rani?" she asked.

"To see that Pandeish is returned to its people."

"But you cannot keep such a promise! The Rajah has an army and great wealth."

"There are wealthy nobles in Pandeish as well. And good friends like Ala Ram to help us. We have what the Rajah of Rambad can never have—right on our side. I must try, Claire, and keep trying. Otherwise, I would be turning my back on all those who have already given so much to save Pandeish."

"And your son? Will he rule Pandeish?"

"Yes. It would do him no good to know his true parentage. I will not condemn him to the life of a half-caste, accepted by neither race. He was born a prince and will remain so. If his father's blood mingles with the soil of Pandeish, it will only make Pandeish his all the more."

"You may live in hiding for years," she sighed.

"Yes."

"And there is no reason that I should expect to see you again."

"No."

She did not sleep that night, knowing that he was planning to leave. In the dawn he would ride into the mountains, following his heart to where the Rani awaited him. In the first light of day, she crept out of the house and, passing a pair of mountain sheep laden with his provisions, went to the stream to bathe.

Sitting on a mossy rock she stripped naked, discarding the plain grenadine bodice and skirt that Mrs. Wester had altered for her from her own wardrobe when she had arrived with only her wedding sari to wear. Parakeets twitted as she undressed, and little hill squirrels scurried among the fern and rhododendron. She planned to remain away from the house all morning, for she did not feel brave enough to tell him good-bye. She swam in the swift water until she was chilled, lying sometimes amid the shallow rapids, like a boulder herself, enjoying the frothing of water over her as it ran down the mountain to join the river, which had brought her and Colin to this refuge. Then, standing, her wet hair streaming over her breasts, she waded back to the rock where she had left her clothes. But the unappealing grenadine was gone. And in its place was the sari, laid out neatly with its jeweled veil.

Someone had exchanged her clothes. Someone who must be watching now. Had the Rajah found her? And was this his way of telling her she was his again? She sank into the current to cover herself, feeling eyes fixed upon her with such a passion that her skin flushed. She glanced in the direction from which the powerful gaze seemed to come and saw Colin lounging easily on the slope above her, where he must have been for some time.

So he wanted a final image of her to carry away with him, she thought. Why shouldn't she give it to him? He had seen her naked often enough before. Besides, she was cold.

She stepped boldly onto the rock and, having stood for a moment in shafts of sunlight filtering onto her pale body from between the pines, reached for the sari and wrapped it skillfully and unhurriedly about her.

Seeing she had discovered him, he came down to her, jumping the rocks in his leather sandals. His loose white Indian clothing made his tanned skin seem darker, and the casually-draped kurta and trousers suggested the broad shoulders and narrow hips beneath. She trembled from the need to touch him. She knew that he longed to touch her, too, and thought that if he did she would be lost. If he made love to her now, she would not be able to let him go from her life forever. Anger flared to save her from her unthinkable desire. How dare he come here?

"Where are my clothes?" she demanded. "You know that Mrs. Wester doesn't approve of my dressing native."

"I don't care about Mrs. Wester. The other dress wasn't pretty. I was sick to death of it. I wanted to see you in the sari again. Besides, it is a wedding dress, and I have been thinking about what I said in Cawnpore. That you would never make a teacher—that you could not do without a man."

She lashed out at him furiously and, losing her footing, toppled into the water. He waded in after her, his eyes appreciative of the way the soaking garment clung to her form. "Have you decided to send me back to marry the Rajah after all? Or to Colonel Todd?" she cried. "I won't go!"

"Hush, my dearest. I told you I have learned my lesson. I've learned that you are not a woman who can be put aside and forgotten. You are a woman who is not likely to do as she's told. But just this once you will do as I tell you."

"You are not my master or even my husband, Colin Whitecavage!" she declared stubbornly.

"But I will be," he said, his face close to hers. "I order you to keep the vow you made in Cawnpore and marry me, my darling."

She thought perhaps she was still floating in the river, dreaming in delirium on the raft; and then his lips met hers, heating her cold mouth with reality and bliss.

They were wed a few hours later in a meadow carpeted with blue and yellow flowers. The little schoolgirls danced and sang and the boys played horns and drums. She came to him across the sweet-smelling meadow, seeing him as a misty vision through the haze of her jeweled veil and her tears.

The ring he gave her was fashioned not of precious metals but of plaited grasses, as he ardently pledged himself to her. She whispered her promises into the clear mountain air; and then Reverend Wester, beaming over his Bible and spectacles, declared them one. Colin Whitecavage claimed his prize at once, lifting her veil and pulling her to him, kissing her with such intensity that her wedding bouquet of white asters was crushed to perfume between them. Mrs. Wester was reduced to helpless blushes at the sight of them.

The wedding feast included fluffy Yorkshire puddings to accompany rice and goat chops, and Mrs. Wester outdid herself with pastries filled with strawberry preserves. But before the sun was low, the wedded pair took their leave. Claire hugged and kissed Mrs. Wester, who told her, "Ah, I knew it would turn out like this. Anyone could have seen that he loved you. And what luck! Where else in Pandeish could you have had a Christian wedding?"

The setting sun splashed against the mountains and the sky in lavenders and reds, like a display of fireworks in celebration, and then, in the dusk, he called a halt, putting up a small tent of skins to shelter them for the night. The silent darkness was perhaps the best of all. Inside the little tent he undressed her with a sureness of possession that made her feel truly married, and she knew a wonder in his caresses that caused her to weep with joy. For the first time she gave her love as it should be given—without shame or fear, without guilt or reserve. She could welcome her arousal like the opening bloom of a rose, and all her soul bloomed with it. There was, for the first time, no need to fight against the currents of her passion, no need to be driven to physical need beyond her control.

He seemed to feel the specialness of the night as well, and took his time to prolong it, kissing her breasts as he held them tenderly in his hands, kissing away each tear of joy that she shed, kissing at last reverently between her thighs while she clung to his hair and gasped as her hips plunged shamelessly. And even then she could not believe that he had married her, that she was his wife, and the ecstasy that consumed her was sanctioned by society and by God. In the midst of their union the makeshift ring he had given her slid from her finger and rolled away in the grass. She drove him to desperation by insisting it be found before they continued.

"Claire—it's impossible. We cannot stop. Afterward—I'll look."

"I must have it." She was suddenly almost hysterical, unable to explain to him the necessity for having the symbol of all she had that day gained and must never lose. But somehow he seemed to understand and with enormous willpower removed his hands from her breasts to look for it.

Replacing it on her finger, he sighed with triumph and slid again into the nest of her love, that home now vouchsafed to him forever.

And Claire was certain that she was dying of a magnificent surfeit of love, the ineffable splendor of their fusion almost beyond enduring. She cried out with real fear and pulled back as though from the edge of a cliff. But in body and spirit he was stronger than she, and he guided her skillfully over the brink. Then both lay helpless and panting, stunned by the grandeur of fulfillment, beyond any either had ever known before. Had the Rajah's men found them neither could have offered any resistance and both would have been too drugged with love to care. Their impulsive union on the Egyptian desert, their desperate passion along the Grand Trunk Road, seemed mere harbingers of tonight. They lay together spent, as motionless as they had been in their shrouds on the raft floating on the mugger-infested river. Perhaps the Rajah's soldiers would have thought them dead, and in a way they were—dead to anything but the boundlessness of their love.

She shivered, and he drew the disarrayed rugs about them, wrapping them as one; and past the tent flap, they noticed how close the stars had come. She realized that it had been more than the words of Reverend Wester that had deepened their love. That love had been fueled with the willingness of each to die for the other. It had been fired with ultimate commitment, of which the ceremony in the flower-strewn meadow was but a small part. At last she slept, holding him tightly, afraid to think of the future. In the morning they struck camp and climbed higher into the mountains before she had courage to question him.

"Where are we going, Colin?"

"To the home of a friend of mine. Vazir Lal is a noble of the old Rana's court and a cousin of the Rani Tamila. The castle is a retreat that used to be kept for meditation, perhaps sixty koss from here. But the distance will seem twice as far over this terrain. We'll have to walk most of the way, it will be too steep for the horses."

"I can manage," she said. There was nothing she could not do so long as she was with him. But he seemed not to follow any path, and the rocks hurt her feet through her thin shoes. By midday she was exhausted; and Colin, frustrated by her stumbling and the need to hurry, became cross. "We are not out for a picnic, you know," he burst out as she paused to rest again. "The Rajah may be trailing us even now."

"Oh, Colin, he couldn't find us here!" The forest of deodar and fir seemed so untraveled and remote that she could not believe that anyone else had ever been here. Yet only an hour before they had passed through a village, she walking behind him like a good Indian wife. No one had appeared to question their disguise, but they had occasioned comment simply by being strangers. The wily Rajah had many spies and informants. Perhaps some one of the mission children had whispered of their presence to the wrong ears days ago. But Claire wanted to deny such possibilities and bask in the sweetness of her marriage.

That night when they camped he knew she was too exhausted for love and made up for his earlier brusqueness by making a little stew to serve to her as she lay inside the tent.

Somewhat restored, she dared finally to query, "What about Pandeish, Colin, now that we are married?"

"Pandeish?" He looked at her in surprise. "Nothing has changed. I told you that I had made a commitment to the Rani. Pandeish will be returned to its people."

"You have made other commitments to the Rani perhaps," Claire suggested. "She is the mother of your child."

"You mean that I have betrayed her by marrying you?"

Claire nodded miserably.

"I haven't, my darling. The Rani Tamila could never have been my wife. There is the matter of religion, to begin with. Hindu widows are not allowed to remarry, and in any case, marriage to an unbeliever would mean loss of caste. Worst of all, it would reflect badly on our child, and people might even begin to look askance at his parentage. Instead of a prince, he would become an object of scorn."

"But you still love her?" Claire murmured fearfully.

"It is over between us. I did love her, Claire, and when I loved her I thought I could never love another. I was doomed by love until you rescued me."

"The Rani still loves you," said Claire with certainty.

"Yes, with all her heart. But she lives for Pandeish. In the beginning she had no thought for anything except love. Then I taught her to reach beyond the zenana; I encouraged her to maneuver power from her husband, the old Rana. I am responsible for her dream of a better life for her people, but it is her dream now, a thousand times more than it was mine when I first came to Pandeish. That dream is all that matters between her and me now, that dream for our son. I must help her accomplish it—someday after the Raj has fallen, after the British presence is gone from India, my son and his descendants will still belong, still give leadership to the land. When the time comes at last for India to govern itself, my son and his sons will make a difference."

She listened to his words and wondered how deeply any man could know the core of a woman's heart. "Does the Rani understand these things? Does she accept that you no longer belong to her?"

Colin frowned, for this was a matter he had not wanted to discuss. "I've told Tamila about you, Claire. I explained that I had to kidnap you from the Rainbow Palace."

"What else did you explain?" she demanded, giving him no peace. "Did you explain that you loved me? Or did you merely explain that you felt responsible for me?"

Colin, who had been lying propped on an elbow beside her, rolled onto his back as though to collect his thoughts from among the feathered fir branches. "I did not—it was only when I saw you there in the palace, ready to wed the Rajah, that I knew. And even then I scarcely expected to live myself. It was in that moment when I walked into the spider's web and my life was a string of rubies to anyone who could pluck it, that I realized that it was you who gave it meaning." He moved to kiss her, and she nestled against him, content for the moment with nothing more than knowing he loved her.

"Don't worry, my love. I'll explain the matter to the Rani as soon as we arrive."

Claire sat up, nearly upsetting their little tent. "Do you mean that she will be there?"

"Of course," he said, as though he had thought it obvious. The little castle had become the headquarters and secret stronghold of the patriots of Pandeish. It was quite natural that he would return to Tamila.

Claire, stunned, felt herself a fool. She should have realized it, but she had imagined they were to have a sort of honeymoon. She should have known that Colin would not forget Pandeish even for that. Colin slept, but Claire lay wakeful, her soul churning with jealousy. He had married her, but now he was taking her to his mistress, to the mother of his child!

And the Rani did not even suspect that he would be returning with a wife! Tamila still loved him. Could she be expected to accept the situation? Most likely she would essay to have him in her bed again. And why shouldn't she succeed? Hadn't she had him before, when she had been the wife of the Rana, when the entire army of Pandeish might have been called to prevent it? Could Claire prevent it now, with the force of her love for Colin?

But perhaps the Rani would use a more direct means of retrieving her lover. Claire thought of Jana and shuddered. Perhaps the Rani would arrange for Claire to meet with an accident. After all, the Rani had lived for years in the zenana. She would be familiar with the possibilities.

Claire was quiet as they continued their journey the next day. The weather was bright but chilling, and when they came to a group of shepherds' huts, Colin arranged to buy her a jacket quilted in a Chinese pattern and a pair of fur-lined boots to replace her battered slippers. A pair of loose cotton velvet trousers completed her new outfit. He bought vegetables and goat's milk cheese; and before they moved on, he told the villagers an intricate story about their travels.

He was exasperated to be making the journey, he told them, but it was his wife's fault. She had had a falling out with her mother-in-law and demanded to be returned to her own home for a time, as was her right during the early years of marriage. He had threatened and cajoled and even beaten her; but she had persisted, so he had had to bring her all this way.

The shepherds shook their heads in sympathy at the distance of the place from where Colin said they had come. They gave him advice as the pair went on their way. He should deny her the honor of bedding with him, one suggested. Colin shrugged and confessed that she was very beautiful behind her veil. Then, said the village sage, be sure that she had children soon, for she would gain status with his mother. Everything would improve then, he advised; and the others nodded agreement.

"Bah!" said Colin, and started off. She followed meekly, walking farther behind his heel than their two pack sheep.

A mile or so later they stopped to eat; and Colin, laughing asked her, "Which shall it be, love? Shall I deny you the honor of my bed, or shall I make you pregnant?"

But Claire's sense of humor failed, and she burst into tears. "I am so tired of pretending," she sobbed.

"There, dearest, another day and we shall be at Vazir Lal's. We will not pretend any more. And those people will never think of us, should the Rajah's men come asking questions. Cheer up; it won't be long."

At that moment two little jet-black hill cubs, drawn by the smell of food, rambled out of the woods and stood on their hind legs to look at them. They were so charming that Claire did laugh after all.

But she was hardly relieved that they were approaching their destination. And more than anything the discussion about children had upset her. She had almost managed to forget how eager the Rajah had been for her to bear him an infant. Suppose that in leaving the palace, she had brought with her an unintentional bit of baggage, a legacy of her shameful nights—a part of the Rajah implanted in her own body, a condition which could not be escaped by any amount of fleeing?

Were the truth to come out, she was certain Colin would

blame her for what had happened. Oh, he might believe her when she told him that she had not invited the Rajah to her bed. He might believe that she had fought him. But he would still hold her responsible if he guessed the whole truth. He would never forgive her for having been conquered by his enemy. He would never forgive her for surrendering, ceasing to struggle, even though the struggle had been hopeless.

She had taken Sevaley's advice to submit and make the inevitable easier, and now it did not seem the easier course at all. She would always have to live with the knowledge that she had allowed herself to enjoy the Rajah's exotic caresses. How could she ever dare to tell Colin what had occurred between her and the Rajah in the Rainbow Palace? Surely she would lose his love. But if she did not tell him, she would be living a lie. If she bore the Rajah's child—Claire could not envision what would happen then.

It began to rain during what was to be their last night on the trip. At first they merely seemed enveloped in a cloud, and Colin called an early halt because it was impossible to see the way over the treacherous granite and mica boulders. At first she was pleased with the prospect of a long evening together. It was cozy inside the little tent as they feasted on cheese and chupatties and sweet blackberries she had found, finishing with cups of steaming tea, themselves glowing with satisfaction like the little lantern that illuminated the tent. He made love to her gently, and she allowed herself to be transported. His fingers soothed her like a mountain breeze, and his lips drenched her with love like the gentle rain pattering on the tent. He bided his time this lazy night, lavishing tenderness on every inch of her body. His lips pressed to the small of her back radiated a soft warmth in every direction. She was as lost in the haze of love as the stars were lost in the misty rain.

Then somehow it all began to come apart. The rain became harder, beginning to drip inside from above and blow into the tent from below as gusts of wind tugged at the sides. The temperature dropped, and Claire found herself shaking, not with passion, but with cold. Colin, his more primal male passions unaffected by the worsening weather, was frustrated by her change in mood.

"It's only the storm, dearest; it frightens me," she apologized.

"Think of the storms we have already endured. We can endure anything so long as we have each other."

"Do you promise, Colin?" she murmured.

"With all my heart," he answered, holding her so closely that she began to feel warm again, in spite of the wind and the plunging temperatures. She clung to him as though to a lifeline as she entered her, his desire roaring like an avalanche in his ears. But though she loved him so intensely, she could not find her way to that familiar glory. She felt deserted as he pursued his quest within her, and when he subsided, she wondered if he had noticed that he had been alone.

He slept and she grew colder, although his arms were still about her. She knew that her inconclusive response had been not the result of the rain and wind altogether. She possessed him at last, and now that she did, she was more afraid of losing him than she had ever been before. And she realized that her worst enemy was fear. Fear was more capable of damaging their relationship than the Rani Tamila herself. She crept closer to him, fighting the dread. Yet it grew, howling about her soul like the wind outside, snapping branches from the fire like wolves breaking the bones of prey.

We can endure anything so long as we have each other, he had promised. And she believed it was true. She could endure the Rani's hatred, she could endure whatever privation might occur, so long as they had each other. But they must have each other! Did the marriage vows they had spoken guarantee that they always would?

It was still raining the next morning when they struck their sodden tent and began the last leg of their journey. Their clothing was soaked, and although they came across an overhanging rock where the weather did not reach, the boughs strewn by the storm were too wet to burn to dry or warm anything. There was no use remaining beneath the shelter under the circumstances so they plunged on, and Claire thought that even the pack animals seemed miserable. Before noon she knew that she was feverish, but she kept on, saying nothing to Colin. There was no use in complaining, since they had no choice but to continue. She might have married an English lord, a man of high station in the Raj, or a king. But she had chosen an insurrectionist, a self-made exile who would never give her a life of comfort. Claire was well satisfied with that bargain, for though other men might have given her luxury, none could have given anything like the richness of his love.

She felt dizzy and a burning in her chest warned her of the onset of a pneumonia-like illness. She felt she could go on no longer; and when he halted suddenly, she thought she must have called out to him that she must rest.

"There," he said.

At first she saw nothing through the veil of rain, but he guided her glance until she discerned the castle almost hidden in the trees, its gray color matching the rain in a perfect camouflage. It would be easy to defend the castle if need be, for it stood on a promontory accessible only by a single narrow path. But the place was a trap as well. Should the enemy be overwhelming, there was no means of escape except over the cliffs. The three-story towers seemed to tremble with age. As they came closer to the castle, she saw they were patched here and there with odd brickwork or masonry. In the center was a higher tower above the gateway. A clock tower, she thought, though time itself seemed incongruous here. Before long a bell began to ring, making muted echoes in the rain, and she knew that it was a watchtower instead and that they had been sighted. People began to pour from the gates, and ragged servitors seemed to appear from nooks in the walls as they emerged from various portals. Sheep and goats grazing in front of the castle began to bleat excitely.

Someone inside had a spy glass to ascertain the identity of the travelers, for now Claire was certain that word had been passed that it was Colin Whitecavage who was returning. Wheezing notes from cow horns joined a general cheer and waving of hands from the balconies. Colin Whitecavage had come home, the Sword of Pandeish, who had walked into the hands of his enemy, stolen his bride, and lived to tell of it. Claire strained to see into the mist. *She* was there, somewhere in the crowd. Perhaps she was running out the gate to meet him. Or was the Rani Tamila breathlessly arranging her hair and veils somewhere inside the castle? Or running up a staircase to have a better view of his arrival?

No, the Rani would not be able to run out the gate. She could not give herself away by the expression of ecstasy which no doubt would shine through her veils. She would have to content herself with granting him an audience. And so Claire's gaze went to the upper reaches of the castle, where at last she glimpsed a scarlet veil, whipping like a flag of welcome. Its wearer stood all alone, seeming riveted on the scene below. Colin, too, looked up, searching, and Claire thought that he seemed to fix his gaze on the scarlet veil.

They passed through the gateway, half closed by a massive, iron-clamped gate, into a court paved with rough stone and surrounded by buildings with carved verandas and latticed balconies protected by carved eaves.

Water gurgled down dragon-mouthed tin rain spouts, emerging into noisy waterfalls. She had just time to imagine in her dazed state that the dragons were clambering down over the roofs to attack her, and then she fainted.

17

A shadow moved above her, and Claire tried to sit up, an effort that caused the shadow to vanish and stars to appear before her eyes against an infinite sheet of black. An immense pounding shuddered through her, coming from her head or her heart or both. Once before recently, Claire had ended a journey in such a manner, and now she imagined that she was back at the mission after floating downriver from Allapore.

"Is Major Whitecavage alive?" Her lips struggled to form the words.

A reply came in Hindustani—a query. Whoever was in the room wasn't Mrs. Wester. Claire moved her head and beheld the most beautiful woman she had ever seen. Her face was unmistakably regal, its features rich with nuance that no sculptor could have created. The proud tilt of chin; the soft texture of mouth—belying its strong set; the exquisite curve of cheekbones; the blending of tones of spice; the long ivory earrings overshadowing her small ears, mixed with breathtaking effect. Her sari of old rose kincob complemented the shadings of her skin as though it had been painted there. The veil was darker—scarlet—with amber gems sewn into its fringes. It was she, the woman Claire had seen watching their arrival.

"My name is Tamila," she said, this time in English, as though she understood a little, but not too much of the language.

"You are the Rani." This time Claire used Hindustani, and

saw a flicker of surprise in the polished orbs that regarded her.

"And you are Colin's wife."

The fact was stated flatly, as though she were still trying to assimilate it. Emotion quivered about the edges of what seemed immense control. Whatever she felt, the Rani was not going to give way. Claire could not guess in what proportion grief and hatred mixed behind her calm veneer, which lay like a shining varnish over her mahogany beauty. Raindrops slapped the mullioned window in the silence, lying between them tangibly, as material as the Tabriz carpet. A fire burned in the stone fireplace, its persistent snapping announcing that it was pine logs that flamed so brightly but with so little heat. Against the glow Tamila seemed carved, her awesome royal pride overriding the pain and betrayal that must lie within. No wonder Colin had loved her!

In spite of her fever and exhaustion, Claire perceived that the Rani was the true sufferer in this room, and she tried to think of some way to express her compassion. It was no use to say she was sorry, she thought. That was untrue. She wasn't sorry that she had married Colin, no matter what the consequences to another woman. Her love had left no room for such considerations.

"I could not help. . . ." That was better, but her mind was fuzzy, and she could not think of how to finish. The effort made the Rani Tamila seem to undulate in waves before her.

"I have brought you some medicine. Drink this; it will break the fever." The Rani's voice was melodious, but again devoid of expression.

Claire felt a cup pressed firmly against her lips. She did not intend to drink and tried to turn her head, but somehow the bitter liquid was between her lips, and she swallowed large gulps. Almost immediately she began to feel sleepy and fought to cling to consciousness. The Rani must have poisoned her, she thought, struggling helplessly as a grainy darkness enveloped her. How Jana would laugh, back in the zenana of the Rainbow Palace!

Where is Colin? she tried to say, but her mouth refused to form the words.

Much later she awoke and heard laughter, but it was the laughter of children in the courtyard, not the dangerous Jana. Sunlight filled the room, and Colin sat beside her, watching her anxiously. "Good morning, my darling. Are you better now? It was brave of you to walk so far. You must stay in bed and rest today, and the servants will take care of you. We are as safe now as it is possible to be in Pandeish. There are troops here who will fight to the death against the Rajah."

Claire did not feel better, and the idea of a battle unnerved her. It had seemed that in the remote hill castle, one might escape the omnipresent threat of violence that had pervaded all her days in India. But he had warned her, even in England, that India was not a peaceful country.

"The Rani. . . ." Claire murmured. She thought that she might have dreamed the proud Queen with her untelling gaze.

"She offered to look after you when we arrived," he said, and his eyes turned secretive, as unreadable as Tamila's, and she wondered what had passed between them when he had arrived with his wife.

"It was kind of her," said Claire.

"She did not wish you a kindness, Claire. It was a duty, a duty that most would have avoided. It is important that you understand these things."

"Yes, Colin," she said, feeling too weak to pursue the subject. "I am still ill," she confessed with a moan.

He rested his hand on her forehead and informed her that her fever had gone. "You're only tired, love. You will be more recovered when I return tonight."

"Tonight! Where are you going?"

He laughed. "I've an army to raise and plans to make, as you well know. And the sooner it is all done, the sooner you and I can begin to make a life together."

She could not argue with that statement, although she longed to. For the moment, she did not want to think of the future, she only wanted him to spend the hours beside her where she could bask in the knowledge that he was hers.

And not the Rani Tamila's. Yes, that was the heart of it. She was afraid that if he were not with her, he would be with the Rani. And her fears seemed confirmed when, some moments after he had departed, she crept out of bed to the window and saw him in the courtyard below. A woman and child were with him, the woman seated with her back to Claire on a stone bench beside a fountain. Colin was lifting the baby into the air and making it crow and laugh. The artless baby sounds drifted to Claire's ears, endowing the scene with the sort of innocence that she had long forgotten. Colin's face mixed pride and wonder as he played with his son. How could anyone fail to see that they were a family?

Quite forgetting that she herself was his wife, Claire envied the Rani the joy of belonging in that little group. Then the woman turned as she held out her arms to take the princeling, and Claire saw that it wasn't the Rani at all, but a servant, an elderly ayah.

Through the morning and afternoon she dozed, waking only to drink herb teas brought to her by salaaming servants and to bathe her aching body in a tub of steaming water. In the evening he returned to have dinner with her alone in a small dining room in their quarters. She did not find it surprising that they ate alone, since most Hindus would not eat with casteless persons, but she was grateful that there could be no question but that the Rani would remain modestly in her own rooms.

The days fell into a simple pattern. Colin was constantly busy, and on many occasions traveled into valleys below with the Rani to enlist the aid of small chieftans in regaining control of Pandeish. Often the distance was such that they did not return at night, and at these times Claire would be beside herself with jealousy. She would venture to the balcony where Tamila had watched that day and watch herself to see if they were arriving. When darkness fell, she would weep and beat her bed pillow angrily, pummeling the spot where his head should have been. If the Rani wished an opportunity to have Colin love her again, she could not do better. And Claire was certain that Tamila wished it. When the Rani gazed at Colin, her eyes told the secrets they did not share when looking at Claire. As for the Prince, there was an advantage that Claire did not have, and the baby was so adorable that she could not help loving him herself. Colin's serious eyebrows were incongruously delightful on the tiny face, and the infant had a merry disposition that made Claire seek him out and appropriate him from his protective and disapproving ayah.

For a time the child was her only relief to loneliness, but one morning an elegant Indian presented himself at her door. "I am Vazir Lal, Memsahib, your host. Your husband has asked that I take you riding. He thinks you have not had enough fresh air since arriving, and he thinks it would be beneficial to your health."

Claire had no wish to ride, although it had always been a favorite activity of hers. A queer lassitude had come over her in the mountain castle. She seemed scarcely to have strength to rise from her bed in the morning. A cough from the respiratory ailment that had overcome her on the journey lingered, and her eyes seemed too large in her wan face. Her appetite had never returned, and Colin, undressing her on his return from his excursions, would notice each time that she seemed thinner as he held her in the darkness.

"I am too tired to go riding," she told Vazir Lal.

But Vazir was not to be dissuaded. "Come now, it must be done," he said, his moustache turning above his silken beard as he favored her with a charming smile. "It is an order from the Major, whom I acknowledge as my commanding officer, and surely even the *Angrezi* expect their wives to obey them."

His manner was forceful, but it was the smile that undid her. She was starved for companionship, and soon they were galloping about a mountain meadow on a pair of sturdy ponies of a breed which Vazir Lal told her had been brought to the castle especially because they could manage the rugged terrain. "This is no place for a fine horse, but these are splendid in their own way," he said, slapping his mount's solid flank as they dismounted. He spread a rug in the sun and brought out red Kashmirian apples and green Kabul grapes. These he had brought for her consumption alone, and he presented them with a gentleness of manner that made her trust him. Away from the castle she felt a small surge of appetite, for she was not convinced that the almost constant queasiness of her stomach wasn't the result of slow poisoning by the Rani's servants. Although she did not believe that the draught the Rani had given her had harmed her, she had not discarded the idea that Tamila might be trying to destroy her. It would be natural, and never in her life had Claire felt so unwell.

Vazir Lal was a comfort, lolling informally on the rug with one sandaled, beringed foot resting on the bent knee of the other leg. His friendly blue eyes held none of the secretiveness that she had seen in so many dark ones, none of the frightening intensity of Colin's. The jewels in his turban and the material of his long Persian coat marked him for nobility. He might almost have been the counterpart of one of her London swains, she thought, with his unusual informal manner and his lavish dress.

But he was different after all. His body was too well honed and seemed too poised to spring into action, even as he lay relaxed. Once, when his eyes caught her, a haunted look flickered. He was a cousin of Tamila's, he told her, and as

children they had ridden and played in this very meadow together before she had been taken away to marry the Rana at
the age of eight.

"So young!" cried Claire.

"Yes. But that was only for the wedding, you see. Then the
Rani returned home, and everything seemed as before. But it
wasn't, of course. We both knew that the time would come
for the marriage to be consumated. It happened when she
was twelve, and I was fifteen. She was taken again to the
Rainbow Palace, and I thought I might never see her again.
We were, you understand, the best of friends. She had no
brothers or sisters, and I was an orphan in my uncle's keeping. Then, in a year or so, my uncle died, and along with his
other lands and houses, I inherited this summer place, where
we had been so happy. So you see, it was natural that the
Rani would flee here when the Rajah overcame her forces,
and natural, too, that I would know without having to receive
a message. When the Rani disappeared, I brought my men
here to await her. It is a great privilege to protect her and to
provide headquarters for the brave Sword of Pandeish, beside
whom I have fought."

"And you and your cousin are together again."

"Yes." But Vazir spoke with a sigh that seemed to mean
that things still were not the same.

Claire smiled, intuiting that Vazir and Tamila had been
childhood sweethearts and that Vazir had not ceased loving
her. Indeed, it must be unusual for two who were not brother
and sister to know each other so well, and she wondered that
Vazir's uncle had not anticipated the problem.

Vazir's emotions must be similar to her own when Tamila
was gone from the castle in Colin's company. It was obvious
that he missed her and wished that he had been able to accompany the expeditions. But he would shrug and say
philosophically that the castle was his to defend and that the
Major expected it of him. Each one bereft, they made good
companions for each other, though neither spoke of this
bond. But in one important respect their feelings were different. It had never occurred to Vazir to be jealous of Colin. It
was laughable to Claire that he should be so completely
blind. In his mind, Tamila's changed attitude toward him had
nothing to do with Colin Whitecavage. She knew it for a fact,
because when she had come to know Vazir better, she ques-
tioned him about his relationship with the Rani.

"Certainly I have loved her since I was a young boy," he admitted.

"And she loved you."

"Yes. But it was hopeless from the beginning. I was a mere child and could not have competed with the Rana for her hand."

"You are not a child now, Vazir. Why don't you marry the Rani?"

He gave her a shocked look. "Why, because, Major Memsahib, the Rani has been married. Hindu women do not remarry."

"Oh, but that is a ridiculous waste. The Rani is young—and quite beautiful. I am sure that she does not grieve for the Rana. Surely she did not love a debauched old man who stole her from her childhood."

For a moment Vazir's blue eyes darkened, and Claire thought she had gone too far in wishing for an ending that would be happy for everyone. Then Vazir's good humor returned, and he laughed, to her relief. "An *Angrezi* would never understand. A Hindu woman's husband is her god, and he requires worship, but not necessarily love. I am sure that the Rani devoted herself to the Rana as she ought, and perhaps she might even have died suttee had she not been carrying the Rana's son. Even now it is a measure of her dedication to the Rana that she is determined to place the Prince on the throne. The Rani Tamila has changed toward me, but it is to be expected. She had put away youthful foolishness and thinks of her duty to her son. We must never speak of this again, Major Memsahib."

And they did not. But Claire knew that it was not the Rana who had changed Tamila's feelings about her cousin. But what would be the consequences if Vazir Lal discovered the truth? Just how deep did his love of the Rani go? Would he be a party to placing a half-caste on the throne of Pandeish for her sake? Or would he perhaps choose violent retribution against the child's father? Claire was reminded of how precarious the Rani's position was. No one must discover the truth, and for this reason only, she thought, the Rani never displayed the slightest familiarity to Colin in public. When, on rare occasions, Claire saw them together, she could never fault the Rani's cool gaze or Colin's formal bow. It occurred to her that her own presence lessened the chances of suspicion falling upon them. Surely no one would suspect a liaison between him and the Rani after he had stolen the Rajah's bride to wed! No one would suspect—except herself.

She continued to feel ill and out of sorts, and gradually she became less loving. When he came to her, instead of greeting him with kisses, she began to berate him about his long absences.

"Claire, you know it is necessary," he would say. "The army must be raised before spring. Before long the snow will protect us, but in the spring, we cannot count on being safe anymore."

"Armies! I am sick of hearing about armies! You cannot possibly defeat the Rajah. He has all the advantage, and he has already beaten you once!"

"Perhaps you don't want to see him defeated!" It was as close as he came to accusing her of her affair in Allapore, but his eyes had a dangerous look.

"I don't see why you should attempt the impossible and perhaps be killed. I don't see why we don't escape over the border with the Rani and the Prince."

"The border is well guarded, but even if it were not, I wouldn't go. I have explained it all to you before."

"I am sick of being alone!"

"There is Vazir. I have told him to look out for you."

"Vazir is not my husband. But perhaps *you* are not alone when you are gone in the same way that I am alone!"

And this was as close as *she* came to accusing him of continuing his relationship with the Rani. But he knew, and sometimes he exploded in anger, throwing her onto the string bed and taking her with exhilarating roughness. Other times he reacted with disdain, stalking away with some comment about ruing the day he had ever seen Cottington Crest, and leaving her alone as before.

At last she dared to speak to him about her stomach complaint and her fears that she was being poisoned. He was more furious than she had ever seen him, his faith in the innocence of the Rani as stalwart as Vazir's. Claire resented the Rani even more after that. She was a woman who pulled blinders over men's eyes—even the old Rana had trusted her, and Claire had learned that her word might be worthless against that of the Rani. What was she to do? For the time being she continued to drink only water she drew herself from the well, and to leave untouched curries in which other substances might easily be mixed with the seasonings.

As for Colin, his worry over her made his manner more

truculent. She was still coughing, and soon the weather would turn bitterly cold. How would she manage that? He was much afraid she would die. He remembered the things he had told her about India being too hard for a woman and wished she had not moved him so with her fervor to go. In his blackest moments he sometimes wished he had not directed William Rutherford to the summerhouse instead of to Claire's father. He had thought to know paradise when he had married, had thought everything would become simple between them. And it had not! He knew that she must have bedded the Rajah, but he wanted to think that it had been by force. He wanted revenge along with the crown of Pandeish for his son, and it did not sit well when she told him it was impossible. Sometimes he wished she were more like the Rani, who, in her Indian way, did not presume to tell him what was possible and impossible to do. He was saddled, he thought, with a wife who had no confidence in him.

One day when snow flurries whipped about the castle, a messenger came from the silk merchant at Allapore advising him that the Rajah had learned the location of his stronghold. Ala Ram predicted that the Rajah would march on him as soon as spring weather allowed. The bearer of the news settled into the castle barracks, fearful of being caught in a blizzard should he attempt to return. Colin studied the letter soberly and made a reluctant decision.

He had been negotiating for weapons to be imported across the mountains from Kashmir, gambling that their arrival in early spring would be time enough. But now he could not wait. He would have to take a caravan from his garrison across the Snowy Range to collect them. And that was another sort of gamble. If the weather held, he might make the journey in two or three weeks. But if it did not—if the full force of winter caught him at altitudes even higher than that of the castle—he might be delayed indefinitely. He might be forced to bivouac along the way to save men and vital pack animals to carry guns and ammunition. If he did not return in time, the Rajah would almost certainly overpower the ill-defended garrison.

He held a worried conference with Vazir Lal, who was the ranking Indian officer and Colin's trusted friend. "One of us must go and one stay here," he said.

"I will gladly lead the expedition," said Vazir. "I have known these hills since I was a child."

Colin thought it over, and then, shaking his head, declared,

"No. I must be the one, Vazir Lal. It is I who can give the best assurances that the Raj will honor the debt incurred for the weapons."

"As you wish," said Vazir Lal, "but you will leave a wife here. Is it not your responsibility as well to stay and defend her from the Rajah's attack?"

"Yes. But I might behave foolishly because of her if the castle were besieged. You will have the cooler head, Vazir."

Vazir Lal salaamed and said nothing of his cousin, toward whom he had feelings akin to Colin's for his wife. And so the matter was settled. For two days the garrison was a frenzy of activity as preparations were made for the departure. Colin said nothing to Claire about his intent to lead the expedition, but she knew it from the intensity of his lovemaking. He touched her as though memorizing each inch of her body—lifting her breasts and caressing them as though to remember their soft eagerness, savoring her warm lips as though to imprint them on his own, reaching between her thighs as though to collect treasures of love to take with him. Claire responded helplessly, her body wracked with dry sobs as well as the tremors of arousal.

But when it was over, she regained herself and lay away from him coldly, not allowing him the sweetness of the aftermath. He knew what was wrong without her telling him.

"Claire, my darling, it is what I must do," he said.

"For the Rani!" she said bitterly. "Whatever you do is always for her! Nothing is for me!"

"No, love. It is only in small part for the Rani. She does not care so much to be a queen. It would be easier for her to escape Pandeish and lead a peaceful life in some other part of India. It's because of the Prince that she will not leave. It is for him and for India that I am going to Kashmir. Ah, Claire, I thought you understood these things. I did not expect such pettiness!"

"Pettiness! To want my husband beside me! And what if you don't return in time, and we are attacked by the Rajah? You know this place cannot withstand a siege. We shall be cut off with no means of supplies or escape!"

He held her limp hand in the darkness, lying on his back and gazing into high-ceilinged blackness. "Surrender yourself at once, in that case."

"Surrender myself! You know what that would mean!" she hissed. "Do you really think—can you imagine. . . ."

"It would only be the last resort, and you are a resourceful woman, my love. Before I go I will give you a revolver and teach you how to use it. Use it on the Rajah if need be. Chances are he will leave you alone if you but threaten him with it. He would not dare order the execution of an English-woman, and if the Raj orders your release, he will not risk facing a new offense over you. Others here will face graver danger."

"The Rani," she guessed.

"She would be executed with our child."

Claire crawled shivering into his arms. "You are right, Colin," she said. "I was petty."

"Oh, my love," he whispered, stroking her hair.

In the morning he showed her how to use the gun, his arms about her as he steadied her hand. She fired with tears in her eyes, and the bursts of gunfire seemed explosions of the pent-up emotions inside her.

She went to the balcony to watch him out of sight and found that she was not alone. The surprise in her eyes was matched by that of the Rani Tamila. Neither had given any thought to the idea that the other would want to watch until the very last sight of him, but now they stood numbly to-gether, bound by their misery. Just before Colin Whitecavage vanished beyond the next ridge, he lifted his hand in farewell, and as he did so, the Rani, with a gasp, placed her own graceful, ringed hand over Claire's as though for comfort. Neither could be certain for whom that last salute had been intended.

18

With Colin's departure, Claire found a new friend in the castle, and that friend was the Rani herself. The love of one man, which had so long separated them, came to unite them in their fears for his safety. At first their relationship amounted to no more than knowing glances, the exchange of a few words.

"There is sun on the mountains today."

"Yes. Thank God for it."

They began to converse in a trickle, using bits of English and bits of Hindustani. But before long the trickle became a torrent, and they spent endless hours in each other's company. For the Rani, her friendship with Claire was a vast relief, for she had never been able to talk to anyone about her love for Colin. But Claire knew the truth already; there was no reason to hide it. Beyond that, Claire understood as only a woman who had loved him could understand. Claire herself had not had a confidant since Jo. Sevaley had been too young, and Abigail, who had been her chaperone in Simla, had been too unimaginative.

The Rani was neither of these. She was no older than Claire, but though she had not been formally educated, her mind was quick. Colin had awakened her considerable intellect along with her desire, and she was eager to have Claire tell her stories of history which she could not read. The Rani would teach her son to look beyond the boundaries of Pandeish, Claire thought.

"I suppose I might have become a suttee, if I had not been pregnant," she told Claire, echoing the thoughts of Vazir Lal.

"I could not have lived the live of a widow, with no chance of love, after what I have known. But the child makes the difference. He is all my reason for living. He will be a great king, and his father and all Pandeish will be proud of him."

The Rani dandled the baby, Daruska, seeming to speak as much to the child as to Claire. It was a habit of hers to talk intently to the baby, who reflected her adoration with a patter of unintelligible sounds and a smile.

Claire wondered if it could really be true that Tamila had resigned herself to never knowing a man's loving touch again. Tamila believed that she had, of that Claire was convinced. And she was convinced that Tamila had not tried to seduce Colin since his marriage, but could she always be so forebearing, loving him as she did? Claire was in awe of Tamila's strength of will. She herself could never have managed as well. Indeed, she had proved she could not. But Claire had not had a child of Colin's whose life and future were at stake.

"How could you bear to have Colin bring me here?"

The beautiful Rani laughed. "Oh, it wasn't easy, I assure you. I imagined that you would be silly and affected and complain about everything like most of the Englishwomen I have seen. I hated his bringing you here. Even though I could not have him myself, I didn't want to see another woman possess him. And when I learned he had married you, I wept. It was foolish. I knew that it was inevitable that he would marry a woman of his own kind one day."

"I could not have stood it," Claire admitted.

"No. But Indian women aren't used to owning men as Englishwomen do. My husband, you know, had three other wives, all much older than I, and they died on the pyre with him. Each of them had had to accept the others at some time, and all of them had to accept me. So, in a way, it's easier for me."

Claire had given up the notion that the Rani was poisoning her, but now it was necessary to look for some other explanation of her dizziness and general lassitude. And the only explanation was the one she had been avoiding. The Rani herself suggested it, and having asked a question or two, declared, "It's true, Claire. It can be nothing else. You're going to be a mother!"

Claire reacted with disbelief. Her illness and the strains of the past weeks had pushed her fear of pregnancy from her mind. The Rajah of Rambad seemed so far away that it seemed that the consequences of those nights in the Rainbow Palace could not reach her. And yet she realized the real possibility that they had. Surely it had not been long enough for her to be certain that she had conceived Colin's child instead of the Rajah's! The same lack of knowledge that had kept Claire in ignorance of her pregnancy prevented her from telling whose baby she carried. Claire was confused and afraid, and during moments when she remembered the force of the Rajah's lovemaking, she was wracked with guilt and felt certain that the child was his. She could not have prevented his taking her, but if she had fought harder, might it have made a difference? If she had never responded to him, would his ardor have cooled before it had happened? She had not been able to control her reactions any more than she had been able to lock her body against him, and the accusations she made against herself were, for the most part, unfair. But she made them anyway, berating herself for being as addicted to the sensations of the body as another might be to opium.

Each day the weather grew colder as they began to watch for Colin's return. And each day that no sign of the caravan appeared, the atmosphere in the castle became more tense. Vazir Lal increased his efforts to add to the garrison's munitions, purchasing every rusty old flintlock that could be had from the peasants in the surrounding countryside and giving orders that all hunting would be done with bow and arrow or with traps to save ammunition.

But as the ragged supply of weapons grew larger, the number of soldiers grew smaller, as the recruits, sensing disaster, began to slip over the walls in the night to seek safer refuge. Those who were left were a rugged lot, each a bear of a hill fighter, veterans of earlier conflicts with the Rajah. They remained out of disdain for the Rajah and love of Pendeish. They could be more deadly with a tulwar than other men with rifles, Vazir said. But would they be enough?

There was some discussion of abandoning the castle altogether. Claire herself urged Vazir to do it. "The Rani and the baby will be killed if they are captured. Can't we hide somewhere else until we are ready to fight?"

Vazir shook his head. "There is nowhere else. We have run as far as we can. If we disperse the army, we will never be able to gather it again. It will mean the end of our hopes for regaining Pandeish. The Major may come yet; until the last day that it is possible to travel, we cannot give him up. And then we will be snowed in. It will be too late to leave."

"But the Rani. . . ."

"It would not be easy to find a place where she would be safe."

Tamila herself put an end to this line of thought. "Prince Daruska and I will stay here and show our confidence that the troops can defend us," she said. "I cannot ask others to place their lives in jeopardy if I am afraid to offer mine and my son's also."

She began to walk among the men, letting them see her and Daruska, talking to each of them. Such behavior was completely out of character for an Indian woman of her standing, but it was obvious that the rough men were charmed by her and touched by her determination to stay in the castle. And Claire saw them vie for the privilege of lifting the baby Rana to perch on the stained shoulders of their sheepskin jackets. Tamila inspired the men more than in the days when she had been a mysterious figure behind fretwork or chiks, and she began to assume a position of leadership that was unusual for a woman in any society.

Claire watched in admiration. The longer she knew Tamila the less she blamed Colin for having loved her.

And then the snows came. The livestock was herded inside the castle walls to prevent its straying in the storm, and it seemed that night came several hours early that day. The snow fell as though hurled, and the wind whipped it into grotesque sculptures, sending plumes flying, like columns of smoke, in whirlwind spirals. Tamila came to Claire's apartment that evening, and they wept together.

"Perhaps he will still get through," Claire comforted.

Tamila nodded. It suited their mutual idea of Colin that he would appear in the morning, struggling through the enormous drifts with his men and arsenal of munitions. But when the clouds finally cleared, there was only the brilliant sun and the empty white snow. In a day or so it snowed again, and they were certain that the high passes were closed. The second time the Rani did not shed tears.

Christmas came again and made Claire long for Cottington Crest. Nobody celebrated, of course, since she was among "heathens." She wondered what explanation Colonel Todd had given her father of their failure to marry and whether her father had disowned her. She wondered, too, if her child would be born before the Rajah attacked the castle. Her figure had begun to thicken, and her appetite had returned. Her health had much improved, and she had felt her infant's first astounding kick.

But Claire was cold in the drafty castle, and the coldness could not be relieved even by standing close to the fire. How would she know if the child were Colin's or the Rajah's, she wondered. If it were very dark, it would be the Rajah's. But if it were light-skinned, that would not be conclusive. Dark hair and eyes on both men. How was she to know? She found herself studying little Daruska. *He* was Colin's son, but she would not have known it if she had not been told. The eyebrows, she had noticed before, were kin to Colin's. When the child's face screwed up in anger, she was reminded of his father. But the rest of his features were too pudgy. He looked like his mother or no one at all, and in the Prince's case, it was a blessing.

How will I know? she wondered. Perhaps she would not be able to tell—ever. And the idea haunted her in nightmares. If it were the Rajah's child, what would she do? Would she love it? And if she did not know, how would she feel then? She caught a chill in February and thought for a time that the matter would be settled for her. What wonder, after all, if she did not survive the winter, with her thin English blood? Her illness was almost a relief to her, but then it was over.

The first mild day was a balm to Claire's chilled body. But in spite of the warm sunshine, something deep inside her did not thaw, but froze even more solidly. The dripping of melting ice from the eaves wracked her nerves, and more than once, she panicked at the rumble of snow sliding off roofs, thinking it was the discharge of cannon. There was still the chance that Colin would reach the castle first, but it was a poor chance, since the lower slopes, which the Rajah would transverse, would warm first. An awful tension was felt everywhere within the castle as the men prepared to fight.

At last the lookouts spotted an army moving among the fir trees. Not Colin's army from that direction, but as it came into view, a stupendous army. More than a thousand soldiers against the several hundred inside the castle, dozens and dozens of elephants, many mounted with one or more cannon, others carrying howdahs designed to give cover to six or seven archers. Through a spy glass Claire saw the Rajah himself, looking smug on a magnificently caparisoned beast. Beside her, Vazir Lal wore an expression as grim as the Rajah's was smug. She did not need to ask if he believed they could hold the castle. Flags waving and horns blowing, the

Rajah rode onto the narrow stretch of land that led to the castle and, halting his elephant just out of range of the castle's guns, signaled that he wanted to talk. Vazir Lal, mounted on a black horse with a saddle inlaid with gold, rode out to meet him. At the end of the conference, Vazir shot an arrow before the Rajah's elephant, and the Rajah aimed an arrow in front of Vazir's steed, in the salute of adversaries before battle.

Returning, Vazir ordered the gates barricaded behind him, and shouted orders to his men. Then he sought out Claire, who was waiting with Tamila. "The Rajah demanded our surrender," he informed them.

"You have refused?" said Tamila.

"Yes. He would not guarantee your life and Daruska's." Vazir turned to Claire. "The Rajah wishes you to leave the castle. He will allow me to escort you to his lines and return. Go and make ready."

"I am not going," said Claire.

"Not going! But your husband would wish it! Those of us who are left will probably be annihilated."

"But our men are fierce fighters and may hold the castle until the Major arrives," Claire said. "I will remain to show faith in my husband, just as the Rani remains to show faith in her defenders. How would it seem if the wife of the Sword of Pandeish went running to join his enemy? And I hate the Rajah! I will never surrender to him!"

"But your child, Claire," cried Tamila.

"I will put my baby's life on the line, as you have put Daruska's."

No one could persuade her to save herself, and when the Rajah advanced on the castle, she was still within its walls. The sound of cannon reverberated everywhere, and shook plaster loose from the ceiling of her bedchamber. Tamila's baby cried ceaselessly. They took turns trying to comfort it, staring at each other with terrified eyes. Tamila and the child faced death if captured. For Claire, her fate was less certain. But the Rajah would have her in his thrall again, and when she thought back on the nights she had spent in his arms, she preferred death to a life on such degradation again. Obviously the Rajah wished her alive, but when his soldiers stormed the walls, she might easily be killed in their frenzy, and her death might be horrible.

The defenders had one major advantage—that the narrow approach prevented the Rajah from unleashing his entire force in a single, massive assault. Since the men could only cross ten or so abreast and only one elephant at a time, the castle archers had opportunity to do their work, and often the passageway became a bottleneck, jammed with the bodies of the dead and wounded.

It was the elephants that gave the most trouble, for they were the Rajah's most powerful weapon. When an elephant entered the passage, the entire garrison loosed arrows—not at its complement of soldiers, but at the animal itself. Claire complained that it was inhumane, and the terrified trumpeting of the injured animals sickened her.

"It is necessary," Vazir hissed impatiently. And it was. One elephant could wreak more havoc than a hundred soldiers with its cannon; the animal itself was almost impossible to kill and if the soldier riding it were eliminated, another ran to fill his place. The trick was to frighten the elephant so badly that it turned in its tracks and bolted through the ranks, breaking formations and scattering and trampling the Rajah's own men.

One dead elephant would effectively constrict the passage, but arrows and rifle balls seemed to bounce off the tough, horny skin. And even hurled charges of explosives were ineffective. Slowly, day by day, the Rajah's General maneuvered the elephants into position outside the castle, and the walls were riddled with cannon shot.

Still the rebels fought on, and Claire thought they would fight until the crumbling fort was leveled about them. Behind the line of fire, the Rajah could sometimes be seen pacing impatiently. Each day, each hour that the defenders held out made it more likely that Major Whitecavage would arrive, and the Rajah was much aware of it.

"He will come," said Tamila, as chunks of the castle were blown away.

"Yes," said Claire, trying not to hear the wailing of the women whose husbands had already died, for whom help, if it came, was already too late.

They had been under siege several days when the Rajah again rode out to request a conference with Vazir Lal. When Vazir returned he came to his cousin Tamila, gazing at her with infinite pain in his eyes. "The Rajah has offered to let the women and children go free if we surrender. He does not include you and the baby, of course."

Tamila had begun to tremble violently. "What will you do, Vazir? Can we fight no longer?"

"We have lost more than half our men, and the rest are exhausted. In a few hours we will be overrun. But the men do not wish to surrender. We will go on fighting until. . . ." Vazir's voice broke. "My dear Tamila, they shall never have you. I swear it. I shall kill you and Daruska myself. They shall not be allowed to profane you."

Tamila crept into Vazir's arms, half staggering. She seemed on the verge of a swoon, but controlling herself, she murmured with royal dignity, "Dear Vazir! Who would have thought of this when we played together as children? It is great favor you do me; death will be less frightening at your hand. You must promise to burn our bodies at once so that they may not be displayed."

Outside, the gunfire had begun again, but Vazir did not leave to direct the fighting. Instead, he sank to the floor with the Rani, holding her tightly against him as the two of them wept. Claire, unable to bear the scene, rushed outside, oblivious that she was now on an open balcony and shot was whistling about her. But suddenly the firing ceased. A shout went up. "The Rani! The Rani!"

For a moment Claire did not realize that it was she they meant. But none of the Rajah's troops had ever seen the Rani, and the mistake was natural. She was wearing clothing Tamila had given her, a flowing kurta and silken trousers and a veiled headpiece, which she affected to hide her frightened eyes from those about her. No other woman in the castle would be dressed so splendidly, and the sight of her standing there so brazenly, like a flushed rabbit, had stunned them.

Claire rushed back inside. "Get up, Vazir Lal! I have an idea that may save the Rani!"

He looked at her dumbfounded, and she went on, "Surrender the fort on the Rajah's terms. We will send the Rani and Daruska to safety with the other women."

Vazir shook his head wonderingly. "That cannot be done, Memsahib. They will be watching for that, and even in rags one would know that Tamila is the Rani."

"They will not be watching. Everyone thinks that I am she, and I will stand on the balcony while Tamila leaves."

An expression of desperate hope began in Vazir's eyes. "But Daruska?"

Claire thought wildly. "A girl. Find a mother who will lend me an infant girl." It would not be so easy to borrow an Englishwoman's daughter. But Indians were less particular about their girls. The baby would be in no danger, Claire reasoned.

The Rajah would not want to bother with her, and her mother would be proud to have served the little Rana.

"Perhaps," said Vazir, rising.

"It is the best we can do. Hurry and explain it to the men before the chance is lost!"

Since the age of six, Vazir Lal had never obeyed a woman, but today he did, looking hard into his cousin's face before he ran for the stone steps. Within the hour the deal was struck, and the castle gates swung wide to permit the exit of a crowd of women and children, cows and goats. No one disturbed the group, for the Rani stood on the balcony, obviously thinking it useless to try to escape. Perhaps she stood there to say farewell to those who had risked so much in her behalf, and many of the Rajah's men were touched by her bravery and by the heartbreaking way in which she clutched her squalling child.

Claire watched them out of sight, holding the little girl wrapped in the Rana's silks, unable to tell which of the women was the Rani, and dreading the moment when the men would put down their guns and allow the Rajah's men to enter the castle. Then she would be at the Rajah's mercy—or lack of it. The idea filled her with loathing. How would he deal with her when he found that she had tricked him? When he found that the Rani had escaped because of her?

When the signal came, and the Rajah's men rushed howling toward the castle gates, she put her hand into her clothing where she had secreted the pistol Colin had given her. For an instant she thought of using it on herself, to avoid the fate of being in the Rajah's power again. She wished she had obtained a promise from Vazir to grant her the same favor as he had been prepared to do the Rani. But then her unborn child kicked and jolted her to reality. She could not take his life with hers, and she bolted for the stairs, fleeing down them as far as was possible into the nether regions of the castle, where the dungeons were. There she hid in the darkness amid spiderwebs and bones, which she feared were human. Surely she could not be found here. Surely they would go away and leave her. But the baby cried, pressing her angry face against Claire's bosom for milk that she could not give. Nothing Claire could do would calm it, and the reverberating yells were heard. Footsteps echoed on the steps and half a dozen men dragged her from her hiding place. With shouts of triumph, they propelled her roughly onto the courtyard, and the senior of them set her on a horse in front of him. Another carried the baby as they dashed off through the lines to where the Rajah awaited her in his tasseled, silken tent. Excited cries filled her ears and hands reached for her. She was afraid that she would be pulled from the saddle and raped or killed. The looks in some of their eyes said they would have done so, while others seemed more interested in touching her or in pulling the veil from her face. She was the prize they had fought for, and they did not want to be denied the moment of victory. But the Rajah's personal guard, in their blue Western-style uniforms, protected her from the hysterical melee around her, and she was carried into the Rajah's tent.

He sat cross-legged on brocade cushions, his handsome features smug and exhilarated. She had seen similar expressions on his face when he had been about to make love to her, and quite forgetting he thought her the Rani, she wondered if he intended doing so now.

"So!" he said. "Your lover has failed you at last! The Sword of Pendeish cannot save you or his bastard now!" The Rajah laughed—a throaty cackle that set her teeth on edge like a scraping of fingernails on slate. She remained silent, remembering now that she was the Rani and wishing not to give herself away for as long as possible. But even as the Rani, he might use her. It might give him special pleasure to possess another of Colin's mistresses before executing her.

"Come here," he commanded. But Claire lifted her head proudly and would not go. She almost felt she *was* the Rani. She would make him come to her. Tamila would have done so.

"Come here!" he demanded again. Again Claire did not go. The Rajah cursed and came toward her, his expression more evil than she had ever seen it. Fury and exultation leaped in his eyes, and she was certain that he was aroused. The foul heat of his excitement seemed to radiate from his body. He placed an arrogant hand on her breast, and his lust seemed to surge through her body like a filthy stream. She felt his power and knew what it meant; her stomach convulsed and she was ready to vomit. And then the Rajah lifted her veil.

Disbelief replaced the frenzy of desire. Without a word he whirled and jerking the baby from where it lay in the basket, tore off its clothing. It was a moment Claire thought worth anything that might follow. The Rajah of Rambad was confronted by a tiny naked female.

He stared at the baby for a moment, focusing on the spot where she should have proclaimed her maleness, and then, dropping her back into her basket like an unwanted kitten, turned on Claire with a cry of rage.

"You! I will never understand you, Claire Cottington! She was his mistress! You knew! And you saved her! Do you know what you risked? If my men had got hold of you, even I could not have stopped them!"

Claire could not help laughing uproariously, and her merriment fueled the Rajah's wrath. She knew it would make him even angrier, but she could not help saying, "I am not Claire Cottington anymore, Rajah. You must address me as Mrs. Whitecavage."

"Mrs. Whitecavage!" he spat. "I don't believe it! There is no one in Pandeish who could have married you."

Claire remembered that the Reverend Wester's mission had been secret, and bit her tongue. But the Rajah was not interested in pursuing the subject. Instead, something else had attracted his attention. He studied the murky outline of her body beneath the loose kurta and placed his hand on her stomach. Suddenly the Rajah's anger dissipated into joy.

"My love, why didn't you tell me? You are going to bear me a son! Ah, Claire, I forgive you everything for this!"

She knew she should not, but she retorted, "Do not forgive me anything. If I bear a son, it will be Colin Whitecavage's!"

Her words had less effect on him than when she had told him that she was Colin's wife. The Rajah remembered their incredible nights of love, and it was inconceivable to him that her child should be anyone's but his. "It will be a son, Claire, and it will be mine! You may pretend it is Whitecavage's to spite me, but you know as well as I that it is mine!"

For the moment her pregnancy was her protection from him. He saw that her time was close and did not exercise his prerogatives with her. She was given a tent of her own, with guards, as she had had on that first trip she had made with him from Simla. But Claire had learned then that the Rajah was capable of biding his time.

He sent out parties to search for the Rani, and the infant girl was dispatched to be delivered to some nearby village where her mother might find her. After sunset, a moonless night sheltered the Rani among the hills that she and Vazir Lal had known so well as children, and Claire dared to feel relief. But the Rajah's men were mad for blood, cheated by Claire's ruse; and in the morning the Rajah decided that executions were necessary.

Vazir Lal was an obvious choice as the commander of the

garrison, and he and a dozen of his lieutenants were selected. Claire pleaded with the Rajah for Vazir's life.

"Vazir Lal is my friend. It will mark the child," she said.

The Rajah scowled. "But I cannot spare his life. He is the leader. If I cannot execute Colin Whitecavage, I must execute Vazir Lal."

"Then whatever happens to your son will be your own fault," she warned him.

The Rajah considered, realizing that she had conceded that it was his son. She had a way of making his life impossible. How would he explain such unwarranted mercy to his men? They had earned the right to see Whitecavage and the Rani executed and now he could not even give them Vazir. "Oh, have it your way!" he cried. "Only see that it is a son!"

Vazir was spared, but others were not, and their bodies were hung by the heels as the soldiers continued an orgy of eating, drinking, and carousing that had been going on all night. The disorderly camp was typically Indian, one part of it given over to prostitutes who plied their trade inside their tents, sometimes not bothering to close the flaps so that other customers might be attracted by the enjoyment of the first. Generally the camp reminded Claire of a circus she had seen when she was small. Conjurers, acrobats, and astrologists wandered about among fakirs, beggars, and tightrope artists, who had attached themselves to the caravan on its way from Allapore.

By noon the Rajah had struck camp. Elephants and pack animals were loaded, and the defenders of the castle were pressed into service as coolies, chained together, carrying heavy burdens on their backs. Claire wondered what fate was in store for them at the end of the journey. The army made a fantastic parade, starting down the slope, many of the men still drinking after their night of debauchery. Now and then Claire, inside her jampan, heard a thud and a curse that indicated that one of them had fallen headlong over some boulder. But the jampan was carried as lightly and tenderly as though it contained the crown jewels.

The Rajah wanted Claire protected from the realities of camp life, and hers was a cushioned little world, bounded by silk tapestries which hid her from the lusty eyes of soldiers. The sense of motion and the sunlight filtering weakly through were her only connections to the world beyond the jampan. After only a few hours' march, they halted again, in a spot where there was now forage for the animals, and where bearers sent ahead of the main body of troops had already pitched Claire's elegant tent. The Rajah came to call upon her, looking at her anxiously and inquiring about her health.

"Oh," said Claire, "I am not well at all. I did warn you that executions would mark the child."

"You said the execution of Vazir Lal would mark it," he corrected. "And I was careful that you did not see the executions."

"I saw the bodies," she sighed. She had decided to bait the Rajah on the matter of her pregnancy. It would do no good, but it pleased her to see him so vulnerable. But she had seen the bodies, and the memory had sickened her all day.

"I'll send you some soup to eat," said the Rajah. "The hunters caught some rabbits today. A good rabbit stew would be just the thing."

"I'm not hungry," said Claire stubbornly, and was gratified to see the uneasiness deepen in the Rajah's eyes. She was glad to torment him now, when he could not do anything about it. Who knew what might happen to her after her child was born? He might insist on a wedding and make her an adulteress. Or merely keep her in concubinage in the zenana. She did not know which idea seemed more obscene, but neither was supportable, now that she was Colin's wife and soon to bear a child. The night was starry, and the pine trees seemed frosted with moonlight, unlike the misty evening that had allowed the Rani to escape.

If only I might escape, Claire thought. But the idea was impossible. How would she manage, with no one to help her—with her clumsy body perhaps only a few days from its time. There were guards at her tent door, and the little pistol Colin had given her would not even get her past them, much less protect her from the bears and panthers that roamed the forests in search of easy meals. She wondered if there were a midwife in the camp, and if she would have need of such services before they reached Allapore.

The rabbit stew arrived, and Claire reluctantly ate it. It smelled delicious, and in her condition, she was always ravenous. But she felt guilty when she had consumed it. It was almost as though he had seduced her with its aromas, just as he had seduced her to respond to him in the bedroom. But it made no sense to weaken herself to spite him.

In the camp the celebrations continued. She gazed from her tent door and saw soldiers sprawled stuporously about, exhausted from revelry and the march. Pickpockets worked systematically, claiming their share of the victory, plucking off jewels, medals, and coins. Claire wondered if the Rajah would try to move the camp at all tomorrow now that the animals were well supplied. They had halted in a wide meadow, full of grass and flowers and wild indigo. There was water, too, from a nearby stream, and Claire wished she could bathe. Modesty prevented it, of course, and while naked soldiers splashed, she slept with an exhaustion she at last could not deny. It was the child who claimed the sleep, she thought as she drifted off. But it was the child who waked her, too. A single pain gripped her; she put her hands on her abdomen and found it tight and hard. *It is coming,* she thought in panic. But the moment passed, and her body relaxed.

She lay dazed with the feeling that something was about to happen. If not the birth of her child, then what? For some moments she remained lying quietly, listening to the sounds beyond her tent. She heard a soft snore and knew that one of her guards had fallen asleep. Sighs and murmurs seemed to flow among the animals. There was the crunch of a sentry's footstep. These things Claire heard and felt that she was hearing something else. Something that was not registering on her conscious mind.

Methodically she picked her way through the sounds, separating them like twisted threads, and then with quick intake of breath, she moved the cushions so that she could put her ear next to the earth. The sound grew louder, and Claire was certain. She had heard such sounds as a child, when she had liked to lie on the turf in Dartmoor and listen for the hoofbeats of the herds of wild ponies.

Something was abroad in the moonlit night. A large number of animals coming closer and closer. But dare she hope? There were herds of wild ponies here, too. And perhaps a bear or panther had frightened them into nocturnal activity. The sound came closer, grew louder and louder, until it threatened to overwhelm her, until her heart beat with the sound and she could not tell where one pounding left off, and the other began.

And then, inevitably, someone else in the camp heard it, someone who was not sleeping drunkenly or busying himself in a prostitute's tent. A cry went up. In a few minutes the camp was in pandemonium. Men and women alike rushed about in various stages of undress—men without shirt or turbans, women with long, unfastened hair replacing veils, abroad without caste marks, with saris in disarray.

But it was too late. The daring night attack began before they could organize. Elephants ran amuck, trampling their handlers as they tried to ready cannon while infantrymen formed a confused, ragged line. Just before dawn, Colin Whitecavage's band of Pandeish patriots burst across the meadow, augmented by wild Kashmirian adventurers, howling with bloodlust and revenge.

By that time Claire was already in the jampan in the vanguard of the Rajah's servants and camp followers who were fleeing the area. She wept with frustration at being so close to her husband, but the Rajah had sent the guards with her, and there was no way that she could escape. She could only listen to the firing and wonder how the battle was progressing. The soldiers of Pandeish had the element of surprise, but the Rajah's numbers were superior, she was certain, both in men and elephants. Colin had expected to defend a castle, and she wondered if he had acquired even one mounted cannon.

The firing went on all morning, but in spite of the distance Claire had traveled, the sound seemed no more distant. She could only surmise that the Pandeishis were driving the disorganized troops of the Rajah farther south.

She looked quietly smug when the Rajah visited her during the mid-afternoon halt, and his fury caused him to reveal his strategy.

"I suppose that you think your Major is going to rescue you, but that is not the case. I am using you again, my dear. Major Whitecavage must guess you are in my camp, and he is behaving foolishly because of it. This morning he inflicted heavy casualties on my troops and caused me to withdraw my position, but he doesn't realize that I am leading him now. He tells himself that he is pressing his advantage, but in truth I am drawing him on to Allapore, where thousands of my soldiers will destroy him. I shall allow him to chase me at will, lull him into thinking that I am weak, until it is too late. He knows better than to follow me close to Allapore, but you are the sugar cube I will hold before him. He will follow to his obliteration."

"He will not!" she cried, and felt another stab of pain.

"Good day, my dear," said the Rajah, and by way of farewell, placed his hand possessively on her stomach. The gesture made Claire feel as dirty as when he had touched her in bed.

When he had gone, she began to think desperately of some way to escape. By the next night she had formed a plan. If only she had enough time! Time must be her ally, or she could not win in such a helpless position.

"How are you, love?" he asked, paying his evening call.

"Oh, I could not sleep all night for worrying about my poor husband," she replied.

The Rajah's lips curled. "You persist in calling him your husband, Claire. That is stupid. There is still a chance that I may marry you."

"I would never marry you!" said Claire. "Even if I were not already a wife."

"You did not say that once," he reminded her.

"But then you promised me Colin's life as a wedding gift. You would not do that now, I suppose."

The Rajah smiled. "No. There's no need. I will dispose of him once and for all, and you will forget about him when you are my queen and have borne my son."

"Never. I will never forget, and I will never bear your son."

The Rajah smirked. But he was uneasy about her tired, drawn countenance. Claire had not really needed the charcoal she had used to accentuate the dark circles beneath her eyes. "I will send you a draught to make you sleep tonight," he said.

"Don't bother," snapped Claire, but with an inward sigh of relief. She had accomplished her purpose, and he did not suspect. In due time the draught arrived, brought by a servant woman, but Claire did not drink it. Instead, she emptied it carefully into a flask and screwed the lid carefully in place. And she slept somewhat better for the mere possession of it.

All through the next day, the battle continued, at a distance, as the Rajah's troops continued their withdrawal. Things were proceeding according to his plan, but the Rajah did not seem as pleased as he had been before. Something was beginning to go wrong. The servant woman again brought Claire a potion and again she saved it, placing it with the first in the flask.

That's two, Claire thought. She was guarded by six soldiers. Would time be her ally? Would she be able to collect enough before the Allapore regiment joined the campaign? She was aware that messengers had already been sent ahead to alert the garrison in the capital city. The Rajah's mood, however, worsened as the march continued, and finally, Claire, noticing the vacant look of the countryside, began to understand why. In the villages they passed, there was almost no

one to be seen except a few old men and women. The fields
were abandoned at planting time, and it did not take long to
guess that the inhabitants were joining the Army of Pandeish,
inspired to fight side by side with Colin Whitecavage and his
intrepid men. What had begun as the last effort of rebel
holdouts had become a popular uprising. And perhaps the opposing force now numbered more than the Rajah's. More
elephants were with the rebels, too, to be used to charge the
enemy line and break its ranks. But the Rajah still had the
cannon, and one cannon was worth fifty men.

Every day the skirmishes grew more intense. Colin, aware
that the Rajah would soon receive reinforcements from Allapore, was trying to force an early surrender, trying to find a
way to block the Rajah's steady retreat. The wily Rajah
evaded Colin's efforts, maneuvering his troops skillfully, one
day managing to reach the ford of a river against which
Colin had hoped to trap him. And now Claire was no longer
kept in the advance section of the army, but paraded along
the front line from time to time, as though to threaten Colin
with injury to her if he pressed his assault too vigorously. On
one occasion Colin was forced to halt the firing because she
was in the way.

That evening, Claire flew at the Rajah, trying to scratch his
handsome face with her nails. He laughed and pushed her
away easily. Top heavy with her pregnancy, Claire toppled
onto the cushions of her tent. The Rajah chuckled indul-
gently, as if proud of being responsible for her clumsiness.
"Relax, my dear, I am only reminding him of your presence.
I would not dream of using your life as a weapon against
him. I will beat him fairly."

"He is getting stronger. He may win."

"He is not strong enough. Tomorrow the Allapore regiment will join us. A courier arrived not an hour ago."

The news made Claire queasy. Or something did. She did
not eat her supper, and it was not to spite the Rajah that she
left it untouched. Tomorrow the two great forces would join,
and the fate of Pandeish would be decided. And if she remained in the Rajah's camp, he would use her in any way
possible to aid in his victory.

But he had used her against her beloved for the last time,
she vowed. The flask now contained six portions of the sleeping draught. When the last was added, she filled it with raki
and offered it to her guards. They accepted happily. Soon all
of them would be asleep; and when she had escaped the tent,

no one else would pay any attention to a woman wandering through the camp. Claire waited with anticipation until she heard snores beyond the tent flap. At last she peeped through to see if all of them slept. In the glow of a campfire, four of the guards were lying in poses of blissful sleep. Heavy beards heaved softly over their large chests; their fierce faces seemed innocent, their weapons lay as harmless as toys.

But two of the guards were wide awake. What had happened? Too late, Claire realized that these guards were of a different caste. They would not have profaned themselves by drinking from the same flask as the others. Claire was devastated, and her sense of physical discomfort grew worse. The baby had stopped its kicking and seemed to have become very heavy. She felt weary, and almost as though she herself had drunk from the flask, she longed to sleep and forget.

But she must escape, and at last she cut the rear of the tent and slipped outside. The guards were expecting nothing and might not see her. The pair of them seemed involved in some sort of engrossing game, as Claire moved slowly away from the rear of the tent, carrying a brass lota, as though she were going for water. A few yards away some men playing a stringed instruments looked up as she went past. Claire turned her head away and pulled her gauze veil across the lower part of her face as any modest Hindu woman would. The men continued their singing disinterestedly.

So far so good. If only no one noticed that she was not going in the direction of the well with her lota! Then suddenly one of her guards glanced up. She saw his attention rivet on her as he spotted her identity. She ran for the place where the animals were tethered, hoping to take a horse and flee to the other camp.

Behind her the cry was raised. Claire stumbled over a tent stake, struggled to her feet, and kept going, tossing the lota aside. It seemed to her that that she was running without going anywhere. The fall had knocked the wind out of her, and she could not regain her breath. Her chest ached, and red and blue sparks shot before her eyes as she reached the horses. She imagined dizzily that the opposing camp was shooting fireworks or that some midnight skirmish had begun. There was no time to put on a saddle, but Claire had ridden bareback at Cottington Crest, where she had often abandoned her awkward sidesaddle. But now she had not the agile girlish form; and as she flung herself onto the horse's back, she was unable to propel her additional weight. She was poorly seated as the animal reared with a whinny and charged toward the elephants. She felt herself sliding, saw the shadow of the huge wrinkled foot, and then a splendid white finale of the fireworks.

She did not lose consciousness, but was aware of a tumult of noise about her. She knew that she was being lifted and placed into a gharry. Then there was only incredible pain, incredible motion, a darkness that no nightglow penetrated. The gharry's panels must be closed, she thought, wishing one might be opened for light and air. She tried to make her wishes known and heard only a moan when she spoke. Some woman of the camp who was traveling with her, made reassuring sounds, but Claire understood none of it. She hoped that the woman was a midwife, for surely she was in need of one. It was impossible that such agony should exist, and then it became worse. She was leaving a battlefield behind, but embarking on a new war. Her body was at war with itself, the injured parts of it rebelling at the demands of other elements that it work at giving birth. It was a battle in which there would be no truce, though she longed for one; nature and new life could not be denied.

It went on forever, until the gharry had stopped and she had been carried inside. She did not know where, for this place was as dark as the gharry. She felt as though she were in a cave; but that was not so, for she could hear the opening and shutting of doors, and she seemed to be lying on a string bed. Voices above her sounded resigned, and she was terrified that they were saying that she could not give birth to her child, that she was going to die.

She would. She would die and fail to bring Colin's child into the world. She had failed at many things, made many mistakes, but this time she would do it right. She focused every ounce of her courage, as she had when she had volunteered to stand on the balcony to save Tamila, and a light seemed to glow inside, a light she knew could be seen only by her. As time went on someone pressed cool water to her lips, and she heard a voice she recognized. "Drink this, Memsahib."

Sevaley. She tried to speak her servant's name, and failing, clutched for the friendly hand. She knew that she must be back in the Rainbow Palace. She was in Allapore, and outside there was a tremendous commotion—the sound of firing and ricocheting bullets. The Rajah had withdrawn to his stronghold, and Colin Whitecavage must be at its very gate.

If only the night would end. If only she could look outside. It was insane to fight a pitched battle at night, but perhaps the Rajah had lighted torches on the city's walls. And she imagined him directing the defense from the imposing height of his howdah, waving his jeweled tulwar to urge his soldiers to victory.

Then there was no room for any thought except that of birth, nothing existed but her grip on Sevaley's hand, and the pressure between her legs. She screamed until her strength was spent and the light formed of her courage began to flicker and fade. There was only the heaving of her body and her desperate, exhausted panting.

The noise outside diminished, and at last a man's footsteps came into the room. A sword clanked as he removed it and threw it aside. "It will be all right, Claire. I'll help you."

The words were tremulous with emotion. Colin Whitecavage, his uniform stained with the blood of those he had slain to reach her, bent to a task less natural to him than warfare. He had been in India enough years to help English doctors deliver infants under adverse conditions. He had accepted the idea of a cruel nature, which caused women to give birth no matter what the circumstances, but he had been unprepared for the sight of his wife in the ultimate throes of childbearing. He had not even known she was pregnant. Now, in a few minutes he would be a father—or a widow perhaps.

"Push, dearest!" he said, and placed his hand on her stomach, pressing down gently to help her. She obeyed him only weakly. "Push!" he said again, more urgently. She tried, and it broke his heart to see how she responded to him even when all her strength was spent. "Push," he whispered for the third time, hating himself for having to rouse her, for she seemed to have fallen into a stuporous sleep.

She heard him from an immense distance and fought to do his bidding. This time he reached inside her and, finding the child's tiny shoulder, drew the baby gently into the world. For a long moment it did not cry, and he was afraid that it was dead. Then he remembered that he once had seen a newborn dipped into ice water to startle it into breathing, and he gave an urgent command. The water was brought and he plunged the child in, soaking his sleeves in the process. The infant howled, and Colin Whitecavage wept.

"Is it—is it. . . ." Claire tried to ask him a question.

"A boy, darling. We have a son." And he dried the child and, wrapping it in a blanket, brought it to her.

"Oh, do let me see him," she whispered, smiling. "Open the chiks, so there is light."

And now Colin wept again, but not with joy. He had been holding the baby before her eyes. The room was flooded with sunshine. But there was no light for Claire, and there could not be. The only light that could shine for her was the light of her courage.

19

The elephant's kick that had left Claire sightless had left her damaged and battered in other ways as well, and for weeks she could not leave her bed. There were severe bruises and torn ligaments. The doctor Colin sent for from Simla thought she should be taken to a specialist at the hill station at Ootacamond as soon as she could walk again.

"Will she recover her sight?" Colin asked.

"That is beyond my competence to say."

This conversation was held in private amid the prismed lights of the audience hall that had given the Rainbow Palace its name. And to Colin that dappled play of colors was a vivid reminder of all that Claire might never see again. In the beginning he had been fearful of her destructive power; how ironic that seemed now. It was he who had destroyed *her*. He had married her, impregnated her, and left her in the poorly defended castle.

He had been delayed in Kashmir by the haggling of tribal chieftains over what they would sell him. He had been beside himself to be on his way before the passes were closed, and the Kashmirians, aware of this need, had attempted to extort him. To their minds an officer of the Raj was always wealthy, but Colin, without the wherewithall to meet their demands, had had to bluster to lower the price, which had been paid mostly with the Rani's jewels. His uncompromising stance had earned him new recruits, but precious time had been lost, and he had been forced to winter in the mountains. If only he had returned in time!

When he had seen the scarred, empty castle, he had

wanted to die, for he had thought that everything he loved was gone. The little Rana and his mother, dead, no doubt; and his wife in the clutches of the Rajah. Claire would be alive, but had she been able to protect herself from the Rajah's advances as Colin had hoped? Whatever, the Rajah would enjoy making sure that Colin did not retrieve her.

Colin had been overjoyed when the Rani had emerged from the secret cave where she had been hiding with a few of her women and retainers. The sight of Daruska, well and smiling, had all but overcome him, and he had been afraid that someone would notice the intensity of his feelings. But all the soldiers felt strongly about the little Rana, and they had only been pleased that their commander did, too, although he was an *Angrezi*.

But happy as Colin had been to see the Rani and Daruska, he had still felt empty, for he had hoped that Claire was with them. Tamila had given him news of her, though, news of the exploit that had saved the Rani's life and news that she was with child. Colin, more surprised by her pregnancy than by the trick she had played on the Rajah, had gone tearing after her. Now they were all together again. Pandeish was in the hands of its rightful heir; and the Rajah, deserted by many of his men, was in flight toward the border. Everything should have been perfect, but of course it wasn't.

"I am with you, and that is what matters," she murmured, hearing him sigh. And then an edge of worry crept into her voice. "You have never really told me about the baby."

Colin frowned. What was there to tell about a baby? "I've told you that he's healthy," he said, staring at the infant, who, oblivious to his mother's ailments, was lying snuggled to her breast making noisy sucking sounds. "We should get a wet nurse," he said. "You are too ill for this."

"No!" She clutched the child to her. "He's mine, and I will mother him."

"But Claire—you would gain strength faster if you didn't. You would still see him." Colin stopped, confounded at his blunder. He wondered what he ought to say to smooth it over, but she gave him no opportunity.

"That is just it. I can't. So if I do not have the pleasure of giving him sustenance, there will be nothing of him for me. I want him to need me, Colin."

Colin gave it up, and glared at the child. Somehow he did not feel as a father ought to feel about his son. He did not love this baby as he loved Daruska. He was irrationally resentful of young Jeremy Colin Whitecavage. He was afraid that the baby hindered his wife's ability to recover from a disaster for which he felt himself to blame. The child was a constant reminder of his guilt.

"What sort of eyes does he have?" Claire asked, continuing her quest for information about her son.

"Blue. All babies do. You should have learned that better than I, being a woman."

"What about his skin? Is it fair?" she persisted, seeming on the verge of tears.

"Oh, a bit darker than yours. More the shade of mine." Colin felt he could stand no more of this conversation. He could not bear it that she could not see the child, and his inadequacy in describing it made matters worse.

"Has he your chin or mine?"

Colin studied the little face in male desperation. It had not really taken form, and was still splotched from its difficult birth. "I cannot tell! For heaven's sake, Claire, it is ridiculous to decide such things about a baby of this age. Try to sleep for a while. I'll come back later."

"All right," said Claire, and turned up her mouth for his kiss. But when he had gone, she did not sleep. She could not. She was in pain, but physical pain was not the larger part of her agony. It seemed that fate had decreed a diabolical punishment for her. Since she could not gaze on her child, she had no way of guessing who had been its father. She must know! But perhaps she never could. She knew that she should be glad at least that her husband had no such doubts, but Claire only felt alone in her darkness, alone with her black thoughts, which she could share with no one.

She could not share them with Colin, nor with Sevaley or with the Rani, who came daily to sit with her. Claire had thought that with the crown of Pandeish restored to the young Rana, she and Colin would soon be leaving the country to return to Delhi. But this, Tamila told her, was not the case. With her consent, the Raj had appointed Colin President of the Regency for the new Rana.

"Do you mean we will live here forever?" Claire gasped.

"Until Daruska is old enough to take over his royal duties," Tamila said.

"But that would be sixteen years at least!"

"Daruska is his son, Claire!"

"And so is Jeremy. And I am his wife!"

"Yes. You are his wife, and it is your duty to follow him

in whatever he choses to do. If you try to come between him and his son, you may lose his love." Tamila's voice had an edge of warning. But warning of what? Claire had seen that Tamila was a strong-willed woman. It had taken more will than Claire could have mustered for her to give up Colin and accept his wife. But Tamila was devoted to her child, and she still loved Colin. Would she try to reclaim his affections?

The idea filled Claire's dark world with horrible imaginings. In her mind she and Jeremy were pitted against Tamila and Daruska in a contest for Colin. To make matters worse, Claire intuited how Colin felt about Jeremy. Was it because Colin suspected that Jeremy might not be his son?

"You don't love Jeremy," she accused him.

"How silly! Of course I do."

"No, not the way you love Daruska."

Colin came to dread his visits to his wife's room, for she was constantly distraught. As weeks went by he came less, and she, noticing, became even more upset. She began to hint that it was Tamila who was keeping him away.

"It's because there is so much to be done to plan the new government, Claire. Pandeish has been in the hands of tyrants for a long while—first the old Rana and then the Rajah. It needs to be turned to new ways."

"And you will do it."

"Yes."

"But I would like to go away from here," she wailed, forgetful of the Rani's warning. "This place is filled with unhappy memories."

Colin sighed. "You're right, of course. You should leave. When you're able, I'll take you to Ootacamond, and we will see other doctors."

"Do you promise?"

"Yes," he said, "just as soon as you are well enough."

Claire took heart. He had mentioned going to Ootacamond before, but she had been afraid he would find reasons to delay their departure. But he had promised. Tamila had been wrong. It was she, his wife, who had the stronger hold over him. And now she found herself planning that once she had him in the lovely English hill station, she would arrange for him never to return to Pandeish. She would not be an invalid forever. She would walk again and dance and ride. And the doctors would restore her sight—that might take them as far away as England. She moved from her bed to a chair and from the chair she began to walk haltingly, leaning heavily on Sevaley's arm.

Sevaley was always glad to help Claire exercise in the courtyard, for many times Vazir Lal would come to join them. Vazir was dedicated to Claire, since she had saved the Rani, and their deepened friendship was a source of great comfort.

Sevaley was incredulous when she heard that Claire had saved Tamila's life. "She is your rival, Memsahib. It was foolish of you."

"I suppose so," sighed Claire, "but I would still do it again."

"I would not have. Not if Vazir Lal were my husband and looked at her the way he does."

Claire laughed, for she knew that her maid had developed a girlish attachment to Vazir. "There are other ways to bind a man to you, Sevaley," she said.

And Claire had begun to think about those other ways. She ought not to allow him to go too long with his needs unfulfilled, and she began to hint that she wished him to make love to her. He approached her hesitantly, but his passions took over, and she was herself triumphant as she felt his desire building. At last he flung her legs open and penetrated her, and she gave an involuntary cry of pain. After that she tried to pull him back, but he was no longer in the mood. Hurting her had made him ashamed of himself. He had never been able to resist her, and it was no different now. He should have had better control of himself.

Claire was frustrated, wondering if he relieved his needs elsewhere. "I am well enough to travel, Colin," she kept telling him.

"Not yet," he would say.

"Oh! It's not that I am not recovered enough. It's that you don't want to leave Pandeish!"

There was some truth to this, and it made Colin angry. He had a duty to Claire, of course, and he was beside himself to have her back in some semblance of European civilization. But the new regime was fragile. Colin was torn; and Claire, consumed with her own selfish misery, did not help the situation.

She did not help especially when she began to intimate that he was putting off their journey for the wrong reasons. "It's not Pandeish you don't want to leave," she charged one day. "It's the Rani's charms that are holding you here."

"Claire——"

"What is to keep you from behaving however you like? I cannot see what you do!" she burst out bitterly.

"Perhaps you have a guilty conscience yourself!" he cried, stung. "Perhaps you are remembering that you enjoyed yourself once in the Rainbow Palace. Perhaps I was a fool to steal you away!"

It was the first time he had given voice to his wondering about her first stay in the palace, and it frightened both of them. The next morning she showed him how well she could walk across the room unaided, and gave him a tremulous smile. The argument was forgotten with relief, and he kissed her and told her he would arrange for their departure immediately.

With a small retinue they traveled toward lovely Ootacamond. Clare rode with the hangings of her jampan pulled back, for although she could not see the spectacular mountains and high summery meadows, she could sense the ripeness of the earth, smell the richness of the pines and hear the chattering of the monkeys and singing of parakeets.

The dizzying loops of the mountain pass that led to Ooty left her lightheaded, and then she caught the scent of the eucalyptus trees which swallowed the white houses. Soon there were more British aromas from gardens growing roses, Canterbury bells, and mauve stocks. Claire had not known how hungry she had been to be with her own kind again, to hear her own language and to taste a meal of roast beef and potatoes and even English peas grown in the little vegetable plots behind the frame houses.

Colin installed them in the central hotel with wings of bungalows connected by low-roofed passages. The rooms had high vaulted ceilings supported by a center beam, and sometimes little garden sparrows flitted in to perch there. Claire enjoyed their twittering sound and scolded Sevaley when she shooed them with a broom. Colin told her that an orange trumpet vine grew outside their door. "They say it means good luck," he told her.

"Oh, I'm sure it will prove so," Claire answered with enthusiasm. She could not help being optimistic about the future in this gentle English place, not even with all her infirmities. Ootacamond was a sanctuary for invalids and so was well-staffed with some of the best physicians of the Raj. Somehow Claire felt confident that they could help her. After more than a year in native surroundings, the British competence of Ootacamond was comforting.

They were together for the first time as a family, for the first time really as a wedded couple. The routine of domesticity pleased her. After a breakfast of papaya and porridge or boiled eggs, Colin might take her for a carriage ride or to fish beside one of Ooty's mountain streams. Then came lunch and a regimen of naps for her and the baby. At four o'clock the tea tray arrived with scones and jam, Madeira cake, and coriander sandwiches.

At this time of day a sweeper girl came, too, and lighted fires of eucalyptus logs in the fireplace. This was a moment that Claire looked forward to, for the wood burned with the same wonderful scent that filled the groves outside. After that, Sevaley would draw her a bath and brush her hair and help fasten her into crinolines and silks for dinner. Colin would come in to approve Sevaley's handiwork and occasionally to add a diamond feather or a coral necklace. Claire waited with riduculous anticipation for his sigh of approval and his assurance that she was ravishing. Such small moments had taken on tremendous importance since her accident.

Evenings were for socializing. Sometimes there was dancing, and Claire quickly recovered enough to participate. These were times she loved, for she needed no eyes to go waltzing about, steered by Colin's firm hand; and during those glorious moments she need not worry about bumping into an armchair or knocking a vase from a table.

The women of Ooty, some of whom had been sent there by their husbands to recover from illness or childbirth, were horrified and thrilled by Claire's adventures as they drew the story from her during long, gossipy conversations. She had come to India to marry a colonel, had been kidnapped by a rajah, and in the end had married the dashing major who had rescued her—and anyone who knew Colin thought her fortunate to have won his heart. Her handicap lent her a certain tragic romance, and as time went on, she was able to deal with it more gracefully. Sevaley became her eyes, always at her side, even when Colin was not.

Claire was triumphant at Ootacamond. At last Colin had left the Rani. She had got him away and had him solely to herself. Her fears were pushed to the back of her mind. He did not sleep in the same bed with her; and she did not ask him to, afraid that he might reject her advances. Neither had he warmed to Jeremy, though all the women told her that the child was adorable, and everyone spoiled him with their attentions. Most of all, Claire fought a fear of returning to Pandeish. She put the idea that he was still President of the Regency out of her mind. And there was another fear, which she kept so well hidden that she did not even give it a name.

The doctors prescribed therapeutic baths and exercise for her injured back, and at the end of a month Claire no longer walked with a limp. But on the matter of her vision she had been given no encouragement. Claire was content to think that it was merely a natural caution. She could not accept the idea that she might not regain her sight. In fact, she did not even entertain the idea.

Colin was aware of this, so it was with a heavy heart that he gave her the physician's report. "They say there is nothing to be done," he told her.

"Nothing? But there must be something to *try!*" It was contrary to her nature to give up, especially without a good fight.

"It is blindness caused by trauma, and there is a chance that someday your vision will return spontaneously. It is a small chance, my darling, but it gives us hope." He held out his arms for her, and then, remembering that she could not see his waiting arms, he embraced her. But Claire, in shock, sat woodenly, not responding to him.

For several days she did not admit him to her dark world, refusing all the pleasure of Ootacamond that she had so enjoyed, paying attention to nothing but her baby, without whom she would as soon have died. Colin knew he ought to be glad for the solace that the child gave her, but when she turned away from him to suckle it, he wanted to seize little Jeremy and hurl him across the room. Instead, Colin would storm out of the bungalow and go to the club, where he would drink too much and allow women to flirt with him.

It had occurred to him that Jeremy might not be his child, and he tried to push the idea away. He tried to tell himself that if the Rajah had bedded her, it hadn't been her fault. But the uncertainty rankled like an ugly, deep-rooted weed.

Colin had never in his life felt so helpless as he did now against Claire's withdrawal. He was a man of action, and it was his character to deal with any difficulty. He felt inadequate; she made him feel it acutely. She would scarcely speak to him, and he supposed he deserved it.

Instead of marrying her, he might have taken her to the

boundary of Pandeish. But he had made her part of a life unsuited to an Englishwoman. He had put her life into danger because he had loved her, because she had seemed different from other of her kind, because he had not been able to do without her! He was utterly to blame. And so, unable to penetrate Claire's armor, he made himself agreeable to other women, when he had drunk his fill, as if by doing so, he could erase her image from his mind.

But his wife was quick to scent the perfume that clung to his clothes from the intimate contact of waltzing, and she flew into rages. "You are nothing but a womanizer, Colin Whitecavage!" she accused. "You leave me here while you disport yourself any way you please. Lord knows what you do! Lord knows you will not share *my* bed! But perhaps you've found one softer!"

Colin was so glad that she had shown animation and spoken to him of something of consequence that he did not take offense. Indeed, he had no desire to fight with his wife.

"I am lonely, Claire," he said mildly. "I will have no need to dance with other ladies if you will accompany me tomorrow evening."

"Oh, you are only saying that because you feel sorry for me," she sobbed, for the nameless fear had overcome her at last.

"I am not! I miss you! Oh, it's not fair for you to behave this way!"

"It's not fair for you to have a blind wife!"

"I have the wife I want!" he cried.

"Tamila should be your wife. She is a whole woman, and the mother of the son you love so much."

"You are a whole woman, Claire. Don't talk foolishly."

But the fear had taken hold of her. She was afraid that he didn't really love her anymore. He was only saddled with her because he had married her. She was afraid that his tenderness came only from duty and pity. And from fear came belief. If only he would behave as a husband should and demand his husbandly rights!

Colin himself could not have said why he did not. Perhaps he was still afraid of hurting her, although her health had so much improved. Perhaps he was afraid of making her pregnant again. Or perhaps the reason went even deeper. Perhaps it was because of his lack of natural fatherly feeling for Jeremy. But Colin's fear that Jeremy wasn't his son was kept locked away. He could not abide the idea any more than

Claire had been able to stand the idea that she might not regain her sight.

She did not go with him the next night or the next, but continued to withdraw, sitting by the fireplace, staring into flames that she could not see. Colin was beside himself. She seemed to be withdrawing further and further, until he could not seem to reach her at all, either with his anger or his love.

She was certain that she was a burden to him and unable to cope with such a situation, she turned away. The warmth of the fire, the popping of logs, gave her company, and if on a pleasant evening the fire was not lighted, she would fly into a rage, calling for Sevaley to send for its tender.

Her despairing husband held long conversations with her doctors and at last made a suggestion. "They are behind the times here, dearest," he said. "In England there have been new advances. Perhaps you ought to go home."

Her face lighted and he ached at the renewed hope he saw there. He thought he could not bear to see it wiped away again. "It is only a chance, Claire, not a very good one."

"It will work, Colin! It must! Everything will be all right once we are back in England. Mama was right about India. I hate India now. We will be so happy at Cottington Crest, love!"

"*You* will be happy at Cottington Crest, Claire," he said regretfully. "I cannot go with you."

"Can't go!" Claire stormed in an agony of disbelief. "I am your wife, and it is your duty to take me!"

"You are my wife, Claire, and it is your duty to understand my needs," he said sternly. "You know I must go back to Pandeish. You have known it all along."

"No! I won't let you go back!" Claire pounded on his chest, hurting her little fist on the brass buttons of his uniform. "You have done enough in Pandeish. Let someone else be President of the Regency!"

"It is my responsibility, Claire. Daruska is my son."

"And so is Jeremy!" she shrieked, as though by loudness she could shut away her doubts.

"I am taking nothing from Jeremy. I will see that you are escorted to England, and when you are ready to return, I will be waiting for you."

"If you don't come with me, I will never return to India," she cried, frightened that she had gone too far, even as the words left her mouth.

She heard his shocked intake of breath. "You cannot mean that, Claire!"

"I do mean it, I do!" she cried desperately. She had put everything on the line now. He must choose; she had made it impossible for him to do otherwise. Silence hung between them; and neither wanted it to end, for it at least chained them together. But at last it was necessary for him to answer.

"I must go back to Pandeish, Claire," he said.

"You are deserting me! she accused. "You're a cad. I should have known in the beginning! I should have known when you betrayed Colonel Todd by seducing me!"

"I am not the only one who betrayed Maxwell Todd," he returned angrily.

It was a truth of which Claire could not bear to be reminded. But she was the one who had first begun to fight unfairly. Now she allowed the quarrel to descend into bitterness.

"Go on, then. Go back to Pandeish! But do not tell me these lies about duty! It's the Rani's bed you are so eager to return to. Certainly you don't warm mine. Go back to the Rani!"

"If I do, you have brought it on yourself," he cried. "*She* is not forever demanding and criticizing like you!"

"Because she is Indian and afraid to lift her voice to a man. She will be satisfied to be your chattel, and that is what you need! You need a concubine instead of a wife."

Claire was disadvantaged because she could not see Colin's face. The storm of fury that knit his brows and set his mouth in a thin dangerous line, the blackness of his eyes would have stunned her to silence. She would have been warned of the deadly mistake she was making in speaking deprecatingly of the Rani Tamila. But Claire, in her lonely darkness, rushed on, out of control, heaping insult upon insult, mixing insult with hysterical sobs and tears. "Go back to her! Go lie with your heathen slut!"

He raised his hand to strike her, but Claire, unseeing, did not step backward. He, even in his rage, realized why she did not, and somehow he mastered himself. He had never struck a woman; and he thanked God that he did not now, but he had never been so tested. He could not believe that he had ever found those lips sensuous and inviting, could not imagine that he had ever been rapturous from kissing them. He opened the door, plunged through it, and escaped.

The next morning he prepared to leave for Pandeish. He was glad to be leaving Ootacamond, for everyone had looked at him curiously at breakfast, and he knew that their argument had been heard in adjoining bungalows and he was the subject of gossip. Somewhat calmer now, he returned to their quarters while preparations for her departure were being made and asked if she wished to apologize. She longed to do so, but his chill tone did not make it easy; and she had her reasons for thinking it better to leave matters as they were.

She had wept all night, and as her anger burned itself out she had regretted everything she had said. She still wanted him to go to England with her, but she did not want to go to England at all if it meant parting from him. If he insisted on returning to Pandeish, she was willing to go with him and give up her chance to regain her sight. But Claire did not tell her husband these things.

She believed herself a burden, and she was too proud to be a burden. She had hoped vaguely that he might beg her forgiveness and tell her that he had changed his mind about accompanying her to England. But that did not happen, and Claire felt more certain than ever that Colin wished to return to his first love, the Rani Tamila. She regretted the harsh things she had said about the Rani. Tamila was an honorable and courageous woman, deserving of Colin's love.

Claire had always been out of kilter in Pandeish, envious of the bonds between Colin and Tamila, of their vision of a new Pandeish. She had thought to prevail as his wife, but now she was convinced she couldn't. She could not compete with Tamila. Tamila had borne him a child he loved, while she had produced an infant which might not even be his. If she returned to England alone, he and Tamila would resume their love affair. If she went back to Pandeish sightless, she would only make him guilty over his desire for another woman. How easy it would be to deceive her if she could not see! How could he resist? She could not bear to think herself so deceived, and so she said nothing to soften her words of the previous night. It was best, for both of them. She would return to Cottington Crest and pretend to be waiting for him to complete his tour in India. Many wives had done the same. It was a fiction that would serve indefinitely. Perhaps it had served others.

"I will arrange for someone to escort you when the monsoon arrives, and the weather is cooler on the plains," he told her.

"Very well," she said.

"I will be in Allapore, should you wish to return."

"I know where you will be," she answered, her voice heavy with meaning.

He went away without kissing her good-bye.

20

She was alone, then, in Ootacamond with only Sevaley and the baby. For long days she did not venture out, for she was as aware as Colin had been that they had become a topic of conversation. Somehow, on Colin's arm, she had not felt herself an object of pity, but it was different now that she was by herself. It occurred to her that even Sevaley shouldn't be with her.

"It is the time when your parents wished to have you married," she said. "I will return you to Delhi."

"No, Memsahib," said her servant. "I will stay with you."

"But Sevaley, I know that it is the fulfillment of every Indian woman to serve her man as her god and bear him children. Without that her life has no meaning. She has no value to carry into her future lives."

"Yes," said Sevaley. "It was I who told you that. And I who said that it was not important to love one's husband. But I have seen now what it is like to love. I have seen how you and the Major care for each other."

"You have seen how it turned out," said her mistress drily.

"No worse than a marriage without love," observed the girl. "But I would like to love a man someday as you love the Major. Even if it ends badly."

Claire sighed. She supposed she had ruined Sevaley for the life she had been destined to lead, but it was far from the worst of her sins. She lived as a recluse now that Colin had gone, never attending the balls and parties on Rajah's Square. But gradually Sevaley encouraged her to go out for the air in the cool evenings, wheeling Jeremy about the neat paths in his perambulator. Sometimes they ventured to the market where they could buy real English vegetables—small pinkish potatoes, bright radishes, beans, and even tender little Brussels sprouts. These were as exotic to Sevaley as the native vegetables were to Claire—the pale brown fruit of the palmyra palm, the lilac brinjal, a long, springy vegetable which amused Claire by coiling around her arm.

Though Claire could savor none of the rich colors, she loved the market for its ministry to her other senses—the smooth cool touch of limes and guavas, the aromas of fresh breads, ladyfingers, and curry leaves. Often they were intrigued by the fortuneteller with his cage of parrots that would pick out a card to tell the customer's future. Claire thought it was a waste of money, but Sevaley had her fortune told.

"I am to see far-off places," she reported, "and that is true, Memsahib. I'm going to England with you. Let's have the parrot draw a card for you."

"No," said Claire. It was a silly game, but what was sillier still was that Claire was afraid to play it. She was afraid of what the future might bring, frightened even of the little light a trained parrot might shine upon it.

"Perhaps the bird will tell you that you will meet an old friend," said a voice at her elbow. She turned in wonder. It was so familiar, but she could not place it. It seemed to come from somewhere so long ago, so far away. The speaker did not seem to know her condition. She sensed him smiling, waiting for her recognition.

"I am sorry; I cannot see you," she said.

His gasp signaled his understanding. "My God, Claire, it is I, Max!"

Maxwell Todd, the man she had so humiliated and betrayed! She obeyed an impulse to run and careened into a neem tree. Max righted her, an arm gently about her waist. "There, my dear, you shouldn't run away. Neither of us should run any longer. The fault was at least as much mine as yours. I could not admit that I was worn out. I couldn't accept that I could not complete my dreams for India."

"And now you have, Max?" she asked, still trembling.

"Yes. You were my last hope; it was a burden I should never have put upon you. After you left, I returned to Delhi and contracted malaria. And now I am going to England when the weather cools. And you? There is no reason you should deny yourself the love of Colin Whitecavage."

"I have not," she said sheepishly. "I am his wife."

"He is most fortunate, then."

"He might differ with that opinion," she said, and he heard the pain in her voice.

"Tell me, dearest," he said gently.

"I fell beneath an elephant. . . ." she began, but her voice tightened in a sob.

"That is how you were injured. But that is not all."

"No. He has returned to Pandeish."

"Ah." Max's exclamation said more than he intended. It told Claire she need not speak of the Rani, for Max was thinking of her already. "Pandeish is his obsession, Claire. His nemesis."

"And mine," she added. "I, like you, am going to England—to see if some doctor there can help me."

"But unlike me, you will be returning, I suppose. You are not saying good-bye to India forever."

"I am not coming back, Max. It is good-bye to India for me, also."

"And good-bye to Colin?"

"I suppose it is the same thing—saying good-bye to Colin."

"Poor love," he murmured, "poor love."

He escorted her to her bungalow, and after that began to prevail upon her to have dinner with him and to go out to the dances. Reluctantly she conceded. He was so tender, so persistent, in his entreating. "Oh, Max, how can it be that you still love me after I treated you so badly?" she wondered.

"But I treated you badly, too," he replied. "We were each other's dream. It was I who filled your head with India. I, who provided the means of your coming here. And all the while, I was doomed, just as the Raj is doomed."

"The Raj is not doomed, Max," she said, pressing his head against her shoulder as they sat in a soft bougainvillea-scented night. "It's only because you are so tired that you think so. There are men like Colin Whitecavage left to fight for the Raj."

"Good men, Claire. But they are all doomed. I am glad that you are not coming back again. At least *you* are not doomed!"

Some days Colonel Todd was confined to his bed with recurring bouts of his illness; and then Claire would go to his quarters, and in spite of his protests that it wasn't proper, she would help to nurse him and sit for hours holding his hand. She had never been one to be concerned over appearances, after all; and she would explain to him that it hardly mattered, since she was already the subject of gossip in Ooty.

His illness frightened her, for he was sometimes in a delirium and dreamed of horrible things. He would cry out to her of fires and murders, mutilations and beheadings, often calling out the names of people she had known in Delhi. "My god, there is Lieutenant Jenkins, sliced to bits! And Mrs. Jenkins—she cannot protect the children—they are pulling young Jamie and Margaret away from her—dear God, they are making her watch! I cannot bear it! The screaming—oh, the screams! Ah, the mother is dead, too. It's a blessing; how could she bear to live? Run, Claire! Don't let them catch you! Hide in the cupboard. They are killing everyone!"

She did her best to comfort him, repeating to him over and over that the inhabitants of the Delhi garrison were going about their business safely. "Mrs. Jenkins isn't dead, Max; she is eating jam cake at a tea party. And the children are fidgeting in the schoolroom."

She would wipe sweat from his brow, and after a time he would seem to hear her. The fever would break, his breathing would become regular, and he would sleep. Then Claire would sit trembling alone, the imaginary screams still ringing in her ears. He made it seem so real; he was so convinced of it. Was the Delhi garrison close to a rising? When a captain of the Delhi cavalry arrived in Ooty on leave, Claire was quick to ask his opinion.

"A revolt?" the Captain hooted. "No, nothing of the sort. The men are perfectly loyal."

"What about the Nana Sahib?" asked Claire, remembering the messenger the Rajah had received in the dahl field.

"Oh, he is disgruntled over our failure to pay him a pension he's done nothing to deserve. He'd like us to pay for his collection of nautch girls, that's all. You must remember, my dear Mrs. Whitecavage, that Colonel Todd is ill. He's a dedicated man who has given more than his share to the Raj. He deserves a long rest—perhaps, ah, a sanatorium would be valuable."

Claire bristled. "Are you suggesting that Colonel Todd is unbalanced in his mind?"

"There, there, dear lady, please don't take offense. I am only suggesting how devastating service in India can be to the best of officers. Speculation is that Lord Dalhousie will leave soon himself from exhaustion."

The news shocked her. Lord Dalhousie, who had had such

dreams. Was he, too, defeated and frightened like Colonel Todd?

The dream was at an end for Maxwell Todd. But even as a shell of a man, he was magnificent. When she had seen him in Delhi, she had thought more of his brokenness and ineffectuality. Now that she did not think of him as a husband-to-be, now that his inevitable destruction seemed complete, she viewed him as tragic, a hero—not of battles fought with bullets and swords, but of a war for humanitarianism and justice. Was that war really lost, as Max thought it was? Would all India someday see the horrors that Max saw in his delirium?

When Colonel Todd was between periods of illness he never spoke to her of anything dire. Sometimes Claire wanted to draw him out on the future of India, but she never wanted to distress him. Having told her once that the Raj was doomed, Max did not bring up the subject again. He thought she had suffered enough; there was no reason to distress her further. Perhaps he was only vaguely aware of the rambling that she heard when he was fevered.

Colonel Todd tried to make her days pleasant, insisting that she come with him for a stroll or a picnic; and Sevaley would follow along with a wicker hamper and Jeremy. Claire would not have given in to his entreaties except that she felt responsible for him, just as he felt responsible for her. She had an idea that she must try to restore him, and it gave her life a sense of purpose. India had used him up, but it was she who had added the final touch to his devastation. It was time to atone, to try to set things right.

"Oh, Max," she sighed one evening when he had danced her out onto the veranda of the club, "if I had married you——"

"Hush, Claire. It was a foolish delusion of mine that it would have made things different. It would have only made it more painful in the long run, to have you share my fate. I am glad that you are the wife of Colin Whitecavage. Men like Lord Dalhousie and I are of the past now, and it is the likes of Colin Whitecavage who must deal with India's tomorrow. You will not be wasted on him, Claire."

"Max," she reminded him gently, wondering if his mind was really leaving him, "Max, Colin has returned to the Rani, and I am going away forever."

"No, Claire," he answered, and she could feel his fond

smile upon her. "Colin will find he has needs that no one but you can fill."

"How can you know that, Max?"

"Because I know Colin. The Rani loves him, but she is an Indian woman and exists for the sake of her children. Since she has become a mother, she lives for her child. Colin needs a woman who lives for *him*."

Claire laughed and laid her hand on his arm. "Dear Max, you do try to make me happy."

She was wearing roses in her hair, as she had been the night they had danced together so long ago at Cottington Crest, when she had been so young and so much in love with him. He plucked one from her hair, in remembrance, as he had done then. "I did tell you, Claire," he said, "India has no rose so lovely as you."

Each of them was caring of the other. And it was only natural that they should return to England together. Claire wrote to Colin asking that Max be her escort and received a simple businesslike answer.

Dear Claire,
    I shall be happy to agree to having you return to England in Max's company. You will be safe in his hands. It would be advisable, of course, to add some other lady to your party, who might be of assistance to you. I trust that you and the baby are well.

                              Your husband,
                              Colin Whitecavage.

It was the only communication he had sent since leaving Ootacamond, and it did nothing to reassure her of his love. When she had maligned Tamila, she had perhaps gone beyond the pale of his forgiveness. Go back to his heathen slut, she had told him, and no doubt he had. Her words had been merely a measure of her own sufferings, but she could not expect him to understand that. At least she had not whined and begged him to stay with her.

She had set him free of her with her threats and her anger. And she was glad that she had had the courage and the pride to do so. If I had not fallen under the elephant, things would have been different, she told herself. But she wasn't sure. She could not know that his heart would not have belonged to Tamila even then. Perhaps she was only using her accident as an excuse for her problems with Colin.

The rains came, and it was time to make the trek across the jungles and plains to Calcutta. Neither Max nor Claire was really glad to leave their sanctuary, though a Mrs. Wilkerson, who was to join their party, was delighted. All along the way she rejoiced to be leaving India. The conditions of the roads, the appointments of the dak bungalows, the spicy foods, and incompetent coolies were endurable only because she was returning to England. Unlike her companions, she was not going because of her health. She was middle-aged and her children were grown. Her daughter had recently married and her son had joined his father's regiment.

"My dear, I am simply not needed here anymore. I have earned this, and I am going to enjoy it," she was fond of saying.

"Aren't you worried about leaving your husband alone?" Claire asked.

"Heavens no!" Mrs. Wilkerson gave a conspiratorial chuckle and patted Claire's knee. "Albert will be well taken care of. Of course, he'll probably install some native woman who pleases him in the cook's quarters, but I don't mind. I have had enough of *that*, too."

Claire was baffled and then shocked, and Mrs. Wilkerson tut-tutted. "Oh, for a young thing like you, it's different, I suppose. But when you reach my age. . . ." She sighed and, intuiting that Claire did not share her own carefree attitude about parting from her husband, said reassuringly, "Dear girl, you cannot imagine that whatever they do with these native women means anything. It is mere animal pleasure and no more to be worried about than their brandy and cigars."

Under other circumstances, Mrs. Wilkerson might have thought that Mrs. Whitecavage's husband was the one who should be worried. She did not quite understand the close relationship between Colonel Todd and Claire. Obviously they were devoted to each other, and Mrs. Wilkerson would have thought that Colonel Todd was wildly in love with Claire, except that it was absurd, considering the situation.

Certainly it would be indecent for poor Claire to be the object of anyone's illicit desires. And obviously Colonel Todd was too ill to be having such thoughts. Mrs. Wilkerson could only accept the story that Colonel Todd was an old friend of Claire's father, and since Claire seemed to have such affection for the Colonel, it was a blessing that she could not see how thin and waxen he was becoming.

By the time they boarded ship, everyone but Claire was

certain that Colonel Todd would not live to reach England.
But day after day he held on, emaciated and shrunken, loyally escorting Claire to the dining hall, urging tidbits upon
her and persuading her to eat, if not for her own sake, for
the sake of the child who depended on her milk.

Max ate almost nothing, but he continued to give Claire
the impression that his meals were hearty, remarking to her
on the deliciousness of the beef or the quality of the wine.
She tried to please him with gaiety, but when inevitably she
thought of her husband and became morose, he charmed her
with tales of shipboard happenings. He described for her the
various passengers, charted for her the activities of a certain
officer who was attempting to court a young lady with a disagreeable mother, related the escapades of cabin boys who
had found it easy to steal strawberry tarts and chocolate cake
from the mess.

She wept only once, when a school of flying fish was
spotted and everyone rushed to see. The shouts of delight
made her sightlessness unbearable, but as always, Max was
there to make the darkness brighter.

"They were so beautiful coming over, Max," she sobbed. "I
wish I could see them again."

"Why, you can, Claire," said Max. "Of course you can."
And he made her concentrate on a picture in her mind, guiding her to draw from her memory the graceful leaping of the
fish, the iridescence of their silvery scales in the sun, the
turquoise and aquamarine of the water, the ivory fan of
spray. Long after they had left the fish behind, the images remained in her mind, and she was quietly happy. After that
Max spent much of his time teaching her to conjure other
visions—teaching her to see the shape and texture of the
wind-filled sails, the glare of sunrise on the water, the white
shadowed gleam of moon. He taught her to touch her velvet
curtains and create the richness of maroon color, and to
imagine people's faces from the sound of their footsteps and
voices.

At first Claire was dubious. "What if the color is blue?"
she asked of the curtains. "What if a man is thin, and I imagine him to be portly?"

"What if, what if?" Max replied. "It is your vision, Claire.
It belongs to you, just as our visions of India belong to us
and shall never fade."

And Claire understood that in a way he lived in a world
like hers now, a world of imaginings—of what had been and

was no more, of what should have been and never would be. Because of Max, Claire's world became rich and vivid. She learned to use her heightened senses as an artist would a palate. She thought that she could distinguish a quick eager step from a quick anxious one or decide a facial expression from the nuance of a sigh. She honed her skills constantly, spending her hours designing a world which in some respects suited her better than the one she had left.

There was only one thing that Claire could not imagine— was afraid to imagine. And that was her baby. Only in her dreams did Jeremy's face appear, and in those instances in which the child bore a resemblance to the Rajah, Claire would waken screaming.

Then kindly Mrs. Wilkerson would light the lamp as though that might help and, patting her quivering shoulder, would ask her to repeat her dream. "That way, you'll not have it again, dear," she would insist.

But the idea of explaining seemed to horrify Claire more than the nightmare itself, and her well-meaning companion soon desisted. Perhaps, thought Claire, her accident had been necessary. If she were to see resemblance to the Rajah in Jeremy, she might not be able to love him. This way she would never know, and Jeremy would have the love he deserved.

Of course, that was if the doctors in London were unable to cure her. It sometimes entered her mind, after one of those dreams, not to consult them at all. Perhaps it would be better. . . .

She longed to discuss the idea with Max, but she could not—even with him—especially with him. She wondered what Max had made of the letter she had sent back to him after her "kidnapping" by the Rajah. Had he understood that it was because of Colin she had wished to travel to Pandeish? Or had he, as the Rajah had hoped, imagined that she had found satisfaction in his bed? Max never mentioned the letter or her departure from Simla. Perhaps it would have been too painful.

Maxwell Todd was content with the present. It was of no use to review the past. He had left Delhi broken and useless, but Claire had given his life new meaning. She could not give him back his health, but he wasn't sure he really wanted it, just as Claire wasn't certain that she wanted her sight. Max knew that he could not have Claire forever, and so he did not mind so much that the days during which he basked in her loving concern were most likely his last.

"Ah, Max, I was a fool not to love you," she said one evening as they strolled the deck.

"I am well satisfied, my darling," he sighed.

Maxwell Todd lasted longer than Mrs. Wilkerson might have expected. They had docked at Malta and gone ashore for the night, when he collapsed for the last time. There in a spare, stone-floored room, Claire clutched his hand as he drew his final breaths—of air perfumed with orange blossoms and scented creeper drifting in with the soft southern breezes from the arcaded garden where geraniums, fig trees, and oleander mingled in the night.

In his dying moments, it was he who comforted her. "It is better here, in this beautiful spot, Claire. Better than on the ship or in London."

"Don't talk so, Max. You are coming with me to Cottington Crest. We'll ride on the moor, and you will get well."

"No. Sir Henry would take me in, of course. But you will go back to India, and I could not bear being without you."

"I have sworn not to return to India, Max," she said.

He opened his eyes and looked at her, as though to fix her face in his soul for eternity. "You will be needed, Claire. You must go back. You are India's finest rose." A ghostly smile played about his mouth, and became a ghostly grimace as Mrs. Wilkerson and Sevaley watched.

"Max?" cried Claire. And then in a voice of panic, "Max!"

In response, she felt Mrs. Wilkerson's gentle arm about her, leading her away. She struggled, trying to find her friend somewhere in her darkness. The shock threatened to overcome her. She had not known the seriousness of his condition as the others had. "Max!" He had never failed to answer her. She had come to depend on him so. At last she found her way to the bed again and threw herself on her knees beside it.

"Oh, Max, I love you!" she whispered. And it was true.

21

As they neared London, Claire wondered how her father would receive her. She had had only one letter from him during her time in India, immediately following her mother's death, but there had been little opportunity to receive another since mail would not have followed her to Pandeish. She had dictated a letter from Ooty, informing him of her marriage and of her need to return home. But Papa was not waiting for her at the dock.

"Perhaps he's disowned me," she speculated to Mrs. Wilkerson. "I was supposed to marry Colonel Todd, you see."

"Tch, that can't be the case, child. Perhaps he was given the wrong day of arrival. Or maybe his carriage has broken down. You'll come home with me."

So Claire helped Mrs. Wilkerson open her white frame house on the outskirts of London. It wasn't as grand a place as Cottington Crest, but it was pleasant. Mrs. Wilkerson was in ecstasy as she took dust covers off her Louis XV zebra parlor suite and unwrapped her Parian cupid statuettes. Claire sent a communication to Cottington Crest, but the days passed and Sir Cottington did not make an appearance. Claire became more and more distraught. She would not blame her father if he never wanted to see her again. He had sent her to India to put an end to scandal, and she had not only created another by failing to marry Max, but she had been the inadverent cause of her mother's death, insisting on her adventurous ways.

But Claire could not believe it. She was his only child, and they had no one now except each other. Meanwhile, Mrs. Wilkerson aided her, obtaining appointments for her with the most renowned doctors in the city, and she reluctantly sent the bills to Colin, fearing that her father had disowned her.

One by one Claire kept the appointments, accompanied by Mrs. Wilkerson and Sevaley, her faithful guide, patient and silent as a loyal dog, glaring resentfully when physician after physician plunged her mistress into paroxyms of tears. "Please, Mrs. Whitecavage, ask your servant to wait outside," they began to ask. Sevaley's hostile presence made them uneasy. They were used to malleable women, women who were impressed by their maleness and position of authority, women who obeyed them and revered them unquestioningly. This strange Indian girl was a threat to all that.

Of course, by nature, Sevaley should have been subservient. But she had been with Claire too long. She had absorbed other values, her vision broadening even as Claire's narrowed, her eagerness for life dimming and her spirit faltering. In Sevaley, self-determination seemed intensified; she wasn't the simple girl she had been when Max had first assigned her to Claire as a servant, and perhaps it wasn't a good thing. Sevaley wasn't fit to live among her own kind anymore, and certainly she did not belong among *Angrezis* either. Certainly Claire's doctors didn't think so. They felt she might cast some foreign spell upon them with those black malevolent eyes.

Sevaley would have if she could, for her mistress grew tense and pale before these occasions and afterward would withdraw to her room and refuse to eat. Each visit made Claire more despondent than the one before. It seemed it would go on forever, but finally there were no more doctors to visit and no more hope. All had told her the same thing as the doctors at Ooty. Her condition had been caused by a shock and might return spontaneously. But it was a small chance and could not be counted upon. Claire withdrew again as she had at Ootacamond, and not even Mrs. Wilkerson's solicitousness could draw her out.

Along with hope for her restored sight, Claire gave up hope that Max had been right that Colin would need her in ways the Rani could not satisfy. She gave up a dream of returning to India, a dream that had sustained her without her even really knowing it existed.

"If only Papa would answer my letters," she sighed. "If only I had someone. . . ."

"You must go to Cottington Crest yourself," Mrs. Wilkerson decided.

"But it is obvious that he doesn't want to see me," Claire protested. Of all the things that Claire could not bear, this was the worst—that her father should hate her so. He had understood her in a way that most men could not have begun to do. It was he, after all, who had insisted on allowing her to consider Max's proposal. If she were with Papa, she might find some sense of solace. But even news of her blindness had not brought him to her side.

"I'm sure he still loves you," Mrs. Wilkerson urged. "If he were to see his grandson. . . ."

"Very well, I'll go, if you'll go with me," Claire agreed at last.

On a blustery December morning they arrived at the gate of Cottington Crest. Mrs. Wilkerson was sorry at once that they had come. Cottington Crest was itself as dismal as Claire, but Claire could not see how gloomy it looked, and her companion kept up an encouraging patter as they alighted.

"What a magnificent place!" she cried. "What fine hawthornes in the dooryard! I adore the garden statues. What wonderful cast-iron figures of greyhounds! I should love to see this place in the spring, Claire!"

Mrs. Wilkerson was rewarded by a wistful smile about Claire's mouth. Standing there on the lane, Claire painted her home the way Max had taught her to paint the flying fish on the ship from India. She heard the wind in the oaks that lined the drive, and in her mind she drew them a summery green—why not? Hadn't Max said that it was her vision that counted? She added hedgerows of sycamore and alder and populated the sky with wheatears and curlews, whose call was the first sign of spring. In the garden her mother's prize asters bloomed, and morning glories twined about the whitewashed bowers.

Mrs. Wilkerson guessed how Claire occupied her mind and almost envied her. For the sight that greeted her own eyes was quite different. Curtains were pulled tightly shut over every window, and part of the moorstone house was stained a dirty charcoal shade, evidence of flames that had licked up its side from an expanse of burned heather. Mrs. Wilkerson had heard of such "fire raisings" in Dartmoor, set by vandals or naughty children who burned heather or gorse for the mere fun of it. It appeared that the house had been only slightly damaged, but it was the fact that the fire had been set at all that bothered Mrs. Wilkerson. Surely no one would have attempted the act had the place been occupied with the usual complement of staff and servants. As for the hedgerows that Claire pictured, they had almost been destroyed, apparently cut down for firewood, which was scarce on the moor.

"Why is no one coming to meet us?" Claire wanted to know, alarm in her voice for the first time.

"I don't know," said Mrs. Wilkerson, and stumbled over a piece of rain gutter that must have been blown down in some autumn gale. The sound of it rattled and echoed, and suddenly Claire was aware of the loneliness of the house; and it seemed to her that her home called out to her with some sad message that she dared not understand. The happy picture in her mind crumbled, and she began to see Cottington Crest with more truth that even Mrs. Wilkerson. The smell of char blew strongly in her nostrils, although Mrs. Wilkerson did not notice it.

Mrs. Wilkerson still entertained a faint hope that Sir Cottington had merely allowed the place to run down without his wife or daughter present to take charge. After all, there were wreaths on the paneled doors. It was the season for such things; she had noticed a number of decorations as they had traveled. But as she reached the marble step, she gave a gasp of dismay. It wasn't a Christmas wreath at all, but a faded funeral wreath which someone hadn't taken away.

Claire could not guess the reason for the gasp, but she understood its import, and before Sevaley or Mrs. Wilkerson could stop her, she had begun to run. The two women rushed after her, Sevaley gathering up the folds of her cloak but hampered by the cashmere boots that had been bought for her in London for winter wear. Mrs. Wilkerson was impeded, too—by shortness of breath—and she struggled on, panting, horrified that her charge would have another accident.

But Claire knew where she was going and needed no one to guide her there. They found her in the little graveyard in the fields behind the house. There, beneath the overhanging willows, Claire counted the gravestones, running her hand over the top of each known marker until she came to the one that was new, the one that should not have been there. And then, sinking onto her knees, she wept.

For a time they couldn't move her, and they fretted over

her exposure in the raw air. She listened at last to their entreaties for the sake of the baby, who had been left bundled up in the carriage, and remembered that a key to the door should be beneath the lip of the well. When this was found, Mrs. Wilkerson ushered them inside, wheezing at the dust as she pulled sheets from the exquisite French rosewood furniture that had been Claire's mother's pride. Mrs. Wilkerson and Sevaley built a fire in the fireplace and made tea.

"I should have known why he didn't come to see me!" Claire said, her first wild grief abating. She was alone now without any male protector, and Mrs. Wilkerson did not want to voice the question that formed in her mind. What was Claire to do?

"You must write to your husband at once," she said. "I suppose he will make some arrangement for you to go to his family."

"No," said Claire.

"But you must. I imagine that you haven't met them and because uh——"

Claire didn't wait for her to finish her awkward thought. "No," she said, "those aren't the reasons." Mrs. Wilkerson was too polite to ask what the reasons were, and she did not guess that pride prevented Claire from disturbing her husband in the arms of his royal mistress.

Claire went up to bed in the room where she had danced in the moonlight on hearing of Maxwell Todd's proposal. Changing into her embroidered cambric nightgown, she climbed wearily between the icy sheets. The coldness seemed to creep into her bones and hover in eddies about the spot of warmth she created with her body. When last she had slept here, she had had little idea of the passions of love. She could not have guessed how easy it was to be undone by love or how unexpectedly it could seize control of a woman's heart. Life had been simpler then, when she had imagined her love for Maxwell Todd would burn forever with a pure white flame.

She wondered if the room had the same sweet innocence it had then. The set of French enameled cottage bedroom furniture was the same, and the same pear-shaped wedgewood pitcher with flowers painted in their natural colors sat on the wash basin. The draperies seemed the same, too. But had the sky-blue color faded and gone gray? Her dreams took her back to India—to a string bed in the Rainbow Palace and the Rajah's triumphant, smiling face above her quivering body. The exquisite Rani hung in her slumber, too, suspended in clouds of gossamer veils; and always, always, there was Colin.

In the morning, warmth stole across her bed, and she imagined that he had come to sleep beside her. But when she turned to embrace him, the spot beside her was empty and waking she realized that the warmth must come from the sun, which always came in on bright mornings. Ordinarily the drapes would have been closed at night, but no one had bothered, perhaps because it wasn't to be imagined that glare would disturb a blind person.

But Claire did not feel disturbed. Instead, she felt a sense of sanctuary. *I cannot bear to leave here again,* she thought. Calling Sevaley, she dressed and went down to the dining room where Colin had surprised her while she was in rag curls what seemed a thousand years ago. Mrs. Wilkerson was already there; and breakfast was ready, but it was nothing like the lavish affair of old. Only a few staples had been available in the kitchen and no servants to prepare them. Mrs. Wilkerson herself had made biscuits and found some jam, but there had been no butter for the biscuits and no cream for the tea.

"There was a cow wandering about, trampling the holly bushes," she said, "but I'm sure I could never have milked it. Ah, well, we have seen worse conditions in India, and at least we shall not be here long. Are you up to traveling today, dear?"

"No, not today."

"Well, that's to be expected. Such a shock. I'll take the carriage and go to the village for some supplies. We'll stay the rest of the week, if you like, poor lamb."

"Please don't stay on my account," said Claire. "I intend to stay longer than the rest of the week."

"Well—we can, if you must." Claire heard the distaste in Mrs. Wilkerson's voice and judged her reluctance more closely than if she could have seen the lady's face, which from habit, she carefully controlled. "But of course, there's much to be attended to in London. You must see your father's solicitor, who has no doubt been unable to locate you, and you will have to arrange the sale of the house."

"I am not going to sell Cottington Crest."

"Not sell it! What will you do with it, then?"

"I'll live here, of course. It's my home."

The stunned silence told Claire her friend's disapproval of her plan, but then she had expected as much. She fought back a smile as she imagined Mrs. Wilkerson's discomfited expression as she sought for a tactful reply. *You cannot live here because you are blind—because you are not a whole person. You must go to relatives who can take responsibility for your son. Surely you cannot expect to raise him alone— even with a reliable nanny he is likely to run amuck with a mother who cannot see what he is up to. And that native girl would never do for a housekeeper.*

These were Mrs. Wilkerson's thoughts. They hung in the air, so audible to Claire that the silence was no silence at all. But Mrs. Wilkerson would not be so crude as to voice them. She pictured her companion plump and nervous, wearing a cap with little floating ribbons. Mrs. Wilkerson reminded Claire of her mother. Perhaps that was the reason she was comfortable with her, even though their natures were quite different.

"Your husband will never allow it," said Mrs. Wilkerson finally and gave a relieved sigh. She had thought of the perfect retort. Of course Major Whitecavage would forbid her; any husband would. Claire must realize this, but Mrs. Wilkerson wondered if the accident had not affected her reason as well as her vision.

"I don't care if he will not allow it," said Claire, giving credence to Mrs. Wilkerson's idea of lost reason. "It's what I'm going to do. Colin's life is in India, and mine is here. He will have to come to England to convince me to leave Cottington Crest, and I believe he knows me too well to bother."

"But how will you manage?" Mrs. Wilkerson gazed around her. If Claire could see the place, she would be less nonchalant about living here. Everything was dusty and disused. The silver service was black with tarnish, through which ran rainbow streaks of red and blue. In one corner of the room the French wallpaper hung precariously, in a gigantic upsidedown curl, where a leak in the ceiling had caused it to work loose. The rest of the place was in equally shameful condition.

But Claire did not see. Nature compensated her that small bit. "I'll post notices in the village offering the servants their old jobs again," said Claire, thinking out her plans as she went.

"They'll steal everything if you can't keep an eye on

them!" Mrs. Wilkerson protested. "And if they don't steal, they will skimp on the polishing at the very least." She seemed to think that one possibility was as bad as the other.

"Sevaley will be my eyes," said Claire.

"Sevaley! Oh, but it's one thing to have her lead you about and quite another to entrust one of *them* with a household."

"Sevaley is a quick learner. She will do beautifully."

Mrs. Wilkerson kept objecting, but Claire could not be swayed. So Mrs. Wilkerson felt it incumbent on her to remain at Cottington Crest, too, for the time being. She could not bring herself to abandon poor Claire, or the dear, dear baby.

"She's quite demented," Mrs. Wilkerson told a visitor to the house several days later.

The woman sitting across from her in her fine silks was obviously someone of note. Mrs. Wilkerson had known it even before she had been announced as Lady Rutherford.

"What a pity. But then Claire always was unusual," the visitor answered sympathetically. The former Jenny Bainbridge no longer wore her blond hair in ringlets, but elaborately crimped from its center parting and puffed over her ears before reluctantly hiding its splendor in a chignon at the nape of her neck. Her wide, round hat with its curtain of lace was like an enormous bowl turned upside down on her head, and her crinolines, which spread over both arms of her chair, gave her a shape like a child's top. She would have made a marvelous show, had she been stood on end and spun; for in accordance with fashion, she wore a gown adorned with stripes of pink and mauve.

Claire might have thought Jenny looked like a circus tent, but Mrs. Wilkerson was awed by her smart appearance. How flattered she was that Lady Rutherford wanted to sit and chat with her! It was only because she was Claire's friend, of course, but Mrs. Wilkerson glowed with self-importance. She was even able to overlook Jenny's fat toddler, who alternated between chewing the fringed tassels of the parlor draperies and poking precious Jeremy, who had been left in Mrs. Wilkerson's care while Claire went for a walk with Sevaley.

"So Claire did not marry Colonel Todd after all," said Jenny, turning the words in her mouth like a sweet.

"No. And I cannot see why not. Such a kind man and so devoted to her. But perhaps it's just as well. Colonel Todd is dead, and Claire has troubles enough without being a widow."

"She is blind, you say?" asked Jenny.

"Kicked by an elephant."

"Claire was always so impetuous. You would never get me to India!" said Jenny, and both women shuddered; Jenny with imagining, Mrs. Wilkerson with rememberance. Mrs. Wilkerson rang a little bell, and a maid entered bringing tea and cakes. Mrs. Wilkerson beamed at the girl's crisp uniform and the attractively arranged tray. She was proud of how quickly Cottington Crest was regaining its grandeur. It was a tribute to Claire that servants had flocked back to her employ, some deserting other positions to fill her needs. Each one seemed to feel personally responsible for Claire, and there was no need for reprimands over careless work, no hint of missing silver. Often they went beyond what was required of them; and if Mrs. Wilkerson assigned candlesticks to be polished, she might find the sideboard they sat upon gleaming as well, with even its drawer handles shining. Mrs. Wilkerson felt she was managing well, and she was delighted with this show of competence before her illustrious guest.

"Whom did Claire marry, then?" asked Jenny, selecting a cake drenched in sugary icing.

"A Major Whitecavage. Quite a dashing sort and young for his rank. The kind of man to turn a girl's head. But too tempestuous for my liking. All Ootacamond heard of their quarrels. In the evenings he used to dance with other women and leave his wife alone in her room with only that native girl of hers. And if one merely got in his way when he had been drinking, he looked as though he would like to clear his path with his sword."

Mrs. Wilkerson shuddered again, and Jenny shivered with her, but her shivering wasn't the same as Mrs. Wilkerson's. Jenny was remembering Colin Whitecavage, and the idea of his anger was more delicious than frightening. A fantasy flitted in her mind. Major Whitecavage was furious with her, seizing her about her tiny cinched-up waist and shaking her while passionate currents flashed over her like a summer storm. His burning eyes seemed to sear away her clothing as she collapsed helplessly in his arms—oh, it was nothing like William, who now and again raised her gown in the middle of the night and inserted himself without ceremony, as matter of factly as though he had been blowing his nose. It hadn't been that way at first. During their honeymoon months on the Continent, he had provoked her to unseemly behavior with his caresses. She blushed to remember it, but remember it she did, almost every day.

Things had changed when she had become pregnant, and after her child had been born, she had discovered that it had not been merely her condition that had kept him from her. William had lost interest, and no coquetry of hers could entice him again. He had his heir, and that was what he had been after. Jenny sometimes almost hated little William Rutherford the Second. Not only was he a sloppy child who spit oozy milk onto her shoulder and made stains in her lap, but he was the cause of her discontent with her husband. She would have been astonished to learn that Claire had a somewhat similar problem.

Jenny was certain that William's eyes had wandered elsewhere. It was too bad that Claire had had such an accident, but it did relieve Jenny's mind. She remembered how infatuated William had been with her once. Why, people had even expected them to marry! Indeed, the main reason for Jenny's call had been to see for herself whether Claire had managed to keep her beauty in India and to judge for herself what sort of threat Claire now posed. Surely she could be none now!

Jenny had been irritated at first that Claire wasn't at home, but soon she was pleased at the way the visit was turning out. Mrs. Wilkerson was a font of information. Jenny had learned things Claire would never have told her. Jenny scented scandal of the first magnitude, and she was only annoyed that Mrs. Wilkerson did not seem to have all the pieces. Mrs. Wilkerson was too obtuse, in fact, to see that there were fascinating parts missing from the story.

"Whatever did they argue about?" Jenny wanted to know.

"I do believe that she felt he was deserting her to stay in India," mused Mrs. Wilkerson, but Jenny wasn't satisfied.

"Was it because of another woman? One might expect. . . ."

But Mrs. Wilkerson wasn't the gossip that Jenny was. She had, in fact, removed herself from such unseemly conversations regarding Claire. Claire had enough to contend with without being maligned, and Mrs. Wilkerson had managed not to hear the rumor that Claire had run off with a rajah or that she had advised her husband to return to his "heathen slut." Mrs. Wilkerson did not care to have such nastiness invade her well-ordered world.

Jenny could learn no more, though she continued to probe.

At length she excused herself, saying that little William must go home to Thistlewood for his nap. Curiosity consumed her as her carriage took her homeward over snowy roads. Bells had been tied to the horses to jingle with a seasonal sound, but Jenny wasn't thinking of the holidays. Instead, she was hatching an idea. Perhaps she might get William to find out for her. She'd tell him he ought to go and see what could be done for Claire. It was his responsibility in a way to see after her, since he was the most important landowner in the area and Claire had no man to protect her. Of course, Jenny would not have dreamed of sending William to Cottington Crest if Claire had not had her accident. But a blind woman—that was nothing to worry about.

William Rutherford was as intrigued as Jenny. But he was less than delighted at the idea that he should put himself out to help her. His grumbling reassured his wife. Nonetheless, William took the first opportunity to visit Cottington Crest. This time Claire was home, her face eager and questioning as his footsteps came into the parlor.

William caught his breath. She was as beautiful as ever. No, she was more beautiful. When she had left Dartmoor, she had been only a girl. Now she was a woman, and he saw as another woman would not have the bloom of maturity that passion had left on her features. She was a woman who had been deeply loved, a woman of appetite. The absence of any vestige of demureness in her frank approach, the proud lift of her breasts above her narrow waist, the sensual set of her mouth, minutely but profoundly altered from a man's hungry kisses—all were signals to William. He wondered vaguely if the change had been accomplished by one man, and thought perhaps it had been more. A woman sheltered in the cocoon of a single love could hardly seem so worldly. Who besides Colin Whitecavage, he wondered, feeling breathless.

"Claire, it's William," he said, for the household was still disorganized and no one had announced him.

"Oh, William, how good of you to come!" She gave him a radiant smile and held out both hands, which he took in his and raised to his lips. She was genuinely glad to see him; she had been fond of him once and, in spite of the front she put on for Mrs. Wilkerson, it was good to think of having a man to turn to again.

William, for his part, felt a familiar surge as he pressed his lips to her warm skin. He had forgotten how much Claire excited him—by heaven, she excited him even more than when he had asked her to marry him. He ought to be grateful to Whitecavage for having carried her off to India, where she had ripened like a mango in the heat. Surely she was vulnerable. . . .

But while these thoughts filtered through William's mind, he was not quite cad enough to decide cold-bloodedly to bed her. Her lightless eyes in her bright face appalled him and moved him to pity. Why had he ever hesitated in proposing marriage to her? He had outsmarted himself; and now, having married Jenny while still in shock over Claire, he was saddled with a wife who bored him. Oh Jenny had all the proper voluptuous attributes of body, but it took more than that. He had been clever for so long, and then he had allowed himself to be entrapped by the sort of woman he despised. Claire's marriage might have turned out as badly, though, to hear Jenny tell it. Could it be that the two of them might—comfort—each other?

William formed no definite picture in his mind as to what form this comfort might take, but he began visiting Cottington Crest more and more, and Claire might have guessed what he was leaning to had she been able to see the expression that sometimes stole over his face.

All in all, Claire perplexed him. She seemed happiest when he talked to her about India, sharing news he had obtained as a shareholder in the East India Company. Dalhousie was leaving in February, he told her, and it was almost certain that Lord Canning would take his place. Claire always said that she hated India, but she would press him for every detail he had heard, a circumstance that perplexed him.

It was her husband, he thought. She hated him and loved him, and hated and loved India; and the two had become inseparable in her mind. She was not over him, but William didn't mind. He was an expert at mending wounded hearts. It was one of his specialities. It was only talking of India that tired him, only seeing that look of longing on her face. William learned little about Colin Whitecavage—only that he was stationed in Pandeish as President of the Regency of a minor princeling.

"It's a dangerous assignment," Claire said, "because Pandeish borders Rambad, and the Rajah there wants his own son on the throne of Pandeish. He once overran the country, and it was during the battle to retrieve it that I was injured. So I came home—so that Jeremy and I would not be a burden to Colin. He has his hands full in Pandeish."

"And his arms?" William almost asked. The story didn't seem quite like Claire. It wasn't in Claire's nature to run away, even handicapped as she was, not if Colin Whitecavage had made her feel loved. No, it must be that Colin had found it all too easy to cheat on a wife who could not see what he did.

On Christmas Day the perspicacious William stole away from Thistlewood, leaving Jenny admiring a diamond feather hair ornament and solid gold enameled bracelet with which he had gifted her, and made his way to Cottington Crest to give Claire a present that delighted her.

It wasn't possible to bring the gift inside, so Claire went outside wonderingly, wrapped against the weather in a bell-sleeved mantle. Then, because she was unable to see what he had brought, he had to tell her what it was.

"It's your mare, Claire. I bought her after your father died when the animals were auctioned off. But she belongs to you."

Claire exclaimed with joy and threw her arms about him briefly before rushing off to do the same to the horse. William grinned and felt himself a fine fellow for having made her so happy. For the moment he quite forgot that he had an ulterior reason for giving her the mare. The mare would give Claire more freedom and that could only work to William's advantage. William found himself hampered at Cottington Crest by Mrs. Wilkerson, who was always poking her head into the parlor, and by that damned Indian girl, who looked as if she wished to kill him. It was as though she could read his mind.

But the sure-footed mare would obey Claire's every command. It had always been wont to pause at every crossroad to await her direction, and so mounted, Claire could travel alone with little fear of becoming lost. Oh, not that William thought Mrs. Wilkerson would allow it. Some groom or stableman would be sent with her on her rides. But if he wished to arrange a secret rendezvous—well, it had been done once before, hadn't it?

Claire rode every day after that, even in bitter weather. Mrs. Wilkerson protested at first, but before long she became used to Claire's excursions. Claire had always loved riding, and her color improved, and the house resounded with laughter as she played with Jeremy. The poor girl deserved a little happiness, Mrs. Wilkerson thought.

"There is really no reason you need stay here," Claire told her friend as spring came on. "You ought to go back to London. You will have flowers to plant and parties to attend."

"I will plant flowers here," said Mrs. Wilkerson, who had grown much attached to Claire and Jeremy. "The baby will be walking soon, and you will need me to keep him out of things."

"The servants can do that," said Claire, "and it's high time I hired a nanny. It's because you want to see his first steps that you want to stay."

Mrs. Wilkerson could not deny it. "We haven't heard from Major Whitecavage," she countered. "I was charged with delivering you to your father, and since I could not do that, I cannot consider my duty finished until we have heard from the Major."

"That may be a long while," sighed Claire. She had sent a simple letter to Colin months before. *I have arrived home safely,* it had said. *Colonel Todd died and was buried at Malta. Jeremy and I are well and plan to stay at Cottington Crest.*

Claire didn't mention that she missed him intensely, though she did, and neither did she tell him what the doctors had said, though he would decipher that from her lack of comment on it. And though Mrs. Wilkerson would have been appalled to learn it, Claire had not told Colin that Sir Cottington was dead. She was determined to say nothing that might bind him to her in spite of his desires.

Meanwhile, Claire kept busy. There were her father's solicitors to deal with, matters of inheritance to be cleared away. She had been left wealthy, though not quite as wealthy as she had expected. Sir Cottington, out of grief for his wife, had allowed his business affairs to mire in the final months of his life, and Claire thought it would be a close thing to manage Cottington Crest on her income. Again Mrs. Wilkerson urged Claire to appeal to her husband to support her, but Claire would have none of it, though she knew Colin would have been willing. She preferred that he not know that her circumstances were doubtful. Instead, she decided to run sheep on the property as her father had done. William helped to select a flock at spring auctions.

Claire loved the outings, the drive through balmy air with perhaps a picnic along the way, attended by song of skylark and meadow pipit. These occasions were made to order for William, since Jenny would certainly not want to come along and breathe the stench of sheep. But how could Jenny complain about William's going? Hadn't she told him that Claire was his responsibility? But William was frustrated, for he had not yet found a way to make his move. At moments when he was about to kiss her, she would move out of his reach, innocently unaware of his intent. And Sevaley was usually along, making his opportunities far between.

"You ought to leave her at home," William would tell her. "She makes everyone stare. Those saris of hers make the horses rear."

But Claire would hear none of it, and so by May Jenny found herself once more pregnant, a situation incurred by his roughly venting his lust on her after one of his fruitless meetings with Claire. The matter made Jenny out of sorts. It was the season to go fox hunting in the kale fields, and Jenny would have to curtail her activities. But Jenny put a good face on her discomfort, flaunting the news as a sign of her husband's devotion. It was a bit of luck in a way. She was afraid that people were beginning to talk. Jenny used her condition as an excuse to upbraid William for his visits to Cottington Crest, and the pair of them engaged in shouting matches.

"How can you be so cruel to that poor girl!" he would cry. "What will become of her if I don't help her?"

"Oh! What of me? A woman should have her husband's companionship at times like these. I'm not well! I was quite faint this morning." And her pained eyes reminded him that it was all his fault that she felt ill.

But such appeals made William feel the entrapment of marriage all the more keenly. "You should be ashamed," he would tell his wife. "Claire's plight is far worse than yours. Give a tea party if you are lonely."

"Claire's husband ought to see to her," Jenny would say, and for a moment her anger would be directed at Major Whitecavage. She had hoped that Claire would confide in William, but apparently she had not, or William had not shared his information. Jenny's ploy had utterly failed.

Little Jeremy began to walk, balancing his body over widely-splayed legs, his arms waving with effort. He made a sound which everyone agreed meant "Mama." Mrs. Wilkerson, having received a letter from her husband informing her that he was returning home, left Cottington Crest at last, and Claire was entirely on her own. The departure unnerved

Claire more than she wanted to admit. She began to depend even more on William and was aware that she depended on him too much. I must see less of him, she thought.

Lord Rutherford, on the other hand, felt like cheering as Mrs. Wilkerson departed. But Claire still had Sevaley and a houseful of adoring servants to look out for her. He would have to get her away from the house, he thought; and while he was wondering what would cause her to ride out alone to meet him, fate played into his hands. He had gone away to London to attend a meeting of the large shareholders of the East India Company and returned with an interesting bit of information. It was information that Jenny would have longed to be privy to, since it concerned Major Whitecavage, but William did not share it with her.

William smiled a lot and made a trip onto the moor to see if the turfcutter's cottage were still deserted. Finding it in disrepair, Lord Rutherford swept it out and put it to rights himself. Everything was ready, he thought, satisfied with his day's work. Whitecavage was a clever dog. No doubt he had intended to seduce her when he had spirited her away to India right under William's nose. But now it was William's turn.

"Claire, dear, there is something important I have to tell you," he said on his next visit to Cottington Crest.

Claire set down her Chelsea bone china tea cup. "Well, then, tell me." She stiffened, for the tone of his voice alarmed her. What could have happened? Had a dog perhaps killed some of the sheep? Was there some trouble concerning one of her servants?

"I can't tell you here. There are too many people about. I wouldn't want it to become common knowledge."

"Well, I cannot imagine what secret——"

"It's about your husband, Claire."

He saw with satisfaction that he had her interest. The way her slender fingers clutched the carved rosewood arms of her chair betrayed her eagerness to have word of him. Her breath came quickly, and she almost seemed to tremble. Poor Claire obviously still loved the man. What he had to tell her would break her heart. And he would be there—waiting.

"I—will send Sevaley away on an errand. Then you can tell me," she said. She could not bear not hearing what William had to say. It had been so long since she had had word of Colin. She was quite unaware of Lord Rutherford's ulterior motives. She thought simply that she was seeing a side of him that had not been apparent before her marriage. In the months that he had been coming to visit her, his behavior had never been untoward, and she thought that she was merely his philanthrophy. One never knew how complex a person was, Claire sometimes thought, musing at the irony of her blindness having given her a lovely new vision of William.

"I cannot tell you here at all, Claire. For your own sake. There is too much risk."

The tone of his voice alarmed her. Whatever there was to learn about Colin would be distressing, and yet Claire wanted more than ever to hear it. Was he ill? But that couldn't be it. William would not need privacy to inform her of that. "Where, then?" she asked.

"We might go for a ride," he suggested.

"You and I alone? That might cause talk."

"Yes," he agreed with a sigh.

"Oh dear!" She squirmed with frustration and anxiety. "Wait, I know." She spoke to Sevaley, and the girl rose, taking Jeremy with her and closing the French doors behind her. "We will meet somewhere where no servants can possibly eavesdrop. You remember the night on the moor?" Claire blushed, but William nodded matter-of-factly.

"The cottage?"

"Yes. I'll meet you there this afternoon."

William feigned astonishment. He had allowed her to think of it herself. He had known she would. He knew how her mind worked. "But you mean you'd go riding alone? What of the groom?"

She didn't seem worried about the groom, he noticed. In fact, she no longer even seemed worried about what he had to tell her. Now she was eager with excitement and conspiracy; marriage and motherhood had not changed her a whit, he thought; and his heart began to race.

"I'll go alone. I'm the mistress of Cottington Crest, and I'll do as I please—especially now that Mrs. Wilkerson isn't here to make it difficult. I'll order the groom to stay home, and he won't dare disobey."

"But can you find your way?"

He knew the answer to this question, too. "Of course I can. The mare will tell me where the turns are, and I have only to take them. I can still map the moor in my mind."

"I will see you this afternoon, then," William murmured, rising and kissing her hand. Outside, he repressed an impulse to leap into the air and click his heels. He was bound to get his way this time, he thought; and it would be all the sweeter for the time that she had thwarted him in the very same cottage.

He had misjudged her then, but he did not think he had done so now. Then, her inherent sensuality had not bloomed, but now she had been loved, she had been married. She must hunger for love after all these months, and he was the one to fill her empty body with passion. William did not see himself as scheming; he was simply arranging matters to their mutual benefit, and the mores of his day did not allow him to do it frankly. He wondered if she had any inkling of his intent, and would not have been overly surprised to find that she was aware of every step of his plan.

Claire, however, was excited not by the idea of a rendezvous with William, but by her freedom, as she rode over the moor to their meeting. She was alone on the moor as she had been as a girl, and sometimes she made the mare gallop for the sheer thrill of it, as the moist smell of peat bogs and the cry of the raven assailed her senses. It was a perfect sunlit day, and Claire did not need her eyes to tell her of the gold glow that lay over the windswept hawthorns. Summer was finished; the land waited in the stillness of autumn. Smiling, she drew a picture in her mind as Max had taught her.

Her pleasure was marred only by the errand that had brought her, and now and again a sudden cold shaft of fear would shoot through her body. Perhaps William wanted to tell her that Colin was dead. He might have died in some battle, in some cruel, tortured way. The screams of the patriots who had been executed after the Rajah had captured the castle echoed across the moor with the cries of curlews. She remembered the corpses in the Hooghly and her journey on the raft with Colin. If he were dead, she wanted to be with him, floating into eternity together as they had seemed to do then. She pressed her heels against the horse's flanks to go faster and bury her fear in speed.

William was waiting to lift her down and lead her inside. The cottage was smoky from a fire he had lighted to take off the dank, and for the first time Claire felt uneasy in a way that had nothing to do with Colin. Memories of that other time washed over her—of how confused and terrified she had been and of how she had made him light a fire, then, too. But then Claire had known nothing of men. Now, she thought, she knew everything. She knew the devotion of Maxwell Todd, the tenderness and completeness of union with Colin, the helpless animal passions of the Rajah's bed. Claire wasn't frightened of the likes of Lord Rutherford.

"Now tell me, William," she said.

He led her to a settee, the only piece of upholstered furniture in the room. The odor of must which annoyed William only slightly affected Claire strongly; and the prickle of its cheap covering came through her riding skirt.

"Claire, he has been court-martialed."

"Oh," she gasped.

William noticed that she did not ask why Colin had been court-martialed, but he was too eager to tell her to think that she might already guess the reason. "He has been accused of trifling with the affections of the Rani of Pandeish."

Lord Rutherford waited, expecting her to swoon away into his arms. Instead, she sat rigid, shocked but composed. "Who accused him?" she asked, her voice small and quivering.

"Why the Rajah of Rambad, whose state neighbors Pandeish. There are witnesses against him, but they are really unnecessary, since he has admitted it. My dear, he is a cad. Please don't waste your grief on him! He doesn't deserve anyone so sweet—so lovely. . . ." William trembled as he cupped her face in his hand and began to stroke her cheek.

Colin Whitecavage had dealt him an ace and he was playing it. Whatever feelings Claire had left for her husband would be crushed beneath the twin weights of jealousy and betrayal. How would she react? She might collapse or she might be wild for revenge. Either way, William would be there to take advantage. But collapse had not come; she seemed to have survived the moment for fainting. He should act quickly, while she was still dazed, he thought, leaning forward and pressing his lips gently against hers.

There was no response, but she did not push him away, and William, encouraged, kissed her more firmly. Claire gave a slight, far-away moan, which William interpreted as arousal. Lord Rutherford fell onto his knees, seizing both her hands in his, covering them with ardent kisses.

"Oh, my dearest, oh my love—*he* has made you unhappy, and *she* has made me a miserable man. Oh, Claire, we are two lost souls, you and I! If we find each other under such circumstances, surely it is pardonable. If I had not been such a stubborn fool, we would have been married before you ever laid eyes on him! All that has happened has been my fault in a way! Darling, can you ever forgive me! Think of what might have been! Think of what *should* have been!"

William dropped his head onto her lap, where it came into contact with her warm thigh. Lord Rutherford felt himself sizzle like an egg deposited onto a hot skillet. Losing control, he threw back her skirt and continued his endeavor of kissing along the soft flesh that had exuded the wonderful warmth. But William had overstepped himself, and Claire, jerked to reality by the unthinkable caress, stood up abruptly and spilled him off onto the floor. Lord Rutherford had only a moment to feel banished, for unable to see where she was going, Claire immediately tripped over his prone body and fell on top of him.

The situation was made to order for William. With a simple reflex action he locked his arms about her, and her little felt riding hat fell off and was crushed as he rolled her over so that he was atop her. Her breasts strained against the silk of her blouse as she tried to push him away.

But William was stronger, of course, and his hands were busy with her buttons, while the pressure of his throbbing thighs against her stomach took away what little breath she had left.

Claire felt the momentary rush of air over her breasts, then the searing squeeze of his fingers. She knew by the way he had shifted atop her that he was also working to undo the buttons of his britches. She was trapped—helpless. She was reminded of the Rajah. It had been that way the first night when he had come to her apartment in the Rainbow Palace. He had dishonored her, and she had not been able to over-come him, not that night or ever. He had held her in a bond-age of lust, and she would not be so imprisoned again, not by any man! But the memory was so real that Claire had forgot-ten that the man atop her was not the Rajah of Rambad. She began to scream with frightening intensity, and William, who had expected only token resistance, was startled into rolling aside, his ears ringing and his ardor cooling.

"Claire?" My God, what had he done to her? He had in-tended to employ his male aggressiveness and strength only to overcome her natural feminine hesitation. He had wished to make her surrender seem inevitable, and therefore easy for her. It was a ploy that usually worked well for him, but Claire had gone berserk. Yes, that was it. The news about her husband had caused her to lose her mind.

William cursed to himself. He should have been more delicate about it, though he was damned if he knew how. Now
what was he to do? He had a crazed female on his hands. His
displeasure was all the more acute since Jenny had banished
him from her bedchamber until the conclusion of her pregnancy. William had been celibate for some weeks, and the
sudden interruption of his pleasure made him double over
with a cramp.

While he was incapacitated, Claire found the door and,
giving the knob a tug, opened it. Her trustworthy mare whinnied as she rushed outside, but Claire could think of nothing
but running. In her confused mind, Lord Rutherford and the
Rajah mingled in a welter of degradation. She would escape—escape to the moor which had befriended her when
she was innocent and pure, before she had loved and suffered. Today the air was clear, but for Claire the moor might
as well have been enveloped in black mist as it had been the
first time she had fled from the turfcutter's cottage.

William Rutherford, recovering himself, tried to follow her,
but too late. To his horror he saw her plunge forward, as her
boot caught on a rock. She tumbled over and over, crashing
into rocks and bushes until she catapulted over a ledge,
falling limply through the sunshiny air like some meadow
pipit shot down by a naughty child. William ran after her, his
checked swansdown frockcoat flying out behind.

"Claire," he whispered, having clambered down to where
she lay motionless on a fragrant expanse of heather. She
made no answer, but she was alive, and rushing to the stream
below, he returned with his handkerchief soaked in water to
bathe her face.

The icy water revived her, and she opened her eyes on a
magnificent cerulean sky. The light pained her so that she felt
as though she had been struck with a mallet of brightness.
She groaned and turned her head away and saw the gray-
green of heather. Every inch of her body ached from cuts
and bruises, but Claire was unaware of any discomfort.

The miracle had happened; the shock of the fall had
restored her vision.

She sat up gingerly, laughing and crying, afraid the
darkness might fall again, brushing away the tears that
blurred the frothy clouds, the wild steep reach of spongy
green that meant home.

And then, finally, she turned her glance on William Rutherford, half expecting to see the dark, compelling face of the

Rajah. Instead, William's face was crimson from his exertion, and his striped toilinette, blue on canary, strained over his midsection.

Claire began to laugh as the nightmare left her and laughter mixed with her joyous tears. "Why, William, how portly you've become," she said, and ended his hopes forever.

22

"I must go to him, Sevaley," Claire said the next morning after William had brought her home to Cottington Crest. She had been put to bed with poultices for her bruises, but Claire's mind was too busy to focus on her pain.

The doctor came and dosed her with laudanum, but it did not have the intended effect. Claire remained awake, her rugged consciousness filled with hallucinations of Colin Whitecavage. The mystical essence of his presence emanated around her. She seemed to breathe his masculine scent. She could almost feel the roughness of the material of his uniform as he embraced her. The graying of morning behind the drawn curtains and the screeching of blackbirds had faded the waking dream, but even so, Claire thought of nothing but Colin.

She heard the baby cry and ordered it brought to her, and not until then had she made her decision. It was Jeremy who made the decision easy, for the baby features that Colin had found so difficult to describe had molded, and her son could be the child of no one but the man she so loved.

"We will go back to India, Sevaley," she cried.

"But he hasn't sent for you, Memsahib," said Sevaley doubtfully.

"It doesn't matter. He needs me. I know it. The trial will be long and difficult. I must stand beside him!" Claire herself was surprised by her resolve. She had sworn not to return to India. He had, after all, been unfaithful to her. He had chosen Pandeish above her, and he had chosen the Rani as well. He had sent her away, turned his back on her when she

315

would have gladly given her all to continue as his wife. Why shouldn't she turn *her* back on him now?

But perhaps she was thinking of what Max had predicted—that he would have needs that only she could fill. Had that time come? Like a fool she would go and see.

She arrived in Calcutta in spring of 1857. Standing on the deck of the ship with Jeremy at her side, she was awash with excitement as the first buff and white pukka houses came into view. A haze of heat hid the spires of the city, and there was the usual putrid reek of the Hooghly, the acrid aromas of the burning ghats, of garbage and excrement. But Claire saw only the green lawns of the Garden Reach as she drove to the hotel. The smell of frying chunna and masala cooking overcame the unpleasant odors; and along the causeway the palette of complexions—cinnamon, sienna, umber, and mahogany—filled her with pleasure. Too long her world had missed the bright saris, the glint of graceful bangles, the earthy half-nakedness of dhotis, and the majesty of turbans and voluminous white trousers. She had been in her room less than an hour when an enormous cockroach ran onto the hem of her crinoline. Claire shrieked but in a way hardly minded. She watched the sun set over the Ochterlony Monument and the splendid blaze of sun reflecting panes of brilliant gold from the windows of the Government House.

Darkness brought the first disembodied cry of a jackal. The sound made her shiver, reminding her of the night when her mother had died of the cholera, which had swept through the streets like an army of fiends, a thousand times more vicious and deadly than the packs of pariah dogs and jackals that roamed the night. The howls reminded her how treacherous India could be, and how deceptive. One afternoon they had been at a tea party and the next—Claire shuddered at the memory of the day she had buried her mother in the hat with the little dotted veil, but she did not shrink from recalling it. India had taught Claire to face anything that life—and death—had to offer.

At dinner, she was delighted to find an old friend calling out to her and hurrying to sit beside her. "Claire, oh, imagine seeing you here! I thought you'd left India years ago. When Colonel Todd returned from Simla without you as his wife, there were all sorts of stories." It was the woman who had spent so long embroidering her buffet scarf with scenes of England.

"What sort of stories?" Claire asked with a controlled smile.

"Oh, ridiculous tales about your jilting the Colonel and running off with some handsome young officer. That kind of thing. You know how it is in the cantonment. We are so coddled, and the truth is usually so dull—it's necessary to invent to survive."

"Yes, I know." Claire remembered the desperation of the garrison and excused everything. And she was amused to think that whatever scandal her acquaintances had fabricated could not measure up to the truth. The ladies of the cantonments were too sheltered to even dream of Claire's adventures. They could not imagine the bestial kisses of the Rajah or the blissful surrender to Colin Whitecavage. They could not guess how merciless were the twin demons of lust and power or of male revenge that consumed women mindlessly and almost unnoticingly.

And yet, Claire thought, women who had dealt with the demons of propriety and boredom in the cantonments were formed of the proper stuff to handle whatever was necessary. She toyed with a plate of prawns and wondered why the idea had come to her.

She sat, hands folded in her lap over her spread linen napkin, while the ambitious servant behind her speared the choicest slice of roast beef onto her plate, his knife blade shivering against that of her friend's server in contest over the meat.

"What are you doing in Calcutta this time of year?" Claire asked her friend. "I'd think you be getting ready to go to the hills."

"I'm going home to England," the woman said triumphantly. "It's because of the rumor, though that's not official. I'm supposed to be going because of my health. I mean, how would it look if the wife of a major——"

"What rumor?" Claire interrupted.

"Why, of the uprising, Claire!" Without glancing at the impassive Indian behind her, she spread a dollop of orange marmalade on a biscuit. She had been in the country too long for the presence of servants to unnerve her.

"There is always a rumor of uprising."

"But there are a lot of rumors this time. There is a tale of hundreds of men meeting on the parade ground with their heads tied up in white cloths so that only their eyes could be seen—and they swore to kill all the *Angrezi*. And there is a story of a plot to seize Fort William."

"Fort William! What an idea. No place would be more accessible to European troops to put down such a rebellion. The Hooghly would be full of battleships."

"Of course it's silly. My husband is certain that *his* men would never be disloyal. It's only the superstition, but it's affected my nerves."

"You mean the idea that the Raj will last a hundred years and no more?"

"Yes, the anniversary of the Battle of Plassey. It will be a hundred years ago this summer. And there was a sepoy, Mangal Pande, who attacked his superior officer. Much has been made of that. The truth is that he had been taking opium and bhang. He was a Brahman, and none of the others would help against him. You know, Claire, our men are as bored here as we are in their own way. The rumors are no more to be believed than the gossip that was whispered about you."

"Probably not," said Claire, and felt a chill. If the stories told about her had uncovered such a small part of the truth, then how much unrest might likewise be concealed?

She told herself it was a foolish notion. It was only that she had been with natives too much herself. It was only that she had been at the edge of a dahl field and had seen the Rajah meet the representative of the Nana Sahib.

"And what are you doing in Calcutta, Claire?" The question interrupted her dark thoughts.

She covered them with a smile and replied, "Oh, I am going to meet my husband in Delhi."

"Your husband. So you married after all. Happily I trust?"

"Oh yes. And we have a son. But I did not run away from Simla with him as your story has it."

"Of course not!" Her friend's eyes were hungry for details, but Claire turned her attention to her meal.

Her companion followed suit, but after a time a thought came to her. There was at least *some* scandal to talk about, something that couldn't be dismissed as foolish rumor.

"Claire, the most shocking thing—that Major Whitecavage who was your escort. He's being court-martialed. The thing is dragging on and on. They are reluctant to send him to prison because of his great exploits in Pandeish, but there is no way they can find him innocent. He deserves prison, the scoundrel!"

Claire tried to look surprised. Obviously Colin had not let it be known in Delhi that they were married. Was it because he did not want her name besmirched with his? Or was he simply not interested in owning up to her?

"You'd never believe it, Claire! He took the Rani of Pandeish for his mistress while he was the president of her son's regency. Who can guess what such a man might be capable of! And how fortunate that you were so well chaperoned while you were traveling in his company. Only think of the danger you might have been in from him!" And her friend gasped as she imagined it.

After that Claire avoided her. She was too curious, and though she rushed to sit next to Claire at tiffin the next day, Claire managed to seat herself between two officers, who were grateful for her company. "Tell me, is it true that the native regiments are on the verge of mutiny?" she asked.

"My dear lady, what an amusing idea! They are nothing of the sort! Why I would stake my life on the loyalty of my men! Wouldn't you, Charles?"

"Indeed," agreed the other. "Of course, it's to be expected that a few rabble rousers would try to make capital of the prophecy, but that is all it is. Or someone sees a comet and takes it for a sign. All nonsense."

"Is the Nana Sahib a rabble rouser?"

"Yes. He is merely trying to frighten Lord Canning into restoring the pension he thinks due him as the titular head of the Maratha Confederacy. Then, there is that wretched matter of the new cartridges, but that will blow over."

"The new cartridges?"

"Some of the men have the idea that they are greased with pigs' fat and so it would defile them to bite off the ends as it is necessary to do. Now a way has been devised for them to tear the cartridges apart with their fingers."

"I heard a rumor that Fort William will be overrun," Claire said.

But both officers assured her she would be perfectly safe at the garrison.

"I am going to Delhi," she said.

"To Delhi! At this time of year! You should go straight to the hills! Think of your child, if not of yourself!"

"Are you telling me that it is dangerous to travel to Delhi? It shouldn't be, if there is no mutiny afoot."

"Dangerous? No more than usual. But the weather! And these days the help cannot be depended upon. They desert at the slightest provocation. We've spoiled those brownies, I'll swan!"

Claire knew that the officers were right in thinking she should go to the hills. Even now, in April, the heat was stifling. Days were spent in her rooms with the Venetian blinds drawn against the scorching breeze, and rush tatties hung over the outer doors of the hotel. Mosquitoes invaded the netting, and the legs of the bed were stood in saucers of water to avoid red ants. Lizards crawling about the floors and walls made grand playthings for Jeremy. Worse, it began to rain, and Claire had to wipe mildew from her shoes each morning before she put them on. Mold grew on her hats, and her writing paper became unusable. No one ventured out until five o'clock, and Claire realized she would have to travel at night on her way to Delhi. The idea of being abroad in the night on the Grand Trunk Road unnerved her, especially with the mood of the country as it was. It was only a day or so after her discussion with the two officers that she saw the first magical symbols scrawled on the walls of the marketplace.

"What do they mean, Sevaley?" she asked.

The girl shook her head. "I don't know, but it's not good." Perhaps even those who had placed them there did not know the exact meaning of the marks. They were there to excite the natives and frighten the *Angrezi,* and that was all that mattered.

The incident gave Claire pause, but she did not relinquish the idea of going to Delhi. If only she could find some party of English that was going! But nobody seemed to be headed there. She was close to despair one evening when she visited the Park Street Cemetery to place a bouquet of roses on her mother's grave.

The wind whipped at her gown and made a shambles of her chignon as she stood there, lost in thought. Certainly Mama would agree that she should go to the hills—or would she? Claire remembered her mother's refusal to flee from the cholera and wasn't sure. The idea of the strength of Englishwomen pressed on her mind again. Mama in her hat with the spotted veil had been strong in her way—as brave as a soldier defending his fort. Mama's fortress had been marriage, its bulwarks propriety. Without women who were willing to risk to maintain it, there would have been no English society in India—or perhaps anywhere. Claire sighed and felt tears come to her eyes. She herself wasn't the sort to be a mainstay of civilization, and yet she thought Mama might have advised her to go on to Delhi after all. Mama might not have approved of her marriage, but Colin Whitecavage was her husband, and Mama would have thought she should be there to hold her head high in the face of disgrace.

Staring at Mrs. Cottington's marker, Claire wondered for the thousandth time why she was so determined to go to Delhi. Obviously she would only increase the scandal by appearing there as Colin's wife, but then surely the scandal was as bad as it could be already. Was it that she wanted to stake her claim to him? Did she want to shame him by standing futilely beside him in his trouble as she imagined he hadn't stood by her? He had made his choice—the choice she had given him, between her and Pandeish, between her and the Rani Tamila. Why, oh why, couldn't she let it be?

But as many times as she asked herself the question, the answer was always the same, it was the answer that would have made Mrs. Cottington throw up her hands in dismay. The answer was simply that she loved him and could not stop loving him; no matter if he loved the Rani, she could not live without him.

"Good evening, Major Memsahib."

As soon as she heard the melodic voice, she became aware that someone had been watching her. Turning, she saw a person she had thought never to see again, a turbaned Indian clad in an embroidered tunic with a scarlet sash, khaki duck trousers, and riding boots. Vazir Lal smiled at her as he had high in the mountains of Pandeish.

He salaamed low in a mark of great respect. He had always liked Colin Whitecavage's wife. How fortunate for Colin that Vazir Lal was a man of immense honor and already hopelessly in love with his cousin Tamila. Otherwise, the rides they had taken together in those high meadows might not have been so innocent. Claire Whitecavage was the one who had saved the Rani and her child from the Rajah, giving them time to escape. It still amazed him that she, a mere woman, had been able to accomplish what he had not. He remembered that he owed her a sacred debt.

"I am surprised to see you, Memsahib; I heard that you had gone to England."

"Yes, to see doctors there. But I am well, Vazir Lal. I can see."

"Praise be!"

"I am going to Delhi to be with Colin. . . ." She stopped

as his face grew fierce, and she realized that he knew what
had been secret before—he had become aware of Colin's
relationship with his cousin and because of it, their friendship
was at an end.

Vazir Lal did not understand the relationship between *Angrezi* women and their men. Had an Indian husband been unfaithful in the manner of Colin Whitecavage, his wife would
have fled back to her family and there would have been bad
blood then between the wife's family and the husband's. A
feud, perhaps.

Vazir asked himself the same question Claire herself had
been considering. Why was she going back to her husband?
She was alone with a small child, and she seemed to have no
family. Perhaps she had no choice. But Vazir took in Claire's
fashionable moire gown with its black velvet Swiss belt accent-
ing her tiny waist, her dainty shoes with pierced work across
the toes, her smart Mousquetaire hat of brown straw with a
lace curtain. No, Claire did not want for means to live. And
he did not really imagine that Claire suffered from lack of
choice. She was a woman who made choices others did not
think existed. She had chosen to remain in the castle rather
than accept safe conduct to the Rajah's lines and had chosen
to protect the Rani. If Claire were going to Delhi now, it was
because she wanted to go.

"The roads are dangerous these days, Memsahib," he told
her.

"You mean because of the unrest? I've been told it's nothing."

"Do not believe it. Have you heard the slogan that is being
whispered among the sepoys? *Sub lal hogea hai.*"

Claire shook her head. "I haven't heard it, Vazir Lal."

"It means, Everything will become red."

Claire felt as though she could not breathe. If she couldn't
go to Delhi, she couldn't live. "You are telling me this because you hate my husband, Vazir. You do not wish me to
go to him."

"It is true that I hate him, Memsahib. I would take his life
if fate gave me the chance. He was the only *Angrezi* I ever
trusted; I fought beside him in Pandeish as though he were
my brother, and he has been the most treacherous of all of
them. But if you are determined to go to Delhi, I will take
you. You will be safe with me."

"Travel in the company of my husband's enemy!"

"You have no choice if you wish to go to Delhi," he said

with a shrug. "We shall leave tomorrow evening. It will be no imposition on me, if you wish to come. I will only alter my route a bit. I am bound for Alijarh to meet friends, but Delhi is nearby. It is a good thing we are going now, for a time will come when even I will not be able to protect you."

"A time? You mean a certain day has been selected for an uprising?"

"I did not say that, Memsahib." Vazir Lal became impassive. "I mean only that the weather is unusually hot this year and there are more flies and mosquitoes than usual. If I take you to Delhi, you must promise that you will go to Simla by the end of May."

She was certain that the uprising would be then, and the next morning she went to the Government House and tried to obtain an audience with the Governor-General. Had she been Colonel Todd's widow, she might have succeeded, but she was not. She was only the wife of a soldier charged with embarassing transgressions against the Rajah.

"Please, it's about the mutiny!" she begged. But the officer in charge of the Governor-General's appointments was certain she was only using that ubiquitous subject as an excuse to ask for clemency for her husband.

Certainly it would be better if the Raj could forget that Colin Whitecavage had ever existed. It was understandable for a soldier to find his eyes and heart wandering among the beautiful women of India, but one didn't take a rani to bed. Even so, Major Whitecavage had been a hero, and the Raj might have closed its eyes to the situation had the Rajah not blackmailed it into action by making his punishment the price of peace in his area. Thank heaven, the matter had not become general knowledge in Pandeish! There would be upheaval if it did, and it would if Whitecavage were not punished. The Raj had tried to keep the charges against Colin Whitecavage secret, but there had been leaks—probably from wives who had pestered their husbands for information about the heroic Sword of Pandeish. But in Pandeish, only the Rajah's spies knew and they were unlikely to talk. The Rajah wanted the information suppressed and a loose tongue would lead to a severed head. But when the time was right, could anything stop the Rajah from using what he knew? The officers of the Raj little guessed just how much there was to become public. The Rajah had omitted the little Rana's parentage from his tale. It wasn't to his advantage to have it known—then Pandeish would lose its statehood and become British territory.

It would be disagreeable for Lord Canning to see Mrs. Whitecavage, and so Claire had braved the morning heat for nothing. The pavement sent scorching waves through the thin soles of her shoes as she returned to her carriage, beneath which lay her coolie seeking relief from the sun and drinking from his lota.

Claire was disappointed and out of sorts, but even had she managed to accomplish her errand it was doubtful that she would have been listened to. There were a thousand rumors, and hers had no more basis than the others. That evening she left Calcutta with the retinue of Vazir Lal. He was accompanied by several hundred cavalrymen from Pandeish, and Claire was glad for the size of their party, though it surprised her. He had obtained a comfortable gharry for her, Jeremy, and Sevaley, with lanterns to guide the horses through the night.

It was cooler in the countryside, and rain dripped pleasantly on the roof of the gharry. Claire did indeed feel safe, for in this large company she needn't worry about tigers or roaming bands of badmashes.

By mid-morning each day the company would call a halt, often, near a dak bungalow, where quarters could be obtained for Claire and for some of the officers whose families accompanied them. Oddly, Claire would often find herself assigned to some small filthy room or presented with nothing but cold curry to eat. On these occasions Vazir Lal would come to her aid with fiery eyes and a flood of Hindustani. Whatever he said brought results. With many salaams and apologies, Claire would be shown finer quarters, while bananas and oranges were produced and sometimes coconut fudge.

She would spend the day resting and bathing away the heat in the tiled bathroom, pouring jars of cool water over herself and the little boy. Claire felt safe, but uneasy at the same time. Her treatment spoke to her of the new attitude in the land. How different from when she had left! The servants were lazy and rude and had to be asked three times to do the simplest things. If she had not been with Vazir Lal—but Vazir had told her that there would be a time when even he could not protect her.

She began to think that she would be wise to do as he wished and go on to Simla. Perhaps Colin would join her there; he would be done with the army and Pandeish. Maybe they could start over together. Perhaps during the coming hostilities the British presence in Pandeish would be obliterated, but Colin could do nothing about it. He could not go running to Pandeish as he had before, and Claire as much as the Rani could claim him. On these quiet afternoons she dreamed that Colin would be overjoyed to see her and that they would settle down together on some sugar plantation in an out-of-the-way spot where the problems of the Raj would not touch them. But this was only a dream. Claire worried about the reception she would receive from her husband. He had not asked her to come.

Another matter troubled her as well. That was Sevaley. The girl had been in raptures on learning that they were to travel to Delhi with Vazir. Claire had all but forgotten how Sevaley had admired Vazir in Allapore. It had seemed a passing attraction, only schoolgirl foolishness. But Claire had not remembered how abiding girlish love could be. Just as her own love for Colonel Todd had survived the years, so had Sevaley's devotion to Vazir Lal. She was as smitten with him as ever, but now there were important differences that made the situation troublesome.

Sevaley was no longer the child she had been when she had first entered Claire's service. Like all Indian women, she had ripened early, as though the heat of the sun had brought her breasts to bloom. Her hair was long and lustrous, a luxurious pillow twined with blossoms against her ear. She had a graceful gait and was beautiful to see when the wind blew her sari against her curving figure. But beyond all this, Sevaley had something that set her apart from other Indian women.

Sevaley had formed ideas unlike those of her peers. And why not? Who among her peers had had an example like Claire? The association had affected Sevaley gradually but profoundly. She had seen Claire turn her back on an arranged marriage and follow her heart after her lusty, adventuresome major. When the Rajah had bedded her mistress, Sevaley had thought her conquered; but no, Claire had achieved a proposal of marriage from her "master." And then she had thrown it away to ride off with her major. All this had impressed Sevaley. An *Angrezi* woman could be more than a chattel. At least her mistress was. Sevaley was at a dangerous age, and she had selected Claire to admire.

She was not happy to be going to Delhi. In Delhi she would be reunited with her family, and her parents would no doubt think the time ripe to marry her to some sowar of good family. But Sevaley was no longer content to have it so. She did not want to marry a man whose face she would see for the first time on her wedding day. She dreamed of becoming the bride of Vazir Lal.

As the days of the journey passed, it became obvious to Claire that Sevaley had set her sights on Vazir. Claire would not have cared about that except that Vazir was nobility, and his caste was higher than Sevaley's.

"Marrying you would defile him, Sevaley," she argued, trying to reason with the girl behind the drawn tatties of the dak bungalow.

"You would not let that stop *you*, Memsahib," said Sevaley, who had bought a new pair of jade earrings in the bazaar in the last village and was evaluating their effect in the mirror, lining her eyes with kohl to make them all the more compelling.

"You will only be hurt," Claire went on, trying not to notice how beautiful her servant was in her kurta dress over flowing trousers, how exquisite her bangled wrists were as she arranged flowers in her hair.

"If it were hopeless, you would not remark on it," said Sevaley. "You were not upset in Allapore, and I loved him then. You have noticed the way he looks at me, Memsahib."

Claire did not deny it. Sevaley was always managing to be in Vazir's presence. When they stopped in some tope, she was always there to bring him a cool drink or an offering of grapes and cheese, and when they traveled she would find a horse and ride nearby so that he would be unable to take his eyes from her. More and more Vazir Lal stayed close to the gharry, feigning excessive interest in Claire's welfare when his excessive interest was in Sevaley.

"She is only the daughter of a shopkeeper, Vazir," Claire said once as the girl played pat-a-cake with Jeremy.

"I thought perhaps she was the daughter of a zamindar given to you for safekeeping."

"You are dreaming, Vazir. You know she is not the child of a great landowner."

"You are right," he agreed. "I *am* dreaming. But she acquits herself like a princess."

Claire sighed agreement. She supposed that nothing she could say would awaken Vazir from his dream. He had been in love with his cousin Tamila, but that futile love had been sullied. Vazir seemed to be suffering much as though he had been a suitor Tamila had rejected, and Claire wondered if that might have had something to do with his leaving Pandeish. Vazir himself was somewhat unusual in his society. Not many fell in love romantically as Vazir had. Love for most Indian men was not a matter of deep, sacred passion. Instead, they desired and acquired women more rationally. Beautiful women were to be valued, but they did not break hearts so often as *Angrezi* women.

Was Vazir's heart broken? Certainly he seemed changed. He was no longer the man she had met in the mountains. His bright spirit had clouded, his expression was often morose; and when he spoke to his men, his voice was sharp and angry. Sometimes when they halted in the topes, Vazir walked away to be by himself. He seemed in the throes of some crisis of the soul, but Claire couldn't persuade him to speak of it. He would not even tell her any more about his mission in Alijarh.

"What friends will you meet, Vazir?" she asked.

"Loyal friends," he replied, and he looked into the distance as though he could see them in the shimmering haze of heat. Friends who would not betray him as Colin had.

Only Sevaley seemed able to lighten his mood. Perhaps it was the combination of her beauty, her obvious purity, and her studied invitation. Sevaley was neither shy nor brazen like the prostitutes of the bazaar. She was a new experience to Vazir Lal. She smiled at him openly, and her smile brought him a vision of a sanctuary of peaceful innocence, some haven he longed to visit and never return from visiting.

Claire worried. She had formed Sevaley in her own image, and she began to understand for the first time how her own mother had felt. Thank heaven Jeremy wasn't a girl! He, at least, could not take after her.

But perhaps he might take after his father, and one could not shackle a man as one could a girl.

The next afternoon she found some dirty little chupatties lying on the dining table in the bungalow. "What are these, Sevaley?" she asked. "They look stale and too dirty to eat."

"A man brought them, Memsahib; and another man is making others to carry to more villages."

"But why?"

"I don't know," said Sevaley.

But Claire knew. It was a sort of message spreading over the countryside. It was magic or a harbinger. It's very meaninglessness terrified her. *There will come a time when I can-*

not protect you, Vazir had said. But that time had not come yet. The end of May, he had said. And May had only begun.

But Vazir Lal could not judge everything. And the tempest would not wait for its time. Vazir was impatient with every stop now. There was an urgency about him. He seemed to need to keep moving, and even when they halted, he paced about beneath the tamarinds and palms, as restless as a station elephant blowing dust and leaves across its back to chase away flies.

The air had a feel to it. Perhaps it was only the heaviness of the heat. But at Calcutta it had been hotter and more humid. Something more ominous than the vicious heat ladened the air.

Vazir was in a hurry to get to Alijarh, where the road from Calcutta met the road from Bombay forming a V from one side of India to the other. There he could hear news from all over India, learn what was being whispered in Rajputana, the land of kings, in Agra and Jhansi, and far south in the Deccan. One could hear such news, if one were Indian, if one knew where to place one's ear. Above Alijarh lay Meerut and Delhi. And far to the north, Pandeish. Would Vazir's travels take him home at last?

She could not believe that Vazir Lal would ever turn his back on Pandeish or put any loyalty before that to his state. But would be still be loyal to the Rani? She guessed that the Rani's perfidy with Colin was still not generally known. But the rumors must be growing—spreading just as the chupatties were spreading, from hand to hand, along with lotus blossoms, bits of goat's flesh, and leaves of brinjal, all of which seemed to have the same strange meaning.

Palace intrigue, Claire thought, and wondered if the mountain winds of Pandeish sang with the same hot fury. Surely some voice would begin to whisper that the little Rana did not have any claim to the throne of Pandeish. Whispers of unthinkable parentage would thread through Pandeish like morning mist through the pines. The little Rana was one of *them*—a foreign devil!

And then what?

Ghastly dreams had haunted her heat-troubled slumber on the string beds of the dak bungalows. The Rani, lovely and brave, her unlikely friend, ablaze on a pyre, perhaps Daruska as well. Tamila, whose crime was no more than Claire's—to have surrendered to a passion for Colin Whitecavage. Without an heir for its throne, Pandeish would become British territory, but in this atmosphere, its armies would ride to protect it and rid it of foreign influence. And the bloodbath there might be ten times worse than when the Battle of Pandeish had been fought at the whim of the aged Rana. *Sub lal hogea hai.* Surely everything would turn to red in Pandeish.

No wonder Vazir was in a hurry, Claire thought. But Claire misjudged. Vazir had not forgiven his cousin for the profound blow she had given him. He had worshiped her as an inaccessible goddess—and found her human.

On May tenth, they paused at Cawnpore, where Claire was reunited with Jo. It was Sunday morning, and Claire allowed herself to be persuaded to accompany Jo to church. Having let Jo's servants iron the wrinkles from an organdy gown that had been crushed into a trunk since England, she enjoyed the admiring glances of the British officers, all of whom came to church rather informally in summer undress uniforms of alpaca frockcoats and white overalls. Punkahs swung, creaking as rhythmically as the preacher's voice. Horsetails swished as flies were flicked away by dhoti-clad natives. Men slouched and seemed to doze. Women smoothed their gowns or toyed with the buttons on their tight little gloves. Claire felt somewhat relieved. Certainly nothing was wrong in Cawnpore. Surely the winds of discontent had not reached here. She was invited by General Wheeler for dinner and let herself relax to the clink of crystal and insignificant station chatter. In the evening she drove along the bank of the mile-wide Ganges with Jo, past the bridge of boats where merchants and fakirs traveled back and forth into Oude, across the sacred gray water. Claire thought of the Nana Sahib, who lived nearby at Bithur on the far side of the river.

"Do you think he's planning trouble, Jo?" she asked.

"No, he's too busy with his dancing girls," Jo sniffed. "He lives in absolute splendor, you know. He wears precious Kashmir shawls and a tiara of pearls and diamonds. He has an extravagant menagerie of animals and an aviary of rare birds. His collection of guns and swords is said to be a marvel. But he does nothing but eat and drink and send emissaries to London to try to get his pension restored. Ah! And play billiards. If the Nana Sahib is up to anything, it's a game of billiards. He played with General Wheeler just last week."

"What a relief that there is no trouble here!"

Jo laughed. "There is always trouble at Cawnpore, Claire. It's a haven for thieves and badmashes—partly because of the river and the bridge, I suppose. The river is navigable for a thousand miles downstream and three hundred up. Policing it is impossible. And Cawnpore is a rich town, with silk merchants and saddlers and gold and silver shops. There are more robberies on the roads these days, but it is nothing to justify alarm."

The moon came up above the river, and Claire was enchanted. Her feelings of apprehension vanished, and she slept well that night. Delhi was growing close, and the monotonous song of the koll, the brain fever bird, in the banyan only lulled her.

But elsewhere the night was far from peaceful. At Meerut the glare of burning houses eclipsed the glow of the moon. Women were dying horrible deaths, murdered and mutilated. Prisoners were being released from the jail. European soldiers who had ventured out to a bazaar to a shop which sold ginger beers were set upon by a mob wielding stones and knives. The Sixth Dragoon Guards, consisting mainly of young recruits with no experience of hot weather, was in disarray.

And through the night came the cry. *Delhi! Delhi! To Delhi!*

Aided by the hot winds, the words crossed the miles, borne on the wings of carrier pigeons. And Vazir Lal heeded the message. It was not love of the Rani or of Pandeish that motivated him now. He had only been waiting, and filled with a hatred of the conqueror, which had been triggered by the treachery of Colin Whitecavage, he galloped north to vengeance.

23

Two miles beyond the red walls of Delhi, where Colin White-cavage was under house arrest at his bungalow, the morning of May 11, 1857, seemed at first like any other. He had muskmelon for breakfast and dressed in his uniform of khaki flannel shirt and red-belted blue trousers with a sash at the waist. Outside the door, the guard changed. A young private settled down sleepily beneath a sal tree, taking a swig from the leather-covered lemonade bottle that had been issued him for a canteen. Colin was bored to the point of desperation. He had been so confined for months; and while he had once dreaded the prospect of being stripped of rank and uniform, he now only wished that the deed were done.

Much testimony had been taken by the military board concerning his case, and officers who had served under him had been called to give witness. Colin had been flustered by the vehemence with which they all defended him. To a man they did not blame him for his transgressions, but spoke of the tremendous contributions he had made in Pandeish, both militarily, in saving it from the Rajah, and as President of the Regency, stabilizing the regime and bringing progress smoothly, with a feel for the sensibilities of the natives. Some would have liked to mention the Major's wife and his devotion to her, but Colin saw no reason to allow Claire's name to be brought up in court. That would only stir up memories of her engagement to Colonel Todd and serve to besmirch her. And the fault was his. He was guilty—of loving Claire and having brought about all her troubles. Of loving the Rani, who without him might have lived a peaceful and uneventful life. Colin was aware that now that the Rajah had gotten rid of him, he would use his information to create rebellion in Pandeish. But the time was not quite right. The Rajah was biding his time.

Colin was ready to take his punishment. In fact, he longed for it. He longed to atone for the Battle of Pandeish in which hundreds had followed him to their deaths because of his passion for Tamila.

He knew he ought to be shot, and he would not flinch from that sentence. But he might only be cashiered, and that was what he hoped for. If he were merely discharged from the army, he might try once again to save the Rani and his child. And then, with them safely across the border into Kashmir, Colin dreamed of going to England. He dreamed of a night when he had been lost in the black mist of Dartmoor and had felt himself pixy-led by a sprite too warm and real to be a vision of the fog.

It was a futile dream, he knew. She had asked him to choose between love and duty; and he, like a fool, had chosen duty. Without either army or his wife, Colin did not know what he would do, but he thought most likely he would be given a prison sentence, and life would go on in the same tedious way. That, beyond all, Colin did not think he could endure.

He opened the door and invited his guard to join him inside. "What is the news this morning, John?" he asked.

The lieutenant yawned and propped his Enfield rifle in a corner. "Oh, nothing much. The order about the execution of Mangal Pande at Barrackpore was read to the troops at parade, and there was quite a hissing and shuffling over it. Thank heaven he's been made an example of. That'll teach those brownies not to trifle with the Queen's authority."

"What else happened?"

"Nothing. What should? Do you want to play cards?"

Colin shook his head. He did not like it. Even in his confined quarters, he did not like the feel of the morning. Another hour passed before he began to hear the shouts outside. He went to the window to see the regiments falling into line. "Go and see what the trouble is," he told his guard.

"I am supposed to stay here, sir," the soldier protested.

"Go!" cried Colin so fiercely that the young griffin saluted and dashed away. When he returned, he reported that there was a disturbance in Delhi. "There are some of the Light Cavalry of Meerut causing a commotion. The Grenadiers of the Fifty-fourth are escorting two guns to the city and two companies of the Thirty-eighth are to go to the powder magazine. Colonel Ripley is headed for the Main Guard at the Kashmir Gate."

Colin was on the point of ordering his horse saddled when he remembered that he was under arrest. Exasperated beyond endurance, he paced the bungalow. In the distance he could hear gunfire, and smoke rose above the city walls as though there were fires. Inactivity in time of battle was alien to his nature, and he railed at his impotence. His instinct told him it was more than a disturbance. He had seen it coming for years. He had kept his ears and eyes open and had known of any number of secret meetings such as the one the Rajah had held in the dahl field. There had been blood pacts and sacrificial offerings, and finally the hatred of the foreigner had crossed religious lines and united Hindu and Moslem.

A cry from outside claimed Colin's attention. Beneath the sal tree, the young griffin was in hand to hand combat with a sepoy, his rifle yards away where he had carelessly left it. Rushing into the fray, Colin fired at the native with his five-shot Adams revolver, and the man dropped, struck through the heart.

"John!" Colin raced to the lieutenant and found him dead with a bewildered look on his face. Colin cursed. The boy had paid dearly for a naive belief in the invulnerability of the Raj. It was mutiny, Colin knew. One sepoy, or even a few would not be so bold alone.

Suddenly, flames burst through the thatch roof of a nearby house. A girl ran out, wearing a ruffle of flame about the edge of her crinoline. Colin raced for her and rolled her on the ground. Then, catching a horse, he rode off with her to the Flagstaff Tower, where he found some British ensconsed, women and children pressed terrified into a tiny space only eight feet in diameter. Thank heaven Claire was in England, he thought, as he left his charge and dashed away to the Kashmir Gate, beyond the ridge.

In the melee surrounding it, he saw some sepoys of his erstwhile command and called out to them to join him. There was a hesitation, and then some of them rallied to protect him as the mutineers in their French gray uniforms rushed him. Passing a cartload of officers hacked and mutilated by their own troops, Colin managed to reach the Main Guard with his band of loyal sepoys. The city shimmered with midday heat, and the corpses of the slain were already creating a stench.

The mutineers had entered the city by the thousands now, crossing on the bridge of boats with pennants flying. The Magazine was being held by nine men, who had laid a line of powder so that they could blow it up themselves if need be. Through the afternoon Colin fought, while survivors of the massacre within the city straggled to the Main Guard for protection, bringing stories of horror which seeped into his consciousness without his being aware of hearing them, without his being aware of anything but heat and thirst and the aching grip of his hand on his pistol.

Everywhere in Delhi, British were being murdered, pulled from cupboards and out from beneath beds. The manager of the bank and his wife had climbed to a roof to escape but were beaten to death by Indians who leaped down from the roof of a higher building. The *Delhi Gazette* had been destroyed even as the news of the uprising was being set into type, the last edition stamped "Extra." The old King, almost weeping with anxiety and exhaustion, had ridden around the city on an elephant to show himself to his subjects, and the head of his British bodyguard, Captain Douglas, had been seen on a pike.

At last an explosion rocked the entire city as the Europeans holding the Magazine blew it up. The great wall around it collapsed, and hundreds of mutineers died beneath it, their uniforms blasted from their singed bodies.

The confusion around the Kashmir Gate became a chaos of hell. Inside the Main Guard the Indian defenders turned on the British civilians, and Colin Whitecavage tossed aside his pistol to engage in combat at close quarters with his sword. A motherly Englishwoman fell soundlessly against him in the confined space. He turned to support her and found her dead. Blood was pouring over her taffeta bodice, and the expression of ladylike resentment on her face reminded him of one he had seen beneath Mrs. Cottington's little spotted veil. He became tangled in her crinoline as a girl beside him began to scream. She, too, was covered with blood. A mutineer had hold of her and was hacking off her fingers for her rings before taking time to kill her.

Again Colin thought of Claire and was grateful that she was in England. He called out to his loyal sepoys to help him, but this time no one answered. Either they were dead or the frenzy of the moment had triumphed. Colin felt the satisfying slice of his sword between the ribs of the girl's assailant, and savored it. Then another mutineer sprang at the girl, and crimson spurted over her face. She looked like a child who had been eating wild strawberries, Colin thought, and then sudden weakness told him of his own wound. A black mist closed in on him, his mind clouded; and as he landed softly on the ample breasts of the dead Englishwoman he thought himself among the cool tors of Dartmoor and saw his beloved through a radiant haze.

It was hours after Vazir Lal had gone before Claire learned the news of Delhi. The ancient means of communication were more reliable than the telegraph, which was still a novelty. The messages from Delhi had been garbled, and then there had been none at all.

Claire had only the sense of immense foreboding as she awakened that morning to find him gone ahead without her. As the truth emerged, a cold despondency settled over her. Her energy and will left her, and she sat for hours, staring out the window into the courtyard of the mission school. From there she could watch Jeremy playing with the native children. He was obviously in raptures, never having had playmates before. The Indian girls argued over who would entertain him, and they spoiled his appetite with sesame seed candy. Claire hardly noticed. Never in her life had she minded being a woman as much as she did now. If she had been a man, she would have gathered troops and gone to relieve Delhi, but the English were in too much confusion and panic to manage it.

Sevaley mooned about over Vazir Lal and pretended to be certain that he would come back for her. Claire paid no attention. What were the chances that Vazir was as devoted to Sevaley as he had once been to the Rani? He was an Indian male, to whom women were supposed to be of little importance. For that matter, what man did put women before war? Certainly not Colin Whitecavage.

For the moment all was quiet at Cawnpore. General Wheeler, the commander of the garrison, had spent almost all his life in India and had had a distinguished career. He spoke Hindustani and had an Indian wife. Cawnpore was in capable hands. General Wheeler confidently sent a force to Lucknow, where matters seemed unsettled.

Nonetheless the British residents were nervous. Abigail, Claire's one-time chaperone, who had married and was preg-

nant, reported that the wife of a sergeant-major had been
told in the bazaar that she would not be alive in a week.
Having heard the story, which spread quickly to all the ladies
in the cantonment, Abigail could not sleep nights.

"Where shall we hide when they come?" Abigail shivered
when she came to tea with Claire and Jo. "The barracks will
never do!"

There had already been one panic, and then the barracks
had filled with all sorts of people. Artillerymen had manned
guns in nightcaps, amid an immense disorganization of ladies,
ayahs, wailing babies, and tradespeople. The roofs of the barracks were thatch or pukka and the buildings were exposed
on the plain nearly a mile above the river. They were not yet
finished, and a flimsy bamboo scaffolding encased red brick,
which was not yet whitewashed as were all the military buildings of the Raj. A trench and a wall were also under con-
struction.

"It would be better to be in the Magazine," Jo said.

"General Wheeler doesn't want to show a lack of confidence by going to the Magazine," Abigail said. "Anyway, my
brother says the General is confident that the Nana Sahib will
fight with the British."

"Oh, he will do nothing of the sort!" Claire gasped.

Her two friends were surprised at her vehemence, and she
had to tell the story of the dahl field.

"Oh, the Major must have been wrong," Abigail guessed.
"The Nana is absolutely harmless, and anyway he is in
Lucknow for the moment."

They spoke of those who were trying to hire boats to escape down the river, and of some who were having Indian
garments made for themselves and hiring houses in the town
itself in which to hide. Claire wondered what plan would be
best for her, and while she wondered, the Nana Sahib returned suddenly from Lucknow, entering Cawnpore with a
retinue of horsemen armed with lances and cavalry swords
and soldiers with matchlocks and blunderbuses.

Claire had to admit that the Nana looked harmless. He
was a picture of utter decadence, with jewels gleaming on his
turban, and his plump cheeks battling with his sleek
moustache for dominance of his face. And yet in the eyes,
she saw a look she recognized. The same veiled, hungry cunning had been in the Rajah of Rambad's eyes when he had
persuaded her to allow him to kidnap her from Colonel
Todd's house at Simla.

She had not known what it meant then, but now she was aware that complete contempt for English intelligence was often hidden by deference and salaams. The Indian mind had not been conquered, and it was long on patience. And that look seemed mirrored everywhere. It was in the eyes of the silk merchant at the bazaar, as she purchased materials with the idea of making saris. She was surrounded, and the power of the Queen of England could do nothing to save her.

She saw that look in the eyes of badmashes and soldiers and even in the eyes of the wizened native who scurried in at Abigail's call to pick up a handkerchief she had dropped and save her the discomfort of bending over in her condition. And then, when she looked again, the eyes would be perfectly blank. It would be easy to think one had imagined it.

Certainly if General Wheeler saw it, he allowed himself to believe that he had imagined it. In fact the General decided to show his confidence by inviting the Nana to protect the government treasury in the suburb of Nawabganj. Claire felt she must speak up, and although she was unable to obtain an appointment to see him, it was easy to get herself seated next to him at dinner. Glad for the privileges of womanhood, Claire poured out her story, only to find the General more interested in her pretty face and in his boiled potatoes and his Yorkshire pudding. Dinnertime was the General's chance to relax and forget his problems and doubts.

"My dear Mrs. Whitecavage, that was a long time ago, and perhaps you misunderstood. I myself am intimately acquainted with the Nana—he is of the same caste as my wife. I am taking all the proper precautions, I assure you. I am stocking the barracks with extra provisions in case of an outbreak, and I advise that everyone acquire a weapon. Have you one, Mrs. Whitecavage?"

"Yes. A pistol. And my husband taught me how to shoot it. I will not be afraid to use it when the time comes."

"Tut, my dear, *if* the time comes," he corrected cheerfully, and offered to pour her a glass of claret.

May waned into June and there was no opportunity of going to the hills as she had intended. Delhi was still occupied by mutineers, while the British had laid siege, waiting for reinforcements. At first no one had expected the mutineers to hold the city long, but the commander of the Army of Bengal had been in Simla at the time, and all was in confusion.

"We can be thankful at least that we were not at Delhi," said Abigail, who was spending most of her days on a chaise longue with a punkah coolie in attendance. She had been supposed to go to Ootacamond to have her child, which was due at the end of the summer.

They had just heard that the European prisoners in Delhi had been roped together and murdered beneath a tree in the courtyard of the Red Fort. The chilling news had filtered through a chain of spies out of the city and across the countryside. "You would have been there in a few more days," she reminded Claire.

"Yes," she murmured, agreeing that she should be grateful. But then she would have seen Colin. She would have known whether he still loved her, perhaps felt the glory of his kiss. Then, thought Claire, she would have been ready to die if need be. Better to die in Delhi with Colin than here. Better where she might have perished at his side than in Cawnpore, not even knowing whether he were alive or dead. Then Jeremy claimed her attention, as he tried to turn a flip in the dusk beneath a kikar tree, and Claire banished thoughts of death to lend a hand to push his little posterior over his head and then to lead him howling away to bathe.

On the fifth of June, when the Second Cavalry sent their families away to the city slums, it was obvious that mutiny was at hand. Among the men of the station and even among the women, there was a sense of relief and exhilaration as the unbearable tension broke. That night the cavalry, aided by the Nana's supporters, broke into the treasury and ransacked it, opened the jail and set the prisoners free, started fires, and finally attacked the Magazine. In the morning, The Fifty-third and Fifty-sixth regiments joined the other, after General Wheeler had had a battery open fire on them to frighten them. The mutiny had come, but everyone thought the worst was over. The mutineers were on their way to Delhi, with the Nana Sahib leading.

"Thank God," said Jo. "We wouldn't have stood a chance if they had come at us."

A thousand people were crowded into the poorly defensible barracks. Four hundred were women and children and another hundred, civilians. Of the men, many were invalids. The mutineers numbered three thousand, not including the Nana's troops and a large portion of the native population.

But the respite was brief. The next day a messenger galloped in with the news that the Nana was retracing his route and had decided to attack the fort.

"But why?" Jo wondered.

"I imagine he thought better of subordinating himself to the King of Delhi," Claire guessed. "He is thinking that he could rule an empire of his own."

"And demand tribute!" Abigail added.

"Yes. And have hundreds of dancing girls instead of dozens, buy new race horses, support his relatives in style. Best of all, thumb his nose at Britishers who denied him his pension."

It was unclear whether the Nana was a patriot or an opportunist, but it hardly seemed to matter. On June seventh, the mutineers sacked Cawnpore, dragging out English who had chosen to hide there and slitting their throats. Claire had been persuaded against hiding in the town by Jo, who had insisted that it would be even more disastrous than being in the fort. The mutineers were certain to go from house to house searching for Christians, she had said; and now as she and Claire worked frantically with some of the other women to make last-minute improvements in the defenses, tears rolled down Jo's cheeks. The children she had taught were all in Cawnpore, and some were from families who had converted to Christianty. Jo had devoted her life to them, and they were being annihilated. "My babies! My babies!" she kept saying as the hem of her merino skirt became stained with the mud of the ditch she was helping to deepen. Claire wondered if she meant the two of her own she had lost as well as those who were just dying.

In the heat of the morning the very sky seemed ablaze as smoke and flames rose from the city into the scorching air. Then came the cry, "They're coming! They're coming!"

Claire rushed to see crowds of sepoys running across the bridges over the Ganges Canal. A horrible whizzing and crashing of bricks and the beginning of the bombardment. To most of the women it was a new experience, but to Claire, who had been besieged in Pandeish, it was as though a nightmare was recurring. They were a small force with little hope of reinforcement, but if they surrendered, then what? The Nana Sahib was a beast, or if he were not, then he could not control the beasts his men had become. There could be no victory in Cawnpore and, her instinct told her, no surrender under civilized terms.

The dying had already begun. General Wheeler's son had had his head blown off by a round shot as he sat on a couch beside his sister. Several others died in a similar manner. A woman was shot in the face, and babies were blown from their mothers' arms. After one barrage a captain, standing in an archway, wrote his name on the wall, and others followed suit. Claire wrote her name and Jeremy's on the list and felt a little calmer somehow. Colin, should he still be alive, would find it someday and know how she had died. She ought to leave a message, too, she thought; but while she considered, the pencil was taken from her hand by another.

Food began to run low. Although at first there had been champagne, tins of salmon, and pots of jam, the defenders were soon reduced to half a cup of peas and a gruel of flour and water. And water itself was the biggest problem of all. The camp had only one well, and that was in an exposed position. The creaking of its machinery brought a burst of enemy fire, even in the depth of the night, and children sucked pieces of water bags, trying to get the last moisture. When the rebel soldiers rushed the fort the Britishers would shoot first at the horses, which they would later risk their lives to drag inside to stew.

Servants were sent out of the fort to safety in the town, and Sevaley went with them. There could be no choice about it; food and water were too scarce. "I will take Jeremy with me," Sevaley offered.

Claire was tempted by the offer, but decided against it. Too many Europeans in disguise had already been discovered and killed. Might not the mutineers be looking for children among the native ayahs?

Every day the mutineers' strength grew as bands led by landowners of the surrounding area filtered in to join them. Then, one day when the siege had been underway almost a week, a large cloud of dust was seen along the road. The Europeans raised a cheer, thinking it meant reinforcements from Lucknow; but instead, the troops, when they came into range of fieldglasses, were led by a magnificent Indian on a bejeweled elephant.

"Who the devil is he?" General Wheeler asked and passed the glasses to one of his captains.

"I'll be hanged if I know, sir. He's not from around here."

"From the hills," observed another. Finally the glass was passed to Claire in deference to her experience of the north, and she, with a gasp, beheld the exultant, self-satisfied features of the Rajah of Rambad. She dropped the glasses as she whispered the news and had to be led away from the wall to lie trembling in one of the small crowded rooms of the barracks. The Rajah was fulfilling the promises he had made years ago, perhaps in that dark dahl field; and the realization of all his dreams was at hand. She did not doubt that when Cawnpore had been conquered, the Rajah intended to sweep across India as part of an overwhelming army that would crush British rule in India forever. She did not doubt that he would claim Pandeish for himself, but Pandeish would be only a small part of what he hoped to claim.

He must not claim me, she vowed. But what could save her this time? Only she herself could stop him from taking her, and she remembered all too well her failure to do so in the Rainbow Palace. She had sworn that he would never have her again, that she would never suffer that humiliation or allow him the satisfaction of humiliating her husband by bedding her.

Claire was certain that the fort would fall. There was only one way out of the Rajah's clutches, and Claire began to assign herself the more dangerous of women's tasks. Twice she crawled to the well for water for the children under heavy fire. And she carried food to soldiers in the outpost, where hats and shakos were hoisted in view over the walls to give an impression of strength.

"Jo, will you promise to care for Jeremy if I am killed?" she asked her friend.

"Of course, but I may be killed as well," came the reply. "You had better plan to stay alive yourself."

There were many brave women at Cawnpore. One guarded prisoners by tying them together and keeping her sword ready. Others tended the wounded, though they themselves were suffering from injuries. And Claire remembered her idea that the women of the cantonments were strong beneath their prim outward appearance. Of all the women, Claire was reputed the most daring, once rushing out herself to drag in a dead dog to be cooked. None of the other women understood the risks she took, except Jo, who remembered a night of degradation on the way to Suez. Afterward, Jo had not wanted to live, and yet her heart had kept beating and her lungs had kept filling with air. Life was necessary, especially if one were a mother, and it was Jo who would talk softly to Claire, telling her to think of her child and to pray for strength to endure what she must.

"I cannot endure any more, Jo," Claire would sob.

"You will find courage."

"No. I have run out of it," said Claire, and she thought

how ironic it was that all the garrison thought her a heroine when the truth was that she was the worst coward of all.

Jo sighed and wished she could take Claire's place. Why not? She, of all the garrison women, had nothing to live for. Long ago she had lost her husband and children. She had watched as the mission school burned and felt her own soul in flames along with it. Sometimes in the depth of the night when the guns had grown quiet and the heat had subsided, the women tried to dream of a future beyond Cawnpore. Many were determined that such a future would be away from India, and they spoke of homes to which they would return. Jo had no such home to dream of; she had been the daughter of missionaries herself. The young, unmarried girls talked of men they would wed and the families they would raise; but Jo knew that love was an impossibility for her.

Oh, she had still been fresh and pretty when she had been widowed, but she had chosen to stamp out the tender shoots of love, chosen not to be hurt again. All that Jo might have given to a man she had given instead to her school, and too late she had discovered that that love could hurt profoundly, too. She was only a withered stalk, left standing after the flowers had blown away. A lassitude settled over her; she did not seem to care what happened to her. Sometimes she forgot to eat or gave her portion to some child, and the stalk became more frail. But Jo did care about Claire, who had Jeremy and perhaps a loving husband waiting. . . .

Jo struggled to hold Claire away from the insanity that was claiming others. Many had a look of wildness in their eyes, and one man began to wander about naked. A woman, imagining a snowy forest on the plain beyond the fort, took her child and ran outside the walls. Other women, to escape the stench of the place, crawled into holes and some died there of the heat, which sometimes rose to a hundred and forty degrees.

Abigail, after a few days of terrified inaction, surprised them by becoming a nurse. They had been afraid that the stress of the siege would cause her to go into labor prematurely, but instead she assisted at the primitive childbed of another. Abigail should have been put out of the room, of course, but they were shorthanded; and Abigail, far from being horrified, was jubilant when mother and child both lived. Her sensibilities were jaded, but the victory of life over death was all-important. It was a small triumph for the Europeans, and soldiers grinned as they heard the news.

But three days later the baby was blown to pieces, and the mother's breasts, where she had been nursing it, were shot away by the ricocheting blast. The same day, Abigail's husband was killed and dropped with his head in her lap.

After that, Abigail's hold on her mind became tenuous. "Oh, what is the use of giving birth?" she would moan. "They are going to kill us all!"

"No, no. Surely there is help on the way. Someone will come. We have only to hold out. *You* must hold out, Abby."

But they had had word at last from Lucknow that they would get no aid there. The commander deemed it impossible to reach the fort, since the enemy held the river. It was the third week in June, and no one had bathed since the siege had begun. No water could be spared for washing clothing, either, and their gowns of organdy or batiste had all begun to look the same—all stained with dirt, grease, gunpowder, and blood as though they were all variations of a single pattern. Everyone's hair was filthy and in awful disarray. Stockings had been given up to the artillerymen to fill with grapeshot for the makeshift loading of damaged cannon. Meanwhile, the mutineers, not bothering to fight with vigor, patronized sweet and sherbert stands along the canal, lay in the shade smoking opium, or visited the abode of Azizun, Cawnpore's foremost courtesan.

"It's insulting!" Claire said. "They don't even take pains to attack any more. They're laughing at us. They have only to sit there and make merry while we die of thirst and starvation!"

"We are not dead yet," said the level-headed Jo.

"Oh, how can you be so calm! Is there nothing that can unnerve you?"

"I don't know," Jo said. Perhaps nothing could. Jo knew that it was not because she was brave that she kept her head. Jo had been numbed as insects numb their victims against the pain of the bite. Jo would have given anything to feel the anguish that others did, to know that she was still human. Abigail, reacting differently, moaned ceaselessly, disturbing whatever slumber they might have enjoyed in their hot, cramped room.

It seemed that the siege would last all summer, and then the Nana Sahib seemed to become bored with it. He was ready to move on to conquer larger worlds, and he was infuriated that the determination of the little garrison was preventing him. An emissary arrived outside the entrenchment in a palanquin, a frightened Britishwoman whose earlobes were torn where earrings had been jerked off. She was shown into General Wheeler's presence, and in a few minutes the news was sweeping the garrison. The Nana Sahib would give all who surrendered safe passage downriver to Allahabad.

"What do you think?" Claire asked Jo.

"We should surrender, of course. What else can we do?"

"I wish the General would not accept the terms," said Claire. "Reinforcements will come sometime. The rains are due, and when they come, we can catch plenty of water."

"The rains will wash away the wall and flood the trenches, Claire," said Jo. "You're not thinking clearly."

"Probably not," she agreed, "but it seems a mistake."

The next morning General Wheeler met with the rebel leaders outside the entrenchments and made final arrangements for leaving the fort. The British were to march out under arms, carriages were to be provided for the wounded, and enough boats were to be waiting to take everyone downriver. Some officers went off to supervise the preparations, and a hysterical celebration began. A cask became a drum, thin voices were raised in song, and emaciated women smiled as though they were at a Government House ball. Even Abigail was happy. But Claire couldn not join in the festivities.

"You're thinking about the Rajah, aren't you?" asked Jo.

"I suppose I am."

"That's silly. The Rajah will never notice you. He's not expecting you to be in Cawnpore. He thinks you're in England. And even if he looks right at you, he won't recognize you. You would see why if you had a mirror. Then you'll be on a boat, bound for civilization at Allahabad. It will be a good trick on him, actually. You'll float right past him."

Claire had to admit that Jo made sense, but she was still apprehensive. "I don't know what it is, Jo," she said. "Maybe it's the look I saw about the Nana when he passed through Cawnpore before the mutiny. He has the look of a man who can't be trusted."

"I'm sure that General Wheeler is not taking him on trust again, Claire. We won't leave unless the proper arrangements are really being made. And the officers have gone to make sure."

A silence fell as the officers returned, and then a murmur like a long sigh ran through the gathering as everyone realized it was time to leave. There was a rush to collect possessions. Men stuffed their pockets with ammunition, while women tied up deathbed bequests in rags to take back to England. They left the fort in a daze, as if startled to find a world beyond that bounded by the mud walls of the fort; and as fresh air swept over them, Claire felt also a wind of fear, an urge to go back into the stinking ruin of which she now seemed a part. She bent and smeared her face with an extra coating of grime and pulled a rag of a skirt over her head as a shawl. Then she was pulled into a bullock cart. Jeremy was handed in to her, and they started off with a jolt. Some of the others were mounting elephants, having to climb up by the tails because the mutineers would not make the animals kneel for them.

People crowded out of the city to watch them pass, but no one tried to bother them as they wound toward a temple ghat with steps that led down to the river. Servants who had been sent away came running to see how their employers had fared. Sevaley ran beside the cart, begging to go downriver with Claire.

"Please, Memsahib! You'll need me to help with the baby."

"No," Claire decided reluctantly. "It's too dangerous."

"Why, Memsahib? Why should it be dangerous?"

Claire could not say, but neither would she change her mind, and as they came to the dreary ghat, near a sandy ravine edged with cactus and broken fences, Sevaley was left behind.

A burning ghat. A place of death. The procession struggled down the ravine and made for the boats, which had newly repaired thatch roofs and bamboo flooring. Claire climbed out of the cart and waded in, feeling a surge of joy as the water enveloped her. Was it possible that there could be so much water anywhere? Water enough to cover her, to cool her? It stretched out before her, lapping and purling; and suddenly Claire felt her faith renewed, and she began to laugh and dip Jeremy up and down.

Too late she saw the Rajah on the shore, saw that her laughter had attracted his glance, saw him look and then look again, and incredulous recognition dawn in his eyes. A cry left his lips, but as it did, it was drowned by a burst of gunfire. Volley after volley hit the water—from a village across the river, from the banks above the stream, from everywhere.

Claire tried to take cover by crouching in the water behind one of the boats, but it burst into flame, ignited by a piece of hot charcoal tossed onto its thatch roof by the boatsman. Most of the other boats were being set ablaze in the same way. Some people were burning as well, as they leaped back into the water. Others were clubbed, and one man had both arms severed as he raised them to ward off the blow of a sword. Jo, thinking to help someone drowning, caught at one at it floated past and was horrified to find no one attached .

The Englishmen tried to return the fire as the water turned red, and clouds of smoke enveloped the river like heavy fog. In the haze it became difficult to see who was friend and who was foe. A shape came at her, and she raised her pistol and fired. But the weapon was wet. A moment later she was glad, for the shape became Abigail, coming to help her with Jeremy, who was howling and clinging to her so that she could hardly move. On the banks, children were being stabbed and burned; General Wheeler had been killed. Only one boat had gotten away.

"There is a drain pipe over there. We can hide," gasped Abigail. They began to swim together, dragging the child between them. Then Claire felt her son's hand jerked from hers. She grabbed for it in the water, screaming. "Abby! Where is he? Where's my baby?" But Jeremy had vanished. Abigail tried to pull her on, but Claire turned back, wild with hysteria. A child's body drifted past and thudded softly against her as though begging her to take it into her arms. She reached for it, and turning it over, looked at its dead face. But it was not Jeremy.

She had not seen him killed, and that should have been a blessing, but in a way it wasn't. She could not stop struggling and searching. Perhaps a mugger had dragged him under. In that case she would find no trace.

The boat that was getting away came by her so close that she might have climbed aboard, but Claire ignored the hands stretched out to her. Abigail was gone, and she did not know if Jo had been killed. But now the firing had stopped, and those who were still alive were being herded together on the shore near the ghat.

Claire was hauled out of the water by two dhoti-clad sepoys. She fought to return to the river, recklessly shoving past the barrel of a rifle. She might have been showered in a thousand pieces of flesh and bone over her fellow captives; but she cried out piteously for her *baba*, and the mutineer, startled to compassion, only pushed her back, almost tenderly. Jeremy might be among the children on the beach, she thought with a burst of hope; and she began to call out for him and search among the little forms, bloodied and sand-encrusted almost beyond knowing...

Then she sank down groaning, her groans like those of the dying as despair settled over her. She waited to be killed and did not care, for she had lost everything she had to live for. Colin had been at Delhi, and she no longer believed he was alive. And Jeremy was gone now, at Cawnpore. Cawnpore. Delhi. To think that such names had once filled her with girlish excitement. If only it had been possible for her to love more sensibly, she would never have come to India at all. But she knew it had not been possible. Her doom had been fated; but now she knew its face. She lay there, trying to summon the will to hate India, as she had hated it when Pandeish had claimed Colin. But now she was desolated beyond even hate.

Around her, numbed, wild-eyed women cowered in wet, bloody clothing, their feet bare, their fingers bleeding or broken from having their rings pulled off. More than one of the wretched captives wished it to be finished quickly, but it was not to be. The Nana Sahib had decided that the survivors would be useful as hostages against British retribution, and the lot of them were put back into the carts and taken to Savada House, part of a former charitable institution near the Allahabad road. Vultures were swooping over the beach before the bullocks had even pulled the carts back up the slopes. "Don't look," whispered a voice next to her, and she knew it was Jo.

"Abby?" Claire whispered, and Jo pointed out the inert figure cradled against her. And then, not heeding Jo's good advice, Claire returned her gaze to the devastation of the river, which had claimed her soul and her child.

24

In Delhi, Colin Whitecavage recuperated from the wounds he had received during the first hours of the mutiny. He had been sheltered in the house of some friendly Indians, an old couple whose son had been in his command. Every day that he stayed he endangered them, for hangings of pro-English natives were common. If he himself were discovered, Colin suspected that he would be drawn and quartered.

Because of the danger to his friends, Colin left their home as soon as he could walk and took up quarters in an underground room inside the walls of the palace itself. Amid the general confusion, it was easy to come and go in that strange world where hundreds lived without any visible means of support. Within that great decadent establishment prostitutes had set up apartments in filthy rooms with ivory and silver chairs. Opium sellers peddled their wares, thieves poisoned their victims to make picking their pockets easier, and girls danced naked in hopes of raising the price of their shimmering bodies.

Everywhere intricate passages, enclosed courtyards, secret doors, and cubbyholes were available for hiding. Colin was well satisfied with his abode. He furnished the place with a mat and a little brazier; and when he was hungry, he stole from the supplies of the mutineers, like much of the populace.

The business of the city was at a standstill. The King had ordered the shops open but the barrages from the British had created chaos, and the doors had been slammed shut again. More than forty thousand mutineers had streamed into the city now, dressed in company uniforms of red jackets with white blancos and brass buckles. Bands marched out to meet them, playing British regimental marches. Hardly a day passed that Colin didn't hear the voices of his comrades on the ridge, bellowing the words of "Cheer Boys, Cheer" in cocky accompaniment to the enemy bands.

The British remained optimistic, though they were only several thousand strong, though the walls of Delhi were impregnable, surrounded by a moat seventy-five feet wide and thirty feet deep, set with thousands of loopholes for rifles, and manned with twenty-pound cannon. Colin always felt a tug when he heard the singing, for he longed to return to his own. It would not have been an impossibility, since native spies slipped back and forth nightly. Colin, now heavily bearded and wearing Indian garb, could have passed. But once back with his side, he would only be placed under arrest again. Colin could not bear the thought. Though it was a breach of discipline for him to remain as he was, Colin thought it more practical to allow himself to be counted among the dead.

Colin Whitecavage was of more assistance to his fellows inside the city than out. By day he lolled in a seeming stupor on the stones of some courtyard, while passersby stepped over him or perhaps gave him a deliberate kick. But by night, Colin wreaked havoc however he could. He attacked the guards of a cannon that had been particularly bothersome and, having murdered them all silently and skillfully, spiked the gun beyond firing.

He overheard secrets and passed them to the native spies. Somehow he always knew what foray was being planned, what forward post would be attacked—the main position at Hindu Rao's house, the crag called the crow's nest, or the Sub-Mundi, overlooking a gorge in which the Grand Trunk Road and the Western Jumna Canal ran toward the Kabal Gate.

Colin became legend in Delhi in the early weeks of the siege. They called him the One Who Knows, or the One Who Destroys, or the One Who Is Never Seen. And then slowly they ceased calling him all these things and called him simply The One. And Colin was blamed for things he did and for things he didn't do. If elephants stampeded or a lota was missing, the sepoys said, "The One has been here." A reward was posted for him, a bounty, as in Pandeish.

The siege dragged on. At the King's durbar, all the factions denounced each other like hordes of squabbling children. The ancient Mogul, not understanding why the English couldn't be subdued was on the verge of a breakdown from the constant clamor of shouted petitions. Now and then someone simply seized the old King by his beard to get his attention.

Outside in the British camp, camels and horses died of starvation, and their bodies bloated and reeked. Among the troops, dysentry had set in. The Guides—fierce Afghans and muscular Gurkhas—arrived to fight beside their old commander, the celebrated Henry Hodson, and repulsed attack after attack on the main position of Hindu Rao's house. It was to Hodson that Colin's spies reported to receive money for their news, and from these spies the British learned about the exploits of The One. The British, no more than the mutineers, knew his identity; but they, too, had ideas. Some suggested Major Whitecavage, who was unaccounted for, and some, including Hodson, who had known him in the north, thought it was like him. But others, who had not known him so well, thought Colin Whitecavage had run away from the disgrace of court-martial and fear of punishment. This school of thought had it that Colin was in the mountains of Pandeish in the arms of the beautiful Rani, and many spoke of it with disapprobation and envy as they made the rounds of the pickets in the rain.

"What I wouldn't give to be where *he* is!"

"Bah! He's a traitor."

"But you have to admit it's better than here! Can you be sure you wouldn't have taken to your heels if *she* had been waiting for you?"

And they imagined the Rani unwinding her silken sari and opening her arms in invitation.

But if the soldiers made allowances for such passions, officialdom did not. Major Whitecavage was missing without leave and subject to a firing squad if found.

The anniversary of the Battle of Plassey came and went, a day of exhausting battle won by neither side but by their mutual enemy, the sun. The hospitals were overcrowded, full of black flies and cases of gangrene and fever. The rain began in earnest and became steam. Horses and men slipped in slime, and there were outbreaks of the dreaded cholera. The smell of the many dead rose from the shallow graves and wafted on the wind, mixing with the scent of cooking and gunpowder in the wet breeze.

There began to be rumors about Cawnpore; and when at

last the truth could no longer be discredited, the hatred of the British for the mutineers redoubled. As they thought of the murdered women and children, of the awful treachery of the enemy that had led to the surrender of the fort, many longed for revenge, not only on the sepoys themselves but on all Indians. During the next days the British shelling grew more intense and even darkness did not silence the guns.

Inside the devastated city, Colin roamed the night, feeling as though there had never been quiet. He himself was feverish, but he had learned of a secret foray to be made tonight into the British camp, and he was intent on sending a message out through some poorly-guarded sallyport. As he made his way through a narrow street near the Chandi Chauk, the thatch roof of a two-story house nearby burst into flame, ignited by the barrage. Feminine screams emanated from the zenana, which Colin knew would be located just below the roof.

Rushing into the house he found the stairs were already ablaze. The screaming grew more hysterical as he hurried out to survey the windows. The fire had attracted a crowd, and people were yelling to the woman to jump. But she, seeming paralyzed with fear, merely clung to the sill and screamed. Colin cursed. The woman was old and would probably break any number of bones if she jumped, but he knew he should not endanger himself to save her. He would make himself obvious, and then it might be discovered that he was British. He might be killed, perhaps in some hideous way by a mob overwrought from the continuous bombardment. What could one old woman matter amid so much death and misery? She could not have many years—he recognized that he was thinking fatalistically, like an Indian. Not one of them was attempting to enter the building. He would be a fool, twice a fool—once for rescuing her and again for not listening to the interior voice that told him better. But he knew he would not leave her to die, for his peculiar British reasoning still insisted that all life was precious. He fought it for another moment, but as he did, he began to circle the house, looking for a way.

A heavy vine, gnarled and tough, grew up one side. He managed to climb up it and into the smoky room. The woman turned with a gasp of hope, but as he reached for her a blazing beam fell onto her. He worked to free her, singeing his own forearm; but weakened by fever and thwarted by flame, he was unable to budge the fiery timber. If only he had help. . . .

Suddenly other hands seized the beam, adding their strength to his; and the beam rolled away. Whipping off his shirt, Colin began to beat at the flames, without thinking that he was exposing his fair skin; but the woman's screams had stopped and her still face was framed in a halo of burning hair.

"It's too late, Sahib," said a dry, familiar voice.

He turned to look at the Indian who had had the courage to climb up after him, and saw the vengeful eyes of Vazir Lal. It was a look that he had seen many times before in the eyes of an enemy, but he had never seen it in the eyes of a friend. Instinctively, he reached for his pistol, not having time to consider whether he could use it. Vazir, who had been as startled to see Colin, made the same move, but more quickly, with more decision.

Vazir would have fired first and killed him, but the floor gave away and both weapons were lost as the two men plummeted into the room below. Recovering first, Colin darted for the door. He had no choice now but to run, while behind him came shouts of *Angrezi! Angrezi!* Dozens took off in pursuit; he eluded them with a skill born of his clandestine weeks. But one pair of footsteps came relentlessly after him, following him as though coupled to him. He grew desperate and weary; his mind fogged with the terrible effort and carelessly he turned into a dead-end alley and found himself against the stones of the city wall.

His pursuer closed in, and Colin was not surprised that it was Vazir with a drawn knife. "I am doing you a favor to kill you," said Vazir. "You would die a harder death if I called the sepoys."

"I don't blame you for wanting me dead, Vazir," said Colin, drawing a knife himself. "But *I* may kill *you*."

"No," said Vazir. A strange sensation passed over him. He had fought others to the death, but never before had he had to fight someone whose heart did not seem in it.

"Perhaps you're right," said Colin. "Why shouldn't I be the one to die? I have lost my commission and have nothing to live for. But you—you should be in Pandeish. The Rani will need you."

Vazir shook his head. "It's quiet in Pandeish."

"The trouble will come. You know it, Vazir."

"Yes. Because of you. But I cannot help Tamila this time.

To stand with her and with her British protectors in Pandeish would be to sanction the crimes you and she have committed. It would be a sacrilege."

"You would leave her to the Rajah? *That* would be sacrilege!"

"The Rajah is not in Pandeish. He is at Cawnpore."

"Cawnpore! The beast!"

"I am sorry, Sahib."

"Why are you sorry, Vazir Lal? You are one of them now."

"Yes. But murdering women and children is not my idea of how to fight a war. I am sorry about your wife and your son."

"What are you talking about? My wife and son are in England."

"No, Sahib! You didn't know? They were at Cawnpore. They traveled there with me."

"You are lying, Vazir!" cried Colin.

"I would not tell you such a lie, Sahib! Not even now."

The shock and grief on Colin's face unnerved Vazir, and for a moment Colin had the advantage. Not even noticing that advantage, Colin struck at Vazir in anguish and sent his knife skittering. But Colin did not press his luck. Instead he began to climb the wall, finding footholds in the crumbling stone. Vazir's compassion vanished and hatred again came to the fore. He lunged for Colin's foot to pull him down, but Colin was over the top. Enraged at his escape, Vazir raised a cry. Shouts echoed as sepoys heeded the call.

But Colin had already jumped into the ditch and was headed for the counterscarp. Unable to bear the thought of his getting away, Vazir followed, struggling after him up the almost perpendicular earthen slope. Halfway up, Vazir succeeded in dislodging Colin and both of them rolled back into the ditch. But Colin, consumed with purpose, kicked Vazir away and fought his way back up. Bullets began to throw clods of earth around them as the mutineers took up positions along the wall. The shots were intended for Colin, but they fell indiscriminately, and halfway across the wide glacis, Colin heard a grunt behind him. Glancing back, he saw Vazir topple from the impact of a shell.

Once again Colin knew that he should not attempt to save a life, and once again he turned to help, racing into the face of the enemy fire to place his former friend's arm over his shoulder. The mutineers shouted with astonishment; but the firing did not cease as Colin unwound his turban and, tying it about Vazir, lowered him over the outer wall. In a moment he leaped down beside him and lay panting. But even then Colin couldn't rest, for he feared that some of the snipers would try to follow him. He thought of leaving Vazir behind, but if the mutineers did not come over the wall, Vazir might die unaided. Or he might wander onto the plains in a delirium and be apprehended by a British patrol.

Colin did not trust his countrymen in their present mood. The news of Cawnpore had given them such a lust for retribution that some of them had been talking of executing prisoners by blowing them from the mouths of cannon. It was a death especially feared by mutineers, both Hindu and Moslem. Hindus believed that their bodies must be cremated or consigned to sacred waters in order for them to reach heaven. Moslems' creed taught they must be buried without mutilation. Colin had heard that such atrocities had already been committed in the station of Ferozepore, and the idea sickened him. So he labored on with Vazir, dragging him through a belt of brush and through a mango swamp, past jungle trees with wicked thorns. Finally he came to a stream and there he made a camp for them, binding Vazir with the turban to secure him. He bathed Vazir's wounds and cut down bamboo for a bed among the thorn scrub and lantana. Then he slept until the jungle cock awakened him, crowing to announce the morning. Vazir stirred and looked up at the sky.

"Are you able to travel?" Colin asked.

"I am your prisoner, Sahib. I will do as you say."

"I saved your life, Vazir Lal," said Colin in annoyance. "You might show gratitude."

"Why? You will only turn me over to the regiments to be shot."

"That's impossible. I am a fugitive from the British as much as you. Anyway, I have other plans."

"It would be a mistake to show me mercy," said Vazir. "I will not show any to you, if the chance comes. We are not friends because you saved my life."

Colin nodded. "I didn't think so. But we may be again one day."

"Never. It is unnatural for Indian and *Angrezi* to live as brothers. The dream is over, and the Raj is at an end."

"It is far from over, Vazir. Do you want to hear my plan? It does not involve showing you mercy."

Vazir shrugged. "Tell me."

"We are going to Cawnpore," said Colin.

"Your plan is like you," said Vazir. "Foolish and impractical. I, too, would like to save your memsahib. But she is most likely dead already."

"There is a chance she is not."

"But there are only two of us and thousands of them."

"True. We cannot save Claire by numbers. We will try another way."

Vazir listened with interest. He hated Colin, but he hadn't forgotten that the Major was clever.

"When we get to Cawnpore, you will join the Nana's camp and find out how she can best be rescued. I will remain in hiding until you return to tell me."

Vazir shook his head. "I may betray you. If she is dead, I will certainly do so."

"If she is alive, you will not betray me, because that would be a betrayal of her as well. I know you wouldn't betray Claire, Vazir. And if she is dead—that is the chance that I take. You have warned me. Give me your lota and I'll fit it. We must be away before the sun is too hot."

Vazir handed over his water jug with grudging admiration. He did not like to be reminded of all the traits he had once found to prize in Colin. About mid-morning they managed to buy a pair of ponies from some villagers and rested beside a tributary of the Jumna. Vazir's wound did not seem to bother him as much as Colin's fever, as they waited for night to cross the shadeless plain. Colin dozed, and Vazir might have stolen his knife and made his escape. But after all, there was nowhere to escape to under the merciless sun. And Vazir was not opposed to going to Cawnpore. He, too, had left a woman there. A woman who haunted his dreams.

The memory of her assailed him. The hot breeze seemed to waft the flowered scent of her warm body, the tantalizing Sevaley, the woman who was like no other he had ever known, even his cousin Tamila. Her gentle, inviting smile shimmered beyond the tope, the mirage of her lips like cool fruit, and he wondered if that were all she would ever be—a mirage. She, like Claire, might be dead, and when Vazir thought of it, he felt as though he would burst with grief because he had never taken the chance she had seemed to offer, never tasted wonders now lost to him forever.

But at other times, when he felt himself traveling closer to her presence, he warned himself against her. It was dangerous to love a woman like Sevaley. He did not revere her as he had the Rani. Instead, he craved her. He had sat at the feet of the sadhus and been cautioned against such appetites. Still he waited eagerly for the cool of evening to send them on their way.

But as the sky grayed, looked charred by the fire of the sun, a band of *goojurs*—wandering robbers—set upon them. Vazir was several hundred yards away by the river when he saw them and instinctively rushed to help Colin save the horses and supplies. It was foolish, of course, since he was injured and did not have a gun or knife. Colin was also unfit from his fever, and the pair were easily overpowered.

The badmashes spit on Colin, and then with special delight on Vazir, for they knew it defiled him. When he cried out in rage and humiliation, they laughed at him. "You are defiled already by being a friend of the *Angrezi*," they told him.

"He's no friend of mine!" said Vazir vehemently.

"Then why do you travel with him?"

"It's not by choice."

"Then you shall part company," laughed the robbers. When they had taken Vazir's money and rings and beaten Colin unconscious, they made Vazir ride away with them.

25

The women and children who had survived the Cawnpore massacre were now incarcerated in a smaller house, soon to be known all over India as the House of the Ladies. But for the moment, it was still Nibihhar, a retreat that had been built by a British officer for his mistress. The survivors had been joined by captives from an uprising at Fatehgarh, and their arrival made over a hundred souls jammed into its rooms with no furniture or bedding except bamboo mats to lie on. Here Abigail went into labor, and after a day of agony in a sweltering, airless room, gave birth to an infant girl. Claire and Jo were exhausted from tending her, having fanned her ceaselessly for more than twenty-four hours. Jo, having had experience, had served as midwife. But as tired as they were, they hugged each other and celebrated. The birth seemed to mean new life in more ways than one. But Abigail wept when she held her baby.

"I wish I had died at the river," she whispered.

"Abigail! Why?"

"Because I cannot bear it now. Not since I have seen her. I cannot bear to die and leave her. Or for her to die. That would be worse."

"You're not going to die, Abby, and neither is she," Claire said. "The worst is over, and we are still alive."

"Claire is right," Jo agreed. "We won't be killed. The Nana is keeping us for hostages. And one of the women who was taken to the stables to grind corn today overheard the sepoys saying that there is a force approaching. It will be over soon."

357

When the sweepers arrived that day with rations of dahl and chupatties, Claire promised one of them Colonel Todd's fine ring in return for extra food and milk for Abigail during the remainder of their imprisonment. "It's a wonder I still have it, Jo," she sighed. She had hidden it in her underclothing, and it had been missed.

"Yes," said her friend acidly, and Claire knew that Jo was thinking of the first time the ring had been in danger—on the Suez desert. "It's a wonder they didn't find it while helping themselves to something more," Jo said with a shudder.

"We've been spared that. It's something to be grateful for," said Claire.

They had not been raped, and they were alive. British troops were on the way. But it was hard to remember that the worst was over.

The Ladies' House was quickly becoming an infirmary. Every day, five or six of its inmates were carried out, dead of cholera or dysentery. Children were left without mothers, and mothers without children. Some formed new bonds from their grief; and often those, too, were shattered. And there were some who ceased to eat and care and died of their grief.

Then one day the Begum, who was in charge of the house and who had been a prostitute's maid, singled Claire out and took her down the road to the big yellow Duncan Hotel, where the Nana Sahib had his headquarters. She was taken upstairs to a room furnished with silken cushions and ivory tables and allowed to rest there beneath the breeze of creaking punkah while she sipped a glass of iced fruit punch. Claire drank gratefully, not bothering to think that the beverage might have been drugged or that she might well have been brought here for some immoral purpose.

The Begum retired, and a man entered. Claire was too stunned to realize that this was what she had been dreading all along. "Good evening, my dear," said the Rajah of Rambad.

"It is not a good evening now," she answered.

"Ah, but it can be." The Rajah was pleased to see that Claire had not lost her spirit. "I saw you at the river that day, and I have been trying to persuade the Nana to allow me to bring you here. I wish I might say you look beautiful, pet, but perhaps when you have had a cool bath and a good meal. . . . Fresh clothes would help. . . ." He came close to her, and she shrank back as he reached out, but the Rajah only plucked a bug from her hair and said in disgust, "Lice.

Those will have to go, too. Then we will see what sort of evening it will be. Do you remember the evenings we used to spend, Claire? Maybe we will recapture old times."

"I am not interested in old times," she replied, but her voice wavered. She knew what the Rajah was telling her. She could leave the House of the Ladies and live here in comfort. But there was a price, of course. Claire felt ill with longing as she thought of the prizes he had offered her. A bath. She had not felt water on her body since she had been immersed in the bloody river. And the smell of roasting meat drifted up from the kitchen and made her dizzy with desire.

She heard the Rajah chuckle and saw that he was enjoying her dilemma. Why did he bother to tempt her this way, she wondered. Why didn't he just force himself on her as he had in Pandeish? She blushed to recall the shameless way her body had reacted after he had pressed himself inside. The Rajah, watching her, laughed aloud. Claire leaped to her feet, or imagined that she did so. In truth, she was so debilitated that she merely tottered erect. She understood now. It was that he enjoyed conquering her in every way possible. He had caused her to submit to him many times, but this time he wanted her to beg him to love her and to weep afterward at the kindness he had shown her in so using her. He was as determined to show her that she was his slave as she was to prove to herself that she was not.

"I am a married woman!" she said sternly.

"Yes. And your husband is in Delhi. Delhi is a long way from Cawnpore these days." He refilled her glass and, dipping his hand into the pitcher, added chunks of ice. "Ah, ice is a luxury, Claire, even for the Nana himself."

Claire's knees buckled, and she sat down again, her eyes fastened on the glass, which dripped rivulets of coolness onto the table. It wouldn't hurt to have another drink, she thought. In fact, it would make her feel better, and she would be stronger to resist.

"I will not stay here," she told him when she had drunk it all. "I will go back to the House of the Ladies."

"Ah, Claire, you disappoint me. We were to have been married once."

"Only because you promised that you would let Colin live if I married you. You could not promise that now, and anyway, he's probably dead."

"Why should you care whether he is alive or dead? He always has chosen to return to the Rani. You're a strange woman, Claire. You pretend to have such pride when I want you, and you have none at all when it comes to *him*. It's a shame that you didn't marry me. We could have been a fine family, I think. Sona and Aleka both loved you. And there would have been our son——"

"He was not your son!" she stormed. "I told you that he was my husband's son!"

"Perhaps that's so," the Rajah sighed, conceding. "I did notice the resemblance, but then it was too late."

"Too late?" she asked in bewilderment.

"Yes. I would not have bothered to order my lieutenants to rescue him from the river that day if I hadn't believed him to be my son."

Claire flung herself at him. "You! You had him snatched away! And he is alive? Tell me he is alive!"

"Alive and well and safe. Shall I return him to you?"

"Yes! Yes!" she sobbed, and then stopped aghast. "No," she said, and her eyes mirrored her thoughts. She could not take Jeremy back to the House of the Ladies, where children were hungry and had no place to play and where some of them died every day.

"You must come here, Claire," the Rajah said softly. "We will all be happy together, and perhaps Jeremy's resemblance to Major Whitecavage will fade. It may be only an illusion. Children change. Ah, Claire, don't feel you are a traitor to your own kind. It's only the times, and you will not be the only woman of Cawnpore to make her bed with her captor. I have heard that there were two others from the river who were carried off and showed their thanks for being saved."

The Rajah rang a bell to call for a servant. "We will see you at dinner, Jeremy and I."

Claire felt her body undulate like the punkah above her. She wanted her child so desperately. And sleeping with the Rajah was so practical! Surely there was nothing she wouldn't do to have her baby again! Colin might forgive her; she might even forgive herself. But if she bedded the Rajah, she could never be sure what sort of woman she was. If she bedded him, she could never come to Colin again as a loyal wife, never live down the accusation he had made about her and the Rajah. But if only she were brave. . . .

"I will go back to the House of the Ladies," she told him again, firmly.

He rewarded her with a look of utter astonishment. "But

Jeremy—how do you know what will become of him with me? Perhaps I'll give him to the sepoys to kill."

Claire shook her head. "You cannot," she said with a sad smile. "You are still not certain that he isn't yours."

Lifting her chin determinedly, she turned toward the door, not looking at the Rajah and yet seeing him out of the corner of her eye in spite of herself. The intensity of his fury swirled about him like a tornado that might touch down and devour her. She fully expected that he would spring at her and strangle her or rape her, and her breasts tightened under the flimsy cloth of her dirty, torn dress. She was certain that he saw and with that for encouragement would throw her down on the cushions.

But the Rajah, in spite of his anger, was stunned and even awed. It was easy for him to see that she loved her child deeply. He had thought to have her easily; he had even imagined that she would respond to him gratefully, overcome with thankfulness that he had saved the boy from the massacre. Instead, she had rejected him with daring and conviction which he had not dreamed within a woman's capabilities.

As she reached the door he felt his rage dissolve, and suddenly he was pleading with her. "Claire! Dearest! If you won't think of your son, think of yourself. You are right that I will not harm Jeremy, but are you prepared to die yourself? What do you think is going to happen to you in the House of the Ladies?"

She paused in surprise. "Happen? Why, nothing, so long as I don't catch the fever. I will be hungry and miserable, that's all. And the Nana will ransom us to the British force, when it comes."

"My poor dear. That is not what will happen. Henry Havelock's army is almost upon us, and the Nana is afraid that the prisoners will be dangerous witnesses. He is preparing to withdraw, and he doesn't want to take his hostages along."

"What will he do with us, then?" she asked, the words a mere croak in her throat. She knew what; she did not really have to ask or hear the Rajah's pained answer.

"Everyone will be killed. There will be another massacre."

"You are lying. You would do anything——"

"No. I have no need to resort to lies. And I could have you, Claire, simply by refusing to allow you to return."

"Is that what you will do?"

The Rajah was disbelieving. "You would still go back. After what I've told you? Leave your son motherless?"

Claire nodded, barely breathing. "Better for my son to know I died honorably than to grow up with a mother he cannot respect."

Rage overcame him again. "So you would rather die than share my bed. You did not find it so disagreeable once! I suppose you think you are dying a noble death, but it is only a stupid one! Go on, then! Your death will atone for nothing, but perhaps it is the only way you will ever be free of your shameful desire!"

It was she, then, who lunged for him to strangle him, screaming insanely as she clawed at him, ripping loose his necklace of jade and pearls, tearing his kincob silk kurta as she sought his throat. Their bodies were close together in the heat, and even as she struggled to kill him, he pressed himself against her so that she could feel the fire of his insolent manhood. She almost swooned, then, as he called out. The door opened and hands dragged her sobbing away from him. And he watched with hateful, mocking eyes.

She returned to the House of the Ladies to lie stuporous on a dirty mat. Abigail stayed in a corner, nursing her pretty baby and singing to it, paying attention to nothing else. She seemed to have accepted their reassurances and had lost herself in a bliss of motherhood. The mood in the house was actually becoming buoyant. Rumor filtered in—news that Havelock had encountered mutineers at Fatehpur and had routed them in only ten minutes. Havelock had captured the bridge over the Panda Nudi, an unfordable river, before the enemy could blow it up, and now nothing lay between the British and Cawnpore. The women who went to grind the corn returned with tales of great commotion around the Nana's headquarters. The hotel was jammed with rebel officers, and elephants and camels were being loaded.

"They'll be here tomorrow; we'll be rescued!" Jo said, but Claire seemed frozen, and her eyes were glazed. "What is wrong Claire?" her friend asked gently. She was afraid that the ordeal had been too much for her at last. "Tell me what happened when they took you away. Did the Rajah——"

"No, no. He didn't harm me. And my child is safe, Jo!"

"But that's wonderful!"

"The rest of us aren't safe. They are going to kill all of us before Havelock arrives."

"Are you sure?"

Claire nodded miserably.

"Then we must try to escape. We cannot sit and wait like rats in a box!"

"There's no way. We are too well guarded. Don't tell anyone."

But the terror was not long in coming. A squad of sepoys surrounded the house, and suddenly all the rooms were filled with the sound of shots being fired into the windows. The air filled with smoke as the women, clutching screaming children, flung themselves against the floor.

It went on endlessly, and then it was over. Reeling, ears ringing, the women looked around. Plaster and debris littered the floor, but not one person had been killed. The trembling women began to laugh and weep with joy. "The sepoys have refused to murder us!" Jo cried. "They fired into the ceiling!"

But the Begum had a dark look when she reentered the house; and Claire knew that it wasn't over. The Begum was evil, resourceful, and weary of responsibility for the lot of them. Claire felt paralyzed with fear when the Begum left the house again, as though bound on some errand. If only by some miracle the British troops might break through and save them before the Begum found those who would not scruple. But hours passed, and there was no miracle.

The door crashed back, and men with swords entered, led by two Mohammedan butchers. One of the butchers seized a child and began to hack it apart, as skillfully and emotionlessly as though it had been the carcass of a goat. Hysteria erupted as some of the women rushed to aid the child. Others, realizing that was hopeless, grabbed their own children and fled back into more distant parts of the house. The assailants, filled now with blood lust, followed relentlessly. Claire saw Abigail trying to hide her baby beneath a pile of clothing in a corner; she looked for Jo and could not find her. Everyone was screaming. Claire was screaming, too, but she was aware of it only because her throat was hurting. She was in breathless agony when hands seized her, and she thought at least she would be able to rest when the knife silenced her cries. Then, before it struck, she mercifully fainted.

26

She could still hear the screams when she regained consciousness, but they were far away and sporadic. A soft breeze came in through a window, and by moonlight she could see that she was again in a luxurious chamber of the Duncan Hotel. A shape stirred in the murk, and Claire gasped, thinking of the Rajah. "Don't be afraid, Memsahib," said a soft voice.

"Sevaley!" she whispered wonderingly.

"Yes. Praise be that you are alive and I am to serve you again." The two women held each other tightly for a long moment, and then Sevaley urged her to action. "Come and I will help you bathe."

Claire followed her maid to the tiled bath without protest. She was beaten now. She had tried her best to die, but the Rajah had thought her too choice a morsel to be wasted in the general carnage. After she was bathed, he would come to join her on the silk-cushioned charpoy, but Claire was past caring. She had seen too much, endured too much. "What is that sound, Sevaley? I hear singing."

"That is the Nana. He has ordered nautch girls for the evening. He wants the sound of the music to drown out the screams."

"I can still hear them."

"I, too. But it is only those who are still dying. The executioners left hours ago."

"Oh, dear God! Can no one help them?"

"No. No one is allowed to go in. Many would like to help.

The women of the Nana's zenana have refused to eat or drink. They threatened to throw themselves from high windows if the memsahibs were murdered, and tonight most of them are crying."

Claire thought of Jo, and of Abigail and her baby, and said with sudden desperate need, "Sevaley, where is Jeremy? Go and bring him to me."

"He is in the zenana, but I am not allowed to bring him here," said Sevaley, holding out a sari and sandals for her to put on. Claire thought she understood why Jeremy could not come now. The Rajah wanted privacy. She sighed as Sevaley brushed out her freshly-washed hair and plaited it in a single braid down her back. A fresh gardenia was fastened at the top of the braid, but Claire, lying back wearily on the pillows, crushed it beneath the weight of her head. The sweet fragrance wafted around her as she lay waiting for the inevitable. She was aware of her body as she had not been in a long time. It was thinner, but smooth and soft in spite of all her trials. She intuited how appealing she would be to the Rajah and began to turn herself into seductive poses, drawing one knee up so that the turn of her hips was emphasized beneath the sari. *I will tell him that I will do nothing with him until I have seen my son,* she vowed. *I will make it impossible for him to deny me.* And she put pillows over her head to keep from hearing the groans from the House of the Ladies several dozen yards away.

She could not have told how much time was passing as they waited, Sevaley seated cross-legged and expectant near the door. The moon set, and the room grew darker. Claire wondered almost impatiently what was keeping the Rajah. Then a door opened quietly and a man was in the room. The faint beam of a partly-covered lantern showed her his face. It wasn't the face she had thought to see.

"Vazir Lal!"

"Shh! We must go quickly. Before long I will be missed at the nautch."

"But Jeremy. I must have Jeremy!"

"It's not possible, Memsahib. He would be missed, and they would realize that you had escaped."

"But the Rajah will know that anyway when he comes and I'm not here!"

Vazir smiled tightly. "It wasn't the Rajah who had you saved from the House of the Ladies, Memsahib."

"It was you, Vazir?" she asked dazedly. "And the Rajah is not coming to. . . ." She stopped in embarrassment, and Vazir, understanding the reason, filled the silence.

"The Rajah is quite drunk and is telling everyone at the nautch about the memsahib whom he sent to her death for refusing him."

"But we must take Jeremy. I can't go without him!"

"No!" Vazir's face was intense and frightening. "Can't you understand? If they find that one of the women has escaped, they will hunt us down, and the Rajah will have to be in the forefront of it, with the bragging he has done. And this time maybe he will not be able to save your son. If you love Jeremy, do not be a sentimental woman. Leave him where he will be unharmed. Save yourself, for you will surely die if you remain as you are!"

Claire ceased to protest and let him lead her away down the stairs, keeping her veil over her face so that anyone who noticed her would think she was an Indian woman. Her legs buckled as they slipped past the House of the Ladies, which still emitted sounds of agony. Jo would be there, and Abigail and the baby, who had had only a week between her beginning and end. Claire prayed that they were already dead and not among those whose suffering was prolonged through the terrible night. Vazir spoke sharply to her, and she recovered herself, remembering that she owed as much to Vazir and Sevaley who had put themselves in danger for her sake. Vazir had horses waiting, tied to a neem tree, and they rode off unmolested in the night.

Claire was dozing in the saddle when Vazir called a halt near dawn. He had found them a place to camp, a mango tope some distance from the main road, where he thought they would be secure. But he would not build a fire to cook, and they had to be satisfied with cold rice and fruit. Even so, it was better fare than Claire had had in some time and was more delicious for being consumed in the sweet air of freedom. Vazir Lal told her how he had come to rescue her, and the story included the news that Colin had left Delhi alive.

"We were to come to Cawnpore, and I was to see how the rescue could be done," Vazir explained. "And after I eluded the robbers I decided to come on myself. I could not leave you to die, Memsahib."

"I will always be grateful, Vazir. But what of Colin? Do you think the robbers killed him?"

"I doubt it. He was ill and wounded, but he is not a man to die easily. I hope that he did not die."

"I'm glad to hear you wish him no ill now, Vazir."

Vazir grunted. "You're mistaken. What happened in Delhi changed nothing. I hope that he is alive so that I may still have the pleasure of killing him."

"You will never do that, Vazir!"

"I will. I swear it."

She knew then that she should think of killing Vazir herself, and she was amazed that the thought even came to her. How brutalized she had become! But without Vazir, she and Sevaley would be unprotected, and for the moment she could think of no way to accomplish the deed.

In the evening they traveled on. Vazir told them they were heading toward Pandeish. He would take them to Allapore where the Rani would shelter them. After midnight they stopped in another tope, but this time more travelers joined them, coming stealthily into the dark grove.

Vazir went to investigate, and returned with the information that it was only a pair of lovers lying together in sweet embrace beneath the trees. When daylight came, Claire saw them standing together, silhouetted against the pinkening sky. The man stood alertly, gazing out in the direction of the road as if assessing the difficulties before them. The woman stood behind him, her arms about his waist, her face pressed lovingly against his back, as though she thought of nothing but the delights of the hours just past.

There was something strangely familiar about the woman, and as Claire watched a breeze rippled her veil and blew it down from her hair. She was a blond woman, a European. She was Jo Baker. But not the Jo Claire had always known. Not the devoted teacher or the dry stalk of the siege. Jo had rewarded the sepoy who had saved her from the House of the Ladies and carried her away across his saddle. Her brave lover had done more than save her life; he had given her new life, and she was transformed.

The horrors she had seen had made Jo admit at last that she was not sufficient unto herself. She had desperately needed an infusion of love and hope. The first night after the massacre at the House of the Ladies, her brave soldier had feared she might die from shock and grief, and he had begun to stroke her comfortingly. His embrace had become more sensual as she had responded to his gentleness and innate decency. In his arms she had found unparalleled release of body and spirit. The soldier, unusually tall for his race, dark and compelling in his forest-green uniform with brass buttons and tufted shoulder straps, had had courage to risk death to save her. And for him, Jo had found courage to go on living.

Jo and Claire wept together when Claire ran from her hiding place, calling out her friend's name. They cried with joy at finding each other and with grief for Abigail and the baby and all the others who had died. The two men agreed to join forces and they traveled on together.

One evening Vazir succumbed at last to the deepest passion that had brought him back to Cawnpore. He had gone down to a jheel with the idea of shooting duck for dinner. And then in the dusk went Sevaley, a ghostly shape slipping through the trees to wash herself as though she did not know that Vazir had preceded her. Doves cooed, lighting in the isolated kikar trees that grew out of the water, as she unfastened her hair, standing at the edge of the reeds, pretending not to noitce him as he crouched concealed, waiting for his shot.

Vazir's voice caught in his throat, and he was unable to give warning of his presence as she unwrapped her sari and let it drop. At last he rose, his emotions in a tumult. She, seeing him, sank modestly into the water; but her eyes addressed him shamelessly. And suddenly Vazir was shameless, too. Leaving his trousers among the reeds, he waded in, clad only in a dhoti.

Sevaley returned triumphant to the tope. But Vazir, having discovered that the deepest urges of love could not always be controlled, became irritable and careless. Several days later, following Sevaley into the darkness, he left his knife behind on the stump of a tree. Claire appropriated it at once and lay trembling. Now she had the means to kill Vazir Lal. When Vazir returned, he took his blanket away to the edge of the tope, and after waiting an hour to make sure he slept, she crept after him, hoping to deal him a quick and silent death. But the knife was never to strike home. Vazir Lal had slipped away, fleeing from his overwhelming love for Sevaley back to the more manageable world of war.

At last they reached the pine forests, and the minarets of Allapore came into view. The countryside seemed as beautiful and peaceful as when Claire had first seen it, but as they neared the city, they noticed that the fields were deserted. Conversely, there were throngs in the streets of Allapore, and it was all but impossible to gain entry at the palace gates.

"I'm a friend of the Rani," she told the guard. "Send word to her that Claire Whitecavage wishes to see her."

They were admitted, and the Rani herself came to receive them in the divan, the beautiful room where rainbows glowed from chandeliers onto fretwork and ivory. The scent of blossoms drifted in from the garden and parakeets sang. Tamila, more exquisite than Claire remembered, kissed her and shook her head sadly on learning that Claire did not know what had become of Colin. Neither woman had to guess whether the other still loved him or whether she longed beyond all else to be held again in his arms. Then the wistfulness left the Rani's eyes, and the purposeful queen shone through.

"There is trouble here, Claire. It will not be easy for you, but I'm glad you've come. You are the only one I can trust. You must help me."

"What is happening, Tamila? Of course I'll help if I can."

"The Rajah of Rambad is on his way here from Cawnpore. He has unleashed the rumor that Daruska is the son of an *Angrezi*, and many of my subjects are rising to join him against me. Will you take Daruska and hide with him?"

"Yes. Where shall I hide?"

"In the old section of the palace. When the hostilities are over, my loyal servants will help you find your way secretly to Simla."

"You should hide, too, Tamila."

"I shall do just the opposite," said the Rani determinedly. "I am going to the front line so that my men can see me. I want them to know that I am willing to fight myself for the just government that Major Whitecavage created in Pandeish. I will inspire them to fight for Daruska."

"You will go to the front line? But——"

"Please, Claire! Take Daruska. What I am doing is the only hope for Pandeish. I have nothing else to live for. It doesn't matter if I die. If you find Colin, love him twice as much for me."

Claire took the little Rana to the unused part of the palace, finding a hidden chamber near the rooms she had occupied when she had been the Rajah's prisoner here. No doubt the wing would be searched, should the palace be occupied, but this remote suite was made for secrecy, with a panel for a door. Claire had the advantage, too, of having explored the labyrinth before with the Rajah's son, Sona, and she made maps in her mind, tracing the way back to the divan and to the outer gate of the palace.

Jo rode away with her soldier, whose home was not far from Allapore. "We may meet again when this is over," she said, kissing Claire in farewell. "But you will have to look for me."

"Yes. I suppose you will never contact British authorities or return to Cawnpore."

"No, never." Jo said with a smile. "But you'll find me, Claire. You'll know where to look."

Jo offered to take Sevaley with them, but Claire's servant chose to remain behind. "You are hopeless, Sevaley," Claire said, as they stood at a palace window, watching the departure. "You imagine that Vizar Lal will be with the Rajah's force and that he may love you again."

"Yes," admitted Sevaley. "It is worth the risk of dying, Memsahib. But even if he doesn't come, I've known love. Whatever happens, I will be content because of it."

Claire sighed. She, too, had known a consuming love and should be satisfied with having been given life's greatest gift. But Claire could not think of death with Sevaley's Indian equanimity. The child close to her was Colin's and depended on her. She had left an even dearer child of Colin's in the zenana at the Duncan Hotel. She needed to live for them, but it seemed to her she had little chance. She had rejected the Rajah; and Vazir Lal had assured her the Rajah had intended her to die for it. He would have her killed if he found her, and it seemed unfair to her that the road to death should be so endlessly long and horrible.

At Cawnpore, General Havelock's troops had routed the Nana's forces, attacking them unexpectedly from the left flank after a severe march through the mango groves in the full heat of the afternoon. Colin Whitecavage, though still feeling the effects of his beating by the *goojurs*, had joined that attack, and now he stood aghast and stricken with other British soldiers at the scene of the massacre at the House of the Ladies.

Inside, clothing was strewn about, children's shoes, petticoats, and bonnets, torn prayer books, a broken doll which Colin at first mistook for a mangled baby. Everything was covered with blood; tresses and plaits of hair lay in leathery clots of dried blood.

A path made by dragging bodies showed the way to the well, and along it hair and clothing were tangled in the bushes. Brains had been dashed out against a tree; an eye was crushed into its bark. And at the bottom of the well, the pile of corpses could be seen dimly in the murk.

Colin reeled as he looked into the well. Claire could not be down there. He could not make himself believe it. Dazed, he wandered about the town until finally he heard of the arch at the fort where many of the besieged had written their names. *Hers will not be there,* he told himself, but he went to see. Her name was written like a final message of love, telling him of the devotion that had brought her back to India to her end. Colin Whitecavage cursed India and cursed himself, for he had never had the right to love her.

For several days Colin gave himself over to mindless grief. He ate nothing and drank everything, becoming a derelict of the bazaar. But finally Colin began to notice what was happening around him as the conquerors dealt punishment for the murders of the women and children. Mutineers were not only being hanged, but before they were hanged revolting tasks were expected of them. Each was required to lick clean a foot of the floor of the House of the Ladies, which had been wetted with water by natives of the lowest caste. Lashes were applied to urge them on, and even that was not enough for some British, who stuffed beef and pork and anything else which would break caste down their throats.

Coming on such a scene, Colin tried to interfere. "Has that man been tried?" he demanded. "Is it certain he was involved in the murders?"

"Certain enough for me!" replied one of the Englishmen. "He's the right color."

"Were our women and children given trials?" snapped another. "No death is hideous enough for the followers of the Fiend!"

"Stop it, by heaven!" Colin commanded. "We are more civilized than they!"

The hostile atmosphere around him grew more intense. "Who are you to give us orders, anyway?" someone demanded.

"An officer." He remembered that his uniform had been discarded long ago. "I am Major Colin Whitecavage."

"Whitecavage! That's a familiar name."

"Ah! I know! He's the one whose bastard is about to be toppled from the throne of Pandeish!"

"No wonder he loves the brownies! He ought to be hanged himself!"

They took after him with sticks and rocks; and Colin, out-numbered, was forced to flee from his own kind. They failed to follow him with more than hoots and jeers, for their native prey was more satisfying. Colin collapsed at the foot of a tree. So the word was out about Daruska. He supposed it had been inevitable. The Rajah would be responsible, of course. The news added a terrible new dimension to his grief. Once he had ridden to Tamila's aid at the head of armies. Now, he had no one but himself. Tamila would die of her devotion to him much as Claire had died for loving him. And Daruska would die for being his son, just as little Jeremy had.

Colin still loved Tamila, though not as he had before. Claire had usurped her place in his affections. His marriage had never ceased to pain the Rani, but for the time he had spent in Pandeish after Claire's return to England, she had honored it. She had helped him keep his vows to Claire, reminding him with her demeanor, when her graceful body might have lulled him into forgetfulness. In his heart Colin thought of the splendid loves given him and paid homage to two superb and courageous women.

He had nothing but himself. He was a man caught between the forces of colossal conflict, unowned by either side. But he *did* have himself, and there had been times when that had been enough. He could try. He could die trying. There was nothing better do do; and shortly thereafter, with a pillaged horse and supplies, Colin Whitecavage galloped north.

The hills of Pandeish seemed to welcome him; he felt gathered into them as into the arms of eternity. He rode toward death with exultation.

Near the gates of Allapore, the Rajah waited to claim his lost prize, the throne of Pandeish. Beside him was his son Aleka, older now, a cunning swordsman. The defenders of Pandeish had retreated almost to the city gates, and the Rajah was certain they could not hold on long. Not against his battering rams, his elephants mounted with cannon. Soon he would attack the walls of the city itself. He was already aglow with the expectation of success.

But on the outskirts of the city Colin was recognized. His brave commitment attracted others. Some who had not yet taken up arms, some who were outposts of the Rajah's camp, now remembered glorious days with the Sword of Pandeish and flocked to fight beside him. He stirred their hearts, riding wild and desperate, more magnificent in his tattered white shirt and trousers than he had been in his uniform. The number of his followers grew. There were a score, then fifty, and finally hundreds.

The sky over Allapore was dark with smoke; the Rajah's men were scaling the walls and battling on the parapets when the new challenge came upon them. The Rajah whirled to face it, shouted orders into the confusion, heard the ominous words, *The Sword of Pandeish.*

The Rajah exploded with gleeful fury. He would put an end at last to Colin Whitecavage. With a cry he galloped toward the approaching force. Many might have struck him down, but all turned away from the Rajah's maniacal countenance. This fight belonged to Colin alone.

"You will die, Whitecavage!" shouted the Rajah.

"Yes, but not before I've killed *you!* Not before you've paid for the murder of my wife!"

"Your wife! *My* mistress!" He leered, his teeth glinting like his sword in the summer sun.

"I will kill you for that, too!"

"What, for giving her more pleasure than you?"

"For honor! She was a woman of honor!" He realized with joy that he was sure of it, and the battle was joined.

The Rajah, with a stronger horse and a better blade, struck from envy and hatred at the man who had so often bested him at love and war. Colin fought with profound grief and a lust for revenge. He fought with determination to save Tamila and his son. When his sword broke against the Rajah's, he lunged for his opponent and pulled him from his horse. They struggled in the dirt until Colin turned aside the Rajah's knife and set his own at his enemy's throat.

And then he plunged it home.

"Sahib!" Someone gave a warning as Colin stood trembling over his slain foe. He looked and saw Prince Aleka, charging him on an elephant. On his face Colin saw the same vicious expression as on that long-ago day when Aleka had killed the monkey his brother Sona had been trying to tame. It wasn't so much the death of his father that galvanized Aleka, Colin thought, as the desire to destroy. As though Colin were the prize lion of the hunt, Aleka was determined to kill him and show himself a better fighter than the Rajah had been.

Knowing he had no chance unhorsed, Colin ran, vexed that he should die beneath the feet of this upstart's elephant and cursing nature, which caused one despot to rise like an ugly weed where another had fallen.

Then arrows from a dozen of Colin's archers struck Aleka, their feathered shafts seeming to ornament his jeweled clothing as he toppled forward in his howdah.

Through the afternoon the fighting went on; the city fell to the forces of Rambad, but Colin's weary, outnumbered soldiers labored to reclaim it. It was obvious they had no chance.

Then at dusk an emissary rode out to Major Whitecavage, carrying a white flag. Colin met the horseman and found Vazir Lal. "Vazir, you swore to kill me." he said tiredly. "Do you wish us to fight now? You are justified in wanting it, and I will grant your wish."

Vazir shook his head. "I no longer wish you harm, Sahib. I have forgiven you—and her. I, too, fell in love unsuitably and learned that love can be stronger than duty. I understand now."

"You, Vazir! Will you marry her?"

Vazir sighed. "If I find her again. I have come to take you to Rani. She has been taken prisoner."

Vazir Lal took Colin to a silken tent, but in it Colin saw only a soldier in the uniform of Pandeish. The soldier was gravely wounded, lying on a carpet gasping for breath. "Where is the Rani?" Colin asked.

"Look closer, Sahib," said Vazir, and his voice was sad.

Colin knelt and, unwinding the soldier's turban, found a woman's soft tresses.

"She fought beside the men, and those who were with her did not care that the little Rana was half *Angrezi*. Justice and courage were beyond people or races for them, as for those who joined you. As they are for me. Speak to her, Sahib. She called for you before."

Colin bent over her, and her name was torn from him in a sob. "Tamila," he whispered.

She opened her eyes and saw him, and her face lighted. "Go to the palace," she murmured. "To the old part."

"Why, dearest?"

She tried to tell him and could not, and he held her in his arms as she had wanted for so long to be held. In those moments she was serene, gazing into his face to hold the memory for all eternity. Even when she breathed no more, he held her, laying his head on her breast. He had lost too much, too much. He could not endure.

Then Vazir touched his shoulder. "I will take you to the new Rajah now," he said.

He led Colin to the tent that had been the Rajah's headquarters, where young Sona, heir to his father's lands and crowns, sat trying to look like a king. "I'm glad you're here, Sahib," he said, and restrained himself from running into Colin's arms as he had used to do. "Sahib, I am tired of the fighting. Let us put an end to it. I do not understand why we cannot be friends again as we were when we traveled on the Grand Trunk Road together."

Colin salaamed soberly. "Let us try, your highness."

Sona smiled with relief. "I have your son for you."

Colin expected to see Daruska, but instead he saw Jeremy, a thin, miserable child, but with his features nonetheless. Claire's child! He was stunned, hardly able to think, and then the child struggled away from Sona and began to cry, "I want Mama! I want Mama!"

"So do I," said Colin, and gathered Jeremy into his arms. If Claire were alive, they would work together to build a new India, an India of peace and respect between peoples. The India that Colonel Todd had caused them both to dream of. If Claire were alive, their lives would be a monument to their great love. If Claire were alive, he would have strength, but without her. . . .

As if realizing that Colin's grief was as great as his own, Jeremy fastened his arms about his father's neck.

"We must honor the Rani's last request," Vazir Lal reminded him. And Sona, on hearing what it had been, offered to lead the way himself.

"I am familiar with the chambers of the Rainbow Palace," he said. They went together, Sona exploring again the corridors he had discovered when he was small.

For a long time they found nothing, but Sona's expert guidance led them at last into a room where a woman sat tending a child. Both Colin and Vazir rejoiced, for the child was Daruska and the woman, Sevaley, who wept happily at being taken into Vazir's embrace.

Unable to bear the reunion of sweethearts, Colin hugged the little Rana and stepped into the courtyard. Hibiscus and bougainvillea bloomed, and water gurgled from a fountain in a pond of goldfish. Feeling he could go no farther, he leaned against a garden wall. But a scent of jasmine came to him, and there had been no jasmine growing there. It was a distinctive scent—not of the flower growing, but of perfume, unlike the scent of jasmine of any Indian woman. He raised his head in disbelief and saw a woman there.

It was she! It was Claire, rising from her bench with an exclamation of wonder.

"Oh, my darling!" he cried.

And with a heart brimming with love, he lifted her jasmine veil.

ABOUT THE AUTHOR

GIMONE HALL was raised in Texas and lives in Bucks County, Pa., where she is working on a new novel. Married to a writer, she has two young children. She is the author of four other historical romances, *Rapture's Mistress, Fury's Sun, Passion's Moon,* and *Ecstasy's Empire,* also available in Signet editions.

SIGNET Fiction to Read

- [ ] **THE CORMAC LEGEND by Dorothy Daniels.** (#J8655—$1.95)
- [ ] **HOUSE OF SILENCE by Dorothy Daniels.** (#E9423—$1.75)
- [ ] **THE PURPLE AND THE GOLD by Dorothy Daniels.** (#J9118—$1.95)
- [ ] **LUCETTA by Elinor J. Jones.** (#E8698—$2.25)
- [ ] **TAMARA by Elinor J. Jones.** (#E9450—$2.75)
- [ ] **CLAUDINES DAUGHTER by Rosalind Laker.** (#E9159—$2.25)
- [ ] **WARWYCK'S CHOICE by Rosalind Laker.** (#E9664—$2.50)
- [ ] **WARWYCK'S WOMAN by Rosalind Laker.** (#E8813—$2.25)
- [ ] **GLITTERBALL by Rochelle Larkin.** (#E9525—$2.50)
- [ ] **HARVEST OF DESIRE by Rochelle Larkin.** (#E8771—$2.25)
- [ ] **TORCHES OF DESIRE by Rochelle Larkin.** (#E8511—$2.25)
- [ ] **GLYNDA by Susannah Leigh.** (#E8548—$2.50)
- [ ] **WINE OF THE DREAMERS by Susannah Leigh.** (#E9157—$2.95)